WILL YOU REACH FOR ME

ROMANCING ME SERIES

S.K. PRESLEY

Will You Reach For Me by S.K. Presley is intended for a 18+ mature audience

Cover Design: R.J. Services

Editing: Traci Bullman

"Alexander and Sarah Sunset" artwork: Anastasia Donets

"Alexander and Sarah Dancing" artwork: Alice Anderson

Contents

Trigger Warning

GRAPHIC DOMESTIC VIOLENCE

- miscarriage
- allusion to racism
- emotional manipulation and abuse
- financial manipulation
- mental health heavy (PTSD, and Anxiety)

Playlist

Apple Playlist

https://music.apple.com/us/playlist/will-you-reach-for-me/pl.u-B NA6rMJF1lxJYAZ

List

Unethical- Faouzia

Caruso-Hauser

Better Than That-Marina and The Diamonds

Don't Love Easy-Nova Blue

Cinnamon Girl (slowed + reverb) Slo & Twilight

Sledgehammer-Mila

Dandelions-Ruth B.

Somebody Like You-Alan Walker & Au/RA

Halo (Piano version)-Daniele Leoni

Symphony- (feat. Zara Larsson)

Breathe Me In-Nova Bleu

A Glorious Purpose-Gimba JR.

Crave You-Slow Burn

Free-Rumi, JINU, EJAE, Andrew Choi

So Easy (To Fall In Love)-Olivia Dean

Still Here-Nova Bleu

Wicked Game-Hauser

If Love Comes Back-Crystal Faith

Only Love Can Hurt Like This-Paloma Faith

In the Kitchen-Renee Rapp

I know- Faouzia

Adiago for Strings-Hauser

To Love You More-Celine Dion

Dedication

For those of us who have had to endure way too much, give up on our dreams, and relinquish our hope...

in silence...

invisible...

...broken...

We are not. You are not.

I am not.

We bend, but we do not break.

PROLOGUE

SITTING IN THE HARDBACK chair by the window in the informal lounge of my home, I tilt my head back solemnly, enjoying the rich musical notes successfully taming my emotions. Not much does these last few weeks. Which is why I'm here. This room, painstakingly designed to be my oasis, feels like the only happy place I have anymore.

Because they say sun is important, and it is, the cream, floor-to-ceiling length drapes are wide open as it sets, affording me an admittedly stunning view of the back yard and my koi pond.

I close my eyes, relaxed, and dare I say it, *serene* as my fingers fly over the strings of my cello. Shadows begin to shift across the floor as the music swells and wanes around me, and I lose myself to it completely. Reverently. Lost in the beauty of my simple creation, my toes lift off the floor and settle back in perfect rhythm as my bow glides smoothly across the strings.

I rock in my seat as I let the music sweep over me...own me...and breathe deeply with my arms firmly in a familiar hold around my instrument.

A sound startles me out of my calm, forcing my eyes to open in irritation. The calm dissipates as my phone lights with a text. The momentary brightness effectively disturbs the serene peaceful state that envelopes me. I readjust my hold on my instrument and lean forward to grab it, beating back hope it's my son, Tyler, who was supposed to call me at four.

My shoulders droop when I see it's not.

> Veronica [5:02p]: Hi, Alexander. Are you picking me up at six to go to dinner?

It crosses my mind to reply back and cancel our date; however, manners prevent me. I put my bow down on the side table, maneuvering further around my cello. The curved maple and spruce wood instrument gleams in the light of the setting sun. Its dissipating rays cast the room in a beautiful orange and pink glow.

I reply back, even though I'm reluctant to part with the peace my music is giving me.

> Alexander [5:04p]: Hello. I apologize, but no, I will not be picking you up tonight. Will you please meet me at the restaurant at six-thirty? I can send you an Uber if you wish.

Veronica [5:04p]: Yes, please. That would be so great. Am I coming home with you tonight?

Alexander [5:05p]: Not tonight. I'm sorry, but we only just started dating four weeks ago. I'd like to take you out a few more times before I bring you home…Please don't be offended.

Please don't be offended… The words stare back at me. Weak. Flagging me as a target.

All the nasty words my ex-wife has called me over the years fill my head and make all the peace I'd just had drift away as if it'd never happened. My trauma being dredged up by a simple text. Perspiration dampens my forehead, and I clench my jaw at the raw need inside me swelling up–demanding I protect myself. My finger hovers for a moment over the send button, fighting to not erase the entire text and cancel the dinner, before erasing just the last sentiment. *Then* I hit send.

I press my lips together, tightening my fingers on the handle. The cello rests against my thigh, waiting.

Veronica [5:05p]: Ok, Alexander. See you at dinner then.

Swiping out of our text thread, I quickly check to see if I have any communication from my son before setting my phone back down and picking my bow back up. Taking advantage of the hour of time left before I have to leave out for my and Veronica's date.

My features soften as I begin to play again, trying to find the serene peace I was so close to achieving before I was interrupted.

I replay the conversation repeatedly in my head, wondering if I should have relented to picking her up despite my gut telling me not to. Overthinking, as usual. A horrible, weak trait of mine: always incessantly worried about how I'm coming across to others. I play furiously as my inner thoughts begin to overtake me inch by fucked-up inch. My skin dots with goosebumps, feeling the cold that everyone laments is trapped inside me, vying to be let free, and I rock a little harder as the music once more infiltrates the lonely and unfulfilled spaces of my mind.

My cello wails, emulating a woman's voice. In a desperate bid to distract myself from these encroaching thoughts, I let my imagination free, daydreaming that she's crying for me. In my heart I swear I hear it as I work vigorously at getting her tone and pitch perfect, responding to her somber yearning. Someone heroic, and worthy.

Not weak.

I shake my head minutely with feeling as I play. My lips tilt at the corner when I finally get the note I'd been working on perfect, but yet, the longing for something more is still there. Leaving me unsatisfied. And as I sway, my heart jerks uncomfortably, letting my emotions run rampant.

Wishing to be *enough,* when it's time. If it were ever time. If I could just stop being so cold.

God, I so desperately want to be warm.

Alexander and Sarah by Anastasia Donets

CHAPTER ONE

UNETHICAL

"No!"

I gasp as my head snaps violently to the side, and red-hot pain washes over my face in waves as my boyfriend's fist connects with my cheek. The sound reverberates out, echoing in the small space, and it stuns me, driving home just how desolate the situation I'm in is.

Locking eyes with him, I stumble backwards, and my fingers fly up to my face.

Discombobulated, I let out a surprised yelp and hit the floor with a sickening thud and land with a jarring jolt onto my left shoulder. The terror deepens when he takes a threatening step forward, and my throat works as I desperately try to inhale, but I can't get much air. My body fights against me, strangling me even as my vision suddenly goes black, and nausea tightens my throat.

Whimpering, I roll to my side and squeeze my eyes shut as I recoil in fear.

Not again.

Ignoring the deep throb in my shoulder, my feet cycle against the floor as I hurriedly attempt to position myself to face the wall next to me. Panic floods my being as Brandon's body looms over mine, towering over where I'm huddled in the corner of our living room trying to make myself as small as possible because maybe that means he'll leave me alone. I should know better, but I still pray anyway.

"Why do you make me fucking do this to you, you stupid *disgusting* bitch?" Brandon yells.

I flinch in disgust when his spit lands on my skin and hair. Knowing replying will only make it worse, I bite back a moan and curl in on myself, intent on protecting the almost eleven-week old baby in my womb. My arms work to cradle around the slight swell in my stomach tightly, pressing myself harder into the wall.

"Just stop, please," I cry out, fearful for Bumpy's life.

He bends down, mercilessly fisting his hand into my hair hard and yanking me around to face him as he pulls back his fist again and snaps it forward. With a stunned cry, I crumple once more to the gleaming dark-walnut hardwood floor, huddling as close as I can against the wall and pulling my knees up to my chest.

"Brandon, no!" I sob. *"The baby! You're hurting our baby!"*

My body jerks, and I gag on my cries as he kicks me so hard I splay flat onto my back. His size eleven shoe bounces off my knee a second, then third time, creating fresh pain for me to deal with.

Rolling back over, I begin to pray as hard as I can that he'll cease beating me, desperate to protect my baby. I raise trembling hands to shield my face as I curl up against the wall next to the tv stand. A loud crash sounds out as I accidentally knock over a decorative blue mosaic vase that was my parents housewarming gift to us when we bought this home. It's contents clatter loudly as it scatters on the floor next to my feet.

"You stupid *slut.* I told you not to perform that song tonight!" he yells. I peek through my fingers, trying to see how close he is and if there's a possibility I can try to run for the door. But to my dismay, he's too close for me to attempt it. "If I hadn't shown up, then what?" he snarls roughly. *"You were just going to get away with disobeying me?"*

The intensity of Brandon's yelling causes his face to turn bright red. His blonde hair is mussed, and he's currently showing a side of himself that I've so far not gleaned in our time together. It terrifies me even further. In response, I crawl into a safe spot inside my head, dissociating from the father of my child.

My college sweetheart of four years is now an unrecognizable shell of the man he used to be.

Brandon's face contorts in anger. The dimples in his cheeks are pronounced as he continues to scream obscenities at me, and his usually pristine hair flops limply over his face as he bends down over me while I cover my ears, shivering. I'm too scared to fight back. Scared this might be the time he'll snap and kill me.

Oh God. Please don't.

After a few more minutes of cursing, he finally stumbles noisily away and narrowly misses tripping over our glass living room table. I keep quiet as he grabs his jacket and keys, slamming the door behind him loudly as he exits the three-bedroom home we'd bought just two years ago when I thought we were happy.

Before the baby.

Finally alone, I sag flat onto the floor in relief as the adrenaline fades, letting my cries ring free now that he's gone. I lay here weeping for long minutes that all blend together in a painfully indiscernible eon of time. My shaky fingers touch my bruised cheek, causing me to wince as a fresh bout of pain slices through my face. In the weeks he'd started abusing me, Brandon has never outright punched me in the face.

Matter of fact, I've *never* been punched in the face before.

A different kind of sorrow fills my body, and I let out a hurt sound at the realization. No woman should be hit.

Moaning, I fight through the pain and sit up, looking down at my stomach. Though I'm not even showing yet, I place a trembling hand over the place where I know my baby, affectionately named 'Bumpy,' rests. The baby I plan on naming Brittany, having just decided on a name this morning. I'm sure I'm having a girl and have been looking forward to the upcoming scan that would verify it for me.

I'm so close that I can taste it.

Pulling to my knees, I pause as the room suddenly spins, forcing me to breathe through the nausea before crawling forward.

"Ow. Ow, ow, ow," I complain, shakily pulling myself up by the brand-new sofa I'd just bought a few weeks ago.

My fingers go to my face again, thinking my skin is wet, but when I pull my hand back, there's no blood. I stare for a second while I get my bearings, before I attempt to walk on my hurt knee. My eyes flick to the television which still has the video stream of the classical station I'd put on to relax. Before Brandon walked in, flipping my world upside down yet again.

Straightening my spine, I wipe my nose with the back of my hand and watch the man on the screen play his instrument. In this harrowing moment, it feels like the instrument is calling out to *me*. It affects me so badly that fresh tears slide down my face as I stare straight ahead miserably, feeling my heart crying out just like the lovely instrument. Wondering once again what I ever did that warranted Brandon to begin treating me this way.

Dejected, I turn away from the screen dismissively, limping gingerly into the primary bathroom to inspect the damage to my body and my new hell. Closing the door behind me, I lock it before meeting my eyes in the reflection warily. They're swollen, red, and tear-stained.

What's completely heartbreaking is that I'm unrecognizable in my sadness.

I don't know this woman staring back at me.

She's not me.

My long, dark-brown hair that I'm so proud of is in disarray, and my skin is washed-out. Lowering my gaze, I lament at the sight of my brand new red dress that's now torn at the strap and hanging off my shoulder. Ruined. Inspecting my face closer, I notice that my medium-tan skin is turning a shade darker at my jaw. Raising my gaze once more to my eyes again hopefully, I grimace as I observe that my spark is indeed gone.

My stomach knots, and my fingers white-knuckle the sink as I search even harder, seeing *nothing.*

Desperate, I lean forward even closer as if that'll help and search again. My lips twist, and my face contorts at the realization that he's beat it out of me. I can't find it because it's not there.

It's gone.

Standing there, being overwhelmed by fresh feelings of inadequacy and confusion, I let go of the sink and wrap my arms around myself in a soothing motion, wondering how on earth I found myself in this situation. Because this is recent...Brandon didn't start physically abusing me until *after* he'd found out I was pregnant.

Once he'd received the news of my pregnancy, he'd started anxiously binge drinking. Shortly after that, he started hitting me, and it's becoming progressively worse as the weeks tick by. Now the hits come accompanied by nasty words fueled by hate. Words I'd never thought I'd ever hear come from him, now come as easily as if he was ordering his favorite Starbucks drink. Except it's unfortunately at *my* expense. Not his.

Knowing that I can't afford to abandon my nightly routine, I take a deep breath and sigh.

Picking up a rolled face towel off the stack nearby, I turn the faucet on and wet it with cold water. Moving slow, I sniff, trying to stem tears that won't stop. My fingers are shaky as I open the mirror and grab my face wash, and I try to calm myself as I squirt some onto the white terrycloth. Going through the motions, I wipe my face, all the while careful to avoid my gaze in the mirror, taking pains to not press too hard into my jaw where a deep throbbing is ensuing. I'm probably not going to get any sleep tonight.

When I'm done, I grab my red hairbrush, pull my hip-length hair to either side of my front, and begin to detangle my hair in short strokes.

Ignoring the slight pain of the bristles snagging the knots, I carry on with my nightly duties with a sort of dissociative stoicism I teach my clients not to have. Feeling like a hypocrite, I blink through the hot sting of tears that won't subside for anything.

Replacing the brush in its holder, I plug in my purple hot brush that I use to straighten the frizziness out in the mornings before work, and turn it on, sighing yet again. I wish I had a routine that was simpler. Because right now, all I want is a warm shower to wash the night away and to go straight to bed without having to worry about my hair. Ashamed, I keep my eyes averted from my reflection as I work by muscle memory to smooth my hair out with the hot brush.

I don't really want to look at this unrecognizable woman in the mirror.

She's not me.

Feeling like I'm having an out of body experience, I mechanically twist my hair into a thick bun at the top of my head. I ignore the painful twinging of my back smarting as I secure it all up the best that I can manage with a clip and turn to start the shower.

I return back to the vanity and look over my makeup stash, picking up the almost empty tube of light-mocha concealer. Irritated, I frown at the realization that I'm going to have to buy yet another bottle as it's running low. I never can tell when Brandon is going to hit me lately, and I'd run through almost two extra bottles than normal in the last month and a half.

My muscles twitch with pain as I gently peel the torn dress off, dejected and upset.

I had such a good time singing at the lounge tonight despite the fact that the crowd requested me to sing a song that Brandon didn't want me to. Foolishly, I thought with him not being present for my performance tonight that'd it'd be okay for once to give the crowd what they wanted. However, because he'd been overbearing lately, he came to my performance when he'd gotten off work and I didn't know. It's what set this whole thing off tonight. Not that it was any excuse for him to beat me like this.

As a therapist who owns her own practice, I *know* that, and I would never advocate for any of my clients to stay in an abusive relationship. Ever.

Turning back to the shower, I place my fingers under the water before securing a plastic shower cap over my hair to protect it from getting wet, and step under the warm spray. I moan quietly as the hot water seeps into my sore muscles, but the stinging of my abraded skin soon has me crashing back to reality.

Knowing I'm safe in the shower, I break, placing my head into my hands and letting myself cry. With nothing but the sounds of the water bouncing off the cap to accompany my sobs, the pain I feel on the inside swells high enough to match the pain I feel on the outside.

My shoulders droop under weight I don't think I'm strong enough to hold anymore.

Slowly sliding to the floor, I ignore my body screaming out in pain, lean against the white subway tiles and sob into my knees, knowing I need to get away from him. But how? I'm pregnant and have no family close by.

How am I supposed to leave?

Early the next morning, I lean into the bathroom mirror and wince, closing my eyes tight in pain as I work to dab concealer onto the discolored bruise on my jaw. Pausing, I stifle a yawn against my palm before moving on to my eyeliner and fight to not blink. Nervous I'd oversleep, I'd set my alarm for a half hour earlier than usual to give myself extra time to get ready.

But all I want to do is crawl back in bed, pull the covers over my head, and shut out the world. I don't want to go to work, especially in pain like this and not feeling my best. However, if I don't, I'll lose clients, won't be able to pay my bills, and my reputation will be smeared. At the end of the day, I need my job; I don't think I could rebound from a hit to my reputation.

Sniffling and trying to hold back tears, I try my hardest to blend it in well enough to prevent the bruise from showing through the concealer. I turn my face this way and that, inspecting from all angles. You could barely tell Brandon hit me across the face like he would a man, I did such a good job covering it up.

I blink again, my eyes stinging from all the crying I've been doing. Reaching into the medicine cabinet, I grab some eyedrops and put a drop in each eye, blinking against the initial sting.

I hate him.

I pull my hand back, wondering how bad it'd be if I was vindictive and ballsy enough to put a few drops in one of his drinks. To pay him back for turning my life upside down. Frowning and chastising myself at the intrusive thought, I put the vial back in the cabinet and then self-consciously squint at myself in the mirror.

For once I thank God for my good looks. Maybe it would help to distract the outside world from the bruises I'm sporting, or anything else out of order. I don't want any of my clients suspecting that anything's amiss. I pride myself on ruling over my little practice of three years with an iron fist. Wrapped in velvet, of course.

I take time to clean the vanity off before exiting the room to the bedroom I share with Brandon. Eying the perfectly made bed, I bite my lip as my mind becomes awash with thoughts, unable to be still. I'm in fight or flight mode as I attempt to think through every possible outcome of this relationship.

Sighing, I deflate, knowing good and well I'm going to have to financially figure out how to maintain my practice while going through an unexpected abusive relationship with no savings at twenty-eight years old. I'm desperate and broke, initially having sunk all my hard-earned savings into starting up my therapy practice, finding a nice house in a middle-class neighborhood to rent out for my office space, and then building it up. There hasn't been any wiggle room or to see a real profit in the last three years.

Not with all the extra financial strain I've been under.

Thankfully, I'm rather good at what I do and have clients galore, but I'm still barely breaking even every month. I have just enough saved to get an apartment, but nothing else, and the thought of being left destitute terrifies me. I'd *just* spent money on our living room furniture, and shortly after had found myself being the sole provider of the household. Paying the majority of the bills and the mortgage has left me with few dollars at the end of the month.

I furrow my brow, thinking hard, contemplating my next steps.

In his current mental state, I'd doubt that Brandon will let me take the furniture or other items because he's not being reasonable right now. I'm going to have to wait until he's at work one day to try and at least get the bed. That's all I'll take. Something to lay on that way I won't have to crawl off the floor with a baby bump protruding.

"We got this." I smile, putting my hands to my stomach and rubbing gently.

Yeah...I don't want the house. No way I'd want to walk through the various rooms and see countless areas where he'd beat me until I was a sobbing mess on the floor.

Turning to walk out of the bedroom, I journey slowly down the hallway before pausing. My eyebrows furrow when I spot the slight blood smear on the wall that I hadn't been able to scrub out. I briefly close my eyes against the memory. Seven weeks ago Brandon grabbed me by the hair and slammed my head into the wall, making me smear blood on the light blue paint.

I hate the memory; it makes me feel sick. My face flushes as my eyes tear up from thinking about all the sacrifices I've made. I'd paid three grand to have the entire house painted not even two years ago, and there are at least six walls I know of stained with my blood.

Wanting to move on, I keep going, stopping at the picture of mom and dad.

The feeling becomes even more intense at the sight of my father.

I wrap my arms around my torso, staring into his gray eyes and wishing I could call him and tell him what's going on. My dad is a stoic man who always hounded me for not wanting to be a lawyer. Our relationship has been strained for years since I moved away to live my own dreams. He never got over the disappointment.

My eyes move over to momma, roaming over her dark skin and beautifully locked hair. I get my short height from her. She tries to keep the peace between us, but even she isn't savvy enough to mend our bond. It's so broken at this point I don't see how it'll ever be repaired. I assess the picture quietly; they're standing locked in an embrace in front of the Eiffel tower on one of their many trips out of the country.

Oh how I wish I could tell you what's going on.

My breath hitches as I put a shaky hand to my cheek, wiping my tears away. I linger in the hallway. My eyes move beyond my parents, landing on the picture of me and Brandon when we were on vacation in California visiting them. They'd disapproved of Brandon because he wasn't a lawyer like they wanted for me. So, we ended the visit early and rented a small home near Venice beach where we spent the rest of the time surfing until we had to fly back home to Connecticut.

No, there's no way I can tell them. All they would do is say *I told you so.*

My fingers dig in my arms as I regard the picture I used to love. Lingering on happy and carefree smiles as we held each other in front of the sunset. My hair was curly after swimming, and that night as we were packing to leave, he'd asked me how long before I could make my hair straight again; it was the first time he'd ever had a complaint like that.

Hurt, I'd promptly locked myself in the bathroom and spent half the night self-consciously straightening my hair. That night messed with my confidence so deeply that I've never gone swimming with him again.

Blinking tears away, I reach up and take the frame off the wall and carry it to the sink. I place it into the empty basin, grab a mug, and smash it into the thin glass frame repeatedly until it cracks into a hundred pieces just like my heart.

Stupid. Stupid. Stupid, stupid, stupid, I yell inside my head, hating that I ignored all the red flags.

Breathing hard, I pull out the picture and rip it into tiny pieces until it's as irreparable as we are; then, I toss the mess into the trash bin before calmly walking back to the bedroom. I smooth my hand over my black dress, walk over to the long-sleeved cardigan tossed across the end of the bed and pull it on. I don't mind that it's eighty-six degrees outside in mid-July. People instinctively know therapists and social workers have a uniform: cardigans.

Though it looks odd in this heat, they'd never question me, and that stereotype sure comes in handy today. I need the fabric to conceal the bruises on my arms that I can't let my clients see, as well as a nasty scratch on my shoulder that Brandon put there last week when he snatched me by my hair.

Heading to the front of the house, I grab my tumbler of ice water off the kitchen island, haul my tote bag over my shoulder, and make my way to my car. I spend the half-hour drive to the office listening to my favorite guided meditation and park in my spot a cool forty-five minutes before the first session of the day.

Placing my forehead to the steering wheel, I take a second to pray for strength. God, I really don't want to do this. I need to find a co-therapist who can help me out when I need to take a break. Exiting the car, I promise to make that a priority as soon as I get a handle on my life. And right now judging by the state of the grass in the yard alone, I better get a handle quick. Feeling minutely better, I dig out my keys to let myself into the modest office space and inhale the scent of the only place that's felt like home to me.

The space instantly lifts my spirits, but I feel like such a fraud preparing for a day of pretending everything is okay when the sad reality of my life on the inside is...I am dying.

CHAPTER TWO

EMPTY

"Uhhgg," I GROAN IN frustration, thrusting fast between Veronica's legs and ignoring her moaning because it's hindering me getting off.

I move slightly to grip the bend of her knee and wrap her leg around my hip, circling hard, trying to chase my orgasm. But it's just not happening tonight.

My skin crawls at the feel of her fingernails scraping down my back, and I force myself to bite the inside of my cheek to keep from saying anything offensive, preferring to remain silent yet hating that I have to. I shouldn't have to force anything...*especially* this.

Gently pulling her arm away, I hold her wrist down on the white sheets of our hotel bed, detesting her touching me. Detesting even more that I broke and slept with her knowing I didn't truly want to. I'd just been so lonely. And she'd been blatant and forward in her advances towards me, wondering why after weeks of dating I hadn't initiated sex with her.

Sneaking a look at the digital clock on the nightstand, I see that I've been screwing her for the last half hour. That in itself heightens my irritation, because the fact I'm just mindlessly thrusting into her and nothing's happening...well...it's a shame, really. What's even worse is it validates my thoughts that I might be broken after all.

To my horror I slow my pace when I feel my face begin to break like my heart feels...like it's cracking to pieces.

I *am* broken.

Grinding my teeth together, I wrestle my features into something I *hope* resembles an expression that won't be offensive and pull back from the crook of her neck. Straightening my arm, I rake my eyes over her body and try to latch on to something—*anything*—that will speed up the process to finish me off. But there's nothing. Disappointed, my lip curls back in annoyance, and I take a deep breath of her perfume that somehow makes it even worse.

I hate that I feel like this.

Truly ready to go, I sneak another glance at the clock. Distracted, my eyes go past it, perusing the lush hotel room I'd bought for tonight. I hadn't been comfortable with taking Veronica to my house as we've only been dating about four weeks, which is five weeks too long in my opinion. I bury my face back into the crook of her neck, continuing to try and ignore the irritating smell of her perfume.

I thrust faster, and minutes tick by where it's no use because I'm broken.

Defective.

My orgasm is holding back, my lungs burn, and my back aches with the effort to not take her the way I want to just get it over with. But I need to be gentle. I'm a big man and will hurt her if I pound into her the way I really need to. I slow my pace a little, feeling my cock deflate slightly, finally accepting that it's just not happening. She doesn't smell right, sound right, *feel* right. I can't do this. I won't.

"*Doctor Richardson,*" Veronica moans, running her hands down my back.

I grimace as she grips my ass hard, digging her sharp nails in. She may as well have dumped a bucket of spiders on top of me because I shrink from her touch, and my skin crawls even more than it already is.

Deciding I'm done with this, I grit my teeth and groan, acting like I orgasmed just like she was acting like she liked the sex we're having. Because she doesn't. She's faking right now, and her antics are worthy of a porn star. What's even worse is there'd been no genuineness in her motions with me tonight, which I believe truly hampered my ability to be all in this with her.

My demons whisper awful thoughts in my head, taunting me with the trauma of my past marriage with my ex-wife, Hannah. And my heart goes cold when I look into Vanessa's eyes.

I don't know if she was trying to make me fall in love with her by using her body and securing a physical bond or if she was just truly curious about what being in bed with me would be like, but I hate myself for folding and giving in just to appease this Godforsaken emptiness inside myself, knowing caving was just a temporary fix. Like slapping a band aid on a wound that really needs attention from the inside out.

It never works.

I observed that every move she'd made so far was disingenuous, so I can't get into the sex. I feel like I'm just using her at this point, and it doesn't make for a good time. At all. Over the last few weeks I've suspected that she's only in this with me so she could say she was with a world-renowned psychiatrist. For my money and status.

Absolved in the realization that tonight just isn't my night, I go completely still and pull out of her slowly, mindful of my big size. She throws me a confused look as I sit on the edge of the bed.

"Hey, what happened?" she says quietly, reaching for me. I stiffen, ignoring her fingers grasping at my arm.

I clear my throat uncomfortably. "Nothing."

Her brows pinch. "But then why..." Her words trail off when I turn to look at her. She recoils a bit, and I know it's because of my eyes. I can't help my icy cold stare. I work quickly to take the condom off, tying it, and stand to place it in the pocket of the pants I'd slung over the chair next to the bed. I'm not taking any chances. What would I look like at forty-three starting over with a baby with another woman who is so similar to my ridiculous ex-wife that they could be sisters?

I clear my throat uncomfortably. "I have to go," I lie.

But it's not a lie, either.

My eyes land on the clock again anxiously, seeing it's almost nine at night. If I leave now, I can work for at least a couple hours before I have to go to bed.

"Are you *serious?*" Veronica asks, her brown eyebrows hit her hairline as shock and disbelief color her tone. She pulls the sheet up to her breasts, leaning forward towards me. Her blood-red nails catch my eye, gleaming starkly against the white sheets of the hotel bed. I turn my gaze back to her, my eyes wandering over her wavy hair. A thick lock falls forward over her shoulder hanging against the curve in her breast.

For a second I hate myself. Veronica's extraordinarily attractive, and I wish desperately that I could feel something for her.

I get that I'm probably jaded on some level, but I'm just so *over* inauthentic women and their games. This one proves no different, unfortunately. My nose crinkles again. However, I note with some relief that it's not just her perfume that bothers me; Veronica smells *desperate*. And that's a scent I've grown to detest ever since I smelled it on my ex-wife Hannah.

Acutely aware of how intense my gaze comes across, I purposefully work to soften my eyes as well as my voice before speaking.

"I'm afraid so," I respond, firming my voice. "I have two evaluations to complete by Sunday night that need to be ready for Monday morning. I apologize for not making that clear beforehand." Pulling my briefs in place, I hurriedly jerk my pants up my legs and turn to her as I button them. "Feel free to stay the night, V. I've already paid for the room, and you can order something on room service if you'd like."

Averting my eyes from the sudden look of hurt that flashes in her eyes, I turn and reach for my shirt, pulling it on and commence to looking for my socks and shoes. I feel awful doing this to her, I do, but I'll feel even worse if I lead her on to believe that there's something here between us that's not. I'm not getting suckered back into a life that I worked so hard to get away from. If I was going to fall for someone like my ex-wife, then I should have just stayed with her and avoided raising my son in a divorced household.

"Oh, *Alex—*" Veronica implores. Sliding forward on one slender arm, she bites her bottom lip in a bid to look more enticing. It doesn't work.

"Refer to me as Alexander, please," I interrupt. "No one calls me Alex."

Because I won't let them. Too personal.

Veronica scoffs. "It's a Friday night. We were supposed to have fun," she says. Keeping the sheet clutched to her chest, she sits up on her knees and raises her gray eyes to meet mine. *"Do you have to?"*

I finish tying my shoes and stand up. She doesn't deserve for me to act like a complete asshole, so I lean forward and brush her hair behind her ear before pressing a soft kiss to her cheek. Veronica pulls her lips into a pout, but I speak before she has a chance to.

"Yes. Unfortunately, there's a cost to being a psychiatrist," I say softly, holding her eye contact. "I'll check on you in the morning and have an Uber here for you by ten-thirty."

Then I can figure out what excuse to give you for not being able to continue this ridiculous farce of a relationship.

Pulling away to walk to the door, her next words stop me dead in my tracks, causing me to turn my head slightly as she lashes out at me.

"You're so *cold!"* Her high-pitched voice rings out harshly, touching that tender spot inside me that's always felt attacked about my demeanor. "My coworker told me to not ask for your number. To not even *try* because you were icier than fucking Alaska. I should have listened to her!" she spits out from the bed behind me, throwing off the covers and standing up angrily to find her bra.

Her words hurt, like they always do.

"Perhaps," I say gruffly. "Goodnight, Veronica." Ignoring the sting, I open the swanky five-star hotel door, exiting the room into the brightly lit hallway.

I'm icy because no one's been able to warm me up.

Though I'd just left her, loneliness swells heavy, familiar, and hard in my chest as I make my way to the elevator bank and push the button.

As I stand there, waiting for the elevator to open, I contemplate on how I'd been unable to thaw out enough to even be comfortable with us driving together to our date tonight. I get it's odd, but I just can't let my guard down with anyone no matter how hard I try to put myself out there. For the hundredth time, I examine the thought that I'm still probably not ready to move on after my divorce. Maybe I'm not healed enough yet. I'll have to let her down...

Like I've done with various women for the last nine years since my divorce.

I swear a career in psychiatry was the best and worst thing that could have ever happened to me. Unfortunately, even outside of work when it's inconvenient, I see everything. I miss hardly anything, except real connections, genuine conversation, and chemistry.

I miss those things, a lot.

When I board the elevator I pull out my phone to text my best friend, Johnathan, not really expecting him to respond since he's been busy with a five-month-old. I smile wryly, thinking about starting all over with kids again at the age of forty-three. No way, man.

AR: Sorry for the piss-poor update, but I don't know man...It's not going to work out with Veronica. I don't like her. Couldn't make myself spend the night. I couldn't even fuck right. It's time for me to step back and just stop trying for a bit.

I run a hand through my hair, pulling the strands away from my forehead as I disembark the elevator, rather absentmindedly than normal.

Listening to my shoes tapping on the marble floor, I muse even deeper. Thinking on how hard it's been for me to keep my boundaries firmly in place since the divorce. A hard lesson I had to learn from being Hannah's doormat for well over ten years.

Right as I make it to the front revolving doors of the hotel my phone pings.

> J. Dawg: It's only been four weeks, Alexander. You have to give it longer. You do this with EVERYONE. You date for a month and then call it quits with every woman you've talked to in over seven years. I find it hard to believe out of the nine women you've dated since your divorce, you haven't found one that fits your high standards?

He doesn't get it. No one in my small circle does.

Shaking my head, I pocket my phone, make my way to my luxury BMW and drive off without bothering to respond. He's got his happily ever after already. He, Colin, and Vincent all do. I just want mine, now. And I don't want to feel judged at the way I go about it. So *what* if I have to go slow to find it? I went fast with Hannah and look where that got me: almost middle-aged with no one to love. That's where.

My chest now burns with irritation because Johnathan's text has my hackles up. He's one of the rare people who can get under my skin and make me doubt myself. Because, though my standards might be high, even *I* know better than to fall for a woman who only wants me for my status. And I keep lucking out and finding all the women who want me for my name and what being attached to me could mean for them and their life.

Though I don't mind having a woman to spoil, and who will benefit from my lifestyle and what I've worked so hard for, I want to feel seen for once. Not used. Not *doubtful.*

Is this really too much to ask? It's seeming like it.

I drive home in complete silence, lost in my thoughts. Determining that I'm just going to cease trying to date, or force anything romantic or physical for a while. I want something more than just special. I want primal love. Magic. It's out there. Has to be.

Maybe it's just not in Connecticut. Is that the problem? Perhaps I should consider a move.

Pulling through the wooden gate and up my driveway, I park outside my home and take a deep breath as I glance at the front door of my house. I scrub a hand down my jaw and settle deeper in the seat, not quite ready to journey into the lonely four walls of my home just yet. Not able to help myself, I pull up my work email on my phone, arching a brow when I see I missed an email earlier in the afternoon from Sarah B. Johnson.

Groaning in annoyance, I tilt my head back on the rest and close my eyes briefly, praying for peace.

"This woman," I sigh. *Major* pain in my ass. Probably an old, stuffy woman with nothing better to do than try to emulate being a psychiatrist because she couldn't financially afford what it took to become one, so now I get to deal with the fucking attitude that follows that.

Not even bothering to get out of the vehicle, I message Sarah about our mutual client. Forcing myself to go back through weeks of emails worth of correspondence to make sure I'm up to date regarding the client we're communicating about. Sarah and I have shared various clients throughout the past two years, and she always, without fail, pushes my buttons. Making me work harder at my job.

Thank God I love my career because *damn.* This woman has sent me some things before that's made me want to join my son in Spain, and say, *"fuck all, sayonara."*

There are times that I know she's right regarding our clients, though, and it's forced me to go back to the drawing board to reevaluate either their diagnosis or the clients' plans. Either way, she presses a nerve inside of me that I wasn't even aware of. One that even Hannah *herself* hadn't been able to reach, ironically.

For the next fifteen minutes, I sit in the dark and painstakingly read through our email chain before thoughtfully typing out a reply I hope touches a nerve that Ms. Johnson didn't know she had either. It's only fair.

Exiting the car, I slip my phone into my back pocket and spare the behemoth stone building that has been my home for the last sixteen years a hard look and curl my lip at the reminder of Hannah. This place hasn't ever felt like a home to me. I only bought the house because *she* wanted it. Craved the status that came along with being married to me. Can you imagine how awful it feels to dump countless thousands of dollars into a place you never even wanted?

I tighten my lips at the sight of the starkly modern exterior made of glass and stone, with fancy exterior lights showing off the place to admitted perfection. To some, this home might look like the epitome of success and the accumulation of two decades of hard work. To me, the enormous structure is a painful reminder of all the sleepless nights I'd spent in the beginning of my career, staying up all hours of the night slaving over notes and evaluations. Tediously pouring over the necessary documents to keep my new practice going.

Teaching myself how to start my own business, and not get sued while I was at it.

Truthfully, I'd bought the house well before I could financially afford it. I borrowed some of the down payment from my father thinking it would make Hannah happy enough to actually want to mother our son, Tyler. But I found out too late that the more I gave, the more she *took.* And took. And took. And took. Then it turned into *Tyler* taking. Until I felt like a sieve, merely a tool for someone to wrap their mouths around to suck dry.

I twist my lips, thinking that maybe our marriage would have been a bit more tolerable had she ever tried to suck something else to make me happy for once. But no, she never could because she was always recovering from lip surgery. A tuck here, a nip there.

Couldn't hardly touch her because she kept slicing and dicing herself up. And when she cut out half of her stomach for no real reason other than vanity, I'd lost it and stopped trying to touch her completely after that. Didn't even try. Moved into a different bedroom and the whole nine yards. She'd become almost unrecognizable over the course of our marriage.

She drained my bank account to afford the procedures so badly that I'd been forced to start boxing lessons in order to get some extra income. Which is how I met Johnathan, who had turned out to not just be a generous benefactor, but a dear friend throughout this lonely time in my life.

I walk inside the eerily quiet house and head straight to the kitchen, my safe spot, to throw open the double-door refrigerator. My eyes peruse quickly, flicking over the ingredients until I see the ones I want. Needing something sweet to make me feel better, I work fast, grabbing my mixer and the bowls I need.

I turn the sound system on to chase away the deathly quiet of the house, desperately trying to ignore the pinging coming from my phone. Already knowing it's *her* now, requesting the money I wouldn't send to Tyler. Neither one of them thinks I know, but she'd been using him to continue to leech from me well past the time her alimony and child support dried up.

It makes me sick to think I spent all those years sacrificing my emotional well-being for what felt like *nothing.* For two individuals who don't care for me other than what they could glean off me. To come home to this empty house with nothing but memories of my failures when all I would have killed for was the chance to be a father to my son, and now it's too late. I'll never have the chance again.

In a rare moment of self-pitying, I begin to work, making the dough for homemade chocolate chip cookies. I'm painfully aware I'm making way too much for one person, but I can't force myself to halve the recipe. Somehow, the thought makes the hurt even worse and makes my solitude more final.

My eyes flicker around the kitchen. There's no life, no movement except myself, and that amplifies my desolate state of being to even greater heights. Hot tears prick as I work to fight it back, and my chest tightens as I try desperately to lock down my emotions, but it's no use.

What was it all for?

Failing to be strong enough to keep up this icy façade, the internal cracks mercilessly deepen and lengthen. I shape the cookies and place them into the oven even as my traitorous body does anything and everything to punctuate how alone I am despite having two dozen cookies currently baking. I can't help but see the one plate and glass in the sink left over from my breakfast. And as I snatch a towel off the rack to wipe down the island, I also can't help but notice the breakfast table with only one charger placed in front of my seat.

The bare wall that used to hold the portrait of Hannah and I right behind it.

I put my eyes firmly to my hands working in front of me and clench my teeth.

My breathing comes heavier, disturbing the silence of my kitchen. It's bad tonight. Hitting me harder than normal for some reason. Maybe I'm so emotional because I fucked up and shared my body with someone I had no business with. I bring up a hand and wipe angrily at my eyes and clear my throat hard. Despite my best efforts, my lips tighten as a wave of anger and hurt meets the desolate loneliness and washes over me in waves. Successfully drowning me.

What have the last twenty years been for, if I'm to be this unhappy and unfulfilled?

Dropping the towel to the counter, I break. A hot tear escapes my eye to slide down my cheek.

I'm pissed with myself. Irritated that in almost ten years I still can't seem to get over the emotional abuse I've suffered. Giving up, I fold my arms, turn to rest my hips against the island counter, and bow my head to silently weep with only the sound of silence to keep me company.

"Fuck," I growl, pinching the bridge of my nose. This was not the life I imagined for myself all those years ago when I was younger. Before the reality of life slapped me in the face.

Thinking of all the years of hurt, I place my head into my hand and let out a choked sob at the very real possibility that I'll never have what I want: true love. I cast a look over, seeing the cookies slowly baking, illuminated in the light of the oven.

I shouldn't be having these alone. I should be sharing these with a woman in bed, laughing and making love all night. *God, is it too much to ask?*

I don't want to, but I embrace the pain, letting myself cry until the oven's timer goes off. Feeling irreparably empty.

CHAPTER THREE

Favorite Feminist Therapist

After a torturous night where I tossed and turned, and dealt with horrible guilt that I came to work and looked my clients in the face as if I was okay, I decided to make a plan to leave and return to my practice the next morning almost an hour earlier than normal. I'm determined to see my way out of this reality.

Operating on auto-pilot, I turn on the lights and glance around the little area like I always do, checking it to make sure the plants don't need sprucing up before the clients start rolling in.

I'm able to see it better than I was yesterday, that's for sure.

The bright room has delicate crown molding, tasteful art on the walls, and two purple couches that sit perpendicular to two light brown leather chairs. Next to the seating area is a small stove fireplace, and I can't wait for the weather to start getting colder so I can use it again. The end tables have picture books to look through, and small plants line the picture window. I walk to the end table to straighten a small sailboat on top of the stack of books and smile fondly.

I'd *just* found this unassuming piece at a thrift shop last week and knew I had to have it.

Nothing else needs sprucing up, so I dust my hands off and make my way down the hall that hosts two spacious offices and a small kitchenette. I only use one of the offices, keeping the other one empty just in case I ever move another therapist in here with me.

Unlocking my office door, I walk into the space, place my keys gently in the ceramic bowl on the corner of my desk and turn my purple desk lamp on, not wanting the overhead light on today. I need dimmed lighting and calming music that will hopefully give me the resolve to think clearly. To plan.

Remembering that I should have gotten paid today, I pull out my cell to check my bank account. At the amount, I feel a frisson of relief that helps to chase away my deep-seated discontent. I sigh at the number: eleven-hundred dollars from the club. Not bad for three hours of singing. I'd need to continue to have a steady flow of money coming in to help pay the rent on my practice. I figure I'll need to at least pay up to two months on our house so that I'd have time to sell it, or to figure out if he will buy it.

Either way, I'm sure I don't want it.

Lowering to my seat, I wince and suck air through my teeth as my sore back presses into the chair. I shake my head, getting back up again to prop a pillow behind my back and pop a Tylenol to help with the pain. I'm certain we're going to be okay. Placing my hand on my tummy, I rub in gentle circles, tilting my head back on a relaxing sigh and focus on pushing positive thoughts to my baby.

We're safe in this moment. It's me and you against the world, baby girl. You have one momma who loves you madly.

I work hard to mentally prepare myself for a long day of clients. Knowing a distraction is what's needed, I pull open my personal laptop to look for apartments to rent nearby. Finding two in my preferred price range, I call to set up an appointment to view them.

Quickly overwhelmed, I place my fingers against my jaw and press in hard when my thoughts turn into trying to stay with Brandon, to see if he will change and help with the continued financial burden that just keeps getting heavier and heavier. They settle as an ache in my neck like all the other ones I'm currently experiencing.

The pain radiates from where my fingers press; a literal reminder that no, the man put his hands on me, and that is unacceptable. Also, I would *never* in a million years advocate for one of my clients to stay in a domestic violence situation. So why would I?

I swipe open my phone and start a group chat with my college besties: Christopher and Jerome.

Sarah Beara [8:30a]: Hey, guys. Your favorite, friendly female feminist therapist here. I know we haven't seen each other in weeks (I'm so sorry), but I have a favor to ask of you two.

Placing my phone on its stand, I close my personal laptop, jiggling the mouse to wake up my desktop work computer. Opening my work email, I check for anything important, starting from the oldest email to the most recent.

I respond to a couple clients: one who said they were wanting to refer a friend to me and enquiring if I have space on my caseload, and another who needs to cancel for the next two weeks. It takes all of five minutes to respond to them with twenty minutes left before my first client's session.

My mouth tips up at the corner when my phone lights up with a reply.

> Jerome [8:35a]: Sarah, the FFFT. Is this another fancy acronym to go behind that fancy name of yours? M.A, LPC, *now* we have to add FFFT, too? You're about to use up the whole alphabet. What's up, baby girl?

His humor reaches through my desolate spirit, and I feel my smile broaden. Jerome can be such an asshole. But he's my asshole.

Sitting back against my pillow I sip more water, and peruse through my email. I scroll down, narrowing my eyes at an email sent at almost two in the morning. I twist my mouth in displeasure because even *I* don't answer emails at all hours of the night. And I consider myself extremely on top of my game...just during business hours.

I bristle, seeing *his* name.

Dr. Alexander Richardson.

I roll my eyes, irritated for probably the tenth time in just a handful of weeks with this man. Leaning over my keyboard, I ignore the twinge in my back as I tuck a thick lock of hair behind my ear and begin to type furiously. God. I've been in an aggravating back-and-forth communication with him about this client for *three freaking weeks.*

I've been killing myself attempting to convince him that our mutual client needs a different diagnosis.

I can't help but feel like he's treating the client for one condition, when I've been been finding through our latest one-on-one sessions that the client is actually suffering from a personality disorder and bipolar. My fingers are stiff with anger as I beat out a quick email; I tell him—yet again—that he needs to push this client's appointment up so we can review the necessary meds, diagnosis, and make the needed changes. The more I type, the more I find myself heating in anger.

Though we've shared mutual clients for a couple years now, and he normally goes along with my requests, he is *unrelenting* on this one for some reason. And I just don't need this right now.

Dr. Richardson responds almost immediately, making me bristle at his short reply. He's not budging. Gleefully informing me he thinks I might be mistaken regarding my thoughts on the client's diagnosis.

"Oh my Goddd," I breathe, pinching the bridge of my nose as I speak to him for the second time today. A record for me. "Please help me, because I can't do this this early in the morning. I just can't."

A scowl breaks over my face because I am *not* wrong.

I press my lips together in irritation and hit reply harder than necessary before feverishly spelling out my feelings on the matter.

> Mr. Richardson,
>
> With all due respect, this method of communication is obviously not working for us. We need to be united on behalf of our client—*he* is the one who is truly suffering. I do not have time for this power trip.
>
> I would like to see you in person this week. Friday at the latest, if you can manage to fit me in. I see our client on Thursday and will have an updated therapy log to add to the ones that I need

you to review that show current symptomatology. I will even bring my personal copy of the latest DSM-V in case you can't remember how that goes.

Please give me a time you can meet after 3p on Thursday, or anytime on Friday. If this continues to go on much longer, and I feel like my client is being hurt, I will not hesitate to go to the Board of Ethics regarding your lack of attention to the issue at hand.

Unkind Regards,

Sarah B. Johnson, M.A. LPC.

Bright Light Counseling, LLC.

Regret instantly fills me as my mouse hovers over the email, because laying down gauntlets is not my thing. It doesn't feel good. However, right is right.

I take the '*un*' off my signoff—because that's unprofessional and petty—and send the email with a deep sigh. Truly ready to go home, I sit back, anxiously rubbing the bridge of my nose. I hate that I had to threaten to do what I didn't want to *ever* do to another professional. But it's crucial in this field that you follow rules, and if I suspect a fellow mental health professional is not engaging in best practices, then I'm obligated to report them. Regardless of the man's top tier status in the mental health field, I do have a practice of my own to maintain and protect.

No offense, Alexander, but it's a dog eat dog world out here.

Killing time, I swivel slowly back and forth in my chair.

I shake my head, trying to dispel these feelings of resentment starting to build up against the psychiatrist. I have enough resentment for Brandon to not be adding Dr. Richardson in the mix of it, too.

Thinking of Brandon again, I pick up my phone to respond to Jerome.

Sarah Beara [8:56a]: Jerome, I will not stop until ALL of the alphabet belongs to me. Anyways, I'm leaving Brandon. I can't really get into it now, but there's a lot of stuff that's been happening, and I need help grabbing my bed from the house. Can you help me? I'm looking at apartments next weekend.

Sarah Beara [8:56a]: I figured since Chris has the truck, we can sneak in there and grab it while he's at work.

My office door rings, and I glance at the clock, seeing my first client has arrived a couple minutes early and has let themselves into the tiny lobby. Taking a deep breath, I patiently go over the clients' last therapy log, preparing myself for our session. However, my phone dings again, forcing my attention away.

Chris [8:57]: What did that stupid motherfucker do? We don't even have to wait till he's gone. I'll bust through that house with my truck and run him over in the process. I'm not scared of him.

Not wanting to get into it right now, I shake my head, silence my phone, and stand up, opening my office door to usher my client in through the doorway to the seating area by my desk.

"Mrs. McDermont, how're you doing today?" I say softly. "You look absolutely *gorgeous*!" I smile at the beautiful redhead fondly as she works to settle herself in the cushy love seat against the far wall.

"Hi, Sarah. I'm doing good. But *look at you,"* she responds brightly, "you're looking very pretty today. I love your dress. That hemline is to die for."

Keeping it simple, I turn to my desk, wishing I felt it. "Thank you; you're very kind." Grabbing my tablet, I arrange my dress and cardigan before sinking down onto the plush wingback office chair and cross my legs with some effort and work to match her bright smile. Putting on an act through the pain isn't easy.

She tucks a leg underneath her and pulls a blanket in her lap, hugging the purple throw pillow to her chest.

I love this about her; she really makes herself comfortable and commits herself to the process. I'd never tell her this because it's not ethical to, but she's like the *perfect* client. She's quite the salacious case, too.

Olivia McDermont is a self-professed masochist who had given up her daughter when she was born. The poor woman started seeing me four months ago after an unfortunate kidnapping spree that had almost taken her, her husband, her sister, and her brother-in-law's life. She's just now starting to come out of fits of depression, finally ready to process the grief of not raising her daughter.

I do all the things. I smile, nod, and listen to her speak. Once I get enough information, I put my head down, writing notes into my tablet. I give Olivia my undivided attention, putting my personal pain to the back of my head.

CHAPTER FOUR

DIFFERENT DAY

THIS IS JUST NOT my fucking day. But I need to get it together enough to at least put on my professional hat for my employees because the show must go on. Nodding at the stragglers in the hallway, I attempt an airy feel despite my emotional discomfort; however, the smile I emit feels more like a grimace. They smile back but turn their eyes forward quickly as we pass.

It stings more than it should because when I'm like this I come across very cold, which is a character trait of mine I *loathe* validating.

Sharply turning the corner, I push through the glass door and then force myself to take a deep breath as I walk to the seat at the head of the table in the boardroom of my practice. I place my briefcase on the table, and I shove a hand through my hair as my heart pounds heavier than usual and causes me to run a finger between my collar and neck for relief.

"Why's it so hot in here? Damn," I mutter, stepping to the side to check the thermostat, thinking Cathy must have set it at the wrong temperature. But, nope, it's seventy-two degrees per usual. I click it down two degrees then go back to my seat.

Feeling uncomfortably hot, I unbutton my suit jacket before shrugging out of it and draping it over the back of my seat. Opening my laptop, I wait patiently, going over my files, while my colleagues and the other psychiatrists who are under my supervision shuffle in with their folders and laptops. They come in staggered clusters, taking their seats and murmuring their hushed greetings to each other. No one speaks to me, content to talk amongst themselves.

Miserable, it doesn't take any effort on my part to put their droning to the back of my head. God, I don't want to be here, but I don't want to go home to that fucking house, either. Shit. I'm stuck between a rock and a hard place. Rubbing a hand across my jaw, I nod respectfully as they all sit. A couple people eventually say hello, but for the most part, I keep my attention on my computer, preferring to not engage in chit-chat until everyone is in the room and quieted down.

Yet still, my newest hire, David, a fellow psychiatrist, pulls out the seat directly to my left. He reaches out and rudely raps his knuckles on the desk next to me just as I'm in the middle of reading an email. "What's up, Richardson?"

Taken aback by the audacity, my hand falls softly to the table as I sharply look up and narrow my eyes, assessing the younger man with an equally as sharp greeting. "Osterkamp."

Before he can see my displeasure, he turns to share a low laugh with his neighbor.

Discreetly, I regard him for a moment for probably the fiftieth time since I hired him. Though he's perfectly nice, he seems to never get a clue.

There's something off about him that I can't place despite two decades of experience in this field, and that's *never* a good sign.

At first, my head colleagues attempted to convince me that I should be flattered that it seems he wants me to take him under my wing, but no, that's not what this is about. I do know that much. Until I figure it out, though, I have to contend with the fact he constantly inserts himself in my space. As a psychiatrist, this is worrying because the man can't pick up on the fact I want to be left alone unless the conversation has to do with work.

It speaks to a lack of boundaries, and everybody knows that irks the hell out of me.

Turning my attention from David, I nod my head in greeting to the late stragglers pouring in before looking back down at my screen, biting back a groan with effort. An incoming email from Ms. Johnson sits at the top, unread. Clicking it open, I only allow myself to read just a few lines before pinning the email, intending to come back to it after the meeting. Since my colleagues are still settling, I take a second to rub my eyes in irritation.

God, I'm so over her shit.

"Ms. Johnson. You're determined to be a pain in my ass today, aren't you?" I breathe quietly to myself.

David immediately snaps his head to look at me. *"Sarah* Johnson?" he stresses, arching a brow.

Lowering my hand, I frown, eyeing the expression on his face. "Yes. You know her?" I don't bother telling him to mind his own business.

David nods.

I contemplate transferring this client to him so that he can take it over, and I won't need to be bothered anymore. *Matter of fact,* maybe I can figure out how to offload *all* of the clients Ms. Johnson and I share so that I can be done with this woman. My personal life sucks enough without my work life becoming a place of discontentment for me as well.

I stretch out my arm and glance at my watch, everyone's cue that the meeting has begun.

When they're finally settled, I begin in a curt tone. "Alright, everyone, thank you for joining me. If you would please, take out your laptops and send me all of your upcoming evaluations, court dates, and where you are at on any currently completed evaluations." I eye them all in turn. "Let me know if there is any assistance that is needed with billing your clients or any insurance snags that we need to work through."

I sit back in my seat, hating how long-winded these meetings get, and click my pen in an agitated move. Everything in me wants to respond to that fucking email that's probably more than likely guaranteed to send my ass through the roof.

"Also," I clear my throat harshly, "if you are requesting time off within the next three months, please send me the dates you need covered so we can make sure your clients remain in compliance. You all know how I like to stay on top of these things." I give everyone a second to laugh before turning to David. "Osterkamp, you first. What have you got?"

By sheer force of will I make myself pay attention, but in the back of my head, I'm furiously crafting my response to Ms. Johnson.

Furiously.

My phone dings, drawing my gaze down as David's voice drones on. I swipe it open quickly, fighting the urge to roll my eyes at Tyler's request. Further irritated that the boy couldn't even spare me a fucking hello. Not surprising, really. It's truly shaping up to be a shitty week.

Tyler [9:00a]: Dad, can you please send me fifteen hundred dollars? Please?

Ignoring the text, I attempt like hell to not let the correspondence ruin my meeting. I place my phone face down and resume listening to David. Pulling up a spreadsheet on my computer, I record any information that's relevant, keeping myself the picture of a person who's in charge and put together. Which I am...to a certain extent anymore, I suppose.

I clear my throat gently, pulling up another spreadsheet. "Thank you, Osterkamp." I eye the man next to him. "What about you, Robinson?"

I move on to the next one, then the next, until I take care of all twenty employees under me.

As everyone spends the morning updating me on their work, I shake my head wearily, wishing I had something to look forward to when I get off besides texts asking for money, and a cold, empty house.

Different day, same old bullshit.

The end of the meeting is beyond disappointing; everyone's full-up, so I won't be offloading any of Sarah's and my clients. See what I mean?

Absolute. Bull. Shit.

A [11:49a]: Tyler, please tell your mother to stop asking you for money. I won't send you any for her to take. Now, I haven't heard from you in a while. How's your day been going?

He doesn't reply.

When I journey back to my office, I spend time looking at the gold framed photo of us that sits on my desk. It's the one of when he was ten and thought he wanted to play the cello, like me. I was so proud, and it reflected in the brightness of my smile. He's posing with the instrument, my arm around his shoulders. I looked down at him, beaming. I remember that day like it was yesterday. I was so surprised and excited that he'd taken up something that I loved. I thought we could practice together, maybe be the start of us bonding. But like everything else, the cello fell by the wayside not even a year later.

Reaching forward, I turn the photo away from me so I can focus on work and not the past.

But at the end of the day, like every single day, I drive home, cook myself a simple meal and eat by myself at the breakfast table. No music today. I want to wallow in my solitude. Once I finish my meal, I wash my dishes, then head up the stairs to the room down the hallway, and push open the only door I keep closed.

His room.

I keep it just like he left it. Same dark green comforter with the planet projector on his bedside table. I walk to it and open the top drawer, seeing the raggedy stuffed animal that he used to haul with him everywhere before abandoning it when he was seven-years-old. Smiling, I pick it up in my hand and rub my thumb over the matted fur, remembering a night, twelve years ago in the winter, when he left it at the restaurant we'd had dinner at. I drove half an hour back to that restaurant that same night in the freezing cold because I couldn't bear to see him cry himself to sleep.

I think that was the last time I felt like his hero.

That night, Hannah made love to me, telling me she was turned on by how fatherly I was, only for us to end up divorced a year later.

My eyes prick, and I place the animal on his pillow before shutting the little drawer. I click on his planet lamp and take a second to marvel at the patterns it makes on his wall while I think about my life, all my regrets and choices. I didn't spend nearly as much time as I'd wanted in here. It would have been magical, snuggled up with him in bed and reading him book after book under the stars.

Truth of the matter is, I didn't even get to read him even half of the books I'd bought, and I doubt his mother did, either.

Fuck, I failed him so badly.

I scrub a hand down my face and walk to his closet where I get out his old cello before going back to his bed. Sinking to the mattress, I roughly dust off the case before unzipping it. The mahogany looks just as bright as when I'd first bought it. Contemplating change, I stare for a second before taking the rosin out of the small pouch and test it. Surprised it's still any good, I brush it over the strings and then stand it up. The bow snags a little as I play a few chords, but it still sounds decent enough for another parent to have a chance to accomplish what I couldn't.

Tightening my lips, I return it to the case, click off the lamp, and leave the bedroom, my fingers wrapped around the handle with a death grip. I'm not quite ready to let go of what could have been, but I know I need to start taking the steps to. My mental health can't take holding on like this much longer.

Just outside the door, I turn my head slightly and allow myself a moment to grieve before meandering down the hall.

I leave his door open for the first time since he moved out.

Placing the cello in the foyer to donate, I journey to my den to turn on the fireplace and put on the television in a rare need to zone out, keeping my phone face up on the cushion next to me. Propping my feet on the table, I keep a hopeful eye on my phone and stay up an extra hour later than normal in consideration of our time difference, hoping he'll respond.

But he doesn't. He never does...really.

I shut the fireplace and television off, both my heart and soul heavy as I make my way up the stairs to the bedroom. Painfully aware it's not just a different day, it's a completely different time in my life, and maybe it's time I start coming to terms with it.

CHAPTER FIVE

SAME BULL

A FEW HOURS LATER, I moan, rubbing the back of my neck. I'm in so much pain that I don't even know how I'm going to be able to drive home. I had all my clients back-to-back, but thankfully I'm now out of session for the day and can focus on administrative work.

Because I spaced out my clients, I was able to complete all their log notes in between sessions, so now all I have to do is check for referrals and my work email. Opening my laptop, I blow out a tense breath. I'd be absolutely lying to myself if I said I didn't think about Dr. Richardson's reply. *If* he even replied, that is.

I pull up my work email first, and there it is, in irritating black-and-white with enough healthy dose of holier-than-thou energy and professionalism to make my teeth grind.

> Ms. Johnson,
>
> In our communications, it would be preferable for you to address me as *Dr.* Richardson.
>
> I am available on Friday between the hours of 6p and 7p. I will go over your notes. No need to bring the DSM-V. In case you weren't aware, I helped to add to the new edition, so maybe I can teach you a few things instead of you always trying to school me in this *insufferably* professional way of yours.
>
> As for the incredibly thoughtful, and *lovely* threat to go to the board, well, that's your prerogative. *Isn't it*?
>
> I'll see you in court.
>
> *Warmest* Regards,
>
> 'DOCTOR' Alexander Richardson, MD.

I feel my face heat up immediately. I didn't take out the *"un"* like I'd thought...

"Oooohh, this freaking man!" I blurt out loudly.

Bending over my laptop, I roll my eyes and reply simply, stating that I'd be there Friday at six sharp. Mr. Richardson is how I greet him, nothing more, nothing less, because he needs to be knocked down a peg or two. I sign my name, no titles, regards, *warm* or otherwise, included. Even though, yeah...it's unprofessional...I do it anyway, feeling absolutely no shame. I'm too tired and hurt to care about being embarrassed or politically correct.

I pop an extra strength Tylenol, wincing against the throbbing pain in my body. I shut down the office and head home for the day to fix dinner: a simple chicken salad. I spend time calling Chris and Jerome on the way home on a group call and verify that when the time comes that they'd be able to help move my things.

I consider myself so grateful that I had the sense to not combine finances with Brandon, as it would have made this sticky situation worse.

Back at home, I breathe a sigh of relief at Brandon's absence. Thanking God that I may not be beaten or degraded tonight, I make dinner quickly because I'm starving. A half-hour later, I'm finally done, and I sit at the glass dining room table with a whimper, feeling my back smart. Thinking about taking a long warm bath when I'm done, I eat my salad.

Bumpy must like it because I crave it so much.

I'm lost in my head, wondering when Bumpy is going to decide to give me an actual bump, when the front door opens, and Brandon saunters in drunk. I put my fork down, appetite gone.

Oh no. Wiping my mouth, I stand up and take my half-eaten plate to the sink. Feeling his eyes on me, my skin prickles with trepidation and discontent.

"Hey," he says in an aloof tone.

Glancing over, I ignore Brandon's greeting, knowing that he probably won't remember this interaction at all considering how drunk he currently looks. Flicking my eyes down his disheveled state, I note his blonde hair is mused, and his shirt is buttoned up haphazardly.

I tighten my lips. He's probably cheating, which is why he thinks *I* am. It's projection at its finest and an old-as-time textbook abuser trait.

My efforts to ignore him are in vain. Brandon comes up behind me, smelling godawful, and presses his lips to the back of my hair. "Hey, baby," he murmurs into my ear, softening his voice.

Not able to help myself, I recoil, wrinkling my nose at the stench of body odor and alcohol rolling off him in waves. My nose twitches, forcing me to pause in the action of rinsing my hands, smelling something different on him this time. The alcohol is *almost* enough to mask it, but not quite. I turn off the faucet.

Was he with another woman?

I sting with betrayal, even though I was so sure at this point that he couldn't have done anything else to hurt me. But I'm done with him. Tightening my lips, I turn to dry my hands on a hand towel, keeping quiet and trying to ignore him hovering.

Out of my periphery, I see him look at me with a sad looking expression on his face, but nothing in me is able to meet his eye.

"I'm *sorry,* Sarah Beara. I won't hit you anymore! Can you just love me, please?" he says, leaning into me. His arm bands around my shoulders, snagging my hair and making my eyes water anew with the small prick of pain that is just a mere layer on top of the other hurts.

I grit my teeth and maneuver myself from under his arm, turning and walking to the living room.

Sitting on the sofa, I reach over for the remote on the table. "There's chicken salad for you if you want some," I say in a light tone.

It isn't until I'm mindlessly flipping through the various apps on the television for something to watch that I realize I'm hesitating to pick a show based off what he might think about it. My heart beat ramps up, stealing my breath and making my chest tight.

If I choose a dating show, would he call me a whore and ask if that's what I wanted? A bunch of men's attention?

If I watch a weight loss show, would he call me disgusting and fat again?

If I choose a competitive singing show, he'd find a way to bring up my singing at the lounge, as that's what made him beat me so brutally the night before.

I frown, finding a problem with every show I click past. My heart races even faster, and to my horror I feel something like hate bloom in my chest as I realize I'm beginning to truly resent him for making me feel this way. It's a freaking TV show, not a monumental decision to be made. I shake my head, lamenting at the four years just down the drain, wasted. My twenties.

My precious youth.

He moves closer, and I turn my head slightly, feeling my face heat as he strolls lazily to me. His footsteps sound out unevenly as he stumbles slightly, under the influence.

"*There's chicken salad if you want some!*" Brandon mocks back at me in a baby voice. "You already cook like those fat southern women," he says in his normal tone, getting an ugly expression on his face. "I guess that's what's coming next, huh? You're gunna let yourself get fat?" He bends down to put his face inches away from mine, cocking his head to the side in a blatant challenge.

Recoiling my head, I eye him, staying silent. No woman should ever be made to feel challenged by a man.

He doesn't relent. I turn my face away to hide as my eyes well up with sadness, this time at his childish, uncalled for behavior. Silently I will him to back off.

"*Bitch*," he spit out roughly, turning and tripping over his feet as he walks back into the kitchen.

At least he's not hitting me.

I can deal with degradation; I just don't want to be hit.

Not knowing where to put my gaze, I just sit here quietly and stare off towards the wall, trembling and upset, wishing I could call my dad.

Craving softness from him. To know that he'd want to protect me and tell me I'm going to be okay.

I flinch when Brandon pulls a cabinet drawer out so aggressively that it comes off its hinges and clatters noisily to the floor. But I continue to stay quiet as he curses about how stupid I am, and how promiscuous I am for performing at the lounge two nights a week like a whore.

My gaze falls to my lap where my fingers fidget. I didn't even need to click on any show, honestly. He's giving me a spectacle to watch, a live experience in degradation. My lips quiver as the image of my fingers distort.

What did I ever do to you to make you treat me this way? I thought you loved me. You told me that we're in this life together...

My heart tugs as I continue to sit quietly.

A tear falls down my cheek as I clench my hands, imagining I'm holding the hand of someone who cares about me. Someone who will hold their hand out for me to take and pull me into them, wrapping me in their arms and assuring me that I'll come out of this thing in one piece. I imagine the hand gripping mine is someone who wants to comfort me. Wants me.

Why does no one want me?

Even my own dad doesn't like me.

The realization makes my heart skip a beat, because it hits me that I truly have daddy issues, and this is why I was so blind to Brandon's antics. I contemplate how he'd never betrayed any negative feelings to me before the pregnancy about my side gig. His hot and cold behavior leaves me reeling and confused. Because Brandon used to *love* my singing and the fact that I was talented.

He would sit in the front row and clap with the others in the audience, smiling brightly as I performed. I guess it turns out it was all a façade. All of it. Every second. And that hurts to the bone, and even deeper, if possible.

I don't know if I'll ever trust again.

Feeling like my heart is shattering to pieces, I begin to grieve the Brandon that I used to know. Mourn the man that is apparently no longer there in any fashion. I hug my arms close to myself and sniff, feeling more alone than I've ever felt before.

I wish I could go home to my parents. If that were a possibility, I'd leave tonight. Start over again.

"Stupid bitch," Brandon mutters.

There's a scuffle as he slips on a utensil he'd stepped on in the kitchen.

Tears slide unchecked down my face as I look back up and do my best to turn on a show to ignore him, keeping the volume low as I wipe gently at my cheeks with the sleeve of my cardigan, trying to not draw attention to myself. I attempt to mentally retreat, worried that if I tried to leave right now, Brandon really would put his hands on me and put me in the hospital.

Breathing deeply, I force myself to calm down. Trying to mentally remember the guided meditation I followed this morning in the car, I place my hand on my tummy again.

Don't worry; I'll love you enough for the both of us, Bumpy.

I try to send all positive thoughts, not wanting the negativity to infiltrate the baby. My little bumpy. *Brittany.*

Just a little over a week until my first apartment tour, okay? It's the week after next, I talk to Bumpy, trying to encourage the both of us. I can't give up on my practice, drop everything and move to my parents'. I try to have faith that it's going to be okay.

It just has to.

Refusing to let him alienate me out of the living room, I curl my legs under me and take a steadying breath. I studiously ignore Brandon's muttering as he sits at the table and eats the rest of the food that he'd *just* complained about. He's selfish, not leaving me any for my lunch tomorrow. I don't let the lack of consideration bother me, because what is the point?

It's not a new feeling to me, the lack of consideration; I've felt it my whole life.

Different day, same bull.

CHAPTER SIX

Until It's Not

I manage to get through the next day easier than the last at the prospect of seeing Johnathan for a few rounds in the ring after work. We're a half-hour deep into sparring at our private boxing venue, and I relish the workout taking me out of my emotions. The familiarity of my muscles straining makes my head clearer, affording me the time to put some distance between me and my emotions. And because of it, I'm going a little harder on him than usual tonight.

My arm snaps forward lightning fast, making contact with the side of Johnathan's head.

He grunts. "Motherfucker, what are you trying to *do*? Knock my brain through my head?" He eyes me as I smoothly slide back into a poised fighting stance, waiting for him to recover and retaliate. He brings a hand to the side of his head and rubs, shaking his head hard.

I bet his ears are fucking ringin'.

I rejoice as sweat slicks down my body, making my shirt stick uncomfortably to my feverish skin. Ignoring the nasty look the big guy is giving me, I pause, ripping my soaked shirt off and throwing it to the side. I slide back into my pose, giving him a wicked grin. This is what he pays me for, so he better buckle up.

"You better be happy I'm holding back. If you were in a *real* fight, your brains would already be plastered all over the floor," I grit, stepping forward quickly and swinging a sharp uppercut, happy to see Johnathan move out of the way just in time. He's been a little slow since the birth of his son, understandably.

I blink sweat out of my eyes as we circle slowly, swaying from one foot to the other, gauging each other's weaknesses. Johnathan doesn't have many, but it seems like I do.

Tonight, at least.

Johnathan steps forward fast, and I grunt as his fist connects hard with my ribs, causing me to retaliate with a sharp uppercut. He grunts as I shoot off a couple of quick one-two punches, making the broad, Middle-Eastern man growl in frustration and back up from me. His sharp brown eyes find mine quickly; mine narrow, observing a simmering energy within their depths I need him to let break free for my sake.

But Johnathan always remains in control, the fucker. I know we could really stand ten toes down in this ring if he wanted to; he just won't. His boundaries are perfect, ironically. I'll never tell him this, but he's the mental health field wet dream.

He gives me a rather abrupt once over. *"No,"* Jonathan rasps, swiping a hand quickly across his brow. "I'm holding back slightly because even though we have this arrangement, it's to keep me sharp because you're the best I've found at this style of fighting. Not for us to fight to the death."

He's irritated, and his accent is a bit thicker, causing me to smile. At the thought that an actual fight might make me feel less disconcerted, I lunge forward, trying to further agitate the big guy.

"God, but it would be so much fun to actually fight, though, wouldn't it? *Really let loose?*" I smirk, trying to egg him on as I pummel his torso with more punches.

My wrapped fists sting as I make hard contact on the fifth punch to his chest. He grunts, giving me another quick look up and down. "So, you broke up with Veronica, huh?" he says in an accusatory tone. "That's the reason you're going in so hard tonight?"

His words make me curl my lips and step forward, trying to get him into a headlock. "Yeah, I broke up with her, man. I can't deal with the disingenousness of it all."

He makes a disapproving sound, jerking against my hold. We move across the ring as we grapple hard, but my arm stays locked around him. "You didn't even spend enough time with her to know her. Two evenings out a week for four weeks doesn't *count*, Alex. You can't know everything about somebody in that short amount of time." Johnathan barrels us forward with a grunt, sending us both to the floor.

"I didn't need that much time." I jerk under him as he wraps his hands around my wrist, and almost like he's got the grip from God himself, he manages to loosen my hold. Impressive. Not many have been able to escape a headlock from me. I plant my feet, our strained sounds reach past the ropes, causing a few bystanders to look towards us, but I keep focused, not making it easy on him. I flex my arm hard, seeing every vein standing out against my skin in sharp relief.

"How much fucking time you need, man?" he huffs hard, his face turning red. "Come on!"

"Not that much." My voice comes out strained as I work to keep him right where I want him, but he decides to go ahead and indulge me in what I so desperately need tonight and damn near breaks my arm off to get free. We stumble back from each other, sweat dripping from our faces, and panting. "I can tell almost right off the bat," I say, a rumble starting deep in my chest when he comes at me again and attempts to get me in a restraint. I let him, for no other reason than so he can practice. "And I'm not wasting either of our time. I'm getting older, brother. I don't have the luxury of wasting years getting to know someone." I make a rough sound, managing to get out from under Johnathan before he dislocates my goddamn shoulder.

We grunt and grapple for a bit, sliding around on the floor of the ring as we display our strength, causing a few others in the building to meander up to the ring to watch. We separate before getting up quickly and sliding into a fighting pose. Back to boxing, not wrestling.

Do I imagine his eyes soften towards me with his next words? I don't know because people don't ever grace *me* with softness. I get why...but it still hurts.

"Alexander, you're *not* going to fall for another Hannah again. You need to give it a chance. At *least* stay with someone long enough to be able to get into the swing of having a healthy sex life. It's been like nine years since you've been in a long-term relationship, right? Hannah was the last, huh?" Johnathan asks.

The man really missed his calling because he should have been a therapist. His words trigger something inside me.

Vulnerable, I put my hands down and look openly at my friend of ten years. I know my eyes are sad as I meet his wise gaze. He's the only one I trust enough to open up like this.

“I can’t enjoy it, man,” I admit, shrugging heavily. I fight against heaving, trying to catch my breath and talk at the same time. “Even when they give themselves over, I don’t like it. It doesn’t feel right...and I don’t like to feel like I’m taking advantage of them. And that’s always how my mind ends up taking it. When I force myself to be intimate with another person *just because*, it feels almost like I’m *raping* her because I’m using her body, and I don’t even want to.” Chest rising and falling heavily, I put my hands on my hips and look away from my friend. “My mind just won’t let me enjoy it.”

Johnathan blinks at me for a second before leaning on the rope. "So....have you always been this way?"

I nod, fighting back the feeling of not wanting to be judged. "I've always been this way." Never one for casual sex. Always needing that emotional connection first before I gave my body over to someone. Even with Hannah, the minute our emotional connection severed, so did our sex life. There's a label for what I am: demisexual.

Feeling too bared, I look away, relieved to see our audience is gone.

"Hmm," Jonathan hums, standing to his full height. He doesn't speak, though; he lets me have my thoughts.

"I know it's not the most manly thing to admit, and I'll probably lose some major masculine points, but soul ties are a *very* real thing. I see people come in all the time needing to be medicated half out of their mind in order to deal with the trauma of having a sexual relationship with someone they had no business being with." I bring my gaze back to him, seeing him staring, giving me his full attention. "And I don't want that for myself."

Johnathan looks me up and down with an assessing gaze. "That's interesting. I respect that completely, my friend, and thanks for sharing that with me. So, you're just going to be celibate?"

"I'm going to have to be."

"Sounds reeaaal depressing."

"Sex is not about *happiness,"* I snap back, shooting him a look. "It's much more than that. It's an exchange of the bodies. An *intimate* meeting of the souls. So no," I hold up a hand and shake my head. "I can't mentally handle fucking a woman who I don't want to fuck just for the sake of it. That's a disgusting feeling."

"I get it, but celibacy is a lonely journey." Now *his* eyes turn sad as he references the time he'd spent mourning after his late wife passed, before he found Vanessa. And in this moment, I realize he understands me a lot more than I originally gave him credit for. "It's been lonely for you?"

I nod somberly. "Of course."

"Yeah, I bet." He clears his throat hard as he glances away, contemplating. "Well. All I can say is it's lonely, until *it's not."*

I feel chills race down my body and my mind pivots. "That's okay. I'll just spend my time fucking up *your* body until I find the right woman to fall into," I joke, needing to lighten the conversation.

Johnathan puts his fists up. "Sounds good to me. And mad respect, brother. Let's do what I pay you to do."

He decides to give me what I need and grunts as he makes contact with my chest hard enough to send me reeling backwards. Elated, I lunge back. We continue to spar for another hour. And when we're done, sporting bruises, exhausted expressions, and thoroughly worn out, Johnathan writes me a ten-thousand dollar check for my services.

He pays me this three times a week, but tonight, I refuse, shaking my head when he tries to hand me the slip of paper.

"No, man, that's alright. Thank you, but I can't accept payment tonight. You did me a favor. I think I needed this way more than you did." I hold my hand out for him to shake; however, he just grins at me as he places the check in my hand anyway and then leans forward to clap me a couple times on my back. It's the first *almost hug* I've had in *months*. Other than my sister, Aurora.

Rolling the windows down, I take my time driving home, feeling better than I have in months. I finally let myself accept the truth that I'd told Johnathan. I'll wait if I have to, and in the meantime, I pray for the right person to enter my life. I deserve it.

Albeit true, that's a fact that's a little harder to accept.

CHAPTER SEVEN

DIFFERENT

THE NEXT COUPLE OF days fly by in a blur, and before I know it, it's Thursday evening.

I'm anxiously awaiting my scheduled apartment tours this weekend. I received a phone call from another building this morning, wanting me to come in for a surprise tour that I was thankfully able to squeeze in about twenty-five minutes from the office. However, this apartment is a luxury one bedroom on the third floor of an apartment building. It has two strikes against it: I need *two* bedrooms, and it was too expensive.

I get out of the office a little earlier than usual and decide to treat myself out to dinner at a nice restaurant across town. My mouth waters in response to Bumpy's incessant demand for fried chicken. I smile brightly at the waitress when I slide in a dimly lit booth, ordering the two of us our favorite fried chicken salad, happy that at least we have each other.

Though right now it's lonely, and probably *looks* as lonely as it feels, it's just not worth it to go home and have to look at Brandon for a few hours before bed. So I pull out my tablet and begin to go over notes for work, relieved there are no more emails from Dr. Richardson.

As I work, it hits me that I haven't heard from my dad in a while.

My heart tugs as those wishes and dreams wither just a little bit more. There was a time I'd kill to be a daddy's girl, but now, it seems like wanting it is starting to kill me. Stirring my salad, I shove that hurt into the place where I store my feelings about Brandon and commence to letting them die together. It'll hurt, until it doesn't. And I'm determined to get to the place where it doesn't hurt anymore. Because right now I feel like every hope and dream I'd ever held close to my heart has been cruelly ripped away, leaving a giant void where love and contentment should be.

I eat my food in silence. Peaceful with the fact there's no one here to hit me, scream at me, spit on me, or take my things away. Right now I'm just a woman sitting in a booth and enjoying dinner. Right now, it's the best, most content feeling in the world.

Until it's not.

I spend the fifteen-minute drive home playing instrumental music to soothe myself; however, the feeling quickly morphs into dread when I pull into our little paved driveway and see the lights on in the front of the house. Brandon is home, and by the looks of it, he's still awake.

Dammit.

I blink back tears as I fight to keep my dinner down. I hadn't wanted to deal with him tonight. *I was having such a good day.*

Walking into the house, I sit my purse and tote bag on the little kitchen counter. He's sitting on the couch in the living room, the television on and muted, and the resentful energy chokes me from twenty feet away. His face is hard, impassive, and he's holding a glass of something dark. Drunk *again.* The stuff seems to seep out of his pores in a vile, sickly-sweet smell, making my stomach roll once again.

Pausing in the little entryway of the living room, I place a shaky hand on my tummy over the top of my purple blouse, willing the nerves to go away. I just have to get to these apartment tours.

God, help me get something and fast, please.

"Where the fuck have you been? You were supposed to be home *hours* ago." The weary tone of Brandon's voice sends dread through me, his blood-shot eyes shooting to mine quickly as I force myself to remain silent.

The hairs on the back of my neck stand up as his energy begins to assault me. The hushed accusation lining his rough tone makes me nervous. I glance at him before hastily averting my eyes, feeling something different in his energy tonight. I wet my lip and shift my weight onto one foot, desperately wanting to put a door in between us. I push my hair behind my ear with a trembling hand and make myself speak loudly, confidently. Trying my hardest to make myself sound strong.

"I went for a late dinner and caught up on some work while I was eating."

He grunts. Hard eyes drift down my body. "Since when have you ever had to catch up on anything, Mrs. Goody Two-Shoes? You think I'm *stupid?"*

"No. You're very smart, Brandon," I say flatly. "Always have been."

Feigning confidence, I take off my cardigan, draping it lightly over one of the two wooden stools at the peninsula off the kitchen. I flinch as Brandon gets up suddenly, slamming his cup down on our new glass living room table, spilling the contents onto the wood frame.

My eyes widen. Not wanting my new table to be ruined, I rip a paper towel off the roll that's on the peninsula and quickly hurry over to the spill to clean it up so the liquid won't bubble the wood. As I bend over to wipe it, I yelp as Brandon's hand shoots out and slaps me across the face.

White-hot pain reverberates through my head, and I fall with a hard thud on the floor, pulling my legs to my chest, and covering my head with my arms.

"Brandon, no! Why are you doing this to me?! Stop it! Please stoopp! *I thought you loved me!*" I sob.

Self-preservation kicks in, and I panic. Rolling over, I try to crawl toward the kitchen, thinking I should just get a kitchen knife and be done with this.

I'm only able to make it a few feet before my knees drag my skirt down. Shaking, I glance up in terror when the sound of his boots bring him closer to me, and I hastily reach a shaky hand back to grab the material so it won't drag off my hips. But before I can, pain explodes across my back as he kicks me mercilessly hard in the center of my spine, causing me to scream before it's cut off by the air shooting out of my lungs at the contact.

Sweat dots my upper lip as I shudder flat on my front and desperately heave, working to suck in another breath.

It's like breathing fire, it hurts so bad.

"Ugghh!" I grunt, my body jerking as he lands another kick to my hip.

He pulls his foot back again, making contact with my shoulder blade now. I screech in pain when he grinds the hard sole of his boot in, almost falling over me with the severity of his movements. "You fucking cheating, *lyin' ass, bitch!"*

In his anger he rears his leg back and kicks me again with a dull thump into my back, over and *over.*

"No, God, pleeaasse. *Please stop it!"* I scream, my eyes widening in fear, and my words coming out garbled with every blow into my back.

"Shut up!" Brandon yells.

I flinch hard as his boot bites into my ribcage once more. Yelping, I put my hands to my ears and curl inward, trying to close off my ears to the sounds of Brandon's furious grunting as his blows land all over my body. Throwing out my arms, I drag myself, but it's no use. He kicks me repeatedly as I attempt with everything in me to crawl over the hardwood living room floor to the tile of the kitchen. By some grace of God, I make it and fall to my side.

He mercilessly ignores my screaming until I'm suddenly overcome with pain and vomit all over the kitchen floor.

Flopping to my side, my body gets hot, and I break out into a sheen of sweat as I lose control of the contents of my stomach. My screams cut off as he keeps kicking me while vomit pours from my mouth and through my nose, choking and gagging me.

Dry heaving now, I choke just as he delivers a nasty kick to my upper back, making me slide into the mess I'd made. An eerie silence descends upon the house, only broken by my cries of anguish. He watches me, laying stunned in the aftermath of his fit of rage. I press shaky hands to my face in terror.

"Are you happy now?" he says hoarsely, running a trembling hand through the disheveled hair atop his head. "Huh? *Are you?"*

I say nothing, feeling the mess begin to soak through my skirt. I find myself thankful that my hair didn't get in it, because I'd never be able to fix it after what he just did to me. This was the worst he's hit me yet. My fingers twitch as I whimper, laying there trembling with my eyes pinned to his chest. Scared to make eye contact, scared to move, scared to breathe...forcing myself to be deathly still until his footsteps fade as he lets himself out the front door, leaving me alone once again.

I lay there for an hour, moaning, crying, and hiccuping until the worst of the pain subsides, and I'm able to sit myself up on shaky arms.

A chill moves over my body, making me shiver as an ice cold sweat covers my body. I sob, in pure disbelief at what just happened. Pulling up my blouse that had fallen off my shoulder, I limp slowly to the bathroom and strip, throwing my vomit stained clothes into the corner of the bathtub before turning the water on to soak them.

I go to the cleaning closet in the hall, not bothering to put any more clothes on. Whimpering and wincing with every reach to the upper shelf, I carefully pull down various cleaning supplies, and for the next hour I clean up the kitchen floor. Slowly, naked, and with tears pouring down my face as I pray.

No use, really, because I feel no comfort; however, I *am* feeling small cramps in my stomach once again. But I have to get this mess cleaned up. If I don't, he for sure won't. But the seconds tick by slowly like molasses until I'm shaking so hard that it takes three times as long to clean up the mess as it should have.

Fatigued and hurt beyond belief, I cry harder, placing my hands on my knees and willing myself to breathe through the pain.

I can't even describe how badly my back hurts as I move slowly to the bathroom to shower, this time not bothering with a plastic cap. I pull my hair into a sloppy, haphazard looking bun on the top of my head, and stand under the spray. Defeated, and worn down. Not even having the strength to soap up, merely letting the water rinse me off.

As I stand there, I try to not let my sanity go down the drain with the water.

Emotionally and physically spent, I dress in pajamas before curling up crying on the sofa. My phone is clutched in my hand, but I'm too scared to reach out to any of my friends. Not that I have many left. They all fell away because of Brandon, from being uncomfortable in his presence. I really only have Jerome and Chris. And if I alert the two of them to the severity of what's going on, I have no doubt they'd try to find Brandon and kill him. It'd make everything worse. Thankfully, I don't have any clients tomorrow and only have to deal with seeing Dr. Richardson. That'll give me most of the day to rest.

Pulling up the blanket, I spend a couple hours trying to ignore the pain, and focus on breathing deeply. Completely exhausted, I shut my phone off, vowing to go to urgent care in the morning to get me and Bumpy checked out. I end up crying myself to sleep.

Wishing things could be different.

So much more different.

CHAPTER EIGHT

I AM DOING NOTHING

Hannah [7:01a]: I don't even know why I married you. I could have done so much better, you asshole.

Hannah [7:06a]: You would really not help me when I'm coming to you damn near begging?! Do you want to see me on the street? Maybe you'd be happy then, you ice-cold prick!

Tyler [7:39a]: Dad, mom won't stop calling me. Will you pleeaassee, please just give her the money so she can leave me alone? She's annoying me, and how can I even begin to study when my phone won't stop ringing? I thought you said my studies were important to you!

Hannah [7:45a]: Look at how you're acting. No wonder no one wanted your ass after I left you! You selfish prick.

Tyler [8:13a]: Dad.

Tyler [8:13a]: Do something!

I AM DOING SOMETHING: nothing.

The texts come back to back. So, needing relief, I play my cello while irritated and trying to clear my head of my thoughts. Painful memories of the past meet the absolute hopelessness of the present and swirl in my head, accompanied by the sound of my phone pinging repeatedly. I studiously ignore it. I'd woken up to a slew of nasty texts from Hannah *and* Tyler, begging me to keep enabling her.

But I won't do it anymore.

I'm through.

Done with shouldering guilt I have no business bearing. Recognizing it was easy, but forgiving myself for settling for a life I knew I had no business living, with a woman I should never have entertained, is the hard part. I fight the feelings of wanting to give up. I want love. I know I'm capable of it, and I know there's someone out there for me. But, unlike with Hannah, who enticed me into ignoring every red flag she possessed, I'm going to make sure whoever I give a chance to that they're going to damn near deserve the world before I open up ever again. But am I ready?

I play steadily, with my phone pinging in the background.

> Sleeping Beauty [8:58a]: Alexander, are you okay? Tyler called me. What's going on? Is there any way I can help?

At the sound of my twin sister's special ringtone, I stop playing and hurriedly snatch my phone up to call her, needing to hear her voice.

God, please don't be mean right now, sis. I don't think I can take your brand of wickedness right at this moment. I toss a prayer up that I'm greeted with a softer Aurora instead of the evil alter ego she sports ninety percent of the time.

"Hi, you okay?" she answers softly, causing my chest to loosen in relief.

Thank God.

"Hey, sis." I clear my throat uncomfortably. "You?"

"I'm good. Just making sure you're okay..." she trails off, leaving me space.

"What are you doing tonight around seven-thirty? Can we grab some dinner?" I ask.

"Sure, I'm free. Want to head out for our usual?" She pauses. "Hey, why so late?"

I blow out a relieved breath. "Sorry...it needs to be kind of late because I have an after-hours meeting with a pain in the ass therapist.

I'm free after we're done; then we can catch up." I go silent, placing my head into my hand, feeling my hands begin to tremble with nerves. "They're driving me *nuts,* Aurora."

"I knoowww; I can *feel* it." Aurora chuckles into the phone. "Sorry, it's not really funny. But remember when I offered to give her brain damage for you, *and you didn't take it?* Remember that?"

I laugh, remembering quite well. When she first brought it up I thought it was a *joke,* but Aurora surprised me by telling me she was dead serious. Although I don't know why it came as such a surprise at the time, she *is* the evil twin, after all.

"Yeah, but then I would have been stuck taking care of her for the rest of her life. Could you imagine?"

She makes a little gagging sound in the phone. "Yuck. You already know I can't. Sounds like a straight nightmare. Alright, see you later at dinner. You make sure you keep your head up until I see you. And don't *break* and give them any money," she says sternly.

I smile. "I won't. I've been firmly holding my boundaries. I love you, sis. Be safe."

"Love you, too."

CHAPTER NINE

I Have To Be Okay

"You took a nasty tumble down the stairs, huh?"

The doctor at the urgent care looks over every inch of my body, tsking at the bruising on my back that I hadn't been able to make myself look at since it happened. Until now. It feels a lot worse than it actually looks. I feel like I should be completely black and blue on my back and not able to see any of my light-brown skin amongst the shadows gracing my flesh.

He'd checked and made sure Bumpy was fine but told me I needed to rest for a few days, so that my body could start to return back to normal.

Stress is not good for babies, obviously.

I accept the prescription for pain medicine and get back in my car to head back home, wanting to clean up and make myself presentable for my meeting with Dr. Richardson. Knowing I have to be one hundred percent on my game for the stubborn man to take me seriously.

As I pull onto my street, my shoulders relax at the sight of the empty driveway. Parking, I inhale a shaky breath and turn off the car, thankful Brandon's gone for the day.

Once in the house, I try to ignore the slight, crampy burning in my stomach while taking extra care to brush out my hair. I accessorize with some sensible earrings, my best tank watch, a flowy blue skirt, a simple white tank top, and an almost sheer, light-blue camisole. Curiously, I turn my back to the little mirror in the bathroom and look over my shoulder, making sure my bruising can't be seen. My hair hangs in a long curtain down my back skimming across the top of my butt. Thankfully it hides everything.

Picking up my phone, I request a ride service, not feeling confident I can make the longer drive myself, and take a second to swallow an extra-strength pain pill before putting on some makeup so I look normal. I'm determined to advocate for my client even if it kills me.

After a while, my phone pings letting me know my ride has arrived, and I ignore the pain with every step, clutching my bag tight to my body and making my way to the front door. Half an hour later I'm walking carefully through the marble lobby of the ultra-modern psychiatry building. I glance at the directory and quickly find Dr. Richardson's name. He's in an office suite on the fifth floor. *Of course he is.*

He's at the very top, much like his attitude.

Trying not to limp, I can't help but roll my eyes as I make my way into the elevator. Grimacing painfully as I move to get the folder housing my client's information out, I commence to flipping through it once more in a fit of OCD. Relieved, I nod, happy to see that I didn't forget any documents. It took *everything* inside of me to make it to this meeting—this is how important it is to make sure my client gets what he needs. I just need Dr. Richardson to see my side.

I shove the folder back into my bag, right next to the DSM-V that I brought. I turn, anxious about my appearance, and work to smooth down my hair and tug at my cardigan anxiously. It's human nature that when you're going through some life-changing event, or even something relatively minor, that we tend to think other people can see exactly what we're going through.

I *pray* that this is not the case with this guy.

This is an open and shut case, so I shouldn't even have to be here that long, unless he's trying to be a jerk.

When the elevator opens, I walk out slowly, trying to appear like I'm not in pain. I press my hand briefly into my stomach over the slight swell of my tummy, right under my belly button that I've always detested, and blow out a breath to keep from the bad habit I have of sucking my stomach in. I've always been curvier and could never manage to get that flat, willowy look that all the other girls seemed to effortlessly attain.

No. God decided to reward me with extra-flared hips and a waist that dipped in on the sides. And being a 34DD, I have larger breasts than I'd like.

Rounding the corner, I make my way to the glass door that leads to Dr. Richardson's office.

Stopping for a second, I glance around shyly and experience a small pang of envy. He seems to be living the life I've wanted for myself: a tastefully decorated office in a big, swanky building with beautiful landscaping, and a parking lot that holds considerably more than four cars at a time.

Brushing the jealousy away, I breathe deeply through my diaphragm, reminding myself I sank my savings into my little office house and fixed it up into a beautiful, shining jewel. I have nothing to be ashamed of. *Nothing.*

I push through the glass doors and sink down into a buttery leather chair, trying to carefully sit without pressing my back to the seat. Looking over curiously, I see the receptionist's desk is empty, and I fight my hackles rising as it looks like they're presumably gone for the day. My eyes flit around nervously as my palms begin to sweat. Am I going to be alone with him?

I don't even know this man.

Glancing at my watch and seeing that I'm just a few minutes early, I force myself to sit patiently. Going over the words I want to say to get him to see our client needs a new diagnosis. He needs help.

My worries rise to the surface again, bringing my eyes back to the hall which seems to house the psychiatrists, according to the plaque on the wall. Surely Dr. Richardson won't hurt me.

He would never threaten the upstanding professional reputation he's curated for two decades.

Biting my lip, I strain to hear the sound of his footsteps. Do I call him Mr. Richardson or Dr. Richardson? My nose crinkles at having to choose. Being snarky in an email is one thing, but to say it to someone's face, especially someone such as he, is completely another thing. I decide on Dr. Richardson and then force myself to stop staring towards the hall. It won't help my case if I look too desperate. I need to appear confident, and a touch aloof. Maybe he'll respect that since that seems to be what he knows, after all.

I anxiously brush my hair behind one ear as I look down at my knees, trying to hold my spine straight, and ignore the twinge in my vagina and the cramp in my lower abdomen. I just need to get through this meeting; then, I can go home and lay down. I can make it. I can.

I just need to meet with Dr. Richardson first, and then I will be okay.

I have to be.

CHAPTER TEN

MD. MEETS LPC.

Beyond ready to go home, I finish typing on my computer and take my glasses off for the day, abhorring my next meeting. Closing my patient's chart, I leave the computer on, knowing that I'll have to start it back up anyway when little *Ms. I'm-going-to-tell-the-Ethics-board-on-you* gets into my office.

In all my years of practice, no one has been able to get under my skin the way this woman has. And lately, my family has had me strung so tight that I question my sanity for agreeing to this impromptu meeting.

Needing a moment of peace, I sit for a second and rub my hand roughly down my face before pushing my keyboard in. When I'm ready, I briskly brush down the lapels of my suit as I stand up. I give myself a quick once-over in the mirror by my desk, arching a brow at my intense irises that are unfortunately more striking than they are calming and the permanent five o'clock shadow across my jaw.

Wait, why the hell am I worried about what this old woman thinks when she sees me?

Checking myself, I smile, convincing myself that Ms. Johnson can't bother me. I'll get through this little appointment, then go stop for ice cream with Aurora to congratulate myself on yet another successful work week completed.

Taking long strides, I round the corner to the lobby and stop rather abruptly, seeing nothing but hair, a long, blue skirt with matching heels, and white-tipped toes sticking out underneath.

Huh. I tilt my head curiously.

Glancing around and not seeing any older ladies in any of the other chairs, I clear my throat, tamping down irritation that the therapist is late. I turn back to the woman sitting there quietly with her face turned away from me, seemingly so lost in thought that she hadn't even turned her head when I walked into the lobby.

Keeping quiet, I take a few steps further into the waiting area, stopping by the receptionist desk to find our intake packet. I never turn away anyone. Ever. Even if it is after hours, the least I can do is get her an intake information sheet and a business card.

"Excuse me, miss," I say loudly, "I apologize, but we're closed for the day, and my receptionist is gone. You'll have to wait until Monday if you would like to come and make an appointment for intake." I firm my voice. "Is this an emergency?"

"No," she says as I'm looking down, reaching into Cathy's drawer for the packet. I grab it and round the desk, flipping through and making sure everything's there. Assured that it is, I raise my head, and suddenly the woman turns her face to look up at me, and I freeze.

It's like my brain stops working as she begins to speak. Holy fuck. I feel the blood drain from my head.

She's *beautiful.*

Her deep brown eyes, lined with a soft-brown kohl, pierce mine, and I stand there, mute. Completely dumbstruck and suffering as my brain literally turns to mush inside of my skull. I can't even tell you how I understand what she's saying to me because I think I'm losing all control of my mental faculties.

I'm not so far gone, though, that I don't see her eyes widen a little when she gets a look at my face. However, she doesn't awkwardly stare like every other woman seems to.

"Didn't we have a six o'clock appointment?" she says hesitantly in a voice smooth as butter, furrowing her brows together in clear displeasure. I'm silent, my throat working around a swallow and I feel my face heat when her eyes lower, catching it. *"My,"* she scoffs a soft laugh, even as the corner of her mouth tips down a little, "maybe I was right to be worried? A little judgmental, wouldn't you say? I'm not here for *intake.*"

Her eyes tear away too soon as she reaches to the floor to grab her tote bag, which was hidden behind the mass of her skirt.

My brain begins to thankfully click back on, I think, and I work to find words to speak to her. I suck in a breath that does nothing to steady me, nor help me to speak. My throat tightens when she turns back to me and arches a pretty eyebrow as she leans forward to stand. Vocal cords frozen, I try again, but it's no use. It ain't happening. The alphabet is gone.

She's taken it.

No—*stolen* it from me.

However, though I can't manage to form a coherent word, as she stands up, I *am* cognizant enough to notice a pained look cross her face before it's gone too soon. I fight to keep my expression neutral, because what's that about?

Her eyes flick towards the psychiatry hall. "Um...where's your office?" she asks in a cool, professional tone, glancing at me expectantly. When I'm still silent, she gestures with a finger towards the hall. *"There?"*

I nod, like an idiot.

Shit. The blood drains from my face as that displeased look on her face becomes more pronounced. She's not happy, and now neither am I because I can't *stand* bad first impressions. Goddammit.

Grabbing onto the bag's handle instead of slinging it across her shoulder, Sarah huffs a long suffering sigh before walking stiffly past me, headed the way I just came. My head turns to follow her as she walks past, and when her back is completely to me, I bring a hand up to rub at the sudden painful ache in my chest that's getting tighter by the second.

My eyes roam greedily, watching her long hair swish thickly behind her back and brushing the round globes of her ass.

My jaw clenches when I get a whiff of her scent, and my cock suddenly jerks to life, surprising me.

Thankfully, despite the lack of blood, my brain decides to stop betraying me and snaps back into action. I narrow my eyes before pivoting smoothly and following Sarah into the hall and through the door of my *own* office.

Because this *is* Sarah Johnson, right? Has to be. And boy, was I dead ass wrong about who I thought she was. This is *nothing* like I'd been envisioning. But it's poetic, though, because here she is proving me wrong *again.*

My mouth starts to water as my cock twitches and forms a heartbeat so chaotic, painful, and unfair that I bristle, now *pissed*.

I'm tired from a long day of helming a difficult client's evaluation. My brain feels broken, and now my cock hurts. And I really want my ice cream sundae. However, I try to play it cool, feigning nonchalance.

"Ms. *Sarah Johnson*?" I enquire in a deep, clipped tone, walking smoothly to stand behind my office chair as she sits down across from me without waiting for me to offer her a seat.

"Yes, that's me," she says absentmindedly, reaching into her large tote bag without meeting my eyes. "Sarah Johnson," she almost sings in a matter-of-fact tone. "You were probably expecting the other Ms. Johnson? I get mixed up with her *all* the time." She gets a tiny grin, as if she's amused, but it's gone a second later.

Placing my hands on the back of my chair, I wet my lips, taken aback once more by the lilt in her voice. I need her gone. Need a minute to figure out what's happening to me. Why my body is doing this.

"Ms. Johnson, I'm so sorry to tell you this, but I'm afraid today isn't a good day for this meeting," I say smoothly, injecting as much confidence as I can in my voice.

Pain erupts in my face as my jaw ticks hard.

My fingers sink rather uncomfortably into the back of my leather office chair as I attempt with everything in me to get a fucking grip when Sarah looks up sharply. A shocked look flashes in her hazel eyes before settling into an infuriated stare, and her nostrils flare slightly in aggravation. I watch silently as her creamy, medium-toned skin flushes a pretty, light-rose color, darkening her skin slightly more. It's the most beautiful thing I've ever had the privilege to witness.

"What?" she half-whispers, and I *love* that. I love that she's not yelling.

I adore her tone of voice. And even though she looks angry at me, I still feel so safe in her presence, oddly enough.

Feeling myself break out into a sweat, I just stare back, completely enraptured. So overtaken I can't even begin to figure out how to function.

She's going to fucking report my ass. I know it.

Unfortunately, I can't bring myself to care. Because the longer she stares into my eyes, the clearer it becomes that something is happening within me I can't explain. My throat bobs uncomfortably, and my chest expands as I feel my erection suddenly lengthen and thicken to its fullest extent. A muscle jerks in my thigh as my shaft tingles, and my balls draw up tight.

My entire being fills with heat, and I pray to everything holy that I don't ejaculate on myself in front of this woman, because I can feel a steady stream of precome flowing from me, informing me that this might be a very real possibility. I can't go down like this.

I need her gone.

My heart pounds so loud I'm sure she can hear it rom where she's sitting. We're both still silent, aside from my harsh breathing and elevated heartbeat roaring in my ears.

At the look in her eyes, I suddenly imagine myself laying her down on the floor, clawing her skirt up her body, and slamming inside of her like an animal. Erasing everything I literally *just* said to Johnathan about propriety around women.

I bite back a groan as my fingers tighten so hard on my chair the leather creaks, protesting under my harsh grip. Precome steadily drips from the tip of my cock, slicking down my length as I struggle to maintain control.

I'm not broken, I realize, staring into her beautiful eyes.

So soulful.

The realization sends a lightning-hot shiver up my spine. Because this has been a serious, almost crippling fear of mine. That something's obviously wrong with me because of how my body and mind react around women and sex.

"We need to reschedule, please." Do I imagine my voice is soft?

Or is this my broken brain now playing tricks on me, making my shame worse?

My body temperature heats up as I'm suddenly assaulted once more by this woman's scent. She smells like a marshmallow, vanilla dessert. Like the exact one I crave every night before bed. How is this happening? And with *her?*

Sarah's lips part in clear shock before she tenses and snaps them shut. "*I'm* sorry, but this is incredibly important, and I've been asking, no, *requesting* your time for a meeting!" she exclaims, her plump, dark-pink lips now pulling tight against her beautiful face.

I tilt my head curiously because her voice does not match her words. She's obviously mad, but she doesn't sound like it. Though everything she said screams obvious irritation, her tone is soft enough for me to lay down and wrap myself up in it.

And in that knowledge, I note I still feel safe.

My eyes lower to her lips, observing a natural dark-pink ring around the edge of them. Stunning.

Thinking truly unholy thoughts about this woman, I wince as my cock jerks hard, causing me to inhale sharply. It takes everything in me to sound normal as I address her with my next words in a soft tone that's really taking me by surprise, "No, I can't do today...I deeply apologize, but I'm afraid I overlooked and overbooked myself," I lie smoothly, keeping the chair in front of me to hide my erection. The true reason I'm pushing the meeting. "Let's plan for next Tuesday at this time?"

I swallow thickly, my Adam's apple bobbing as I see her features change into one of anger.

"Of freaking *course* you can't," she hisses quietly to herself. "After I wasted my time coming all the way out here!" She pulls out her phone and taps a few buttons before looking at me sharply, and all I see is hurt in her eyes. "Do you know how hard it was for me to come here today?" I hate what I've just done to her. Her voice is now tinged with hurt and quivering like she's trying to hold back from crying. I tighten my lips and shake my head once. It's all I can give her. *"You know what? Forget it!* It doesn't even matter because you couldn't care less anyway." Her voice rises slightly with how upset she is, but again, I still feel safe.

"I care," I stress, feeling a bead of sweat trickle down my back.

I care so much that I won't be offloading any of her clients now. Not a single one. I need to be able to see her. To talk to her again. Though it's not the norm for psychiatrists to dally in meetings with therapists, my mind races to try and think of ways to get her into my office. Or get to hers.

Sarah has an angry, disbelieving look on her face, and she scoffs, looking to the side as if she can't believe I'm saying this to her. My eyes widen as I take in her beautiful side profile and cute nose.

Yeah, she's gotta go. I need privacy.

"I apologize," I repeat, softening my voice even more. And at my tone, her eyes relax a little. I don't even have to second guess if it does; this time I know without a shadow of a doubt Sarah softened towards me. "Whatever you think of me, I *do* care. This is not how I intended our first encounter to go."

Truthfully, I can't believe I'm pushing this meeting either.

Needless to say, I've never been this unprofessional before, but I can't hold the type of meeting she wants if I can't get a handle on my reaction to her. I'll be better prepared next week. I'll just have to have long self-pleasuring sessions to survive our next meeting, apparently. Because this shit I'm going through right now, right here, is *ridiculous.* I've never in my life been taken over like this by a woman.

It's diabolical.

"Yeah. *Okay."* She twists her lips, keeping her face averted.

Sarah shoves her things back into her bag, sucking air through her teeth before clicking her tongue and pushing up to her feet a little unsteadily without looking at me. She's got a pinched look on her face as she shakes her head without even a goodbye as she storms out my office.

I feel like shit doing this to her. But I keep quiet, forcing myself to follow behind her way more calmly than I feel to the hall outside and watch her advance through the lobby.

I groan when she pushes angrily through the office doors, then go back into my office and slam my door hard, making my degrees and awards rattle on the wall. "Mother*fucker,"* I growl, my fists balling as I catch her sweet scent lingering in my office.

Sitting down in my chair, I undo my button-up shirt and unzip my pants, pulling out my erection. Eyeing it warily, I see it's swollen and angry looking, slightly wet at the tip with my excitement. It springs free from my boxers and smacks me heavily in the abdomen. I wince as the cool air from my office slicks over my damp skin, and I take it firmly in my left hand with a hiss.

My shaft is so sensitive that this shouldn't take too long.

I take a few tissues and begin to work my fist up and down my erection roughly, gasping as my pre-come slicks the way for me. I tighten my fist as hard as I can, letting out a shout on a rough tug and downward pump, imagining Sarah's tight pussy slamming down on my dick, and the scream that'll no doubt rip from her throat at the shock of how thick I am spreading her out.

God, I bet her pussy gapes so prettily.

With that mental image it takes no time, and I quickly ejaculate with a rumbling growl that rips through my chest, startling me. Thick white ropes of semen spurt from the tip of my cock, draping over my hand, and thankfully not getting on my pants. Gasping with aftershocks, I tilt my head to rest against the back of my chair and sit there for a minute, shuddering. Trying to get a grip over my emotions.

I'm shaking, so overwhelmed I can't think straight.

Because when Sarah left, she took the fucking alphabet with her, and I still can't form a coherent sentence in my brain to save my life.

Cleaning myself up with a couple more tissues from my desk, I lean back in my chair, breathing deeply. I glance down again and sigh miserably at my half-hard length.

"Fucking hell! *Sarah!"* I groan.

I'm a man possessed as I inhale deeply, still smelling her scent lingering in the room. It's torture because she smells like dessert. My weakness.

CHAPTER ELEVEN

UNCOMFORTABLE

LINGERING INSIDE THE DOUBLE door entrance and waiting for the driver to show, I replay the last twenty minutes, feeling myself getting angrier and angrier. Not much of a curser, I let it out in the privacy of the empty lobby. Balling my cardigan to my mouth, I screech, "*Fucking infuriating asshole!* Fucking meeennnn!"

Wiping my fingers under my eyes, I breathe hard and try to get it together before the driver comes. Not even five minutes later, I'm gazing quietly out the glass door, and I have my breathing firmly under control by the time the driver pulls into the lot and flashes her lights.

My mini breakdown only helped so much; I fume all the way home, upset beyond words at Dr. Richardson's behavior. However, I'm shocked out of my anger at the psychiatrist when I see Brandon is home in a good mood, with flowers and my favorite tea, wanting to watch a movie and asking about my day...thankfully, not drunk for once.

And I'm so pissed at how this afternoon went that I accept the gifts and company without complaint.

I smile slightly as we recline on the couch together. He has his arm around me and his hand on my belly, rubbing gently. A small frisson of hope blossoms in my core, making me feel wildly off-center because I know better. I *should* know better. But I'm weak right now, I can admit that.

"I've been calling the baby 'Bumpy,'" I say quietly.

Not comfortable sharing the name I picked out, I keep it to myself and place my hand over his, wishing things could be different. Contemplating quietly on everything. I'm afraid that I will always hate him for how he's treated me over the last few weeks. Even if he started acting perfect right this second, and stayed that way, I'm not sure I could erase the fact that he's beaten me and treated me the way he did.

That night, I fall asleep on the couch, not comfortable sleeping in the bedroom with him. Thankfully, he doesn't get angry and leaves me alone.

The weekend flies by uneventfully. I spent most of it in bed. It only took a day, but Brandon reverted back to his usual drunk self, becoming even more vicious, if possible. Probably because he'd been nice to me. So far this weekend he's criticized my cooking, all because I'd made my favorite dish: oxtails and rice.

Then, desperate to make myself feel better, I forced myself to relax and was busy giving myself a hot-oil treatment to help with the heat damage to my hair when he came home. He took one look at me and started a fight. In criticizing my curly hair, he called me a racial slur - which, coming from him, is new and threw me incredibly off guard.

I'd never heard him say anything remotely racist before.

In shock and crying, I went into our bedroom and grabbed as many clothes as I could fit into a bag, along with all of my toiletries and makeup. I grabbed my keys, snagged my favorite blanket, got into my car and drove straight to my office. I'm done.

If he has the audacity to be racist towards me, how will he treat our child?

Four Days Later

I've been staying at my office since I left, sleeping on the tiny couch in my room. It's been peaceful, being by myself, and gives me the right amount of time to convince myself that I can do this alone. I'm less scared than I was before and a bit more confident in myself.

However, by Thursday evening, I realize I need to go back to the house to grab some more clothes and toiletries. I trudge along, not wanting to see Brandon, and pray he's not there, so I can just waltz in, grab what I need, and leave.

Letting myself into the house after work, I walk quietly through the living room, gasping in fear as the lamp suddenly turns on, illuminating the space. There Brandon sits, looking *incredibly* drunk. My eyes roam his body, seeing his hair and clothes disheveled. My nose crinkles as the overpowering smell of tequila wafts over here at me from several feet away; I swallow hard, fighting my gag reflex.

Empty liquor bottles and trash litter the brand new table in front of him.

I try not to panic as my eyes meet his in the barely lit space. The hair on the back of my neck stands up, my fingers clench, and I shift my body weight to my right foot. The air becomes heavy and thick with tension as we lock eyes, and I feel my heart pound just a little faster. My lips part in fear as I try to take a deep breath, but my windpipe begins to close with terror at feeling something different in his energy; I can't manage to get in anything but a trickle of air at a time.

Brandon sits forward in his seat with his legs spread and his hands clasped between his knees as his eyes rakes over my body in one long, slow movement. I swallow thickly past the lump in my throat, feeling dirty and violated with just that simple action. I can't believe I ever let him touch me, and I can't believe that I ever let him inside of my body.

In this moment, I realize I never want to be touched again.

My fingers dig into my forearm as I take a step back away from him, ready to leave without anything. Coming here tonight was an obvious mistake.

Brandon sneers at me, making my flesh crawl. "He's been fucking you good, *huh?* Is that why you were gone for three days you fucking, stupid, nasty—" my breath catches at the racial slur that slides out of his mouth, yet he continues, "whore, *bitch?*" Brandon curls his lip as he pins his eyes on the apex of my legs, making my stomach drop. "You weren't even there to perform at the lounge tonight. Guess he was hitting it so good you didn't even want to go to work, huh?"

Oh my God! I swallow, feeling truly sick.

"I'm not trying to fight. I just want to get some things," I say quietly, inching my way to the hallway.

I stumble back a couple steps, yelling out as Brandon suddenly launches himself from the chair, stomping over to me.

"No, Brandon, *no!"* I cry out in shock as he knocks my raised hands away and snatches the hair at the crown of my head, smacks me, then pushes me into the wall so hard I bounce off the painted drywall with a pained scream.

"What are you doing? *Huh?"* Brandon snarls. "Where the fuck do you think you're going? In the bedroom? *For what?"*

He crowds into my space, completely uncaring while I slump to the floor, coughing and crying in pain. I moan, closing my eyes against the black floaters suddenly obstructing my vision, and bring a hand up to my head to try and stop the throbbing.

"You're not taking *nothing,* you whore. You think you're going to take *my* things out of this house so some man can *fuck you on it?* You want our bed? No, bitch. I'll kill you before you ever fucking think you can take what you want from me!" As Brandon yells into my face, his spit sprays from his mouth, some getting into my mouth and eye, making me whimper and turn my face away from him as I cower against the wall.

"Please, Brandon, I just want my stuff! You can have the house. I'll raise the baby by myself; just please leave us *alone,"* I shout.

I sniff, and my hand raises to wipe the snot that's gathering under my nose as my shoulders hunch up unconsciously to try to protect my face. I scream again as he suddenly grabs my arm hard and hauls me off the floor, throwing me in the direction of the living room.

Thrown off balance, I trip on the area rug. The world tilts, and I cry out when I slam into the arm of the couch. I instinctively twist to protect Bumpy; however, I overcorrect and yelp when I collapse to the side. A flash of pain bursts through my head when I hit the living room table before landing on the floor.

A searing pain rushes through my midsection at the jolt. And as the pain settles deep inside, unmoving, unyielding, I start sobbing, trying to crawl away. Something's wrong. Very wrong. But I can't attend to it because I need to get away from him.

Footsteps sound out loudly as he stomps to where I lay on the hardwood floor. I shiver, trying to shrink away, but this new Brandon is merciless as he hauls me up again and pulls his hand back with a truly evil look on his face.

"Brandon," I plead, raising a hand in front of my face and trying again to appeal to the man I'd shared my home and body with for the last four years. "You don't have to do this. You don't have to hurt me! Just let us go. Please. *Please!"* I beg with everything inside me, but it's no use.

My eyes flit from his back to his drawn back fist, feeling adrenaline surging through my body.

My need for self-defense kicks in. I scream, managing to punch him in his face first, although my fist merely grazes his face. Panicking, I try to follow up with my right hand and hit him much harder this time, nailing him in the eye.

Stunned, his lips pull back, and in a move I don't see coming, he shoves me hard in my chest.

In the midst of my screaming, I feel myself fall back into our glass living room table. I have a half a second of awareness as the thick pane shatters loudly before collapsing underneath me, and my body falls awkwardly onto the sharp shards, the trash and liquor bottles, and wooden frame.

My face contorts in pain, fear, and hurt as I cry and lay there stunned. Unable to move.

I don't want to die. It's not time.

I sob. Not knowing if I should move, or be still...I don't know what to do.

My body heats uncomfortably as Brandon walks a couple of steps to me with his fists clenched, and his gray eyes flashing with evil. Oh my God. *This is going to be the last thing I see on earth.*

My heart finishes shattering. The pieces that were held together by adrenaline and hope dissipate as if it were never there to begin with.

"Nooo. Oh God, *no. Please don't,"* I whisper, awkwardly trying to shift against the frame and the glass before slumping back down.

The sharp blades of glass dig their way into my skin, layering over the hurt on my back. A cramp burns hotter in my belly, and I sob as I lay here helpless, too scared to move, not wanting to cut myself.

"Fucking bitch, watch where you're going. Clean this shit up before I get home," Brandon barks in a rough voice, grabbing his jacket and making his way to the front door. He swings it open and doesn't even close it all the way as he leaves, letting the mid-summer air into the house.

Finally alone, I make a ragged sound of relief as I realize he isn't going to kill me. Not tonight at least.

Frozen by fear, I lay here moaning softly, crying as I hear his car start up and make its way down the drive. I gasp for breath, my entire body aching as I use the wooden table frame to pull myself up carefully. Wincing and crying out when I feel a slice go into my hip and my right hand as I struggle.

Maneuvering carefully, I manage to weakly inch my way out of the glass before doubling over in pain.

Trying not to vomit, I grab my phone out of my tote bag where I shakily call the paramedics to the home. When they see the mess, I work to quickly explain it away. Stating I tripped, disoriented possibly from falling down the stairs last week - the same excuse I'd given urgent care.

The paramedics take me to the hospital for testing and order me to go on a brief bed rest.

I get out of the hospital around one in the morning and drive straight to my office, falling onto the couch, and sleeping almost immediately. My stomach continues to cramp, and I wake up the next morning crying, not even able to open my eyes before fresh tears glide down my cheeks with the memory of last night.

I can't believe he pushed me through a glass table.

I stand wearily in my office bathroom, trying my hardest to make myself presentable in the bathroom mirror.

I arrive at Dr. Richardson's office at just before six in the evening, exhausted, and limping slightly. Overcompensating. Trying to hide the extent of my pain. I'd performed my usual hair and make-up routine, making sure that nothing's out of place. I had to use more concealer than I'm comfortable with. Inspecting my skin in the reflection of the mirror in the elevator, I frown, thinking it looks too caked on.

I cry further when I see the damage on my back. I'd donned a cardigan to hide the injuries, but in my haste I'd grabbed the wrong one. A sheer one that shows more of my skin than I'd wanted, but it was too late to go back and switch it. So I pray he won't see.

I wait in the lobby again, much more dejected than I was last week.

Sitting in the same seat as before, I attempt to straighten my spine, but the effort's too great, forcing me to slump forward again and sigh heavily, further defeated. Entertaining thoughts of leaving, I put my head in my hand as I lean hunched over my lap. The only way I can be even semi-comfortable. My features pinch tight, thinking if I'd just been able to have the appointment like planned last week, then I could be in bed comfortably right now.

I frown. *No, not in bed. On the itty-bitty uncomfortable loveseat in my office.*

Taking a deep breath, I force myself to be patient. I *can* be patient. Because this won't be the rest of my life.

CHAPTER TWELVE

PATHOLOGIZERS

GOD, I'M IN SUCH a good mood at the thought of seeing Sarah again.

This week has been absolute *shit*, and my heart was racing out of control last night for some reason. I spent most of the night tossing and turning in discomfort, but I chalked it up to my excitement for our meeting today and got up a full two hours earlier than usual since I couldn't sleep anyways.

Though I'm not one who normally has anxiety attacks, I also can't help but wonder if this shit with Hannah and my son is about to come to a nasty head, contributing to why I've been so off-kilter this past week. But I put all that to the back of my mind because I'm about to see her after seven long days.

At the realization, my heart tingles, and all the other bullshit...it falls away with every step that brings me down the hallway and closer to her. My heart beats harder with every step, and I feel so crazy I might let her bite my head off over this client if that means I can be near her.

Floating on cloud nine, I can't exactly help the pep in my step as I round the corner into the lobby of my practice. Which is so not like me. I've been anxiously thinking about how our next visit is going to go all week, and to be honest, I'm a little surprised by how elated I am that it's now six o'clock.

Self-consciously yanking the lapels of my light gray suit, I pause at the sight of Sarah sitting in the same leather chair she was in last time. Except this time she looks much stiffer, and curled in on herself...

Hunched over legs that are not crossed...

In heels that are much lower than the ones she had last week...

Her fingers are clenched tight in her lap.

So tight, the skin at her knuckles are pale, and so lost in thought is she that she hasn't realized I've come in the lobby to join her.

I clench my jaw as my skin becomes hot, and my chest tightens with worry that I feel might be inappropriate, due to the fact I don't really know her, to be so concerned with her demeanor. However, my eyes narrow slightly, not caring for her posture.

Finding my legs again, I walk halfway through the lobby and stand patiently, waiting for her to notice me. But just like last week, she doesn't.

"*Ms. Johnson*." I tilt my head as she unfolds her limbs and reaches down for her bag, still not looking up at me.. "Are you ready? Good to see you again," I offer kindly, beginning to wonder if I've offended her beyond forgiveness.

My brow furrows as she continues to stare off to the side, and I take another step forward, doing a quick assessment across her body. That sensation from last night returns.

Something's wrong.

At her continued silence, my peppy mood begins to dissipate. My jaw works, my good mood souring. Playing it safe, I'd masturbated this morning and felt I had a pretty good grip on my lust...even feeling more mentally clear than I did last week. But seeing her again, I'm wrong. I harden again as soon as my body realizes the source of its desire is but mere feet away. Until she stands up, that is, and she's just moving... *wrong*. It almost kills me to keep a neutral expression on my face.

"Hi," I say softly when she finally looks up, but refuses to meet my eye.

"Hi."

Shit. Her voice sounds tired and short. Full-bodied with stress.

My brows rise, and I frown as she begins to make her way to me. "May I take your bag?"

Sarah shakes her head. "No, thank you. I got it."

Nodding, I hold my arm out to usher her to my office, noticing her slight limp. She's incredibly stiff as well, her hips not having the same gentle sway they did last week. I tilt my head down curiously as she passes by me and can't help but to take a deep inhale.

She might be moving oddly, but she smells delicious.

"Please, have a seat," I offer once we're in my office, but Sarah's already two steps ahead of me, slowly lowering into a chair opposite mine like she's scared to move too much.

Picking up on this action, I keep my gait controlled and my eyes sharp on her as I round my desk. I also note her eerie silence as she begins to take items out of her bag one by one, staying quiet when she unceremoniously moves the wooden plaque that boasts my name over to hang out behind my monitor.

Noticing she really doesn't seem to care for or be overly impressed by titles or formalities of status, I try not to let that bother me and instead get comfortable in my office chair. I place an ankle across my knee and rotate my chair slightly side to side, amused when she slaps a folder down that's tied-up with twine, along with another folder, and wouldn't you know it: the DSM-V.

The bible of the mental health field.

I chuckle because she's a *very* serious little thing, and that in itself is a turn on.

Sarah throws me a rather filthy look, and I arch a haughty eyebrow at her in response, silently challenging her to say something. To be the first one to break the tension between us.

Not able to help it, my cock jerks in my pants at her expression, biting back a groan as she stiffly holds out a lithe arm and presents me with the most beautiful set of chocolate-tipped, almond fingernails.

"Just *Sarah*, by the way," she snaps, obviously irritated at me staring.

My eyes keep hers as I reach forward and take her hand, not too firmly but not too soft either. I don't really do anything but press my hand into hers, until I notice a small cut on the side of her right hand and frown.

What on Earth...

"Are you aware you're hurt?" I ask, attempting to throw her off, not elaborating on the cut.

Don't get me wrong; it's not that she *needs* throwing off. I don't know her and can tell something's blatantly wrong. I've been a psychiatrist too long to not know when something is off. And something is off with Sarah. *Majorly.*

"Of course I am, Mr. Richardson," she replies in a subdued tone.

I tilt my head, wetting my lips as my gaze drops to her mouth. Looks like we're going to be here for a bit. "*Doctor* Richardson, please," I respond, trying to get her riled up so she can say more than two words to me.

My mind races as I work hard to figure her out. I anxiously flick my eyes across her form with a pleased look at the sight of her heavy breasts straining against the fabric of her tank top under her cardigan.

Why is she moving like that? I wonder to myself, rotating my body a little more to the left and tilting my neck a little to try to see through her near sheer camisole at her delicate shoulder blade that's momentarily turned towards me. There's a shadow there.

A tattoo maybe?

Nah, she doesn't seem the type to get a tattoo. Though you'd never know. She turns back, facing me, to make room to open the folders, bringing my attention back to her mouth and seeing she'd been talking the whole time. *Fuck.*

My eyes rise back to hers, and I work like hell to get a grip over myself. They narrow slightly as I stare with a carefully placed, impassive look on my face born from two decades of professionalism, forcing myself to listen. Though it's the last thing I want to do, to be honest. She's explaining why she feels our client's diagnosis needs another review, but I hear it as if she's talking to me through a tunnel.

My gaze lowers back down as she rather harshly slaps a paper on the desk between us, clearly aggravated.

"This week's log, showing my email to you saying what symptoms were present that indicated bipolar disorder." She slaps yet another paper on top of that one, amusing me as her dark nails click slightly as they tap it. "*And here's this week's* log showing *another* email to you saying what symptoms were present for a personality disorder."

Seeing I don't need to respond yet, I stay quiet, just observing. Impressed that, though I can tell something is wrong outside of our professional bounds, and she's clearly upset at how I'd been handling things with this client so far, she keeps her speech professional.

Sarah slaps four more papers in front of me, one by one.

I know she deserves my undivided attention, but my sense of propriety and my usual iron-tight grip on my self-control has diminished considerably. I can't stop staring at her lips, the shape of her winged eyebrows, the little gold nose ring in her left nostril, how long and shiny her hair is; I tilt my head, wondering if it's naturally straight.

No. Of course it's not.

My eyes land on her teeth, which she's busy sucking air through.

"Doctor Richardson, are you listening to *anything* I am saying to you?" Sarah says before a pained grimace momentarily contorts her features. Her arm snaps around her stomach, and her lips form an "O" shape.

She tosses me an embarrassed look, forcing me to take pity on her. I don't meet her eyes and acknowledge I saw this embarrassing-to-her moment, but rather busy myself reaching forward, slowly shuffling the papers together. Propping an elbow on the arm of my chair, I hold them up between us, turning to give her my side profile and to get the vision of her out of my eyesight. Ah. That might explain it...

It's not my business if she's on her period or not.

I think to myself as I read the papers slow enough that I can thoroughly memorize every line of her notes and the slant of her writing. She likes a fine tip pen, which is nice. She's got elegant handwriting, and my eyes eat up the embellished calligraphy with pleasure.

Painfully aware I've said less than forty words since she's been here, I keep my eyes glued to the papers, not trusting myself to speak. This is not like me at all. I can speak in a room of thousands, in a room of one, and everything in between.

A detail in her notes catches my attention, and I frown slightly, pausing as I get to the last page, giving it about three times more attention than I did the others. I put that one down, too, jiggling my mouse to wake up my computer and using my left hand to type the password.

A quick glance over shows me her cheeks are flushed pink. My eyes slide back to my screen and I pause again, wondering why.

Staring at the screen for a second, I take a steadying breath before I click the client's folder open and begin to peruse through the multiple clinical notes I'd written. Maximizing one, I clear my throat, moving the papers around until I find the page I want and compare it to what I'd documented on our client.

"Hmm," I say contemplatively.

She's correct.

"What's *hm*? What does that mean? Do you not know how to talk? How are you a psychiatrist who doesn't know how to talk?" she scoffs as a frown tips the corners of her lips down.

I note that she doesn't say it in a nasty way. She's been genuine so far with the questions she'd asked, and I'm sure I'm confusing her because she's also correct in this instance as well. I've barely said anything to her since she got into my office.

I put the papers down and swivel my chair back to face her.

"Why are you so *bothered*, Sarah B. Johnson?" I ask smoothly, *anything* for an excuse to say her name. It rolls off my tongue like sin, and I grin as a sharply winged eyebrow rises when her eyes lock on mine in our first true time making eye contact, and I am *lost.*

Such fucking beautiful eyes. So soulful.

Her mouth drops open slightly as a breath catches in her throat, but she recovers quickly. "That is *such* a male thing to say," she responds softly.

Disappointment colors her tone at the same time it colors my heart blue with hurting her feelings.

"I apologize," I reply, keeping her eye contact while I hold out the papers for her to grab.

As usual, she's right about the client, but I don't admit this to her right away. I want to push her buttons and keep her here longer to find out what's wrong. It might be presumptuous of me, but I wonder if there's a way I can be of help to her.

"I think we need to discuss this more," I say simply. "I'm curious, Sarah, because you seem to feel like you know how to do a psychiatrist's job better than I do?"

Sarah scrunches her nose, and her eyes flash with renewed irritation. I'm pleased to see some fight instead of the desolate spirit warring within her to override what I know to be her true nature. Don't ask me how I know this, but I do. This Sarah in front of me is not the Sarah that I've been engaging with the last couple of years.

"The last thing I need is another *man–" Bingo–* "trying to make things harder on me than it already is. We have a client who is needing help, not for the *helpers* to engage in a pissing contest. And I am not leaving until I am sure you will help him!" she spits out, slapping the papers rather rudely in front of me.

I have no clue why, but the need to see this woman broken, raw, and splayed open crashes over me in waves so tall I'm dwarfed with the sensation.

Her obvious distress in turn feeds my new feelings of anxiety; however, I force myself to sit here coolly and as if I'm unbothered. Feeling I'm overly tense, I relax my ankle over my knee and lean an elbow on the armrest of my chair. I continue to stare at her as I work to search within myself the reason for my need to know this woman with everything in me.

Maybe now is the time? Am I ready now?

With *her?*

Contemplating this, I glance at the desktop where her nails are spread rather prettily over the notes, then back at her. My eyes pierce hers, observing how visibly tense she is, and it's interesting to see when the realization hits her that I see too much. See *her*, and she can't hide.

Will *not* hide from me.

"Man trouble, huh?" I dig deeper, feeling my fingers twitch because whoever this fucker is needs to be taught a lesson.

She does not look like a woman who is loved properly. At all. Nothing in Sarah's demeanor suggests she's full or satisfied. A rather hungry and desperately sad look crosses her face, causing my eyes to flicker all over her face and to her hands, her torso, searching for other clues.

There's so much pain in her eyes I can't think straight.

It throws me off-center for a moment and makes me lose all sense of keeping my typically cold demeanor under wraps, working to figure her out instead.

Sarah gasps, obviously offended. Her chin tucks in as she throws me a filthy look.

"Stop fucking *pathologizing* me!" she hisses, leaning forward and slamming the DSM-V onto the desk between us so hard my plaque bounces. "I'm not a client. I know what you're doing!"

Sarah winces as a pained expression dominates and diminishes her feisty gaze. Closing her eyes, she averts her face from me, biting her lip against a small sound as her hand flies back there, trying to reach, before straightening her back once more. Her head lifts up, and my whole world comes crashing down at her next words.

"Sorry *I-I fell...*y-yesterday. Down the stairs," she half-whispers, her eyes averting quickly to the side and away from mine.

I go stone still in my seat; equal parts red-hot anger and disbelief rise in my chest so hard it momentarily clogs my throat. "You're *lying* to me!" I snap.

Leaning forward in my chair, I look her boldly in her face, causing her eyes to go wide.

I watch carefully, feeling this need to protect her fill me so fast that it makes me desperate. Sarah licks her bottom lip before clearing her throat, braces a hand to my desk before rising from her seat shakily, and snatches up the papers to shove them back in her bag. Her face pales, and she suddenly breaks into a very fine sheen of sweat that alarms me.

Her hands tremble slightly as she attempts to shove the other items haphazardly in her bag. All while I free-fall my way into hell.

"Don't go," I say quietly. *"Sarah."*

Desperate, I think of ways to keep her here. She can't leave. I have to figure out what's wrong. *Fix this.*

But I can't keep her locked in here either.

The papers crinkle as she shoves them in the bag without even bothering with the folder, in a rush that does much to cause my anxiety to skyrocket. Her chest rises and falls rapidly, and all I can do is sit here while it looks like she's fighting off a mental breakdown.

"I'm s-sorry. You know, *it's okay...* we can do this another time," Sarah whispers, looking like she could be sick as the rest of the color leaves her face in a rush, as it does from mine at her next words, "Maybe this isn't the best time. We'll just reschedule, *again.*" I stare, horrified.

Oh, God, what the fuck is going on?

What the hell's wrong, baby?

I stand out of my chair slowly, my eyes assessing her. Her breath catches on a ragged inhale, and I'm so fucking worried about her that I can't even find pleasure in that simple action. Her movements are wrong; her breathing is wrong; her words are wrong.

"Sarah—" Her name rips from my throat in a tortured, hoarse groan, before going quiet again as she moves to bend forward. "Wait..."

Her hair shifts heavily to the side when she leans over to grab her bag, and I get a good look at her back through the near sheer material of her cardigan. My blood runs cold as I launch myself out of my chair, feeling my heart draw to a stop.

Bruises, not a tattoo like I'd first figured.

"Sarah, why do you have bruises on your back like this?" I ask sternly, walking around the desk to her. "*Who did this to you?*"

Terror leaps into my chest when Sarah makes a scared sound in her throat, causing me to come up short when she raises a pair of terrified eyes to meet mine as she topples back a few steps, tripping on the chair next to her. I reach forward to try to catch her, but she takes another fast step away from me. Her hair swings heavily as she rights herself before flinching so hard she doubles over.

A sharp scream rips from her throat as her arm goes around her stomach again. My arms hang uselessly at my sides despite wanting to pull her to me, but from the way she's acting, it would only make her more afraid.

"Sarah, how can I help you?" I implore.

We have two seconds of silent communication where I can literally *see* her calling out for me, before her features contort in a pained expression, and her eyes squeeze shut hard, breaking our eye contact once more.

"*No*. Oh, nooo," Sarah wails as her knees collapse.

The next few seconds are so bizarre that it's almost in slow motion. I watch her grapple with the chair next to her as she sinks down.

Fuck it, I curse to myself, hurriedly reaching forward to grab her up by her arms before she can hit the floor, hauling her to me. I'm thankful for my fast reflexes.

She pants, and I look down at her, confused as tears fall out of her beautiful eyes, fast and unchecked.

"Bumpy!" Sarah cries, clutching the front of my shirt. "*Bumpy.* Bri-*Brittany!*" Goosebumps erupt across my skin as she leans her forehead heavily against my arm. She lets out a keening sound, her mouth opening in what can only be described as shock and horror. "Nooooo! *No!* Oh, oh God, no *please,* please don't do this to *m-me!*" she sobs true, gut-wrenching, *mournful* cries into my chest as I work to figure out what the fuck is going on.

My eyes go wide, flicking down her body in concern, and shock of my own, to be honest. *"Sarah—"*

"The baby!" she wails.

I frown. *Baby?*

Sarah's fingernails dig painfully into my arms as I work to clutch her tighter against me, feeling an uncomfortable trembling start from deep within my soul.

"*Baby?*" I ask, feeling my own face flush as I look down into her eyes. "*What are you talking about, Sarah?*" My voice sounds hollow even as the words leaves me with urgency.

A rough sound leaves my throat, and my heart beats strongly, forcing blood to rush in my ears. Causing my brain to work overtime as I struggle to piece it all together coherently.

"Losing it. Losing Bumpy," she grits between her teeth as a pained whine escapes her mouth.

Tears continue falling down her cheeks, and my heart swells uncomfortably tight. I tighten my arm on her and reach over and snatch up my desk phone to dial the police when full blown awareness of the situation finally hits me. It's like a slap to the face.

Oh my God. She's having a miscarriage in my office!

Sarah trembles before going limp in my arms.

I don't fight it. Something shifts deep in my spirit as I sink down to the ground with her, with the phone cradled tight between my ear and shoulder. My arms band tightly around her, arranging her with her back to me in between my spread legs. I keep her cradled close and rock her, forcing myself to keep my voice level as I give out instructions to my office to the dispatcher. My eyes remain tight on her while they assure me an ambulance is on its way.

Sarah's crying, curled over my thigh on her side, shivering and moaning in pain.

"I'm here. I'm here, and I got you," I murmur, pressing my lips to the top of her head.

I rub her shoulders, not able to offer her any reassurance about the situation with the baby. From the blood staining the back of her skirt, there's unfortunately none to give. My own blood runs cold when her cardigan slips, and I get an up close and personal look at the extent of the damage done to her back; small cuts and bruises mar her flesh.

She flinches when I brush my fingers lightly against one on her shoulder blade.

"No!" she cries out. *"D-Don't touch—"*

"Okay. Okay, honey," I hurry to reassure her, immediately withdrawing my hand. "I won't. I just want to look, not touch. I need to see how bad it is and to see how hurt you are, honey, so I can tell them when they get here. So they know not to make it worse. Okay?" I keep my tone of voice low and calm, placing my palm directly on the side of her head and rubbing, trying with all my might to lend her my strength.

She rocks against me in a self-soothing motion, wailing her loss.

Swallowing hard, I know what I'm getting ready to witness is about to break what's left of my fucking heart, but I grasp her cardigan between my fingers, and pull it away so I can get a better look. Her reaction is immediate; the wailing ceases, and she flinches, wrapping her arms around herself. Her slender fingers grasps mine tightly as she attempts to grab onto my hand to keep me from seeing. Scared.

"You don't need to be afraid of me," I say quietly. My thumb brushes hers as I rock us gently, exercising patience. Her little whimpers are breaking my heart. "Shhh, you're okay, Sarah. It's alright. I just want to look. I'm safe, okay, honey? Let me look," I croon.

Small gasps leave her mouth as she pulls back slightly, finally letting me see the damage on her back.

"Thank you. You're so *brave,"* I praise, squeezing her fingers and not letting her pull away just yet. "You're so brave to show me what's hurt you."

Letting her know that, even though she's trusting me to look, I'm willing to go slow. Make sure she feels safe.

But when I finally get her cardigan pulled away, my eyes go wide at the dozens of tiny cuts welted on top of huge blue and black bruises. Squeezing my eyes shut tightly, I look away, biting my cheek hard as I begin to rock us both now.

You gotta be fucking kidding me. Oh sweetheart...

Anger rises up in me so hot that it's a struggle to keep my movements slow and gentle so as to not scare her.

I feel sick.

Who did this to her? I silently rage. Outwardly I hold her calmly and rock her while she cries and cries, her tears soaking my arm through my shirt.

"*Bumppyyyy*. My little bumpy," Sarah sobs. "I'm so sorry! I tried to get away before it was too late. Mommy tried, my love."

I sit, helplessly feeling my heart break as I listen to her speak to the baby she'd just lost. I put my hand on top of hers that are cradling her stomach, squeezing her delicate fingers, trying to give her comfort.

The paramedics show up a few minutes later with a stretcher and strap her in. On her stomach, because I wouldn't let them put her on her back.

Sarah's so inconsolable that they had to sedate her to calm her down.

Feeling uncomfortably turned inside out, I busy myself packing up the rest of her things into her bag and grab her purse from the chair. Ignoring my phone starting to ping with back to back messages, my eyes sweep my desk thoroughly to make sure I'm not missing her keys or phone.

"You next of kin?" one of the paramedics asks, pulling my attention away as his gaze assesses me quickly.

"No. But she was with me when it happened, and I have no idea who to call on her behalf. Sarah's a colleague of mine. Can I come so she won't be alone?" I ask, leaning over to grab my keys from the drawer in my desk, before following them out at the man's nod of assent.

Steadily walking into my future.

CHAPTER THIRTEEN

Perpetrator Toilet Swims

Hours later, I sit here in the hospital chair next to Sarah, looking at her in concern. We're in a private room with the lights turned off, and it's so silent. Been silent for quite a while. Neither of us knowing what to say, I think. And honestly, she shouldn't even feel the need to talk. She doesn't have to with me.

I see her.

She's curled under the blanket and just staring off into space. Every now and then, she'll blink. But that's it. Understandably so. My heart tugs because I can only imagine what's going on in her head right now. Her soul.

About an hour ago I gave her her bag and purse, watching as she texted a number.

I sat here next to her silently while she told the medical officials about the abuse that's been going on and saw her muster up a rather steely resolve when they informed her that they needed to take pictures for their records. When they asked if she was hurt anywhere else, she showed him her jaw, having to use a wet wipe to remove the foundation hiding the bruising there.

Watching the dark bruise being revealed really fucked me up on the inside. But thankfully I could keep my emotions locked down, successfully hiding what I really think from her. Because this is about her, not me.

They x-rayed her just to make sure nothing was fractured.

I left the room for a second, too angry to feel like I could continue to sit there calmly. But now, I'm back in and by her side.

I look over at her small body huddled underneath several warming blankets in the hospital bed; her almond-shaped, light chocolate nails clutch the blanket under her chin. Her stunning hair spills down her front and side in a near black waterfall of loose waves, slightly mussed.

My face tightens as she sniffs delicately, holding a tissue to her reddening nose.

My heart thumps uncomfortably as I think about Aurora, who'd suffered four miscarriages before the doctors told her she would never be able to have children. My palm itches to grab my phone, but it dings with an incoming text before I can.

Sleeping Beauty [9:58p]: Hey bro, you ok? I feel off but there's nothing going on with me.

I sigh as I lean forward to reply to Aurora, who never misses the mark.

A [9:59p]: No, I was actually just thinking I wanted to text you but thought it might be too late. You won't believe what just happened to me. Well....to my colleague. A therapist came to my office this evening to discuss a client.

Sleeping Beauty [9:59p]: The one from last week? The appointment you postponed?

A [10:00p]: Yep. She had a miscarriage in my office tonight.

Aurora sends a string of broken heart emojis and shocked faces.

Sleeping Beauty [10:00p]: Oh my gosh, Alex, is she ok?

A [10:01p]: Not really, sis. She's so....listles s....it's heartbreaking.

Sleeping Beauty [10:02p]: Are you ok?

A [10:02p]: I'm enraged. Her boyfriend was beating her, Aurora.

Sleeping Beauty [10:04p]: Is anyone else there with her? And standing her up....tha t's not like you at all. Well...things happen for a reason...maybe you were supposed to stand her up last week, so you could be there for her tonight.

“You can go,” Sarah whispers so quietly that I barely hear her.

My eyes flicker to her, momentarily startled by her voice piercing the quietness of the sterile hospital room. I catch her eye, and my heart tugs at the emptiness and pain I find there. Leaning to the side, I slide my phone into my back pocket and hope like hell my eyes look kind as I regard her.

Because our bullshit professional stand-off dissipated the minute I sank down onto that floor with her in my arms.

“No, I’m staying. Why would I leave you? You have no car, no nothing,” I say softly. Cognizant of her abuse, I purposefully keep my tone low and non-threatening as I lean forward and clasp my hands in between my knees. Not even able to imagine what she must be feeling right now. “Do you want me to contact anyone? Your parents...or a sibling, maybe?”

Her gaze averts away, letting me know that this is a sore spot for her.

“No. No one knew about my pregnancy," she replies, blinking and resuming her stare at the window next to me.

I frown, biting the inside of my cheek before pressing, "Are...Are you sure? It's no problem, I promise—"

"—My parents live in California," she interrupts me quietly, "and...we’re just not that close, honestly. I messaged my best friends to come. So, you can go. You must be very tired.”

Curious that she's mustered any energy to care about how I'm feeling has me tightening uncomfortably. Staying still, and silent, I stare at her profile as she continues to look off towards the window, her eyes scarily blank. Selfishly I want her to look at me. But it's not use because it wouldn't help. I wish my eyes could offer hope and warmth like other people do.

Maybe I could help heal her if they did.

The nurse verified she was twelve weeks pregnant, right at her second trimester. The fact she was so far along and hadn't told anyone about it is just as concerning as it was heartbreaking.

My hands clench helplessly as a singular tear slips out of her eye, falling across her nose and hitting the pillow under her head. She stays unmoving. Needing to be closer to her, I rise and drag my chair up to her bed. "I'm not tired, sweetheart," I murmur. Daringly, I reach forward and wipe gently at her face with my thumb, smoothing her tears away, caressing her soft skin.

There's just something about this woman that speaks to me.

Sighing to myself, I lower my hand and place it onto hers, feeling she's ice cold. She's got her delicate fingers wrapped around the blanket, but I work my hand over hers and grip it tightly. Rubbing my thumb along the veins present under her skin, I take a deep breath before speaking.

"*Sarah*, you're going to get through this." I lean forward further, tightening my hand slightly more on hers.

She doesn't squeeze back. The blank look in her eye is worrisome; the girl that was so full of life in my office just last week looks like she's dying. She stays silent, and a pinched feeling starts in my chest.

I don't want this for her, no matter our professional history.

"Can I get you anything? A change of clothes? Anything?" I enquire quietly. The door opening and the nurse walking in grabs my attention, forcing me to cut my words off. She gives us a quiet greeting, and I observe carefully as she looks at Sarah's vitals before leaving us alone once more. Sarah turns her head to glance at me and takes a slow, deep breath.

"My friends are coming to get me, and then they're going to stop by my office so I can change my clothes." She pauses. "You really can go...it's very late—"

"Please don't ask me to leave you again," I say hoarsely, feeling my face warm. My eyes prick with emotion too acute for me to name right now, but I do know this: I'd rather walk on glass right now than leave her side.

"Okay," she whispers, her eyes welling with tears. "Thank you for staying with me."

I take a second to observe her quietly, seeing the rosy flush to her nose, her cheeks, and the red tint to her eyes. The poor girl looks tired, distraught, lost. I frown, her words finally sinking into my consciousness making a warning bell go off.

"Your office...for a change of clothes?" I parrot back, trying to understand.

Just then, there's a loud commotion in the hallway, and a young, fit but slender African American man comes barreling into the room.

He spots Sarah quickly, and a distraught expression crosses his features before he quickly schools his expression into one of quiet strength. As the man marches up to the bed and leans down into her face, I get up hastily, preparing to throw myself at this person. However, the man starts talking, ignoring my presence.

"*SJ!* Look at me, baby girl," he says, his tone strained. His black eyebrows knit together as his hands came out to move her head slightly to look at him. Concerned, I look down at Sarah, seeing she stays staring, like she doesn't hear. The man continues, "Sarah, *Brandon* is here!" His brow lowers into a thunderous expression. "And what the fuck? *He did this to you*?"

"Brandon?" Sarah's squeaks. Her eyes go wide with fear as her hand tightens on mine, becoming clammy and cold.

"Yes, and Christopher!" His eyes flash with worry and anger as he shoves both of his hands over his head and half-turns. *"Fuck,* Christopher is going to kill him!" He blows out an exasperated breath before

flicking his eyes to mine and then down to my hand in Sarah's. "Uh, who the hell are *you*?" He glances sharply at me.

Not willing to let go of her just yet, I take my free hand, holding it out to the stranger. He takes it in a light grip and shakes it abruptly. There's another commotion outside. I flit my gaze down the man's body, arching my eyebrow.

"Dr. Richardson," I reply. "So, *who's* Brandon and where is he again?" I purposefully keep my tone nonchalant, yet feeling anything but.

"My name's Jerome," he replies curtly, "and Brandon's her boyfriend. The fucker that did *this* to her. He's out in the hallway with Christopher. The nurses are about to call security." Jerome's face is pulled tight with barely restrained fury, but I'm out the door before he can even finish saying the last sentence.

I round the doorway and see two young men loudly facing off in the hallway. I don't know who is who, though, having never seen them before. My steps slow as I take them both in. There's a black haired, stockily built guy, and a taller, blonde man with dimples who looks like he could be a model.

"Brandon?" I call sharply, tilting my head. My gaze flickers between the men.

The blonde-haired man turns first and a sick, hot wave of hate washes over me. I detest a lot of things, but women beaters and pedophiles are always my top two on the list of hates. Anger simmers just beneath the surface of my sanity as I calmly walk up to him, feeling my muscles straining. The need to sink my fist into this man's face is vicious.

"Sarah's ready to see you now," I lie, taking Brandon by the shoulder and maneuvering him towards the door to Sarah's room. My lip curls at the look of relief on his face.

"Wait! He can't go in there! Who are you?" The other man I assume is Christopher walks up next to us before pushing into the room before us, putting himself between us and Sarah as we maneuver our way through the doorway.

There's no need. I never intended to let him talk to Sarah anyways. I just want to get him alone to teach him a lesson.

I close the door swiftly behind us hearing Brandon say, *"Baby!"* and then see the sudden fear on Sarah's face before reaching forward and clamping my hand hard on the back of this piece of shit's neck. Tightening impossibly hard. Christopher frowns, and his eyes go wide at my actions, but I ignore him.

I lean into this rare feeling of losing control, ignoring everything but the need I feel to put this man in his fucking place.

Brandon grunts in surprise, trying to jerk away from me, but I move fast, opening the private bathroom door and shoving him in and knocking his head on the wall in the process.

The sickening thump of his head hitting the wall sounds wonderful.

Brandon groans as he rights himself, his hands flying to his head in shock. His gray eyes squeeze shut in pain as a trickle of blood moves down his face from his temple, and I enjoy a momentary delightful prick of pleasure at hurting this man who caused such damage to the woman that's got me turned inside out.

I wish I could slam his head into the wall until his brain leaks out of his skull. But I'm at a hospital and need to have decorum.

"What the *fuck,* man?!" Brandon yells, turning in the small space to face me with rage in his eyes.

I move fast, sinking my fist into his stomach, doubling him over and stunning him before snatching his hair and yanking his head back. I know my eyes are ice cold as I regard this disgusting, sorry excuse of a human, but right now every derogatory name that's been hurdled my way regarding my looks is worth it at the look of fear in his eyes.

Brandon gags as my fingers tighten hard on his scalp, feeling some of the strands rip from it.

I take a deep breath through my nose. "You like beating up pregnant women who can't defend themselves?" I snarl down at him. Brandon's gray eyes morph from fear, to downright terror. "Lie to me. *I dare you,"* I say roughly.

I see the lie in his eyes before he says it, and it sends me through the roof.

"I didn't—"

Brandon yells as I pull my fist back and punch him in the face, not hard enough to snap his neck like I'd like to but hard enough to stun him.

I use the momentum to turn him and kick him in the back of his knees, making his legs collapse, and pull him to the toilet where I shove his head in, plunging him into the water inside. Listening to him gurgle for a few seconds, I relish the thought of drowning him before I snap out of it and call out for Jerome. A second later, the bathroom door flies open, and Christopher appears instead, Sarah's other friend, poking his head in.

His brown eyes narrow as he sees me nonchalantly drowning Brandon in the toilet.

Christopher's eyes flicker up to mine, and he leans against the doorframe in a relaxed stance with his arms crossed, as if he sees a man being murdered every day. Maybe he does. Hell, I don't know. And if he does, who am I to judge?

"Yeah, man. It's *Christopher* by the way; Jerome's the other guy," he says conversationally and with a hint of a smile at Brandon's predicament. "Not sure what you plan on doing with him, but *I'm* going to claim self-defense, just in case anyone asks."

I nod at the unspoken agreement that passes between us. Brandon's arms flail, trying to make contact with me, but he's unsuccessful as I work to shove his face harder into the porcelain.

"Give me two minutes and then have the security officers come in here. I should have my point across by then," I say firmly.

I like to think we'd just shared a brotherly bonding moment, me and this stranger.

Christopher frowns, nodding his head several times. "Let's make it three, *juuust* in case," he says, pushing off the door frame and closing us back into the little room once again.

Feeling his fight leave him, I yank Brandon up. He sags in my grip, pathetically wheezing and struggling for air. His face is bright red, and his hair is wet just at the edges of his face as the water trails down it.

Hospital toilets are low flow, apparently.

I give him half a minute to catch his breath. "Now, I *asked:* did you beat her up?"

Brandon nods his head yes, still choking. I watch with disgust as a trickle of water slides from the corner of his mouth. He's about spent, but selfishly, this isn't enough for me. It's not near good enough.

My lip curls. "You're disgusting."

Irritated, I shove him back into the toilet and hold him there firmly, uncaring of him flailing and trying to get away. After another minute, I pull him back up, aware he's fighting to stay conscious.

"Now that I have my point across, this is how this is going to go. The police are about to come in here, and you're going to confess to what you did to her *in front* of her, so we all know you got the facts straight. You live with her?"

My eyes flick across his face, memorizing him.

Brandon nods.

"Then, at some point, she's either going to come get her stuff, *or* she'll stay in the place that you two are living in. And whatever she wants to do, you're going to respect that, and you're going to leave her the *fuck* alone. Aren't you?" I say, narrowing my eyes..

"Fine," Brandon hisses as his gray eyes flash in anger, his nostrils flaring.

I cock my head, feeling murderous. Because I instinctively know this attitude he's showing me, albeit I just knocked him around a little bit, is nothing compared to what I know he's unleashed upon that beautiful, helpless woman laying in the next room.

With bruises on her back so big and dark that I know he's taken out a lot of his anger on her, and didn't spare her any thought or mercy.

"I don't give a shit how angry you are," I say decisively. "If I hear you are fucking around her again, I will personally come take care of you myself. Promise." I let go of him and rise fluidly. "Oh," I click my tongue and tilt my head, giving him a nasty once over, "I'm *Dr.* Richardson, in case it comes up for any reason. Nice conversation, Brandon. Let's go."

I escort him from the bathroom, out of the door, and into the hallway, away from Sarah. I don't even let him look at her until security comes, and we all go in together to give them a report. I walk to the other side of the bed, keeping myself in between her, Brandon, the officers and her friends.

"You're going to be okay, honey," I whisper into her ear.

Seeing she's shaken up, I press the side of my head against her temple, nuzzling her briefly, trying to give her some of my strength. I slide my hand back into hers, not giving two fucks about what anyone in this room thinks about it. She needs to know someone's in her corner.

That I've got her.

Opting to stand next to her instead of returning to my seat, I exchange a mutually infuriated look with Jerome and Christopher while we listen silently as Brandon hollowly confesses to beating Sarah almost daily for the last several weeks. And to the beating that caused her miscarriage. My fist clenches.

The fucker threw her through a fucking *glass table.*

I should have killed his ass in the bathroom.

I rub her soft skin with my thumb as Sarah quietly corroborates in her soft voice, correcting and interjecting where needed. Brandon stands there like a pathetic idiot, red-faced and quiet as the police officer reads him his rights and then places him in handcuffs. I hand Sarah a tissue, as she can't get through the statement without crying. Brandon doesn't mention what I did to him, and we all watch silently as they take him away in handcuffs.

Sarah's fingers tremble in mine the entire time.

Having been strong the entire report with the officer, as soon as they disappear through the door, her face contorts with pain as she breaks down crying again. She buries her face in her hands, and her sobs rip through my being, digging her way into my soul where I feel her settle deep.

Pressing her head to my chest, I stroke a heavy hand down her hair, needing to feel a connection just as much as I know she does.

Jerome and Christopher's eyes nail themselves on her back, where the hospital gown sags open. They widen in shock.

"Motherfucker," Christopher curses and turns to stalk away, rubbing a rough hand across his jaw.

Jerome's face is tight with sadness as his eyes flick from her back, to mine, then to her back again. He brings a hand up to cover a ragged gasp, and a tear slips down his cheek. It's quite difficult to watch as these friends who obviously care deeply for Sarah get a good look at how bad the damage actually is. They stay silent though, and there's not much to say really without making it worse.

Though riddled black and blue, she's flawless to me.

Her tears cease, and she suddenly stiffens and pulls awkwardly away from me. "Sorry," she murmurs, swiping her tissue across her eyes again with an ashamed look on her face.

Sitting once more, I lean back in my seat and look away with a scowl, wishing I would have just went ahead and drowned the sorry excuse for a man. Surely going to jail would have been worth the rage that just bubbled up in me, hotter than anything I've ever felt before. It's a disconcerting feeling.

A feeling admittedly and uncomfortably worse than my anger at Tyler, who's busy screwing and bar fighting his way through Spain.

The anger I swallow is hotter than the rage I feel at Hannah, who never seems to take ownership of anything. Always delegating the hard stuff to me and not wanting to be a mother to her own son. Alienating me from my own family with her antics.

Christopher comes back in and slings an arm around Jerome's shoulders and says something quietly in his ear. They distract me just enough for me to take a deep breath. Getting a grip, my eyes flick slowly back to Sarah as she seems to struggle to breathe for a moment. I feel myself melt even more. She's so beautiful, even in her melancholy state.

She looks at me suddenly, pinning me with her beautiful dark, almond shaped eyes. "Thank you, Dr. Rich-*Rich—*"

Sarah's words are cut off, muffled by her hands.

Christopher wraps her up in a hug and rocks her; his hands band around her head so as to not disturb the raw skin of her back.

"Aww, you called me rich. That makes me feel very good," I tease in an effort to lighten this screwed-up night and her truly unsettled mood.

I lean forward as the men chuckle and run my hand down her soft arm and then squeeze her hand gently, comforting this woman who is technically still a stranger to me. I ignore her friends looking at me curiously and focus on how good her skin feels against mine. So warm and fragrant.

Sarah looks over at me, gasping through her nervous laughter and tears, and my eyes soften as an emotion swells inside me. Something I can't explain, because I've never felt it before.

CHAPTER FOURTEEN

A Lesson in Sadness

I LOOK UP AS a night change nurse enters the room, animated and boisterous.

"Okay, okay! Let's aalllll back awaayyy. I have a change of clothes for the beautiful woman. Missy, I gotta say, in all my years I have *never* seen an abuser admit what that man just did and walk up out of here voluntarily wi' handcuffs. But there's always a first time for ever'thin', isn't there?"

The southern woman picks her way around Jerome and Christopher and gently hands Sarah a bundle of clothes. I can't help but fight her trying to remove her hand from mine, and I grip until I feel her nails scrape my fingertips.

The nurse throws me a curious look that I return unashamedly. Her blond hair is in a high bun with streaks of grey running through, giving her a warm, matronly look. I clock her blue eyes, just like mine, and like her instantly. Wishing people would see warmth when they looked at my eyes like I see in hers.

Sarah gives her a tentative, shaky smile. "Hi," she says shyly, probably still shaken up after all the back and forth of staff and police officers, and then, of course, my altercation with Brandon.

"Hi, beautiful! I found these in the lost and found. I guessed your size the best I could. I know how hard it is to hold the girls in!" the nurse says with a laugh, her chest jiggling as if to reinforce what she just said.

That does it.

Sarah holds a hand to her mouth and lets out a hilarious laugh through tears that understandably never seem to end. She nods her head slightly in agreement, wiping them away even as she giggles.

It makes me smile, though she can't see it. God, the sound of her laughter is intoxicating. As a matter of fact, her voice is adorable, too. Soft and slightly sensual. Unassuming. Calming.

Soothing.

There we go; the alphabet's coming back.

Spreading my legs, I settle deeper into my seat and rub the back of my neck, feeling a tiny bit more in control. The nurse begins to fuss over Sarah, sweeping her hand down her hair, plumping up her pillow, laying the clothes across her lap and showing her what she'd found.

Her friends and I look at each other, amused and maybe even slightly embarrassed.

"Well, uhm, I think Jerome and I can go to a little waiting room and wait for you to get dressed. We'll be back in around twenty minutes. Care to join us, Dr. Richardson?" Christopher says confidently, jerking his head toward the door. I tighten my lips, and heave a small sigh.

Shit. Here we go.

The nurse gasps theatrically, putting a hand to her breast as her head snaps quickly to me, making me wince. My lips twist with a little half-smile. I already know what's was coming and really don't want to take any attention for myself. Tonight isn't about me.

"*Alexander* Richardson?" she says in a high-pitched tone.

"Yes," I answer quietly, flicking Sarah a look and giving her a reassuring wink.

Her face flushes, and she smiles so broadly I can see every single one of her teeth. "Oh my *gosh,* I am *so* honored to meet you! You're a legend around these parts, Mister!" I feel my face heat up when she turns excited eyes to Sarah as she continues rapidly, "My gosh, Ms. Johnson, you're so lucky you were with him when—*well.* He's like a *God* around these parts." Sarah's eyes slide to mine and widen, and I can't help but give her a very tiny nod as the nurse keeps going. Sarah's lips part a little as she turns her face back up to the nurse and just stares, entranced, as are Jerome and Christopher who are watching this scene unfold with a mixture of horror and fascination. "The doctors and nurses talk about you all the time. They *love* you, Dr. Richardson. Just absolutely love you! You are highly respected in the psych ward."

I give her a very toned-down version of my usual smile, not feeling like the occasion calls for such pleasantries, and clear my throat gently, not wanting to startle Sarah. "It's an honor to meet you as well, ma'am. You flatter me." I turn back to Sarah, who is picking at her hospital gown with a little faraway look in her eyes. "We'll be back in a bit. Alright, sweetheart?"

And because I can't help myself, I place my hand lightly on her head and rub down until my hand falls away. Her hair tangles in my fingers until the strands, whisper soft, fall away.

Sarah blinks at me rather blankly. "A-Alright."

Christopher and Jerome share a *what the fuck glance* but stay silent as I follow them out.

"Uh...Who are you again?" Jerome asks, frowning as his brown eyes meet mine.

"Dr. Richardson," I repeat, as if the nurse didn't say my name about half a dozen times just now. "I'm a clinical psychiatrist—" I rattle off before being interrupted.

"Oh, no. *I got that.* I mean...was Sarah seeing you when...?" Christopher asks hesitantly, his brows knitting in confusion.

The need to protect Sarah rises hot and heavy inside me, and I work to make sure her reputation is not stained in any way. Even with her friends. "In a professional sense, *yes.* We have a mutual client. Here, let's sit in this waiting room and talk," I offer, ushering the men down the hallway.

Although, my mind's still very much back with Sarah in the hospital room behind me.

Ten minutes later we're sitting at a round table and bonding over a cup of disgusting hospital coffee. We get to know each other and sort out how we know Sarah, and the events that happened today in my office. I listen intently, sipping on my coffee while Christopher sits with his legs spread, his stance completely open for me to observe.

Christopher's right hand settles on the back of Jerome's chair, while he periodically shoves the other through his long black hair in irritation.

"She told us last Tuesday that she was leaving him and was going apartment shopping this weekend. She said something's been happening, but she never said what. We didn't even know she was *pregnant,*" he bites out with a hurt look on his face. "Brandon kept her so secluded. She barely could even sing at the lounge anymore. He was restricting all the good songs she wanted to perform, and it was starting to cause issues for her." Christopher glances to the side and shakes his head. "Fucking hell! I can't believe we didn't know; she's our *best friend.*" He throws this part at Jerome, who's looking especially tortured.

Propped up on his elbows, Jerome has his head in his hands and rubs at his temples for the dozenth time on a groan. His eyes are red. They're especially close, Sarah and Jerome. I can tell without it even being verbally confirmed. The unsaid hurt rolls off him in waves as he begins to speak. "Do you need another pain pill?" Christopher asks him quietly, but Jerome just shakes his head and sighs. He folds his arms on the table and pings his eyes between the two of us.

"When you two were in the bathroom with that fucker, she told me he called her the N-word, a whore...disgusting. A *bitch.* He threw her into their *glass living room table* which is how her back got all fucked up, amongst other things," Jerome says quietly.

I freeze while lifting my cup to my mouth, but then jerk when the hot coffee spills over onto my fingers. "Fuck," I curse, snatching a few napkins and wiping up the spill. My chest tightens, and his words echo around in my head making me immediately regret not ending the man's life when I had the chance. She never *once* told the officers about Brandon's use of the racial expletive, and to hear Jerome discuss it in the interim is jarring.

Christopher lets out a growling noise, his features tight with rage.

Jerome suddenly puts his hand on Christopher's thigh and squeezes with a worried look on his face.

"That fucker!" Christopher spits out. "I *knew* I didn't like him for more than his bullshit antics with Sarah. Fucking disgusting, racist, *slimeball*. Probably got off with being with a woman of color to control her." He sits back heavily in his seat and heaves a hard breath.

"Abuse victims are good at hiding. Abusers are good at masking," I say quietly, looking over to the side. "It's a cycle that can last years if left unchecked."

"But that's the thing. *It didn't use to be this way.* I think he *just* started doing this around the time she got pregnant," Jerome explains. "How the fuck can you be with someone for four *years,* then start beating them because they're pregnant?" His eyes go to Christopher who stares back intently. "Can you imagine how on Earth that must have made her feel? And she didn't have anyone to talk to about this. She didn't even come to us! And we're the closest to her...*we l-love her.*" Jerome's voice breaks, and I can tell just how hurt he is that he couldn't be there for Sarah when she needed it the most.

"Around one in three women are victims of domestic abuse when they are pregnant. It's not really that uncommon, unfortunately," I inform them.

My lips tighten because the fact that Sarah's part of that statistic really burns my ass up.

They shake their head.

"I should have helped you finish the fucker off," Christopher says, his jaw is so tight it looks like it might snap in half if he clenches his teeth any further.

Feeling restless I fidget in my seat at the realization that I miss her. I look at my watch, ignoring Christopher momentarily. It's been twenty-two minutes since we left Sarah's room, and that's more than long enough.

"Hey, can you give us a ride? I rode with her in the ambulance, and I have no clue where she's going. Do you two know?"

They shake their heads, glancing at each other.

"No, she said she's been staying in her office. But we can figure something out." Jerome heaves to his feet. "Our place is cramped and, well, she doesn't like our place because she thinks it's haunted."

"It *is* haunted, baby. There's no thinking to it," Christopher says with a chuckle. He holds out a hand to Jerome, and it solidifies my thoughts that they're a couple.

"Well," I sigh. "Let's find out, shall we?"

We don't need to figure it out, because I'm going to make sure she's okay. From now on, she's my responsibility.

"Thanks, you guys. I love you so much. I'll call both of you tomorrow, okay?" Sarah says softly as she leans forward into Christopher's and Jerome's embrace.

It's been a long night. They took her key and retrieved some of her clothes from her house with a promise to be back later for her bed. Currently she's swimming in the long-sleeved shirt and sweatpants that the nurse from the hospital had given her. She had to tie the pants up with a hair tie to keep them from falling. She looks adorable.

It came as no surprise to me when she didn't want to stay in her home, even for one night. Too many bad memories to haunt her and give her nightmares, she'd explained.

I wait patiently as they take their time fussing over her. I'm basically running on pure adrenaline alone. It's almost midnight. Christopher dropped us off at my car at my office, and I promised them to take her to her office from there, considering she shouldn't be driving so soon after her miscarriage. She said that's where she'd been sleeping. And, feeling protective, I want to check it out to make sure it's safe and suitable.

I insisted that I needed to take it from here.

Their car doors slamming and the engine turning over disrupts the quiet night air. They give us a wave as they pull away, and I turn and eye her. She looks so tired.

"Ready?" I ask softly, opening my passenger door for her.

She nods but keeps her eyes averted from mine when I help her in gently with a hand on the side of her waist, trying to be mindful of her back. My fingers brush the deep swell of her hip as I pull away and gently close the door behind her before getting in on the driver's side.

Taking her cue, I drive in silence while the navigation system chirps directions from the car's computer system. As we pull in, I take in the small blue and grey stone house curiously. Cheap lighting illuminates the front. It's adorable, and to be honest, it looks like it fits her perfectly.

"This is me," Sarah says, but I remain quiet as my eyes sweep the property.

The house has an oak wooden door, a bay window in the front, and that's it. It's small, and the driveway holds enough space for maybe four cars. I get out and round to her door, opening it and helping her out. Crickets break the hushed silence, and I ignore the overgrown grass tickling my ankles as I stand patiently waiting for her to place her hand in mine.

"Can you walk?" I ask.

“Yes. Thank you,” Sarah says softly, leading the way to the front of what she’d called her little office house. The slow pace has me itching to pick her up, but I need to respect her boundaries after her traumatic experience. "Sorry about the grass."

I arch a brow, a grin tipping the side of my mouth. "There's no reason to be sorry for something like that."

Her skin flushes pink as she walks to the door and unlocks it. Waiting behind her, my smile broadens just a bit at how her bone straight hair is looking a little puffy in the back, and she keeps putting a hand back there and smoothing it down. I erase it off my face the moment she gets the door open and turns the light on.

I step into the house she’s converted into her practice and get a good look, immediately hit by how soothing it feels in here.

My eyes roam greedily, trying to take in everything at once. She painted the place light gray and topped it with molding I wouldn't have expected to see in a house like this. My shoes slip a bit on the well-maintained wooden floors, and when I look down as I try to catch my balance, I can see my reflection in the wood it's so polished.

I'm a bit jealous at how cozy her place is compared to the sterile environment of my office. A tiny stove for warmth is the main focus of the seating area which boasts two plush purple couches and a weathered leather chair. Lots of little plants sit in the bay window, and there's so much beautiful art. It's gorgeous. And to top it off, it smells good.

Like autumn and warmth.

There's even a little kitchenette through a door in the back that I bet is well stocked. I turn my head, looking past a small bathroom to see two other doors down the small hallway, with a little sound machine on the floor outside of one of them.

She heads to the back, and I follow her. Keeping an appropriate amount of distance between us as we head towards the door that has the sound machine on the floor next to it in the hall. I allow her space to enter into the office first and watch her be swallowed momentarily by the darkness, making me frown. But not for long.

"Hang on," she says in a weary voice, fumbling around for something.

The space is suddenly illuminated in a soft golden glow via a lamp on her desk. My eyes flicker around the medium-sized space that holds a desk, computer, a small sofa, and a wingback chair. I briefly wonder where her file cabinets are and any other junk. She seems really tidy. My eyes return to her and roam her body curiously as she rounds her desk, pulling out a drawer and dropping her big tote in with a light thump, keeping her phone in her hand.

"I like your place. It looks like you," I mumble. My eyes wander around the room again, then flicker to her eyes. "Not that I know you well enough to know what looks like you. I don't mean to be presumptuous." I half-smile at her, seeing that she's still pressing down on the back of her hair self-consciously.

She doesn't say anything, remaining quiet. Understandable after what she'd been through today. Empathy tugs at my heart at the little bags under her eyes and deepens the hurt I feel for her. She looks incredibly tired. Worry causes the muscles in my face to harden as my eyes roam down her body again, seeing her press her fingers into her stomach and rub little circles.

Renewed sadness wells up inside of me at the action. Poor baby.

I square my shoulders, determined to not let her fall so soon into a melancholy state. I want to make sure she's okay, and I'm damned sure going to make sure I get her into some trauma counseling. Biting the inside of my cheek, I narrow my eyes slightly as I pivot to her open office door. Where's she going to sleep?

Oh, she's got another bedroom. I see the closed door across the hall and mentally slap myself.

"Where are you sleeping? Is it this room right here?" I ask curiously, giving her a little *"may I?"* look, and stepping out into the hallway to open the other door that's closed without waiting for permission.

However, there's nothing to see as it's an empty, dark room.

I frown, closing the wooden door back with a soft click, and walk back to her office. I lean my shoulder against the doorframe and assess her for a moment. "Sarah, there's not a bed in there. Where are you sleeping?" I ask quietly.

Ssrah looks dead on her feet, and the speed in which she averts her eyes has my hackles rising. "Uhm, I've been sleeping on the couch for the last week or so. I was just going to stay here until I pick an apartment," she replies in a hushed tone, her fingers tangling in her hair as she stands there, swaying gently.

I fight to keep from clearing my throat. She can't mean this loveseat I'm currently staring at. I know she can't.

My eyes nail themselves to the small, dark-blue couch against the far wall. I frown at the very thin throw blanket laid across the back of it. And it's not big enough for a five year old child to stretch out comfortably on it, much less her. Now it's my turn to blink.

Silently I push off the door frame and journey back down the hallway, walking into the kitchenette where I open her little refrigerator and her freezer. She has nothing but ice, an almost empty jug of iced coffee, a bag of grapes, and two bottles of water. My eyes narrow in annoyance.

Fuck that. Uh-uh.

She's coming home with me.

Striding back into her office like I own the place, I walk casually around her desk to where she stands. Ignoring her little flinch away from me, I open her drawer back up, bending down to grab her tote out. Swiveling, I carefully pick her up bridal-style, being extremely careful of her back, and ignore her squeak of protest.

"Dr. Richardson, *what are you doing?"* she sputters.

Too bad for her she's too exhausted to really put up a fight because I'm not letting this go. I won't. As if she knows, she seems to give up before she even has a chance to fight. She lays her head on my shoulder, her body going limp in my arms.

My heart races at the feel of her in my arms, and how close our faces are. I stare down at her, watching her eyelashes flutter against her cheeks as she fights to stay awake. The sight is arresting, and innocent. Giving me enough pause to be momentarily lost in the color of her skin. She is one arresting woman.

She has blue-green veins visible underneath delicate skin that I've seen flush several different shades of pink tonight. She reminds me of a beautiful sunset, with every color imaginable available to me if I just know which buttons to push.

Thank God she's too tired to argue. I think.

I speak to her in a calming, low tone. "We can either go to a hotel tonight, or you can come to my house. I'm not leaving you alone, and you are not sleeping on that *thing*. It's not even a couch. You won't be comfortable, and you need to be able to stretch out after what you just went through," I say, swinging us in the direction of the sofa so tiny it's barely made for two people to sit in. "Your choice."

"You don't have to-" Sarah whispers weakly.

Oh, but I do.

"Hotel or my house?" I gently interrupt, rocking her in my arms as I wait patiently.

Thankfully, more of her resolve leaves her. She wets her lips, opening her eyes. "Well, if you promise not to do to me whatever you did to Brandon, I'll go to your place. You probably want to get out of your clothes," she says wearily, and I feel her resolve *completely* leave her.

Single-mindedly focused on getting her to my house by any means necessary, I turn to walk down her hallway.

Sarah stiffens. "*Wait,*" she says sharply, her eyes snapping back open. God, her particular shade of brown is to die for. "I need my hair...stuff."

"Where is it?"

"Bathroom. O-On the left."

I turn and walk four steps to the other room, leaning us in. She reaches forward to grab a plastic shower cap, a brush, comb, hair oil, and a hot brush, and shoves it with the rest of the things in the tote.

"I'd pay good money to see your curls one day," I admit, making her stiffen and scrunch her nose. "Maybe you'll come terrorize me at the office another day, and you'll grace me with the sight."

I want to keep her talking so she doesn't have much time to slip into the sadness I know will be coming once she gets alone. Desiring to hold it off just a little longer for her tonight.

She rests her head on my shoulder again, and this warmth in my chest burns just a little bit hotter. Melting me further.

I try to be as gentle as I can, but she makes a little sound as I bend to grab her bag of clothes, walk out the door and turn back to face it again so she can reach and lock it. She flinches and heaves a little gasping sigh.

"Are you okay?" I ask her gently.

Concern knits my brow.

"Just...I'm hurting," she whispers, her brows furrowing with pain, and I know I did right by making sure she's not alone tonight.

"I'll have you comfortable in no time," I assure her. "I'm only about twelve minutes from here. I have one of those heating pads that you warm up in the microwave, too, to put on your belly if you want it."

I place her carefully in the car, not concerned with the seat belt. Once I'm in the driver's seat, I glance into the back, making sure her hospital bag is there, suddenly worried we'd left it with the guys. I just want to make sure she has what she needs. I'd overheard the nurse tell her about needing to change pads and all the stuff that happens after a miscarriage, and I don't want her to have to worry about a thing once she's in my home. I turn my head. She's reclined in the seat, her long eyelashes flutter against her cheeks as she succumbs to her exhaustion.

I know it's inappropriate, but I reach out a hand and lay it on the soft swell of her stomach, right under her belly button. The loss she's experiencing is unimaginable, and she deserves to have someone hold space for her, so I will.

Turning, I place my hand on the back of her headrest, reverse efficiently out of her little driveway, and head down the road for the fifteen minute drive to my house.

Sarah is sleeping hard when I pull through the gate, so I park out front, not wanting to be bothered with the garage. Taking the steps fast, I open the front door of the house and go back to the car, gently lifting her out before carrying her inside. Her hair is so long I can feel it brushing the front of my legs through my dress pants.

I carry her slowly up the stairs, careful to not jostle her back, and turn to the right to one of three guest bedrooms, and push the door open with my foot.

I'm not ready to put her down, I realize.

I pause momentarily, relishing the warm puffs of her breath against my neck. I cradle her body gently against mine, also realizing I really like the weight of her in my arms. She's so soft.

Walking to the queen-sized bed I maneuver carefully, yanking back the sheets and laying her down as gently as I can manage. Seeing her hair caught, I frown at how uncomfortable it looks snagged underneath her.

I click my tongue, lean down to pull her head back up slightly, and firmly pull her hair out from underneath her and to the side. I watch with furrowed brows as the long mass spills down the side of the mattress. That can't be comfortable either. It takes a lot of maneuvering, but I finally get it. I think.

Feeling the fatigue settle bone deep, I blink tiredly as I pull the blankets over her.

I leave my guest room to grab all of her stuff from where I left it in the foyer, and bring it to the bedroom. Trying to be quiet, I glance at her as I place her things in a small guest chair, happy she's still sleeping peacefully. Her hand rests against her cheek as she sleeps curled in on herself.

I open her hospital bag and pull out her soiled clothes, hoping I'm not overstepping.

Taking her clothes into the laundry room, I unload the bag. There's just a skirt and tank top. The underwear is gone, letting me know she wanted to keep her skirt. I bring it to the sink and open the overhead cabinet, looking for cleaners.

Finding the stain remover, I plug the sink to let it fill up and soak her blood-stained clothing with the stain remover before scrubbing and soaking again. I put it to the side, promising to finish it in the morning.

Exiting the room once more, I pad to the master bedroom and hurriedly throw myself in the shower, getting out and dressing in a pair of pajama bottoms and a muscle shirt. As I'm yanking it down, my eyes snap to my bedroom door as that new burst of warmth glows in my chest. She's right down the hallway, and I miss her. I don't want her to be alone.

And I don't want to be alone, either.

Toweling off my hair, I go back to the bedroom with Sarah and tentatively crawl into the other side with her before falling into a light sleep. I'm exhausted myself, having been up since four-thirty that morning.

A few hours later, I stir at the sound of a tortured moaning and sit up in bed, blinking away the sleep from my eyes. My head tilts to find Sarah's curvy body in the moonlight, turned away from me.

The moaning continues, followed by a sob. Then another sob and sniffle.

"Hang on, sweetheart," I say.

I get up to grab her pain medicine, then kneel by her side of the bed, and hold water to her lips to help her drink. She's trembling and still half-asleep.

"It h-hurts. My back, my heart...*everything just hurts so bad,*" she whispers, closing her eyes and putting her head back on the pillow. "What did I ever do to deserve this?"

Jesus... How many times can a man's heart shatter in one day?

"You don't deserve this. No one does," I whisper back, brushing my thumb down her cheek.

"I obviously do."

My heart cracks further at the raw pain in her voice. Carefully climbing back into bed behind her, I reach over, brushing gentle fingers down her arm before moving closer and curling myself around her from behind. I know this is forward, but I have this innate, primal desire to comfort and protect her. Wrapping my arms around her, I rub small circles into her belly holding her through it.

My soul mourns for this woman.

I press my lips into her hair, smelling her unique scent, and say a quick prayer for peace for her.

"You're going to be okay." Feeling her hand reaching for me, I grasp it hard in mine, holding both of our arms to her front as I rock her slightly. "The pain won't last always, sweetheart. I promise." I smooth up and down her arms, her belly, and even her hip. Everywhere I can think of touching her to reassure her that she's okay. "I'm right here. No one can hurt you," I murmur, offering her comfort until she stops crying and falls back asleep.

Restless, I stay up a little longer, taking in her scent as well as her sadness. Determined she won't carry it alone.

At least, not tonight. This day has been a lesson in sadness for the both of us.

CHAPTER FIFTEEN

No Assuming

I WAKE UP, SWELTERING hot, to the sun shining brightly through the curtains, and a thick pair of strong forearms wrapped around me. One hand is on my belly, and the other wedged underneath me and wrapped around my breasts, cradling me intimately. The first thing that hits me is how *right* this feels, how good his hands feel against me, even the breaths that puff against the back of my neck so intimately.

Oh my God.

My mouth falls open, my heart pounds hard, and my cheeks heat up to what I know has to be a fire engine red. I turn to peek through my hair, lamenting that I didn't have a scarf or anything to tie it up.

Squinting, I see Dr. Richardson's face through the frizzy strands. My racing heart suddenly skips a beat.

He's somehow even more handsome in sleep.

I turn my head again, pulling his hand very slowly off my breast. I slide, worm-like, off the mattress, standing up and then gasping as my pants fall down to the floor. Peeking back up quickly, I check he's still asleep before bending carefully, ignoring the cramping in my stomach.

I grumble as I pick them back up and see the bag of clothes on the chair by the door. I grab it, spotting an en-suite bathroom near the closet. Alexander suddenly groans and then rolls onto his belly, into the space I'd just vacated. The gray sheets of the bed pull with his movement, exposing more of him to my gaze.

My eyes flicker down the muscles peeking through the shirt he'd put on to sleep in. Pressing my lips tightly together, I go into the surprisingly expansive bathroom, closing the door before locking it. Pulling my hair up into a bun, I turn the shower on, feeling a slight cramp in my tummy that makes me twist my mouth in pain, making my hand fly up to press into the hurt.

Brittany...

I close my eyes against the nauseating, fresh wave of pain.

I sigh miserably, remembering the nurse said I might bleed for a few days after the miscarriage. Waiting for the water to warm up, I pull down my pants and look down into my panties. There's not a lot of blood. Not as much as I expected. I roll up the pad, wrapping it in a bunch of tissue before shoving it into the trashcan, lamenting that there's nothing in there for me to hide it under. I pull off my top and bra, turning in the mirror to take in the swell of my tummy. I hadn't been pregnant long enough to have any real physical changes, and that swell that's there has always been present.

I put on my shower cap and and step under the water, seeing the shower stocked. My mind whirls as I go through the motions of lathering a rag. I can't believe what happened. Here I'd been doing my absolute best to advocate for my client with the most hardheaded, *arrogant* psychiatrist—

I stop soaping myself up, pausing to take a good look around me.

I'm in the hardheaded arrogant psychiatrist's *bathroom*. In his *home*. After he wouldn't leave me alone last night to be by myself. I bite my lip, remembering the way he held me on the floor of his office while we waited for the ambulance, and what he did to Brandon at the hospital. How tenderly he comforted me last night when I was breaking down crying. My eyes sting. I've never been treated so nicely before in my life, and...maybe there's a chance I've greatly misjudged him?

I have to send him some flowers and a thank-you card.

I'm not even sure why I believe that that would be enough of a thanks, but it's going to have to be. My bank account can only take so much, and now I have a hospital bill to worry about as well. I wince, sighing as I turn the water off and reach over to the rack, wrapping a thick towel around me and tucking the edge in at my breast.

I step out of the shower onto the low-pile gray rug, ripping the cap off my head. Walking up to the vanity, I give my hair an admonishing look, parting my hair in the mirror, truly detesting having to go through the motions of being normal. I don't feel normal.

Nothing is normal anymore.

I plug in and turn on my hot brush. Giving myself a once over in the mirror, I spray my hair with a heat protectant, and while I wait for the brush to get hot, I moisturize my body. Then I spend ten minutes combing out the strands with the hot brush, paying careful attention to the back of my head where the curls and frizz are trying to make a vicious comeback.

Ignoring the pain and wanting to put my best foot forward with Dr. Richardson, I carefully make my hair into a silky curtain again that flows over my breasts and down almost to my belly button.

Satisfied I'm presentable, I pull out a pad and shimmy my underwear up before donning a burnt-orange strapless dress. Out of all the clothes I could have grabbed, why on Earth did I pack something that shows my back? I must have been way out of it. Had to be in order to let this man bring me to his house.

I wipe a tear away, feeling another pang of loss for Bumpy.

But I try to put my loss to the back of my mind as I put on a light coat of mascara, exiting the bathroom to find the bedroom empty, and the bed neatly made. Stepping out into the hallway, I turn my head left and right curiously. The hallway is a huge space with contemporary vases and pieces of art standing on pedestals instead of pictures on the walls. The hallway is very sterile, with plain white walls illuminated by recessed lighting. It's the type of no-life look that elites strive for because their everyday life is so busy and hectic.

I don't care for it.

Apparently, being a psychiatrist of Alexander's stature is a lucrative career, and he does very well for himself. No wonder he didn't want me sleeping in my little office house. It wasn't good enough for his standards. My eyes sting.

If I'd felt inadequate before...

Making my way down the hall, I walk towards a glass staircase that's ironically right up my parent's alley and follow it down slowly with my hand on the banister, feeling the pain shooting through my back with every step. Lost in the thought of my parents, I completely blank out for a few seconds before pausing halfway down when I realize I'd forgotten to put on my cardigan. I turn and look back up the staircase, not sure I have it in me to re-climb them and then come back down.

I'm stuck for a minute, self-conscious about my bruising. But what does it matter? He's seen them anyway.

I smell bacon, so I follow my nose. It makes my mouth water as I remember I hadn't eaten at all yesterday, and I am *starving*.

His place is quite impressive, and I can't help but glance around at all the glass, marble, and contemporary art. It's all icy, just like his damn stare.

Padding over marble tile, I pass underneath a tall archway and into a vast kitchen that's surprisingly *not* very modern looking. Alexander's at a six-burner gas stove, dressed in a pair of slacks and a plain black T-shirt, cooking. He hasn't noticed I've come down, so I take a second to observe him for the first time in more normal clothes.

His tallness gives my eyes plenty of room to roam, observing rippling biceps with not an inch of fat on them. His arms are covered in a light dusting of hair, partially hiding the veins and cords that stick out. Though his stature is lean, his shoulders are *broad,* and his back muscles flex against his T-shirt as he cooks. They taper down to a set of hips that's broad and muscular, too. His body is thick and strong. It's obvious that he takes very good care of himself.

Steeling myself to face him and tackle a new day, I walk into the kitchen, making my presence known. "Good morning, Dr. Richardson." I clear my throat and come even closer, until I'm almost pressed against the huge island that separates the two of us.

Alexander turns around with a spatula in his hand. I almost want to smile at the red and black checkered kitchen towel thrown over his shoulder. When our eyes lock, he pauses as he gets a good look at me. I feel myself stiffen as his striking blue eyes meet mine, before slowly dragging down over my neck, my breasts, and my hair.

I roll my lips, tucking my chin in and flushing. It's quite overwhelming being *seen,* but I don't feel picked apart. So there's that.

"Good morning, Sarah." He gives me a handsome smile that makes me feel funny. "I think we can do away with pleasantries now, don't you?" My body relaxes at the low, smooth tone of his voice, and I'm ashamed to admit it does something to me deep inside. I cannot imagine this man raising his voice. I bring my eyes back up to his, which is a big mistake, because it sucks me in even deeper. "Unless you'd like me to call you Miss Johnson, feel free to call me Alexander. Only Dr. Richardson at the office, please," he says with a little smile in his voice as he turns back to the stove.

I crane my neck, watching him flip pancakes next to a bunch of bacon, and lick my lips as my mouth waters in hunger.

"Uhm. I guess that's fine," I say, pensively. My mind is positively spinning, because aren't I supposed to be busy not liking him?

He turns back to me again, jerking his head pointedly at the breakfast table nearby. "You shouldn't be standing. Go sit until I'm done."

Furrowing my brow, my mind pivots and I suddenly realize I don't have my car. Where's my purse and keys?

I anxiously stroke my hands down my hair. My lips purse, about to fire these questions off at this intimidating man in front of me. Nevertheless, before I can, Alexander moves, placing the steaming pancakes to the side before walking around the island.

Fear suddenly hits hard, tightening my spine and making me freeze in place.

He's moving way too fast for my comfort, making me stiffen further as my nerves get the better of me. Before it can consume me completely, I *also* see his steps hesitate as he observes my eyes widen. I take a couple quick steps back. A look of concern settles into his features, and he ceases walking now entirely, puts a hand flat on the top of the island, and leans back giving me space.

"How're you feeling this morning? Anything I can do?" he asks quietly, his eyes flickering over my body again as if he's searching for something.

To my horror, my eyes well up, and I furiously blink back tears as both of my arms come up to wrap around my stomach protectively. His eyes catch it, making me ashamed.

I look down at my feet. "I'm okay."

He stares at me with a rather pitying, yet disbelieving look on his face. His next words take me aback. "Can I give you a hug?"

The request makes me tear my gaze from my feet to meet his, shocked. He swims in my vision as tears well so thick in my eyes I'm not sure how they aren't spilling over. I tense, realizing I really, really need a hug. One of those big bear ones that swallow you up.

I swallow hard, nervous. Because though I've been in a relationship for four years, I'm not used to physical touch. Even before Brandon, I wasn't used to physical touch from anyone other than my momma or Jerome.

I miss it.

Biting my lip I nod, feeling my heart beat just a little faster. "I-I'd like that." And even though I just gave him permission, I can't help my eyes from widening even more as he takes a few very slow steps into me. The first thing that I notice is his scent. It's so warm as it greets me first. And as his arms wrap around my body, pressing his chest and his abdomen into me, it forces me to loosen my arms to wrap around him instead of my torso. His body heat meets mine, making me fall into it. But when he puts a hand on the back of my head, cradling me, and the curve of my ass so as to not agitate my back, those tears I've been fighting back break free.

He hears me cry and just holds me to him. Not rocking. Just holding me gently...yet firmly.

"I am so sorry that this has happened to you, Sarah." His voice is tender, but instead of making the tears worse, it actually helps. It hits me then that that's why I like his voice so much; it's healing. There's something safe about this man I can't place.

Do I need to?

I sniff. "Thank you. Me... me too."

We stay locked in our embrace for way longer than I know should be normal, but it doesn't *feel* abnormal. Hugging Alexander feels like the best thing that's ever happened to me. And that's odd, because he's a stranger. I clear my throat, hating I blush so visibly, and reluctantly pull away. He's just as reluctant, it seems, because his fingers tighten briefly before falling away.

His obviously respectful demeanor shifts my sad thoughts to this morning, to how he had his arms around me.

I feel guilty.

"Uhm..." I tuck a lock of hair behind my ear self-consciously. Really wondering if I should tell him how he was wrapped around me. As a man though, maybe he wouldn't care as much. Am I making this a big deal? Probably. I'll keep it to myself. "I have an apartment showing at three, if you could take me to my car?" I ask hesitantly. "It's still at your office."

Alexander tilts his head, his eyes like a blue abyss. "It's not at the office anymore. Your friends Frick and Frack have already driven it here, but I'm afraid I'm going to insist on you not driving today. I can take you on the apartment tour. Come on, sit at the breakfast table with me. I didn't know what you liked, *so* I figured pancakes would be a safe choice. I wasn't sure if you were vegetarian," he says, startling me with the admission.

I was about to comment on his nickname for my friends, but his last words take me aback, causing me to frown slightly, tilting my head to the side, mirroring him.

"Why would you think I'm vegetarian?" I enquire.

He smiles a teasing smile and takes my hand gently, pulling me next to him. I turn my head to look up at him as I take a seat at a small buffet table tucked away in the corner of the kitchen next to a bay window that overlooks a beautiful backyard with a small koi pond tucked amongst some beautiful landscaping.

The birds fly around, catching my attention.

Alexander goes back to the island before coming back over with the food and a few plates, setting it all down efficiently. The pancakes look fluffy with slightly crisp edges, just like I like them; albeit, I don't let myself eat pancakes very often, having a love-hate relationship with carbs. But it's a free breakfast and one that another person cooked for me, so I won't be complaining.

"It's just that Indians are oftentimes vegetarian, and I didn't want to assume. I would have made eggs too, but I ran out and didn't realize," he says easily as he slides in across the seat from me.

Surprised, I let out a giggle, placing my hand over my mouth.

"What is it?" Alexander says as he throws me a slight smile, placing some pancakes on my plate.

I'm so hungry I can't answer him right away. He watches me with interest as I reach forward and snag a piece of bacon and chew on it. Moaning as my hunger hits hard.

"Oh my *God*. Thank you so much. I didn't get a chance to eat at *all* yesterday." I snag another piece of bacon, and before I know it, I've eaten four pieces before he's even put food on his plate. He'd been busy staring at me with a rather amused expression on his face.

Gosh, he's so handsome. It's almost nerve-wracking.

No, it is. It's so nerve-wracking how handsome he is. And those eyes! My God, I can barely hold his eye contact because they're so striking.

"So, *not* a vegetarian, then?" Alexander asks, his eyes crinkling with humor.

I shake my head. "No, and I'm not Indian either. Dot *or* feather," I say absentmindedly.

He barks out a laugh. "*Did you just say that*?" He asks incredulously.

His laughter warms me, and I grin back, choosing to not ream him about the faux pas of him assuming my race so blatantly.

"Yeah, just like you just said what you said," I tease him with a giggle. "Which one did you think I was? It wasn't *specified*." I crack a little diagnosis joke, cutting into my dry pancakes and placing a bite into my mouth. I lean my head back, biting back a moan because it's so good.

Alexander clears his throat and pointedly glances at my plate. *"You don't like syrup?"* he asks, rather accusatory.

"I don't eat a lot of stuff. And yet, I *still* can't get this fupa to go away," I say, putting another bite of pancake into my mouth.

To my surprise Alexander chokes, beating his hand to his chest, making me throw my silverware down, prepared to do the Heimlich.

Who am I kidding? I don't know the Heimlich. I could try, though.

Again, who am I kidding? I don't think I could wrap my arms around his broad frame. Thankfully, he gets it together, and I don't have to intervene. I push his water towards him. The best I can do right now.

"*What*? What's that?" he asks, his brow arching.

"Yeah, I have this place on my tummy that I can't spot reduce for anything. I perform at a nearby lounge and there are so many pretty dresses I want to wear, but I can't because everyone wants a super flat stomach, and I can't seem to get it, so...*why* am I even telling you this? I'm sorry," I whisper, horrified at my rambling.

I put the tip of a piece of bacon in my mouth and chew slowly, mortified.

Alexander's eyes flit to my stomach, and a look I can only describe as hunger crosses his face, but I don't feel afraid. He doesn't say anything, though.

"I didn't eat at all yesterday, so I'm just a little hungry. I'm sorry," I continue. My chin lowers as I suddenly throw the bacon back on my plate.

I shouldn't let him see me eat like this.

"Nuh-uh," Alexander says. He snatches up the syrup and pours a healthy amount on my plate, along with some more bacon. "Eat. You deserve sustenance."

Slightly horrified because he just poured about five hundred extra calories on my plate, I look up before lowering my eyes down to my food again, swimming in syrup. I hesitantly pick up my fork, seeing the syrup drip off it, and swallow nervously.

CHAPTER SIXTEEN

SOMETHING SWEET

I CHEW MY FOOD quietly, thinking to myself. I can not—*would not*—scare this woman who'd been through something as traumatic as she'd been. My eyes go down to her breasts, admiring her curves. She's beautiful. Curvy, plump and soft. My entire being hardens and fills with lust. It's so inappropriate, but I can't help it.

She's going to eat everything on her plate. Period. *I'll be damned if she loses her curves.*

I blink. Where did that thought come from?

Sarah gives me a little look as she puts a forkful of food in her mouth. The tines disappearing behind her dark-pink lips make me tighten as I attempt to lock my body down.

Do not have inappropriate sexual thoughts about a woman who just suffered a fucking miscarriage, you idiot! I chastise myself, keeping my expression still calm and neutral on hers.

I'm proud of myself actually; I don't even think you can tell by looking at me that I'm quite possibly having an existential crisis. Just when I realize my behavior might be coming across weird, I open my mouth to say something, but she beats me to it.

"This is the second apartment I'm looking at. The first one wasn't good enough because it only had one bedroom and was on the third floor of the building. I wanted this one, a two bedroom—*for obvious reasons.* But I think it might be a bit...much for me now," she says sadly, yet conversationally.

Just like a therapist.

I cannot wrap my mind around the way she talks. Her rhythm of speech is perfect and caresses my brain just right. She reminds me of a quiet lullaby in the nighttime when you can't sleep and need something soothing to calm the spirit. How that man fumbled this gem so badly, I'll spend the rest of my life trying to figure out.

"What do you mean by that?" I ask, leaning back and stretching out my legs.

I watch as her eyes flit to mine momentarily before lowering to her plate. She takes a hefty minute to consider my question.

"Welll..." My ears prick at the trilled out word as it almost sounds like she's singing. "It's a luxury apartment, and I just...I don't *know.* I guess I'm not used to it."

I watch riveted as Sarah puts another bite in her mouth. Her eyes narrow, and she scrunches her nose as if the thought of living in something luxurious is distasteful to her. I don't like that. She's more than worthy of a wealthy life.

I clear my throat, taking a sip of my drink before responding. "Everyone's gotta start somewhere. I can't wait to see it. Maybe *I'll* rent it before you have a chance to and give you this place," I joke before sobering, biting the inside of my cheek at how serious I actually feel at the thought.

I'd only bought this house because Hannah wanted it. I never really considered it my home.

"What was that look there?" she asks, taking me by surprise.

My eyes rise to hers. For a minute I'd forgotten she was a therapist. Observant, astute, just like I am.

I put another bite in my mouth, stalling. After a split second, I decide to share. "This house isn't really my style. My ex-wife wanted it. We divorced years ago, and I just never bothered selling it. Too much hassle when you're busy," I say truthfully, instinctively knowing not to lie to her.

"Hm." She chews for a second. "When did you get divorced?"

"Nine, almost ten years ago," I answer. "Worst mistake of my life."

Sarah's eyebrows rise as she scoffs, and I watch, fascinated, as an intriguing spark enters her eyes that chases the sadness away for a moment. Something that wavers in the holding space between challenging and defiance. My skin burns suddenly, adding to my dilemma. I watch as she takes a slender hand and tucks a thick lock of dark hair behind her ear. Noting with pleasure that her almond nails give her fingers a beautiful shape.

"So....in *nine years* you haven't figured out time to sell a house? Why do you live in something you don't like? Pay absorbent amounts of money for something you don't even *want?* That's interesting," Sarah says, holding another bite to her mouth.

Tilting my head, I'm intrigued she didn't run with the "worst mistake of my life comment." I want to tell her that money is of no consequence to me, but it's not the right time. And it'd be rather uncouth to flaunt my wealth when she's in this predicament, and I don't want to even come close to hurting her feelings.

I watch as her fingers leave her hair to play with her nose ring briefly. "Now look at who's pathologizing who," I retort, referencing her comment at my office yesterday.

She narrows her eyes at me. I'd also forgotten in the midst of all this mess going on that we've also had a professional rivalry because I put that to the side. But for Sarah it seems like old habits die hard.

"It's not pathologizing when you're stating a *fact*," she says, her lip curls rather sexily as she reaches forward for her water, bypassing the orange juice I freshly squeezed for her.

It's my turn to crinkle my nose. "You don't like orange juice *either*?" Not able to control myself, I put all the judgement I can into that one sentence.

"Too much sugar," she states simply.

No. That's not good enough for me. Sorry.

I pin her with a stare. "When you're in *my house* you'll eat *all* the things, and you won't complain about anything being too much in *any* aspect at all, got it?" I say sternly, moving her orange juice closer to her before sitting back and picking up my own.

I watch as her face goes from a light mocha color to a deep dusky rose as she picks up on my double entendre.

Jesus, I've never seen skin like hers before, I lament, itching to touch her again. *I need to call Johnathan, because what the fuck kind of person lusts after someone who just had a miscarriage*? I wonder, thinking Johnathan would know.

The man's brother is quite fucked-up in the head, and I'm starting to think I might be, too. I haven't felt like I've had a sane thought since Sarah looked at me from her seat in my lobby the first time we met.

Is this what a woman does to you? Makes your brain mush?

I tilt my head, regarding her. Sarah gives me a small, nervous smile and puts another bite into her mouth. I watch as her free hand strokes the wooden table absentmindedly, and I'm noticing that stroking movements are a soothing reflex of hers.

Jesus fucking Chri—

I clench my jaw as my erection now tightens to the point of pain. Likewise, Sarah is obviously in pain herself—for a different reason. The thought instantly calms me. The harsh bite of desire lessens as I realize she's not betraying just how much pain she's in. And though she's not complaining, I know she's in pain.

Because I saw up close and personal last night that her back is in awful shape. It sobers me instantly.

"I have some pain meds for you, for your back. Do you need me to rub some ointment on it?" I ask, wanting to take care of her.

Finding myself needing to do for this woman what I never could for Hannah. I flinch at the sudden, intrusive thought. Because though I'm aware I've been severely emotionally abused, I'm still not proud of how coldly I treated her, especially towards the end of our marriage. I was just too shut down.

"Oh, uhm..." Sarah looks away, finishing her last bite of food, looking briefly lost in thought. "No thank you to the ointment, but I'll take some pain medicine. Other than that, I think I'm fine. I need to do what I can to get on with my life....I can't let this suck me down. I have clients who need me healthy and mentally stable, you know?" I do know, baby. A lot more than you'd think. "My livelihood depends on it."

Her eyes are sad, and I can't stand this for her. She should be able to be allowed time to heal from this. Not have to keep pushing.

My mind whirls, wondering what I can do to help ease her burden. But I stay silent, only offering her a nod, not wanting to push her. She's been through so much since yesterday, really since her boyfriend started beating her, and the last thing I want her to feel right now is pressured into anything.

I finish the last of my orange juice, pulling her empty plate out of her hand before she can stand up.

"I got it, sweetheart," I say. Seeing her flush at my term of endearment for her gives me so much pleasure. "Tell me where this apartment is while I clean. It's almost two o'clock, so we should probably get a move on. While I clean up, let's talk more about our client. One of your case notes intrigued me with a specific behavior."

I figure I'll provide a distraction for her.

Sarah stands up slowly to follow me to the island. "Okay, but I can help you wash the dishes, or at least clean off the counters?" she asks softly, wringing her fingers.

She doesn't need to be awkward with me.

I smile as I half turn to glance at her. "*No,* you've been through enough. Just sit there." I jerk my head to one of the six stools at the island. "Sit there, rest, and let me do it," I say, turning to place the dishes in the sink to rinse under hot water.

Let me do it.

I work to try to remember when I stopped saying those words to my ex-wife. I don't know. But what I do know is, when I think about Hannah lately, it doesn't sting so bad. Her bitterness begins to fall away from my psyche, whisper-soft.

Being replaced by something much more sweet.

CHAPTER SEVENTEEN

SYRUP SKIN LICKS

I LOOK ON, IMPRESSED as we pull up to a great fancy apartment complex with a big circular fountain out front. It looks rather a lot like a high-end hotel. I park and glance over at Sarah, who's nervously looking out the window. Her head tilts as her big brown eyes stare up at the seven-floor building.

She's gorgeous. Literally the most breathtaking woman I've ever had the pleasure of sharing space with, and in this moment, despite our circumstances, I feel so lucky I may as well be floating on cloud nine.

Giving her the moment she obviously needs, my gaze licks down the curve of her neck and I stiffen at the tiny drop of syrup shining against her collar bone. It's presence dropping me from heaven, back down to earth, and even lower. If possible.

Oh fuck....

My knuckles turn white on the steering wheel. Could you get an award for self-control? Because if so, I think I might deserve it. My mouth waters, and my flesh burns to lean over and lick that small droplet off her. But instead, I swallow hard, open my car door, and slide smoothly out of my vehicle instead.

I leave it there, not even telling her to wipe it off. I'm content to just watch it on her flesh all day, torturing me while I think of ways to secretly wipe it off with my mouth.

She opens her own car door before I can get to her. "Stay there," I say sharply, tsking as I make my way around to her side. Her legs swing out of the vehicle, her knees and heels pressed firmly together, before sliding out of the seat with a hop.

Her calves are so curvy. Gorgeous. Flawless, actually.

As her heels clack on the asphalt, I notice her little wince and slide my hand in my pocket to hide the fist I'd just made. Painfully aware this isn't my place to have an opinion, I can't help but be a bit angry we're even doing this. She should be in bed right now, resting.

"I wish you would have worn flats," I say simply, feeling bad for her.

"I'm just used to heels."

I nod, dropping it.

Closing her door with a soft bang, I tighten my lips and force myself to be quiet. I can't believe we're doing this while she's in *heels* no less, after being in the hospital until almost midnight and the trauma she'd gone through. But before we left, she explained to me that she desperately needs to get her own place, so she couldn't blow off this tour. She didn't want to sleep where she works, and there has to be a clear boundary for her there.

So, though I didn't want to, I respected her decision and decided if she looks like she can't keep walking comfortably, then I'll just carry her around. Problem solved.

My eyes take in the light gray stone of the building with it's glass awning and doors with its welcoming chandelier and step a little closer, placing my hand on her lower back lightly, over her now flawless silky hair. It feels perfect.

I wish she felt well enough that I could push her in the fountain by accident just to see her curls once her hair got wet.

Sarah's eyes slide to mine as she tilts her head up slightly to look at me, her gold nose ring glints in the sun. She takes a deep breath, and I feel bad for even entertaining a thought like that. Although it's true. I think I'd give my left arm to see her natural hair.

"I need a miracle," she confesses.

Her hand goes to her tummy. She's thinking about Bumpy, based off the way her eyes water.

"Miracles happen everyday," I say. "How about we just go in and see what they have to offer?"

I press gently onto her lower back so as not to hurt her. Going as slowly as she requires, I ignore every instinct to throw her across my shoulder and drive her home to lock her away. Instead, I lead her through the glass doors and disappear into the air conditioned building to meet our tour guide, Shelly.

Twenty minutes later, we're in the model apartment. And to be honest, if she didn't need it so bad, I'd take this damn place for myself. It's great.

"Are you impressed? You look like it!" Shelly laughs as she finishes walking me around the lush two-bedroom apartment on the second floor.

"I am," I admit with a smile.

Shelly and I stand in the gleaming white kitchen complete with Carrera marble and gold cabinet pulls. I glance at the warming drawer and the small wine refrigerator; then, I stare across the small space of the living room and outside to the covered terrace, which hosts its own beautiful view of the grounds of the property, overlooking a nature park and a sparkling lake with a fountain.

"Do you mind me asking what the monthly rent is?" I inch closer to Shelly, talking quietly while Sarah takes her time in the back of the apartment.

Sarah did share with me that her only real requirement was enough bathroom space for her hair stuff. And I hope to God that this apartment, or the one she saw a few days ago, has what she needs because she's planning on going back to her office with a blow-up air mattress tomorrow. She only conceded to staying one more night at my house. But only because I'm adamant she needs oversight for at least one more day just in case of any medical complications.

She's tough, I think. But she *did* just go through a medical trauma, and to be honest, I'd feel more comfortable if I could keep an eye on her for another two weeks.

"It's nineteen hundred a month."

"That's it?" I ask, surprised.

Her eyes sparkle with humor. "Yes, it's a much smaller floor plan than the usual layout, and to be honest, the receptionist who took Ms. Johnson's call for the tour held this aside especially for her." She lowers her voice further. "Apparently, her niece saw Ms. Johnson for counseling for a year after some family issues, and Ms. Johnson worked *miracles* for their family. She turned down over *fifteen* tours of this apartment to give Ms. Johnson first bid on it. If she wants it, that is."

A miracle. There's that word again.

I nod, rubbing my hand on the sleeve of my t-shirt absentmindedly, thinking about my religious father who made sure that Aurora and I grew up in church and became decent people—by his standards anyways.

"Does the place come furnished?" I ask.

"Yes," Shelly says, "We can add that to the monthly rent, or she can buy the package outright and take it with her when she goes."

I rub my tongue on the side of my teeth, working my jaw and thinking.

"Hm," I hum. "If she chooses this apartment, I'd like to buy it for her. Separately, though... and I don't want her to know. If she signs a lease, draw up another document for me, and I'll sign it separately and pay for it. Here's my email." I dig into my pocket and pull out a business card.

Shelly's eyes widen. "Don't you want to know how much it is before committing?" she asks.

Shelly looks down at my card before her eyes widen somehow even further, barely even hearing my response of, "Not really."

"*Dr. Richardson*?"

I wince, because *heerree we go.* I can't even go to a regular apartment tour without someone knowing who I am. Maybe I should go out of the country, give myself a break. I plaster what I hope is a nice smile on my face and give her a small nod.

"Oh my gosh, I saw you speak at a conference a few years ago! I was far away in the audience, but I remember your face now. I should have recognized that bone structure! Oh my goodness! *This is so cool!"* she gushes, even breaking out into a blush.

Just then Sarah's heels click across the hardwood floor towards us, thankfully saving me from having to respond. Appearing around the corner, I see she has her arms folded and her cardigan pulled tight against her. Her hair flows across her shoulder and down her breasts, tickling her navel. I want to run my fingers through it, touch her belly, feel her skin against mine.

To feel like she desires me.

I feel myself melting as she slowly approaches.

"Well," she says rather breathlessly, with a small smile, "I like the bathroom *a lot*. And the back grounds are beautiful, and I would *kill* for this kitchen set up." She glances at Shelly with a hopeful look. "How much is it again?"

"Nineteen hundred dollars a month." Shelly answers, slipping my business card in her back pocket. "But that includes security in the lobby, all the amenities like a gym, sauna, pool, and we even have a small grocery store and a coffee shop downstairs. *And* we provide internet. We can sign a six-month lease. We do offer that, too," Shelly adds quickly, reaching over to place her hand gently on Sarah's forearm, making her smile.

She turns her head away for a second, and I can tell she's doing some mental calculations. We both wait patiently while she taps her fingers against her arm, and I can almost feel when she comes to a decision. "What are the requirements?" she asks, keeping her gaze on Shelly.

"You need a two-thousand-dollar deposit and first month's rent due up front. And if you have any pets, it's a five hundred dollar deposit fee plus an extra sixty dollars a month."

"Okay...can I fill out an application?" Sarah asks hesitantly.

"Absolutely! Just come with me."

We make our way downstairs, and Shelly shows us to a quaint coffee shop area for us to sit while she fills out the paperwork.

I quickly excuse myself while Sarah sits and scribbles quietly.

Perusing the glass case, I grab us a scone each, a cup of coffee for me, and a chai tea for her, just taking a wild guess as to what she'd like. Then I order a raspberry flavored tea, along with a regular tea and one with lemon just in case, so she can have options.

I bring it all back to the table, watching as she efficiently flips through the pages, looking up at the items I brought over; she smiles before she sees the scone and then frowns.

I push it to her, ignoring her brows lifting.

"I know you don't expect me to eat that. I just had pancakes two hours ago," she whispers rather loudly.

"I can hear you," I whisper back.

Her eyes bounce back and forth between the drinks I'd set in front of her, and I'm curious to see which one she'll pick. Her hands go to the raspberry iced tea, and she pulls it to herself carefully. "Thank you," she says in a normal voice, her eyes on me as she wraps her manicured fingers around the cup.

She's endearingly polite.

I watch greedily, as she holds the cup to her plump lips, swallowing a small sip; the tip of her tongue lashes out to lick a drop of tea off her lip, causing my heart to race.

The simple action sets me on fire.

As if my body is not my own anymore, my eyes flicker to that small dot of syrup on her collarbone, and my cock tightens again, making me feel feral.

Her gaze drifts pointedly to the treats, and I clear my throat to respond to her question, though it does absolutely nothing to help. "Hmm-hm. I do expect you to eat it, *actually*," I say rather harshly.

I can't help it. I'm trying everything in my power to get my erection to go away, and so that means other things get put by the wayside.

Such as the tone of my voice, dour and clipped, because I'm working overtime censoring how badly I want this woman.

Sarah's lips part in surprise, and we both watch as she slowly reaches forward and places her fingers against the napkin that holds one of the scones, and pulls it towards her slowly before she picks it up and bites into it. A shower of crumbs rains down, falling on her cleavage and sticking to her mouth. I suck in a sharp breath, and my fingers clench on the table.

My efforts were in vain. *Jesus. Fucking. Christ.*

My chest expands as my cock unfortunately forms its own painful heartbeat.

Turning my face to the side, I close my eyes and breathe deeply through my nose. Wishing I knew EMDR, or some other technique, to help me in these times that she is absolutely wrecking my mind for absolutely no reason. It's astonishing because I just met her, but the intensity of my attraction to her is damn near suffocating.

My mind fights with my body over what is right, reminding me that I am just a man: weak, flawed.

Once I manage to get somewhat of a grip on my emotions, I rise, grab a napkin, and come to stand in front of her. Aware that I'm being incredibly inappropriate, I brush the crumbs off her chest lightly before leaning down to her ear and ignore her eyes widening. It's interesting, her reaction. She doesn't lean back, or act like she's afraid; no, she leans further into me.

Her scent makes me drunk, I swear.

"I'm going to take a walk, and be back in about ten minutes, so eat your scone, please. I've asked you rather nicely. Can you indulge me?" I ask quietly.

And because I truly can't help it, and I'm a fucked-up person who probably needs my own psychiatrist at this point, my head dips down, and my tongue laps at that drop of dried syrup on her skin. Once. Twice. Slowly dragging my tongue along her skin, tasting her unique scent. And I cannot help but let out a small groan.

If I was drunk before, then right now I am having a straight, raw, unfiltered hit. Guaranteed. Because this woman is a *drug*.

Her mouth falls open, and her breath hitches as my tongue caresses her yet again, letting me know I'm not in this attraction alone. I straighten, catching her eye briefly before walking away without a word. Thinking she can sue me for sexual harassment for all I care at this point. It was worth it.

Outside the coffee shop I sit on a bench and slide on a pair of sunglasses to block out the harsh sun. Relishing the taste of her on my tongue, I take out my phone and check my notifications, seeing I've already received an email from Shelly.

> Dr. Richardson,
>
> As long as her payment is processed, the apartment is hers. The furniture package is attached to this email, along with a way to pay. The apartment will come furnished with everything you saw in it today, as well as the dishes in the kitchen. Please let me know if there is anything I can do for you. Ms. Johnson can move in by Tuesday when the payment is processed.
>
> Best,
>
> Ms. Shelly Tremaine

I smile as I pull up the attachment and do the online payment process for the furniture. It doesn't take long.

Pulling my messages up, I ignore a message from Hannah asking for money, and then find Johnathan's text thread.

AR: Hey man, how's it going? Was wondering if we could meet around noon on Monday?

You free? I just licked a woman who I just formally met yesterday, and I feel like I need to talk to someone about how fucked-up my brain has become.

I slide my phone back into my pocket and stand just as Sarah comes out of the building, slipping on a pair of sunglasses to no doubt hide her eyes from me. She raises a hand and sweeps her hair over one shoulder, taking her time caressing the ends. A harsh grip of jealousy tightens my jaw so hard a flash of pain works its way across my temple, and it's all I can do to look and sound normal.

By the way, being jealous of a woman because she touches her own hair is *not* normal.

"You good?" I ask, walking to her and placing my hand on her back, over her hair once again because I just can't help myself.

"Yes, I'm good," she answers softly, tilting her head to look up at me. "Thank you for asking."

She's so polite. Jesus.

I wonder if she's this reserved in bed. I hope not. If she is, I'll be fixing that as soon as possible.

"No problem." I tuck her under my arm—she really fits so perfectly against me—squeezing her shoulder, and trailing my hand down the soft skin of her upper arm to settle somewhere above her elbow as we make our way through the parking lot. Once at the car, I open her door just as her phone pings. Watching her slide in slowly, I keep my hand on her arm at the wince of pain that crosses her features. I wish she'd let me put the ointment on her like I offered.

And then I also wish I would have kept my tongue to myself because now I'm wondering if I crossed a line with her that she won't let me come back from.

Once she's healed, I definitely want to see where this can go between us.

To my delight, she doesn't seem in the least bit bothered by how inappropriate I was.

"Hey, I got approved!" she says excitedly. "I just gave her that application like ten minutes ago!" Pulling off her sunglasses, her eyes narrow as she reads through the email. "It's a contingent based on my payment," she mutters almost to herself, "which is fine. It'll take all my savings, *but I don't care!* Who needs furniture?"

She turns her face to me and smiles brightly.

A spark of joy enters her eyes. Yet, I keep my smile to myself, not bothering to tell her I bought her furniture packet. Somehow, I know she won't like that. I muse it over in my head, deciding I'll contact Christopher and Jerome and let them know so they won't be bothered with trying to get anything from that asshole's house.

Pulling out my phone, I do just that, texting them in a group chat as I round the car to get in on the driver's side. I see Johnathan messaged me back.

> J. Dawg: YOU licking someone you just met *yesterday?* How utterly interesting. Wait, like licked her *how?* I'm having lunch with Ally at her school Monday. Can we do after work on Wednesday, 7p.m.? Maybe we can meet up at your boxing venue for a round or two?

I'm pleased with the reschedule because I didn't want to leave Sarah alone. She should be moving into her apartment on Tuesday; surely, she would be okay with staying with me until then. I can't have her sleeping on that poor excuse for a couch in her office or an air mattress.

"So, I think that I *should* be okay to move in sometime next week, it looks like," Sarah says, looking at her phone as I drive off. "I know my payment will go through, and I have *just* enough wiggle room to pay up my rent on my office building one month."

Turning my head, I accidentally see her banking account information and immediately become so pissed my foot hits the pedal too hard, causing my engine to rev.

"*Alex*!" Sarah's sharp scream pierces my ears as we shoot forward.

Her hand yanks on the grab bar above her window and a look of pure panic fills her face, making me feel so shitty I slow us to almost ten miles under the speed limit to make it up to her.

Fuck, I curse to myself.

"Sorry. The car is a bit...touchy," I say.

I put a hand to her leg and squeeze before placing my hand back on the wheel. Little pants sound out, her hand is slightly pale because of her death grip, and her eyes are wide as she stares out the windshield making me feel even worse. I'd never want to scare her. She's had enough of that the last few weeks.

My jaw ticks in displeasure when my thoughts go back to her account. When she said she would be using all of her savings to pay for the apartment, she'd *meant* that. She would only have maybe eighteen hundred left over after paying what she needed to...but she'd also just said she would be paying up her rent on her practice.

Theoretically, realistically, she's going to have nothing.

Nothing.

If she was living with that fucker for four years, then how did she not have money? Did he not pull his weight in bills? Fuck that, why didn't he pay all the damn bills? My fingers tighten even harder on the steering wheel, but I manage to keep my speed steady.

After a minute, she calms. I listen carefully as her breathing regulates and purposefully keep my expression the picture of focus when she gives me an unsure glance before going back to her phone.

“What’re you feeling like for lunch?” I ask absentmindedly. Stretching my leg out, I put my left arm on the ledge of the window and my fist against my lips, contemplating.

“Alexander, I *just* had a scone, and besides that, I have a car I can always drive—“

“*Negative.* No, you cannot, missy,” I interrupt sharply, glancing at her over the top of my sunglasses. “Jesus Christ, you’re *hardheaded,* aren't you?” I tease, trying to remember what restaurants are in this area.

Drawing a blank, I pull up local eateries in the area. I just can’t think straight when she's around.

“Okay! I know how to doordash, so can I order food to your house just for today?"

"No." I chuckle. "What are you in the mood for?" I repeat.

"I’ve inconvenienced you enough. And some of the time, I’ve been *made* to inconvenience you against my will," she says rather shrilly, turning away to look out the window. "What a freaking conundrum.”

I fight back a chuckle at her verbiage because it hits me just now that she doesn't curse, something else that endears her to me. She's just so *sweet.*

“Hey, that’s my lounge!” she says happily, pointing to a brick building.

“Oh, Rosalie’s Cigar and Cocktail Lounge? Yeah, I’ve heard of that place. I’ve been meaning to go there to grab a cigar with my friend, Johnathan, for the last year or so." I glance at her, turning my signal light on and making a right at the light. "Do you like spaghetti?”

Sarah giggles. “Who doesn't? I loovvee a good bolognese,” she mutters, looking at her phone and pulling the doordash app up despite me turning that offer down. “So, can I order some to the house to thank you—“

"No," I repeat simply. *No is a complete sentence, don't explain yourself, Alexander—* "Because you're my guest, and it's my responsibility to feed you," I finish, flinching because mentally I'm just all over the place, and I know it and *still* can't help myself.

I tap my fingers on the steering wheel, slowing to stop at a red light. Together, we watch an older lady cross the street with a tote bag, her cane not doing much to help her. She's so slow.

I turn to face her, since it seems like we're going to be here for a minute. "Since you're not hungry, I can drop you off at the house so you can rest while I go to the store to grab ingredients to make bolognese. *Or*, you can come with me...but only if you're up to it." Her eyes flicker from mine to my lips and back again, focused so intently on me that I can't help warming under the collar of my shirt. "It's been a minute since I made that dish, so I don't think I'll have everything at the house. Up to you." I look back at the old woman who is just now making it to the curb. "What are you comfortable with?"

The light turns green, and I pull off again.

"I have a choice?" Sarah snorts in amusement, pausing in looking up from her phone to throw me a teasing look with her pretty mouth twisting up into an amused smile.

I can't help the wicked grin that crosses my face. "You always have a choice, sweetness," I murmur back, forgetting myself. I suck air through my teeth at the obvious misstep. The second one in less than an hour.

Sweetness? Where the *fuck* did that come from? I'd never even had a nickname for Hannah.

Her eyes widen slightly, and I pray to God she doesn't comment on my nickname for her.

She doesn't.

"I'll come. It takes a while to make it correctly anyways, so let's just get the stuff so we can get started on cooking. I'd like to sit at the island and help chop the ingredients. Um...a bottle of wine sounds nice as well," she adds hesitantly.

"Now that, I *do* have." I smile, looking over at her appreciatively. She meets mine with one of her own, and I feel myself melting. She really is beautiful. I turn my face forward, saying decisively, "Only way I'll allow you to help is if you take a nap for me afterwards."

Her stare bores into the side of my face, but I don't break and look. "You know, you're kind of *bossy,"* she says suddenly, arching an eyebrow when I break and look anyway.

Her sunglasses hide her eyes from me, but I imagine they're full of mirth. "I know," I grin. "But it's for your own good. So, what's it going to be? You gunna take a nap for me?"

God. Thoughts of sleeping in bed with her again fill my mind.

She heaves a deep sigh before shifting in her seat a bit, confirming my fears that we've done too much today. She should be home resting. In my bed. Where I can watch over her.

"I don't think I really have a choice." She half-laughs, looking out the window.

"Nope." I bite back a self-satisfied smile. "But I really wanted to make you think you did. It's the gentlemanly thing to do, after all."

We laugh together, heading to the grocery store.

CHAPTER EIGHTEEN

It's Alex

An hour later we're back at the house, and I'm sitting at Alexander's expansive marble island and chopping celery on one cutting board, while he stands across from me cutting up carrots on another cutting board.

We take turns dumping our ingredients into a big bowl, setting it to the side to later add to the sizzling veal and ground beef cooking on the stove. Such a mundane chore, yet all I can think about is how incredibly comfortable I feel right now, and it's helping a lot to keep the tears at bay.

I only cried once: in the bathroom at the apartment when I was praying I could make this transition work.

A chill station is playing over the surround sound, and I'm enjoying myself, even feeling playful, as I attempt to chop the vegetables to the beat of the music. I can't help but smile, finding a rare moment of joy in something I haven't been able to in such a long time. Brandon never cooked with me nor ate hardly anything I prepared.

Actually, he barely ate with me most days.

Aware I've been silent for a while, I peek up quickly, seeing Alexander regarding me as I finish up chopping the celery. I'd taken longer than normal because I'm still in pain but won't lay down. I love to cook and was eager to help. I get I'm being stubborn, but I really want him to see how much I appreciate what he's done for me so far.

He turns and adds the ingredients before stirring the sizzling food and placing a lid on the pot. He dusts his hands together, then turns back to me to pin me with a rather indescribable look that takes me aback.

"It's smelling *so good*."

"Yeah," I say breathlessly. "It is."

He leans his hips on the counter next to the stove. When he braces the heels of his palms on the counter, I can't help but notice his eyes growing a bit tight as he regards me for a silent, tense moment. He breaks it quickly, though, jerking his head to the side; his eyes roam over the pot on the stove. "I almost forgot how much I loved this dish," he says, voice deepening with sudden emotion that has me blinking in surprise. "Thank you for bringing it up," he says. Still keeping his eyes averted, he takes the kitchen towel off his shoulder and places it on the counter.

"Oh." I shrug. "It's nothing, really," I reply lightly, tipping my wineglass for a sip because something tells me this man isn't usually this uninhibited, and I don't want to do or say anything to make it weird, or cause him to be uncomfortable.

Not much of a drinker, I hum appreciatively when the flavor hits my tongue.

He's got great taste in Pinots.

A movement catches my attention, and my eyes lower. Alexander fists his hand momentarily before clasping his wineglass, meeting my eyes when he lifts it to his lips for a deep sip. I flush, a little flustered that he's showing obvious signs he's attracted to me. In any other world, any other *time,* we might be free enough to explore whatever this is that's happening between us. But the fact of the matter is I'm not just getting out of a four-year relationship. I'm trying to heal from a miscarriage.

I work to take our minds off it.

"So–I heard from a little birdy that you were going to be speaking at the Vancouver conference this year. I'm going as well, to get my educational credits for this year," I say conversationally, wanting to talk about something other than the crap we'd been dealing with the last two days.

"Really?" Alexander's eyes bore into the center of my very soul it feels like. I nod, and he tilts his head, eyes roaming my face slowly for a moment before he continues, "Yes, I uh...I speak on the second day." He pushes from the island to place his hips back against the counter and then glances down at the pot again before facing me again. "We speakers normally get put up at this fancy resort. Do you know where you're staying?" he asks, lifting his glass and forcing my gaze to his fingers.

They're so beautiful. Long and elegant.

"Oh, no. I don't know yet..." I blush. Needing a moment from his intense stare, I turn my head. Through the threshold of the kitchen, beyond the foyer, I can just make out what appears to be a cozy library.

"Well, I'll sneak you into my room if you'd like." My heart races, and my eyes widen in disbelief as I turn my head back to look him dead on, but he doesn't falter in his speech. Either uncaring or uninterested at what he'd just implied. "We normally get a pretty big suite, and I don't need all that space. Up to you if you'd like," he says, kindly.

Kindly.

My lips twitch before I lose the battle and smile. I don't think he understands the effect he has on people, and it's quite interesting to watch him navigate what seems to be his usual politeness and the slight attraction that's simmering between us. "I'll let you know if the hostel turns me down." I take another sip and hope my little smile doesn't look goofy.

There's a tense silence for a few seconds as his face morphs from a flirtatious look to one that's a bit...pretentious, and almost even *judgmental.*

"You're joking, right?" he quips, placing his wine down on the counter. His eyes narrow, and a brow arches, letting me know he wants an answer.

I shake my head, a little laugh escaping me. *"Yes,"* I giggle. "A girl's gotta do what a girl's gotta do," I say, gingerly sliding off the stool, going to the pot and taking the lid off before stirring the meat. "Gosh, this looks *amazing*; you're doing such a good job. It already smells like that Italian place by my office."

I keep my gaze averted while I work to replace the lid. When I turn, I gasp in surprise as he's *right there* next to me like he appeared out of thin air.

Alexander grabs my wrist, pulling me a couple steps to him. Making my heart pound painfully in my chest. "Do you really mean that?" he says, with a seriously handsome and cheeky grin on his face. My traitorous heart begins beating so hard that it's stealing my breath. He's looking at me with something akin to awe, even a touch desperate as he waits for me to validate him again. It's in this exact moment that I realize that I'm not scared of him.

I'm desperately *attracted* to him.

Like panty-wetting, clit-throbbing, melt-into-a-puddle-on-the-floor attracted to him. I nod, glancing down quickly at his hand on my wrist.

"I do. Hm-hmm," I hum breathlessly, pulling my wrist away and stepping back a couple feet.

It feels wrong, and I instantly miss the feel of his warm skin on mine. I glance up just in time to see a flash of hurt in his eyes before it disappears behind that careful mask he wears.

"Add the wine. It's ready," Alexander says, handing me the bottle of merlot.

His eyes crinkle with amusement as I take it from him without a word. He turns back to the stove and then puts the towel on the little stainless steel knob. Shoulder to shoulder, he removes the lid again and watches as I pour a couple of healthy splashes in the pot.

Replacing the lid, he turns his head to look at me. "Now, we let it work for a bit. It's time for that nap. I can wake you up when it's ready." We stare at each other for a minute. I'm so ashamed that I'm wondering if he means for us to lay down together. But he continues, his next words making me relieved and disappointed at the same time, "I have a few client folders to look over. I'm going to set up over there in the nook while the food cooks."

He wets his lips, exhaling deeply through his nose as he rakes his gaze across my face. I wonder what the all-knowing, *powerful* psychiatrist sees as he so blatantly assesses me. He tilts his head.

"You've had a long couple days, and I'd feel so much better if I knew you were getting some rest instead of trying to keep up when you don't have to."

I work to stay standing, because something deep shifts inside of me at being so thoroughly considered when I've been so starved of anything of the sort for so long that I'd forgotten the feeling. That pang of shame deepens.

Am I a whore for wanting to spread my legs for this man right after losing my baby? Am I really *that* messed up?

Also, does this man have any *clue* of how intense his bright blue gaze is? It's not even the color of his eyes, really, but rather the *shape* of his eyes. The set of his brow. It all merges together in one seriously overwhelming feature that I feel like might have the power to tip me over into a straight faint if I'm not careful.

I roll my lips and look away briefly. Not wanting that day to be today.

"I guess I haven't been treating myself very well, huh?" I concede softly, wrapping my arms around myself, backing up a few paces and turning away. "I think I'll go lay down. Thanks, Dr. Richardson."

He blinks once at how smoothly I transition back to his professional name, but he stays silent, and for that, I'm grateful.

I grab my phone off the island and make my way to the stairs, but I hear him walking quietly behind me. Placing my hand on the railing, I raise my foot, but I don't even make it up the first step before he swoops me up in his arms. My eyes fly to his as I feel my curves mold to his hard muscles, and I see a little amused grin tip his lips up at the corners.

"Is this okay, Ms. Johnson?" he asks with a hard glint in his eyes.

Him asking me for consent is the sexiest thing ever.

"Yeah..." I answer breathlessly, my eyes flicker back and forth between his when he begins to climb the stairs. I'm completely lost. But funnily enough, I think he's more lost than I am. Our eyes stay locked as he climbs so slowly we're barely moving.

"Sarah?"

"Yeah?" My poor heart.

"It's *Alex*," he rasps.

It's an intimate request, and I feel my breath catch.

I pause, staying silent as he carries me into the same bedroom from last night and lowers me to the sheets. He then covers me up. "Okay. *Alex,"* I relent.

Clear happiness melts the hard edge to his eyes as they fall to my lips, and for a split second, I swear I can tell he wants to kiss me. But he just pulls away.

"Get some rest," he says hoarsely.

Do I imagine the hint of pain in his voice? I don't think so. Ironically, him pulling his arms away from me hurts more than my body does. Rolling over, I settle down deeper into the covers, forcing myself to relax.

To not miss him next to me.

CHAPTER NINETEEN

AREWEHOS VS OREOS

TWO AND A HALF hours later, the sauce is set to a lazy simmer on the stove, and I've made us a mouthwatering side salad with all the fixings to accompany our pasta. I'm anxiously looking forward to having dinner with Sarah and hope to spend time with her tonight, but I'm exercising patience, letting her get the rest that she so desperately needs.

Whatever's happening between us, it's too fast, and I need to distract myself from it.

My eyes peruse the document in my hand, going over the last client's file that I'd been proofreading repeatedly, until I'm sure I get their log notes and evaluation correct. I work diligently to put the finishing touches on the document, going over it once more before hitting save and turning my laptop off.

I gave this client a little extra time, considering it was a woman who's in danger of losing her kids to the foster system. I always make sure I pick through every sentence with a fine-tooth comb, getting my wording right, ensuring I'm doing my client justice in case I need to testify in court for them.

Leaning back into my chair, I nab my phone out of my pocket to reply to Johnathan's text from earlier.

AR: I licked her… as in I bent down and licked some syrup that was on her collar-bone.

J. Dawg: Wow man…. I don't even know what to say about that. Is the pendulum swinging the other way?

AR: NO. It was a momentary lapse in judgment. That's all.

J. Dawg: Uh-huh. That's what we ALL think/say.

Shaking my head, I walk up the stairs, stopping at Sarah's slightly cracked door before knocking when I hear no response. I venture in quietly, seeing the ceiling fan on high and the gray, feather-down covers pulled up to her neck. The clothes she'd been wearing are bunched up on the covers. The burnt orange fabric lies next to the matching black lacy bra and panties, just as innocently as she is lying there, teasing me.

My eyes rise, greedy. Her bare shoulders just above the sheet taunt me further, validating she's naked under the covers. My body tightens up hard in response, and my fingers twitch with the need to snatch her clothes up and smell her.

Assaulted, no—*overwhelmed* by her scent, I step back a foot before turning away and getting control over myself. If this was any other woman, maybe.

Maybe.

But she's not. Sarah deserves reverence. To be respected even when she's not looking.

My heart begins to beat just a little bit harder. Taking a few deep breaths I turn, resisting the urge to smell her clothes, and walk to her side of the bed and sit on the edge, just beside her hip. I place my hand at the sheet bunched against her shoulder, keeping a firm pressure there so when she wakes up and moves, the covers won't slip and embarrass her. It almost kills me to restrain myself because I *desperately* want to see her naked...but I acknowledge that it won't be happening.

No matter what I feel for her, we'd just officially met, after all. Lick or no lick.

"Hey, Sarah, come on. Time to wake up. The food's done," I call softly.

My gaze eagerly travels over her face, lax and innocent in sleep. Her eyelids flutter open lazily, lashes brushing almost to her eyebrows; they're so long. She focuses on me for a brief second before squeezing her eyes again, as if in pain. I rub her shoulder soothingly, comforting her.

I know it has to hurt; to wake up in a stranger's home, with no baby, your back on fire, and your whole life blown up in your face.

"What time is it?" Sarah asks quietly. Her voice is slightly husky coming out of sleep, her eyes open again, and in that split second, everything I'd just thought fills her eyes. She thinks of Bumpy the second she wakes up because the pain I just saw isn't natural.

My heart tugs as she closes her eyes and nuzzles deeper into the pillow. When she takes a deep breath, I do, too.

"It's almost seven. I'm sorry to wake you up, but I didn't want you to sleep too late and miss dinner," I say apologetically.

"It's done?" she asks, almost with a smile.

Her lashes flutter open again. When she finds my gaze, I smile back at her, encouraging her to let hers free.

"Yes, and it's *perfect*. The noodles aren't too mushy, so come on," I quip, chucking her gently under the chin before getting up. "I have your pain medicine downstairs." I rise off the bed and head to the doorway, gripping the knob in my hand before turning back to face her, my eyes falling to her clothes. "Why don't you put something more comfortable on than that dress? Relax a little. Let your hair down."

Stepping through the doorway, I make my way down the hall.

Twenty minutes later, I'm back to sitting at the table, the food already spread out, and the table set with plates, bowls, and silverware. I put on some soft, moody music in the background with a woman vocalist, thinking as a fellow singer Sarah might like this artist and be a bit more comfortable.

Waiting patiently, I read the comic section of a newspaper with my ankle crossed over my knee, the folded newspaper in one hand and a glass of wine in the other.

My ears prick when I hear her at the threshold, and I look over my shoulder, seeing she's in a pajama set with a cardigan on top that says, "cute, or whatever" in the Cola logo.

Oh yeah, you are, baby. You're more than cute; you're adorable. Tightening my lips, I keep quiet, watching her make her way to me. Scared I'm going to say it out loud because I've fucked up too many times today. One more misstep might not be tolerated.

"I like your pajamas," I say, before turning back to my paper for no other reason than to prevent the white-hot arousal threatening to take me over. It's not easy, but it's certainly more bearable when I'm not actively drinking her in. "You look much more comfortable."

"You realize you can do that online now?" Sarah says, ignoring my compliment. "And you should have started eating; you didn't have to wait for me." As she passes, she places her hand on my shoulder and gives me a little squeeze.

Already tight with anticipation, that small unexpected gesture makes me tense.

Shaking it off, I slide out of my seat and step forward, pulling hers out.

"Well, where would the fun be in that?" I tease, moving to returning to my own seat. I watch carefully as she lowers, sitting in a way that's obvious she's trying to not jostle her back. Reaching in the seat next to me, I grab a small pillow before standing once more. "Here," I say quietly, "lean forward."

Her eyes meet mine for a second, and her slender throat ripples with a swallow that causes my chest to tighten. I wedge the pillow behind her back, pleased at her relieved sigh as she leans back on it. Rounding back to my seat, I pick up the newspaper and give it a little pop that makes her smile before folding it and putting it to the side.

Eager to learn her mannerisms, I watch her carefully put rather a lot of salad on her plate instead of the salad bowl I'd provided. In a split decision I reach forward quickly, before she has a chance to grab the utensils for the spaghetti, and snatch up her plate with a tsk. I scrape the salad into her salad bowl, and then I grab the two serving forks for spaghetti and put a serving on her plate.

I relish her wide eyes flickering from me to the plate as I take my sweet time, almost comically scraping all the sauce and leftover meat from the utensils on top of her mound of spaghetti with a cheeky grin. Then, I shred some parmesan on top with a little flourish that makes her grin before I plate my own food. Curiously, she doesn't mention me taking over, and I don't either. I watch, silent, as she takes the little jar of ranch and pours an incredibly small amount on her salad. Really, it's not even enough to wet it.

"I like your shirt." My eyes meet hers.

Sarah flushes before averting her eyes. "*Thanks.* Do you have any olives by chance?"

"What kind?"

"The green pimento stuffed ones? I like to eat them when I have spaghetti and salad," she replies. Sipping the glass of wine I'd poured for her, she brings her eyes back to mine.

"I might. Let me check really quick." Working fast, I grab it out of the fridge and hand it to her. "Seems like it's your lucky day. Here you go," I say, opening it before sitting it next to her bowl.

She's too busy eating her first bite of bolognese to say thank you, though. I watch with pleasure as she tips her head back much like when she was eating the pancakes, letting a small moan out of her mouth. My cock goes hard again, and I curse to myself because eating dinner with an erection is not fun.

No. It should be: her as the appetizer, then we eat, and then I eat her again for dessert. That's the order my meals should be in.

I mentally pin it for future reference

My eyes fall to her plate and then the big serving bowl of spaghetti, narrowing at what she'd done. *The little minx.* The muscles in my forearm flex with agitation.

"This is better than that Italian spot by my office. Oh my gosh, Alex, you can *really* get down in the kitchen," Sarah compliments, opening her sparkling eyes and throwing me a pretty smile before twirling more spaghetti on her fork. "This is a good meal."

I warm uncomfortably at her admission. Hannah was always on some diet and never ate what I cooked. As someone who shows their love language through food, it was hurtful to stifle that part of me. So, needless to say, I was never complimented or appreciated for my skills in the kitchen.

Therefore, her attention is refreshing and so, so welcome.

Relaxing into my seat, I give her an easy smile back. "Thank you. I do okay I guess. *Sometimes,*" I reply cheekily. Lying but trying to be modest. I take a bite of my own, nodding my head. I really did a good job.

She swallows her other bite, then bites her lip as she shifts in her seat.

"So, I sent an email to the hostel before I laid down, and they replied that they can get me booked in time for the conference," she says, pulling her salad and bowl of olives closer. I stare, a frown tugging my mouth as she pops one into her mouth.

Hostel?

Something hot, fierce and protective rises up inside me while I quietly watch as oil from the olives pebble on her bottom lip before spilling over down her chin. Losing my mind, I reach over without thinking and wipe it off with my thumb, ignoring her breathless gasp and wide-eyed expression. Yet *also* noticing she doesn't flinch or pull away from me, and God, that causes me the most pleasure of all.

Keeping my eye contact, she slowly places the napkin over the spot I'd just touched, as if in a trance. I work to regulate my sudden, ragged breathing.

Fuck girl, what on Earth are you doing to me?

My phone rings with Aurora's ringtone, startling us both out of the spell we've fallen under. Leaning to the side, I hurriedly pull it out before silencing it and setting it on the table. "No," I answer automatically, as if my brain is on autopilot, "you're *not* staying at a hostel."

Thankfully, I have the sense to not sound like an asshole when I say it. Practice makes perfect.

Popping another bite of spaghetti in my mouth, I chew slowly, waiting for the response I know is coming because she's hardheaded.

I look down at my phone when it dings again.

> Aurora: What the fuck's the matter with you? I feel nothing for *years,* now all of a sudden you give me every fucking emotion in the span of three days. Do you even care I might fuck-up someone's life by nicking an artery?! I'll answer that for you: *NO. You don't.*
>
> Aurora: So, is it the therapist? What's going on? Stop it.

I ignore my sister, who's more cold-hearted than I ever was, and watch Sarah sputter, amused at the flush rising in her pretty cheeks.

"Excuse me?" Sarah says with a half-laugh. "You don't have any say in where I stay! I'm an adult, a *single* adult!"

My eyes narrow because I don't like that for us.

Yes, there's going to be an us, but I continue to watch silently, letting her get her words out.

She continues, "We aren't together. I *will not* be staying with you." Indignation colors her tone, but it doesn't bother me any.

Continuing to chew, I stare her down, taking all the time I please. I couldn't care less about her attitude. What I *do* care about is her happiness and her not fucking staying in a hostel where God knows *what* goes on.

"I will *staple* your ass to me if I have to," I say quietly, albeit a little threateningly. "Drag you up on stage to present with me—I don't care, but you *aren't* staying at a hostel."

"You aren't responsible for me!" She keeps my eye contact as she stabs her salad rather forcefully, making the tines scrape the bottom of the ceramic bowl.

I smile at her temper before clearing my throat. She's not about to like my next words; I'm willing to bet my savings on it.

I take a healthy swallow of wine for fortitude.

"I beg to differ," I rasp. "The moment you walked into my office you became my responsibility—my *professional* responsibility, I would go to my death arguing." I wipe my mouth with my napkin, lean an elbow on the table, and point at her. "You once threatened to go to the board for my supposed neglectful behavior once; surely you would have no problem with *me* keeping tabs on *you,* considering the unfortunate situation you have found yourself in." Her mouth drops open, so I pivot quickly. "That we have *both* found ourselves in, whether you like it or not." I lean back at her angry gasp, continuing despite her obvious displeasure at me. "I'll be making sure you stay out of harm's way. Making sure you take care of yourself... prioritizing your self-care, making sure you eat. Which you will do. *Eat,*" I say sternly, leaning forward and pushing her spaghetti closer to her. "Finish this."

Sarah's face is comical.

When she leans forward in her seat, her cardigan slips off her shoulder, giving me the full view of the front graphic of her shirt, the curve of her collarbone, and her heavy breasts straining against the thin fabric. Her mouth opens and closes, but she doesn't say anything. I've got her hook, line, and sinker. A spicy defiance simmers in her eyes that I want to reach inside and feel burning me up.

Fucking hell.

She's an angel, but I bet her *everything* tastes like sin. I cock my head and smile at her in amusement at the play on letters.

"And another thing, you'll be staying here until you move into your apartment on Tuesday." I throw that in on a whim, watching the color in her face deepen now into a beautiful rosy-flush.

Leaning forward, I take her hand that's holding her fork into mine, then shove it back into her spaghetti. My fingers prick with the thrill of having her skin on mine.

"Y-y-you!" she stammers, setting my blood on fire. "You *can't*."

Noting she seemed to have a contrary streak, I give her an amused chuckle, letting her know that I'm not trying to mean mug her, but I'm willing to utilize every tool at my disposal to make sure she's okay. Until I can make her mine, that is.

We aren't quite in that spot yet, but still.

I think it goes without saying.

"Yes, I *can,* actually. I'm going to look out for you, and you're going to let me. I'll give you space, but I'll be checking in periodically." I take another bite of my food, dabbing my lips with the napkin before leaning back, cocking my head at her and showing her how serious I am. "The one thing I *do* know is you will be staying with me in Vancouver. No hostel, it's *not* safe. *End of,*" I say sternly, firmly declaring the topic closed.

Sarah doesn't answer, only shoves another bite of her noodles angrily into her mouth, making her cheeks puff out and chewing fast.

Swallowing hard, she finally glances across the table, opening her mouth to speak, but I interrupt her, "Let someone take care of you for once."

This time, I can't hide the desire plain as day in my voice. What's more is: I don't want to.

CHAPTER TWENTY

LET ME

BOLDLY, I LEAN FORWARD and brush my fingers across her knuckles. My heart pounds at the contact.

God, baby, you feel so right.

Her hazel eyes land on my hand before they flick to mine sharply and widen. However, she doesn't move; rather, her fingers flex under mine as I continue to boldly stoke her. She licks her lips when I move higher and caress the soft skin at the top of her hand.

Her breasts rise and fall a little harder, and I can tell I'm affecting her. I just wonder if it's as deeply as I'm affected right now.

"I'm not...doing *anything* with you... I don't even know you, really. I just got out of a relationship—*I just had a miscar—*" Her breath hitches, her eyes well up suddenly, and she glances away, clearly overwhelmed.

Squeezing her hand minutely harder, I work to settle her. Because whatever is driving her nerves, I'm not about. At all. And I need her to understand that. "I'm not asking for any of those things, Sarah, I promise," I say reassuringly. "We don't even have to talk about them if you aren't ready. I swear I'm not pushing you in *that* way."

But, contrary to my words, my heart pounds painfully hard in my chest, stealing my breath. My sanity.

But God, do I want to. I wish I could. My lips tighten. I want this woman with every fiber in my being. *This fucked-up situation, Goddamn it.*

Why did I have to find her at the wrong time, wrong place like this?

As our hands pull back from each other, her eyes dart to mine almost as if she heard me, and she hesitantly puts a small bit of lettuce to her lips, chewing.

I sit there patiently, waiting for her to gather her thoughts. As I wait, I find myself drinking in her pretty dewy skin, the curve of her shoulder, the litheness of her arms. I busy myself looking at the charms on her small bracelet that fall down her forearm.

The hug we shared enters my mind, throwing me off center. The feel of her against me is nothing like I've ever experienced before.

I inhale a sharp breath as she suddenly speaks, startling me out of my thoughts.

"I *do* want to say thank you." Her eyes flick side-to-side, as if she's desperately searching for her words. "You didn't ask for any of this. I was just doing my best trying to advocate for my client, and then it all went to *shit*. It just went to *complete shit*!" Sarah spits out.

Her use of expletives throws me off guard, but then her face pinches as she becomes even more overwhelmed with emotions. To my horror, she lets out a sob, throws her fork down, and puts her face in her hands with her elbows on the table.

Her tears break my soul.

I put my own fork down and get up to sit in the chair beside her. I understand the past she's coming out of, but I'm not that fuck-up of a man, and she needs comfort, badly. She's incoherently sobbing into her hands, hiding. I try to not let that bother me because I desperately want to see all of her, so I reach forward to tug her hands away from her face.

"Come here, sweetheart," I murmur, leaning into her and wrapping my arms around her gently. "Shhhh."

When she shudders and sags against me, I click my tongue, gently pull her into my lap, and rest her head on my shoulder. I take only a second to revel in the feel of her soft body on mine. Rubbing up and down her arm gently, I press my lips to the top of her head, enjoying her silky hair against my lips.

Her tears soak my shirt.

My heart races as she wiggles before settling a little too perfectly into the nook of my body. Biting back a groan at the feeling of her pressing into me, I lick my lips, feeling an unusual warmth saturate me.

Intimacy.

I wonder if she can feel the beat of my heart as she lays here. My hand itches to hold hers and press it deeper into my chest. To make her feel me. It's what I desire the most. What I've tried and failed multiple times over the years to express to Johnathan. What I never could get from Hannah. What I've hopelessly searched and searched for within various women over the span of a decade.

I bury deeper into her. "You have nothing to be sorry for or ashamed of," I say quietly, stroking down her hair. "Bad things happen, and they tend to happen to people who least deserve it. I don't consider you a burden, and I am glad...*blessed,* really, to be able to have been there when you needed it the most." Resisting the urge to kiss her temple, I keep my focus on calming her, not on what I want.

God, she smells so good. So good. Like warm, vanilla, marshmallow, pillowy softness....

Sarah sniffles and pulls back slightly, turning red eyes to me, and brings up a hand to wipe the wetness off her cheeks. "I didn't deserve it?" she asks tearfully, almost bringing my heart to a dead stop.

"No, sweetheart. You didn't deserve any of it." My eyes flicker between hers, and I beg everything that's holy to let her believe me. *"None,"* I stress.

Let her believe she's worthy.

"Are you sure?" Her bottom lip quivers. "I've been such an *ass* to you—"

"No," I murmur, but she carries on, frantically talking over me.

"—Even though I meant what I said to you in that email. I really take my job seriously, you know?" Sarah says, pulling her bottom lip in between her teeth and biting down.

At the mention of our rivalry, I can't help as my eyes crinkle slightly as I assess her face.

I hum, soberly. "Oh, I know. I mean, you were three seconds away from having my license revoked!" I wink at her, then grin, my eyes lowering to her lips for a split second. There's a little crease in the middle of her bottom lip that's just so *distracting.*

Sarah's eyes dilate, and all too soon she's shifting to get off my lap, her cheeks staining pink again. Turning shy.

I clear my throat, thinking it best to change the subject. "Let's finish eating. You think you might be up for a documentary after dinner?" Standing back up, I reluctantly go back to my seat.

As I sit, Sarah gives me a watery smile. "I love documentaries, especially animal ones. But I hardly get to watch anything. What did you have in mind?" she asks. Her momentary sadness disappears, and she twirls her food on her fork, making me relax.

"There's a documentary called *The Longest Third Date* that looks promising. Or you can pick whichever one you want. Want some more wine?" I ask, pushing my plate away and topping off our wine without waiting for a reply.

"Okay, well, let's see what it's about then!" It delights me that she sounds a bit more perky.

She throws me a bright smile, causing me to feel a little helter-skelter as I hold my glass up to my lips. I get up from the table and hold out my hand to help her up, seeing she'd eaten almost all of her plate, and that pleases me greatly.

I'd like to know more about her.

"Hey, when's your birthday?" I ask, looking down into her face while we walk towards the lounge. I tuck her arm into mine under the guise of keeping her steady. But really, I'm wanting her closer.

"Oh!" Sarah's brows pinch, and she looks caught off guard. "It's August third. I'm...I'm twenty-nine," she replies rather disdainfully.

"Hey," I say slowly, "your birthday's during our trip!" I pull her to a stop just before we get to the lounge and face her head on, crossing my arms. My feelings are a bit hurt. "Were you even going to say anything?" I ask accusatorially. Trying my hardest to make my tone playful, I arch a brow at her. "And what's wrong with twenty-nine? That's a good year!"

It really is, too. I was twenty-nine when I got the building for my practice.

Sarah smiles at me. "Oh, come on, I'm like *this* close to being a washed up spinster," she jokes, scrunching her nose up and forcing my eyes to the tiny hoop in her nostril.

"I like your nose ring a lot. It's so delicate, a lot like you, I think..." I say quietly, catching us both off guard now.

"Oh," Sarah says, rubbing her hand down her arm and turning to the side slightly, obviously feeling vulnerable. I take her hand this time and pull her deeper into the lounge. "And yours is July second, right?"

I glance at her with a cheeky grin. "Yes," I reply. A little thrill goes through me at the fact she'd noticed that from the code to my house. "Is your favorite color purple?"

"Yeah," she giggles. "Like Barney."

"What's that?" I ask inquisitively, making her break out in peals of laughter. She doesn't answer my question, merely giving me a little head shake. "I'm assuming it's before your time."

I scoff. *Ouch.*

I keep her hand in mine as I lead her to my plush living room; it's the only other room besides the kitchen and the study that I'd worked very hard to make mine, erased completely of Hannah's influence.

It's a dark green room with cream floor-to-ceiling drapes that are electric powered. There's a rich golden leather couch that faces a huge, mounted flatscreen television that hangs over a stone gas fireplace that's lit. The room boasts recessed lighting that's currently dimmed, giving the room a romantic glow.

In front of the couch, there's a long, chunky wooden table that looks like a weathered trunk. I'm so thankful I don't have any glass tables. Under the tall, glittery expanse of windows sits a long cream-colored chaise lounge, and I momentarily imagine laying her there to kiss her.

She sits on one end of the leather couch, the rich leather creaking softly under her weight. A hesitant, tiny spark of pleasure flickers in my chest at the thought that with enough use, the couch might actually get broken in. Visions of her lying right there, just like that, night after night until the leather gets soft and smells of her becomes a want that settles deep inside me, becoming incessant.

"Hang on, darling," I say, reaching into the trunk and grabbing a couple of chunky beige blankets. Our eyes lock when I spread one over her legs, and something passes between us. Tingles erupt across my skin, and not wanting anything to come across wrong, I break it before reaching for the remote.

"Thank you," Sarah says with a smile, sitting back and curling her feet under her.

"Get comfy; this is going to be good. I hope anyways," I mutter, finding the show and hitting play.

I walk behind the couch and over to the end table next to her to turn off the lamp, just leaving the recessed lights dimmed behind us.

She throws me a shy look as I sit down on the other end and kick my legs up on the table in front of me. We sit back comfortably as the movie starts, nursing our glasses of wine and staying quiet. I notice Sarah's fingers rub together, and I wonder if she's still feeling the grip of my hand around hers.

I know I'm still feeling hers.

We watch the show, and I truly get a kick out of her gasps and breathless *"Oh my Gods."* She's so expressive

As we near the end of the movie, Sarah gets quieter. Curious, I look over and see she slid deeper into the cushions and has tilted further onto her side and tummy. Her eyes flicker, and her chest rises and falls slower and slower. Simply watching, I take a lazy sip of wine when a soft snore comes from her. Chuckling, I lean forward and adjust her blanket further onto her. I pause when I feel something press into my thigh and draw my gaze down. My chest heats with pleasure at the sight of her small feet poking out from under the blanket.

I go still at her pretty, chocolate tipped toes. Boldly reaching forward, I brush my fingers over them, admiring the feel of her soft skin. Her lips part on a quiet whimper, and her toes wiggle.

I wonder when the last time was that she had her feet rubbed.

My eyes roam up her body, still seeing her deeply asleep, and I take one of her feet gently in my hand, pressing and circling my thumb into her soles, and finish the rest of the movie before getting up and lifting her carefully in my arms. I walk slowly, cradling her weight in my arms, careful not to press her breasts against my body.

No need to overly tempt myself if there's no need to.

Rounding into the spare bedroom, I lower her to the mattress and once again fuss around with her hair, ending up twisting it into loops onto the pillow. Covering her gently, I make sure the fan is on high like she seems to like it and leave her bedroom to clean up the kitchen, not minding in the least the clean-up after cooking.

Taking my time, I fold up the blankets in the lounge and instead of putting them back into the trunk, I place them over the back of the couch. Getting a whiff of her scent from the blanket as I fold it up, I harden and groan, shaking my head. I've masturbated more times than I care to think about since she came into my life.

I journey back up the stairs, shower, and then slip into bed with Sarah who's still soundly sleeping, not having moved even a single inch.

Realizing, I feel at peace.

CHAPTER TWENTY-ONE

We're Losing Ourselves

THE NEXT MORNING I open my eyes, blinking lazily. It's Sunday.

Hair day.

I yawn and stretch my limbs with a little moan, sliding lazily along the crisp grey covers of Alexander's bed. The first thing I notice is I feel incredibly refreshed and at peace. The second thing I notice is my baby's still gone. My eyes sting at the reminder.

I tilt my head around and see the other side of the bed empty. Sitting up I wince at the painful twinge in my back, looking around the room.

Where is he?

Getting out slowly, I flex my toes against the embossed rug, feeling the slightly scratchy woven wool against my feet. I pad to the bathroom to relieve myself and to check my hair. It's not too bad, so I run a brush through it and then wash my face and brush my teeth.

Seeing the slight shadow of the bruise on my jaw has finally faded to not be noticeable, I just brush my eyebrows out and put a very light coat of mascara on, leaving my face bare and then head to my bag of clothes. Needing to feel something soft and comforting against me today, I put on a slightly loose calf-length mocha colored dress.

The material is soft and flows over my curves just right, and I can't help but hope that he likes what he sees when I say good morning.

Jesus, I feel kind of like a whore. Why do I care what this man thinks of me? Furthermore, how am I having these feelings of attraction while I'm grieving? My eyes widen as it clicks into place. I'm fucking trauma bonding with this man. I have to be. No one catches feelings this quickly. Do they?

Now, I'm more desperate than ever to get myself into counseling. I have too much to navigate. My daddy issues, the miscarriage, my abusive relationship, and now whatever this is that's budding to life between Alex and me.

Biting my lip, I ponder for a moment. Have I been wearing blinders during my grief, and I'm just making myself think he's attracted to me? I'm so confused.

I turn to the doorway, pausing at the sight of a white pair of slippers placed in front of the door. Directly in front, so I had no chance of missing them. Something blossoms in my heart at the prospect of him thinking about something so simple, and I slide my feet into them before exiting the room, making my way downstairs to find him.

Pausing halfway down the stairs, I grasp the iron and glass railing and feel the hairs on the back of my neck stand up as I hear haunting instrumental music come from the lounge near the foyer. The music gets slightly louder with my descent and the passion of the melody, and my ears prick curiously.

My mouth drops at the next note, and my flesh breaks out in goosebumps as I suddenly hear what sounds like a woman trilling passionately for several tense seconds.

I step off the bottom of the stairwell and turn into the the foyer when I see him. My heart begins to thud in my chest.

He's sitting in a plain wooden chair, dressed in all black with his sleeves pushed up his forearms. He's donned a very nice button-up shirt with the first couple buttons open, revealing his smooth chest, and he's surprisingly barefoot. I swallow hard, feeling tendrils of desire settle deep in my belly at how handsome he is. How insanely *talented* he is.

How incredibly at peace he looks with his body curved over a dark, wooden cello, playing a song about a man's longing to fall in love.

Placing my hand to my chest, I feel my heart skip a beat as I watch him almost *lovingly* caress the strings as he sways with his instrument. His eyes are closed, completely lost in the music as his fingers tremble on the strings, drawing out the beautiful, almost *human* sounding notes that had made my hair stand up on the back of my neck on the stairway.

I've never heard anything this beautiful before. Because what Alexander offers as he sits there, unaware I'm watching, is a gift. Something raw, innocent, and true. Something rarely seen in the theater. This is pain, a longing for hope. A wish in musical form.

Too bad there's not a star anywhere around here, I'd be wishing on it right about now.

Staying silent, because I don't want to disturb this trance he's in, I take a few steps in the room; nevertheless, despite how quiet I tried to be, his eyes suddenly snap open to meet mine. I freeze. The startling blue irises pierce straight through to the center of me, keeping me in place with one foot stretched out as he plays without missing a single note. I stay completely still even as my body catches on fire from the inside out.

Split open, we stare at each other for long moments as he continues to play, and he hits a note so perfect, so *beautiful,* that my lips part in surprise as I inhale a shaky breath. No part of us is physically touching, but I've never had a moment with anyone this intimate before. Something passes between us in this instant. Something I can't decipher before he closes his eyes again, bowing his head over his instrument, and continues on.

Losing himself once again.

My heart flutters as I observe. Suddenly, in my mind's eye, the cello disappears, and I imagine a woman straddling his lap. That's how he looks as he crouches over his instrument... as if he's caressing a lover instead of wood and strings. And I become sad.

What I wouldn't give for someone to hold me like that.

At this new-to-me revelation my eyes prick, and my lips tighten at the fierceness of my desire to be wanted. For someone to feel just as lost in me like Alexander so obviously is lost in his music.

Needing something to hold onto, my hands shake as I lift them to my belly and bunch the material there. I need to hear more, memorize this feeling and hold it deep inside me so when I am able to try again, I won't settle for anything less than what this feeling does to me. I deserve to have something just as raw.

Our eye contact now broken, I inch my way to a seat and settle down, crossing my legs and placing my chin into my palm. I quickly find myself mesmerized by his movements, and I cant help my eyes narrowing slightly as I concentrate on his hands, his long fingers, and the light dusting of hair on his forearms. My own fingers flex, sliding up to my throat. Wondering what it must be like to get an instrument to make the sounds he's evoking from his cello. I know how to play the piano but not with the same passion and precision Alexander wields.

My throat immediately burns, reminding me that I *am* the instrument.

As the music stops, the last note reverberates around us as my eyes flick up, meeting his and seeing he'd been watching me as he ended the piece. There's an interesting moment where we regard each other quietly, almost as if either one of us is scared that talking will ruin the peace filling the room.

Feeling shy, I look away to take a deep breath, blinking watering eyes. I hadn't even been aware I was moved to tears. That's how hypnotizing Alexander is.

"A-Alexander... that was absolutely beautiful. You make her sing something special." I tilt my head back to meet his gaze, my fingers sliding to my shoulder and squeezing lightly, trying to ground myself the best I can.

Alexander's eyes lowers to where my hand is clutching, and his features tighten slightly. Again I wonder if I'm wrong about being alone in this attraction like I think I am, because it really looks like there's something there.

"Thank you. I can't remember the last time anyone heard me play," he says, standing up fluidly and turning to put his instrument back on its stand in the corner.

Shame immediately fills me. What was I thinking intruding like this?

Because I wanted to *feel* something?

"Oh, I'm so sorry. I wouldn't have come in and made myself comfortable if I had known you wanted to be alone." Now ashamed, I apologize profusely, rising from the couch and turning to face him. I bite my lip, giving him an apologetic look across the couch between us.

Alexander takes a couple steps towards me and wraps his hands around the back of the couch, his fingers digging in as he looks at me for so long I wonder what he's thinking about. He's quiet for long seconds as he just...*stares.*

Once again under his rather raw and blatantly unashamed assessment, I feel my face heat up, and my brows furrow slightly. In a fit of self-consciousness, I tuck my right arm across my torso, and his eyes fall to watch my fingers wrap around my left elbow as I work to hold myself. He doesn't seem to miss much, and it's a bit discombobulating to be laid so bare for him.

A tingle fills every part of me at how naked he just laid me.

Alexander's eyes rise back up to me, and he wets his bottom lip before replying. "I didn't say I wanted to be left alone. If I wanted privacy, I wouldn't have brought my instrument out to play, sweetness."

A nickname...I slide my hand up to my shoulder; the movement pushes my breasts up slightly, and I suck my bottom lip between my teeth at the hard bob of his Adam's apple as he works to swallow. Pure feminine pleasure fills my being. Something that's been dormant inside of me for so long I almost didn't recognize that's what it is.

"Okay," I say softly, looking away towards the fireplace, which boasts a big, beautiful black and white drawing of a ship above the mantle. A lot like the little statue in my office, it's sails flap in the wind to an unknown destination, but it's the birds in flight that catch my eye, making the piece stand out.

"Do you like it?" he asks, pulling me out of my musing.

My nostrils flare slightly, and my shoulders rise as I suck in a deep breath, yet staying quiet. Can I tell him I feel like a ship with no direction, when all I really want is to feel like the birds flying free and high in the clear blue sky?

No...I'll keep this to myself.

"Are you hungry?" he asks, thankfully not reprimanding me for not answering his first question.

My head turns. "Well, it depends on what you have in mind to eat," I tease, blinking slowly at him.

A smile broadens my face before wavering as a very obvious look of pure hunger, accompanied by a wicked smile that makes my heart skip a beat, crosses Alexander's features before it's quickly schooled into the regular, polite expression I've come to associate with him.

"My favorite."

"Oh, yeah? And what's that?"

"A ham, cheese, and spinach omelet," he answers. His fingers loosen their grip on the couch, and he walks around it to stand in front of me. "So you wouldn't bitch about carbs, I thought I'd feed you something healthy," he finishes, completely taking me by surprise.

What?

His lips roll together, and his eyebrows lift in amusement as I sputter at his crass word.

"I don't *bitch*," I huff, giving him a look and scrunching my nose up.

He smiles brightly, making my heat drop again. "Oh my, she *cusses?"* he says while arching his brow with amusement, making my jaw drop on a scoff.

"No, I don't!" I put my hand to my mouth, glaring at him.

"Ohhh, you may not cuss, but you definitely *whine, don't you?"* Alexander teases further, his blue eyes sparkling as he looks down at me.

My mouth falls open with an offended gasp, and he just continues to watch me with open amusement. Just like a psychiatrist.

I feel the color rise in my cheeks as my face turns so hot I know he can see. "I do *not*!" I say. My fingers fly up to wrap around my throat as if to hold the words in because I *totally* just whined.

Suddenly, it hits me like a ton of bricks that he's *flirting with me.*

"W-Well, how can I help with breakfast?" I attempt to change the subject, but I have a hard time getting even those simple words out.

The amused look on Alexander's handsome face makes me breathless. Even grieving, I'm not immune to him. He's handsome, but I'll get over it.

Er...Maybe not.

I fight to keep from trembling as he raises his arm to my shoulder, turning me gently as he walks us out of the lounge and towards the kitchen. I notice with pleasure that he likes to touch me a lot. At the knowledge, I feel even more shy, hunching up my shoulders as I dare to peek a look up at him.

"You can sit there and give me company. I hate cooking alone. It's nice to actually have someone to cook for," he says, walking me to the island and pulling out a stool for me to sit on before continuing on to the double-sided refrigerator and pulling out ingredients.

He washes his hands and tells the sound system to play the soundtrack from *The Gladiator.*

I settle in my seat and force myself to sound normal as we converse while he fixes us breakfast. Listening intently as he shares with me how he'd gotten into playing the cello. That because he used to be teased mercilessly in school over his musical interests, he had to learn to defend himself. "My parents enrolled me in boxing lessons, and the two passions sort of grew out of me simultaneously," he says.

Now I'll admit, it's incredibly difficult for me to believe that the obviously confident and charismatic Alexander Richardson standing in front of me now was ever bullied. "I guess you just never can tell where people come from, can you?" I say softly, watching while he works.

He throws me a pointed look. "No," he chuckles, before turning back to the stove. "That's the highest fallacy a person could make, assuming to know anything."

My eyes roam his strong arms as I nod my head, now aware as to why he's so fit and his arms so muscular. It's not a vanity thing with him; it's a self-preservation thing. I've gleaned in the last couple days little pockets and glimpses of his vulnerability, and I hope I make him feel safe enough to keep sharing these little bits of information.

I lick my lips and speak, sharing with him something of myself, so I can focus on my words and not my improper thoughts.

I hope he doesn't catch me staring too hard at him as I stammer, struggling to get the words out. I'm content with Alexander possibly feeling like I'm simpleminded and not lustful.

I shouldn't be lusting after a man so soon after what happened to me.

Alexander pays attention to the food, listening avidly while I share that I was forced to learn how to play the piano as a child. But I don't play much, preferring to sing more.

"You *can* have more than one passion that you nurture, you know. Who said you have to choose?" Alexander asks, pouring the eggs into the meat and vegetable mixture in the stainless-steel skillet.

My parents. I scrunch my nose up, looking a little harder at what he's doing. "*That's not going to stick?*" I ask, my brow arches as I watch him work over the eggs, stirring them slowly. "I threw my stainless steel pans away because everything I cooked stuck or burned."

"Threw them away?" His gaze meets mine again, and his eyes flicker to my lips and back as he pins me with an amused expression.

I nod, suddenly feeling foolish.

"If you heat a stainless-steel skillet on the stove on medium for several minutes, it'll close the pores and become nonstick." His eyes bore into me, not letting me break away. Then he points the spatula at me, making me smile. "That's what's wrong with most people. They're always in a hurry; never wanting to be patient enough to wait for good results. They would rather eat something broken and torn up, because they couldn't wait for their product to heat up enough for their results to come out whole and intact." My brows raise.

Oh my God, is he using food to allude to what I think he is? My heart races, the feeling not letting up even when he turns from me back to the stove.

"Patience is better, helps flavor, and the overall dynamic of the experience," he quips, turning off the stove and sprinkling sharp cheddar cheese on top before setting the lid on the eggs to finish melting the cheese.

I scoff, blinking as my eyes flicker side to side, never having thought about anything the way he'd just described a simple meal.

"So, you consider yourself a patient man, then?" I dare to ask. My fingers resume stroking down my hair, steadily rotating one hand over the other.

A devilish smile broadens his lips as he takes the folded dish towel off the counter and grabs the skillet before turning to place it on an iron rack in front of me. "One of my better qualities," he muses in a low tone, turning to grab two plates and two forks.

"Oh, yeah? What's one of your worst?" I ask, leaning to look into the pan when he lifts the lid off. The steam rises before dissipating and revealing two perfectly cooked cheesy omelets side-by-side in the skillet. It looks too delicious. My mouth waters, and I lick my lips, grabbing a fork from him before stabbing it into one of the omelets straight out of the skillet and promptly eating a forkful. "Oh sweet Jesus, it's *perfect,*" I moan, tilting my head back and swaying as the salty tang of the ham and cheese floods my tongue. I freeze at the eerie silence.

Wait. *I just made a blatant sexual sound in front of him!*

Trying not to choke, I hurriedly swallow my bite and then open my eyes, blinking rather embarrassingly at the hungry look that's on his face again. Except this time it doesn't disappear as fast as it did a little bit ago.

"I'm sorry," I say shyly, biting my lip and looking down at the plates. "I-I shouldn't be eating out of the pan. It's rude."

I grab one and then look up confused as Alexander's hand suddenly plucks the plate away and grabs the other one, putting it on the counter behind him. Turning back, he pushes the skillet on its iron stand in front of us, stabbing his fork into the other omelet before catching my eye and putting a bite into his mouth and groaning himself.

I smile, feeling seen, and proceed to dig in alongside him into a perfect omelet just simple enough to heal the soul.

CHAPTER TWENTY-TWO

QUALITIES

I MELT AT SARAH'S grin before she stabs her fork again into her omelet. We eat for a minute in silence while I contemplate her question.

"One of my worst qualities is that I'm demanding." I pause, gauging her reaction. She stays open in her body language, chewing her omelet and keeping her eyes on mine. Good girl.

"Demanding how?"

"Emotionally." Her face stays perfectly calm, and now it's my turn to chew quietly, debating how much to share. "I divorced my ex-wife, Hannah, because she was so busy being a trophy wife she couldn't be bothered to raise our son, Tyler. I just couldn't tolerate it anymore. I took so much emotional abuse from her during our relationship that I vowed after I left her that I wouldn't tolerate any red flags. So, I've been single all these years afterwards; I haven't had a serious relationship since the divorce."

Sarah continues to chew silently, and I can tell she's mulling over my words. "You didn't try to date?"

"Yes, several times. I can tell pretty quickly when it's not a good fit. Especially for me."

"Is it a standards thing?" she asks curiously, tilting her head just a little.

"Sure," I quip. "And an emotional needs thing, an emotional intimacy thing, a physical thing...it's multifaceted."

"I get it. That's a long time to not be in a committed relationship, but it's worse to be in a long-term relationship where the relationship is based on a lie, and you aren't satisfied, you know?" She puts her fork down and sits back, sighing. "Because that shit is harder than what people realize. I think I'd rather be single myself, too. So I can't blame you."

I clear my throat, feeling validated with just a couple sentences from her. "Thank you, because I've felt very judged for a long time. From male friends especially..." I trail off, not wanting to get into all of that.

"So...you don't jump into sex with women? I do find that interesting because you're pretty prolific, no offense." Sarah whips her hair to the front of her body and begins to stroke down the tresses in what I'm noticing is a nervous tic with her.

I smile humorlessly, finishing off my omelet. "Hmm-hmm," I reply simply, "I guess I am. Makes it harder for people to see the real me. All they want to see is the money and status. It's annoying and makes it hard to have a sexual connection when all I can think about is what else they want from me."

"I'd be annoyed, too," she responds almost to herself. Her fingers leave her hair to begin a slow rapping on the countertop. "Uhm... so do you not, like, *want* to provide? All you want is the emotional and physical connection?"

I stare at her for a second, fighting to not narrow my eyes. "Do you not see this house?"

Sarah looks around, arching a brow. "Yes, it's pretty."

"I bought it for her because *she* wanted it. I provide very well... she just didn't deserve it, and I don't feel bad telling you that at all. Is being provided for something that's important to you?"

She bravely holds my stare. "I think it'll be a hard adjustment for me, but I'd *like* for it to be. I'm not worried about it right now, anyways. I can take care of myself."

I grunt softly and stab another piece of the omelet, deciding to change the subject. "So, what do you normally do with yourself on a Sunday?" I ask, watching her grab her orange juice without complaining like she did yesterday.

"I do my hair, watch a show, refresh my nails, and make dinner," she says, deadpan her eyes falling to her fingers momentarily.

"Are you up for doing any of that today?" I ask, my eyes falling to her fingers as well and see her polish slightly growing out. I frown, not liking that for her, and an uncomfortable feeling settles inside of me because I know this bothers her more than she's letting on.

"No, just my hair and dinner. No mani or pedi today," she sighs with a crestfallen look on her face.

"Why not?" I say, putting the last bite of food in my mouth.

"Well," she sighs, "I'm about to spend a ton of money, and I don't think that I can spare the expense. Something's gotta go, and since I need gas in my car, a phone for work, and a place to live, then I think I can give up my nails for a while," she says somberly.

"I see." I take a slow swallow of my orange juice. "What are you thinking about for dinner tonight?" I ignore the uncomfortable feeling at seeing her have to sacrifice anything, especially something that she takes pride in, like her appearance.

"I'd like to make a pot pie. Do you like pot pies?' she questions, putting her fork down with several bites of her omelet left. So I help myself, slicing through her omelet from the other end easily. Noting her amused grin.

"I absolutely do," I half laugh. Glad I'm not the only one who craves fall time foods in the summer.

Sarah rubs her arm nervously. "Ok, well, I'll pop over to the store, grab some stuff, and I'll make it tonight. But I gotta disappear for a couple hours," she says, giving me a pretty smile as she pushes a lock of hair behind her ear.

My heart skips a beat.

"*We'll* pop over to the store. And what do you mean you have to disappear?" I ask, raising my brows as I place our forks into the skillet before turning to place it in the dishwater.

"I have to lock myself in the bathroom and do my hair."

"Oh." I can't help the disappointment in my tone. "Well, I'll take that time and mow the backyard then." I turn back to the sink, scrubbing the pan and rinsing it.

"You don't have someone do your yard for you?" Sarah says with a slight frown. "That's a pretty big backyard."

"I enjoy taking care of my own home. And I like it mowed a certain way," I reply absentmindedly, wiping my hands on a dishtowel.

"I hear you. On Fridays I get down on my hands and knees—" I flick my eyes to her suddenly, and she sucks in a surprised breath. "And I scrub the baseboards and clean at my practice," she trails off, her lips twisting slightly as she tries to hide a smile.

God...

"Hmm-hm." I grunt softly. "Well, I'm off to mow. Let me know when you are done with your hair, and we'll go to the store," I say, giving her a look as I saunter out of the kitchen to go up to my bedroom to change to go work outside.

Ten minutes later I pop in my air pods and crank up the lawnmower, pausing momentarily to look up at her window. My blood rushes at the knowledge that the subject of my desire is just beyond the pane, undressed as she washes her hair. I shake my head and think about an hour ago and how perfectly I'd played my cello. Wishing it was her I could wrap my body around and play instead. But I'll just have to be patient.

Another one of my not so great qualities.

CHAPTER TWENTY-THREE

FRIENDS

I CRACK MY EYES open on a low moan. Dimmed beams of light shine through a crack in the curtains, showing me it's the next morning. I eye the clock on the nightstand, seeing it's a quarter to seven. Turning my head, I see the other side of the bed empty, making a frown grace my lips as a pang of disappointment fills me that he's not lying next to me.

I feel so safe with him.

My eyes narrow as they settle on a note folded neatly on the pillow beside my head. Hurriedly sitting up, I lean back against the headboard, noticing I'm thankfully still fully clothed in my pajamas. I have a tendency to rip my clothes off in the middle of the night while I'm asleep.

Opening the note I smile, thinking he's so old-fashioned because he could have totally texted me this information, but there's something so intimate about knowing another's handwriting, and the fact it requires more effort and thought than beating out a quick text.

Sarah,

I wasn't sure what you planned on doing for work and didn't want to wake you to ask. I did set the alarm for seven a.m. just in case you needed to go into the office, though I'd prefer you didn't, honestly. You need your rest to recover. However, I know what it's like to have clients you can't cancel on, and I just want to let you know I sympathize with you. How about we work on finding you a backup therapist to help shoulder some of your work load so you can take time off when you need to?

There's coffee in the pot in the kitchen, or hot tea in an electric kettle, as well as a breakfast sandwich in the warmer downstairs. I also made you lunch; it's in a glass container in the refrigerator. Your car keys are next to your purse by the door, and just in case you forgot, the code to lock the house if you leave is 070280.

Don't even think about not coming back! You are supposed to stay here until you move into your apartment, so I'll be expecting you for dinner. I'll have it ready by 6 p.m.. Do you like salad enough to have it for a main meal?

AR

Out of all the things he wrote, his last sentence pierces me straight through the heart, leaving me flushed and feeling very considered. And I've not even gotten out of bed yet.

Folding the note carefully, I roll out of bed, ignoring my phone for the moment in favor of using the restroom. A few minutes later I pad back into the bedroom and grab my phone off the nightstand, hearing the soft melody of the alarm of the clock beginning to chime. Smiling, I turn it off, swiping my phone awake.

Pulling up my text app, I find Alex's name under Dr. Richardson and click it.

> Sarah B: Dr. Richardson, thank you so much for your hospitality. You really didn't have to. I could have stopped somewhere and gotten something on the way, but I'll enjoy it. I hope you're having a good morning. What time do you usually take lunch? P.S. - You'll probably be getting a work related email from me at some point today.

I shower, taking time with my makeup and putting my hair into a thick bun at the top of my head, leaving a few tendrils to frame my face. Smearing a berry lip gloss on my lips, I take a second to admire my dark, sharp-winged brows and decide I don't need blush today because I'm not having any problem keeping color on my face lately.

Going through my clothes I find a red button-up romper that hangs mid-thigh and pair it with some nice golden sandals.

> AR: It's Alex, please. Lunch is around 1p for me today. Why, what's up? (eye raised emoji) What's the 'B' stand for anyways?

I pad downstairs carefully with a hand on the rail, still feeling rather shaken up.

Rounding the foyer I see I missed a text from Shelly stating the apartment will be ready to move in tomorrow, and I can get the keys any time before five in the evening. Yelping with excitement, I enter the kitchen with a joyful smile on my face.

Sarah B: I'd like to bring you lunch as a thank you. B stands for Bella. My apartment will be ready tomorrow. I love salad. Buffalo fried chicken salad is my weakness.

I pour myself a to-go cup of tea, grab my sandwich out of the warmer, and turn the coffee pot off before unplugging both appliances.

My phone pings again just as I get in the car right on time at eight-fifteen. When I start it, I see my gas tank is full, making me furrow my brows in confusion thinking that maybe I fell too hard on Thursday. I *know* I was almost on empty before Friday.

AR: I would love lunch, maybe we can go over Vancouver plans? Set an itinerary? Sarah Bella is quite beautiful, bravo to your parents.

Unfortunately, I didn't have enough time to properly prepare to reschedule my clients, so I have to see them. I feel a pang of guilt knowing I'm going to have to source a backup therapist just in case of emergencies and decide that it's going to be a project I'll begin in the next few weeks. I have that empty office, and it would help me out to have someone split the bills. But I'd need to furnish it first, and that's going to take money I don't have yet.

Sarah B: Hey, I said that I was okay, remember? I'll get to Vancouver fine on my own, Dr. Richardson. You've done enough.

AR: It's Alex, remember? And do you not remember what I said, hmm?

I bite back a smile, putting my phone away before beginning my drive out of the driveway. I'm never late, and I'm not going to start being late today because I was texting my sexy friend psychiatrist.

The thought gives me an immediate pause and makes me frown because... *are we friends*?

Hearing another text from my phone, I decide to ignore it until I get into my office fifteen minutes later.

Sitting in my office chair I finish texting my parents, letting them know of my new apartment and the breakup with Brandon, keeping it simple. Next, I text Jerome and Christopher my new address, and that I'll be getting the keys about five tomorrow afternoon if they want to come and veg out on Chinese food. Albeit, they'll have to bring a folding chair as I won't have any furniture.

With that thought in mind, I realize I'll have to stop by the store and get an air mattress. I work fast, clicking through a few work emails, responding to some and deleting others that aren't relevant, when my phone dings again showing me that Jerome texted.

Jerome: Hey Sarah Beara, pick one- white or dark blue?

Sarah Beara: Hey J, what am I picking for? I need some context! (laughing face)

Jerome: I'm getting you a new bedding set for your new place. I was just going to pick it out for you, but I figured you might want to have input on the color. Christopher's getting you something too.

His kindness makes me smile, causing my heart to tug at all the nice things the men in my life have been doing for me lately, especially after all the hurt I'd been enduring for weeks. My stomach cramps slightly, and I put my hand on my tummy, thinking about Bumpy.

> Sarah Beara: Thank you, J. Blue is fine. Love you, friend.

Suddenly an email from Alexander pops up on my computer, startling me out of my musings. A warmth starts in my chest, surprising me.

> Sarah Bella,
>
> Did you make it to the office? Hope you don't think I'm being too forward; I just saw you're online so was worried that you haven't responded to my text. You doing okay?
>
> AR

Interesting. My brow furrows. *He's a little anxious...*

It hasn't been that long, but that warmth burns just a bit broader at thinking he'd been waiting to hear from me.

> Alexander,
>
> I believe you said, "I'm every woman," with regard to our conversation about Vancouver.
>
> I have clients all morning, but I'll see you at 1pm with lunch.
>
> Sarah Johnson

The front door chimes as I hit reply, informing me that Mrs. McDermont has arrived for her nine a.m. appointment.

CHAPTER TWENTY-FOUR

I WONDER

RUBBING MY SORE ARM with a sigh, I exit the car with the burgers I'd picked up on the way to Alexander's office, enter the glass building and board the elevator.

I took a few minutes to cry in the car because I'd had to inform Mrs. McDermont that I had to drop her as a client. I'd unfortunately become triggered when she'd wanted to talk about her feelings about her husband hitting her during sex, and I became so uncomfortable that I knew I couldn't keep her as a client. It was all too soon after Brandon had been hitting me.

So, I'll have to find a new therapist to take my place.

I take a second to look at my reflection in the elevator mirror and wince. My nose is slightly red, and my eyes are still watering, betraying my emotions.

I walk into Alexander's suite, and my steps hesitate at seeing his receptionist has gone to lunch. A bit nervous, I shift on both feet, seeing his door slightly cracked and him busy typing at his desk. I pause for a second because his jaw is set tight as he focuses on whatever he's working on. He's got a no-nonsense look on his face, and it's kind of hard to believe this is the same man who'd just slept the night away in bed with me only mere hours ago.

Walking through the expansive space, I knock twice, waiting for him to call me in and keeping my eyes off the crack of the door. I hear him push away from his desk before walking to the door and opening it the rest of the way for me with a smile that quickly falls when he sees my face.

"*Sarah*, what's wrong?" he says, making my eyes water even further.

Alexander's brows furrow as he reaches out and takes the bag of food from my hand and ushers me in, closing the door behind me quickly. He pulls out a chair for me to sit in, his eyes glancing over my one-piece romper. I see his eyes linger on my hair that's pulled up into a loose, fat bun at the top of my head with tendrils that fall here and there, and his lips twitch like he's not able to help the smile that wants to grace his lips at the sight.

"I had to let a great client go. It was the first time *ever* I've had to tell a client that I couldn't see them. And I really liked helping her," I reply thickly. My eyes fall to the desk as another tear escapes my eyes. *"I'm really upset about it."*

Alexander pauses on his side of the desk as I bow my head and wipe the errant tear away. He grabs two tissues and holds them to me gently before lowering into his chair.

"I'm sorry to hear that." His elegant voice is awash with hesitancy that seems foreign to him. "Can you tell me why you had to let her go? You don't have to give me any identifying information," he assures, leaning back in his chair and getting comfortable.

Staring at him for a second, I entertain thoughts of physical touch from this man who seems so *cold.* What on earth makes a person so detached and clinical? I wish he'd walk back around his desk and put his arm around me the way he'd done the night before; however, I have a feeling he won't. It'd be too forward, and I don't think that being forward is in his personality.

His lip twists in annoyance, almost as if he'd had a displeasing thought, and I wonder what he's thinking.

I wonder if he desires human touch the way I do. His eyes flicker lazily over my face, and I hate that he sees me in my sadness when generally I'm such a happy-go-lucky type of person. Not anymore, I guess. He's broken me. Picking at a loose thread in the sleeve of my cardigan, I avert my gaze from the piercing azure of his stare and try to muster up the courage to reply.

"She triggered me during our session today," I start softly, keeping my voice low, "she's a masochist, and she was wanting to talk about them...*what they do*...in the bedroom." My eyes flick to his before averting immidiately. "He slaps her in the face and other stuff while they....you know." I put the back of my hand to my cheek and blush hard.

I glance up in enough time to see a muscle in Alexander's jaw jumps in his cheek as if to try and hold back a grin. His brow rises cheekily as he swivels his chair slowly side to side. Something mischievous flickers in his piercing blue eyes before he smiles in earnest, although it looks tight like he's not able to help it.

Alexander's eyes flicker back to mine warmly. " *Well*... I'm sorry that someone's sexual kink triggered you, but everyone's got a kink. You know that, right?" he asks, reaching forward and fussing with the bag of food between us.

"Oh, yeah?" I scoff. "What's yours?" I ask without thinking.

I slap my hand over my mouth, my eyes widen, horrified. Alexander pauses in his motions of unpacking our burgers, laughing at my distress. His blue eyes are full of humor as they meet mine.

"*Booyyyy*, you therapists just can't help yourself, can you? No filter *whatsoever.*" He chuckles. "*Eating* is mine." He smiles as if savoring a delicious secret.

Whoa.

My mouth falls open, because did this man just say his kink is *eating pussy?* I didn't expect him to be quite that bold.

I decide to deflect his comment. "Really? You don't look like you eat a lot," I say innocently as my eyes pin themselves to the two boxes in between us. But they fly back as Alexander surprises me with a deep, obviously sexual chuckle.

"I keep myself in shape so I can eat *whomever* I please." He grins at me as I look away from him in surprise, but I can't help the smile on my face.

What the hell did this man just say? I huff a shocked laugh, wondering if he meant it to come out that way. I turn back to him.

"You mean *with* whomever you please..." I say testily, arching a haughty brow, wondering how he's going to respond. This interestingly stoic, yet *oddly* emotionally attuned man. My lips quirk, thinking about his birthdate, and it hits me that he's a Cancer. The emotional astrological sign.

Alexander shakes his head, arching his own brow at me almost as if in a challenge, but it doesn't intimidate me....not in *that* way. We stare each other down for a tense few seconds before he speaks, "Which one is yours?"

Huh? Is he wanting to know *my* kink? I feel my eyes get impossibly wider, to the point I wonder if it's possible they'll fall out of my head.

"The burger, Sarah," he clarifies, keeping his eyes trained on mine. Does he know how intensely he comes off?

"The lettuce wrapped one, of course," I mumble as I pull it closer, thanking God I can order food with no bread. "I swear I think I've gained five pounds over the weekend thanks to you." I'm still looking down, but I can see in my peripheral vision his head tilts.

"Hmm-hmm. You're *welcome*."

My heart skips a beat, and I flick my eyes back to his in surprise, where we again have another tiny standoff. His lips twitch again, but he's very good at keeping that wicked smile of his under wraps. Controlled. Everything about this man screams discipline, control, and class.

I can't imagine him being unhinged in bed, though I do wonder how he'd be.

Alexander clears his throat, picking up his burger once more. "Now, back to the email I sent. I got you a first-class ticket to Vancouver, and we'll be flying out together. I've already ordered a driver to pick us up and take us to the airport, so we don't have to worry about parking fees and such. The flight leaves at five in the morning, so the driver and I should be at your house by three. Will you be able to get up on your own, or do you need to stay at my house the night before?"

"Huh?" I admonish. My brows lift, and I put my burger down, pinning him with a stare. "You did what? Alexander, what are you talking about?"

Just then, a sharp tapping sounds on his office door, interrupting us. Alexander turns his head and frowns, displeased at the disruption.

Ironically, so am I; I want as much alone time with him as I can get. Because something about him calls to me, begging me to figure him out.

"Come in," he calls, grabbing a napkin to wipe his fingers.

I look over my shoulder and see none other than David, an associate of mine, walk in. David gives Alexander a kind smile before his eyes slide to where I'm sitting, finally seeing me, and I break out into a big smile of my own as we lock eyes.

I giggle as David breaks out into a laugh of his own. "Sarah *Beara*! What a surprise to see you here! You look *gorgeous*!"

Excited to see him for the first time in person after over a year, I stand up with a skip, making my way over to him and throwing my arms around him. He laughs. "Dr. Flemming, oh my God! I didn't know you had an office here! I didn't see your name on the plaque downstairs! It's so good to see you again!"

A sudden blast of icy energy hits me hard, and I stiffen, feeling the vibes in the room immediately turn cold. David's in the middle of rubbing my arm when my skin breaks out into goosebumps as Alexander clears his throat rather rudely. My smile slips, and I half turn to look back over my shoulder, seeing Alexander sitting rather stiffly in his seat.

His eyes are sharp with a smoldering intensity, and, dare I say it, something akin to *jealousy.* My heart skips a beat, wholly unprepared to see that particular expression on his face.

"Oh," I whisper, rolling my lips and taking a tiny step away.

I turn and give David an apologetic look; however, David's busy looking at Alexander, not me, and I can tell the second he clocks the energy shift as well. His smile wavers, and he takes a step away from me cautiously, throwing Alexander a perplexed look. But David pivots easily, fixing his face back into his usual kind expression almost effortlessly.

"I uh.... I *hope* I'm not interrupting anything?" David asks, folding his arms and throwing me another fond smile.

I keep my eyes purposefully off Alexander's as I walk back to my seat and sit down. I look back over my shoulder at David and scoff. *"Nonsense—"*

"*David,*" Alexander interjects smoothly, turning his eyes to him. "If you kindly would excuse us, I can stop by your office at two o'clock when we're done."

I turn my face back to Alexander, surprised at how effortlessly *he* pivoted, effectively shutting down any hint of David third-wheeling our meeting. I keep silent, chalking it up to inter-office issues; maybe there's something going on between them I don't know about. But I wonder how David feels, having been dismissed so thoroughly in front of me.

Nervous, I peek again to see Alexander raise a haughty brow at David, who bites back a grin and backs out of the office. He pauses, though, on the threshold with a hand on the doorknob, and his eyes meet mine once again as he gives me a wink.

"Bye, Sarah Beara, I'll email you soon. Maybe we can have our own lunch date to catch up," David says, clicking the door shut behind him. For a second I tense as he uses my nickname again, all of a sudden feeling very awkward with it being said in front of Alexander.

I turn back to Alexander, gaping at him. "Alex, that was a little *rude*!" I chastise.

I can't help my eyes narrow, but when his gaze leaves the closed door and finds mine, I can see he couldn't care less. Yet it's hidden under the usual carefully veiled arrogance and confidence.

"So, *Sarah Beara,* huh? How do you two know each other?" he asks, obviously ignoring my chastisement of him and trying to keep his tone light and innocent despite the redness under his color.

I lean in further, staring into his eyes. Getting lost in them, rather.

"I think you might be the *only* person who doesn't get this. Maybe you're too prolific to see it? We *all* run in the same circles, *duuhhh.*" I wave a hand dismissively as he chuckles at my admittedly juvenile expression. "He was kind enough to let me interview him for an assignment while I was in grad school getting my counselor degree, *and* he also wrote me a letter of recommendation." As I tilt my head, my eyes fall to his lips, watching him chew slowly while he regards me with an expression that, if I didn't know any better, I would classify as stony. "I remember emailing and asking *you* for an interview back then too, but somebody was just. Too. *Busy. For me.*" I smile softly, wanting to see that expression crack just a little before biting once more into my bunless burger. "But David wasn't."

He visibly stiffens. The tension ramps up even hotter between us, and it's all I can do to keep my hands from trembling as I continue to eat as if I'm not affected by him. But that's insane because anyone with half a brain would be affected by this charismatic, handsome, and, hell I'll say it, sexy-ass man sitting in front of me.

Alexander gives me a little grunt as he puts his burger down, licks his lips, sits back in his seat and wipes his hands very slowly with his napkin. My eyes are drawn to his movement, seeing him rub the napkin with his fingers; though, there's nothing on his hands to clean off. My heart begins to race as his eyes remain almost unbearably hard and cold on mine, causing me to shiver as he doesn't relent and let me into his warmth.

A tiny thrill goes through me at the seriousness behind his eyes. And I wonder what it would feel like to have all that intensity trained on me in the bedroom, burning it down with me between the sheets.

"Uh-huh. So, the nickname?" He circles back. "Why does he call you that?" His eyes fall to my hands holding my burger, and I see a little glimmer of judgement, or maybe even displeasure, in his features, and I wonder why. Noticing that he's been picky about food since I've been around him, I wonder if he's got a past history of being hungry that makes him so finicky around food.

Thinking of Alexander's possible "what-ifs," I soften my tone out of my teasing one and give it to him straight, picking at my burger.

"My close friends call me that. They did all the time in graduate school. David saw it on a group email thread one time between me, Jerome, and Christopher, and now he teases me every time I see him. Which hasn't been a lot in the last couple of years. I only speak to him lately when I refer clients to him via email."

Alexander stays silent for a second, watching me eat a small piece of my burger. I suddenly feel very vulnerable around him.

He tightens his jaw, and I wonder what he's thinking about.

CHAPTER TWENTY-FIVE

CRAVINGS

Oh no, baby. You will absolutely not be going to lunch with him.

I sit back in my seat, having stunned myself with the fierceness and vehemence of my thoughts.

One thing for sure, this woman's a *brat.* Her last comment about David proved it, and she knew it'd get to me, which is why she said it.

I tilt my head for a moment, thinking. I have nothing against David, absolutely nothing. I can't find any fault in the guy, other than he's annoying, really. He's passionate about his job, and thankfully his work ethic is admittedly solid. But the thought of Sarah speaking to him while he uses a pet name for her, and gets to put his arms around her, and then the fact that she sends some of her clients to him makes me irrationally angry.

So I gotta work to cool myself off. And what's better than to focus on a trip where I get to have her all to myself?

I don't want her to think I'm rude, so I hum a response before clearing my throat and jiggling the mouse to wake up my computer. Thinking of having her to myself, I change the subject back to what we were talking about before we were interrupted.

"So, I upgraded the hotel suite in Vancouver for two beds and a kitchenette. We're staying four days, flying back on the fifth—"

"*Alex*," she whines, interrupting me.

The low sound in her soft voice surprises me, turning me on so viciously that I'm momentarily speechless. My half-erection comes back at the sound, and it's all I can do to keep the smile I feel tugging on the corners of my mouth from showing. I don't want her to think I'm overtly interested, especially so soon after what's happened to her.

And especially when I'm trying to finagle my way into convincing her to share a bedroom with me.

"*Yes,* Sarah?" I tease her back with a little laugh. My eyes hold hers a few seconds longer than I know she's comfortable with, but I don't waiver. Her eyes are like twin pools of dark brown chocolate, inviting me in with their sweetness. If only she knew how much I love sweets. Crave them.

Unbeknownst to my inner turmoil, she scowls at me before leaning forward; the top of her cleavage peeks out from her neckline and makes my mouth go dry.

"I had only planned on staying for three days," she says, successfully making the grin I've been holding back break free.

She does this thing with her voice where the inflection of her tone goes down, and she whispers some of her words; it's the fucking *sexiest* thing I've ever experienced in my life.

"Well, now you're staying five. *And bring a swimsuit*," I whisper back, tenting my hands together on the desk. I rub the tips together slightly, wishing to feel her skin on mine again.

"Fine! And I don't swim. I can't get my hair wet." Sarah's eyes flash at me, and her nose scrunches up, making the tiny hoop in her nose glint in the light coming through the window.

"If you don't bring one, I'll be forced to provide one for you... and do you really want to see what I'd choose to put you in?" I say, resisting the urge to lick my lips, turning my head back to my computer screen. But she's not having it.

"Ugh, if I'm *hardheaded* like you said in the car, then you're a stubborn *ass*," she says under her breath.

I give her an amused laugh, listening to her adorable, infuriated mumbling as she stands up and picks up her bag, and stomps to the door. "See you at home," I call out after her with not a care in the world as I browse through internet pages of things to do in Vancouver during our down time at the conference.

She's traveling in first class whether she likes it or not.

She's staying in my room whether she likes it or not. And she's going to enjoy herself, *even if it kills me.*

Heading out an hour earlier than normal, I see my receptionist, Cathy, gape at me as I pass by her desk. At her expression, my feet slow to a stop. "What's the matter, Cathy, cat got your tongue?" I tease as I move my briefcase to my other hand so I can grab my phone.

Damn, I'm in a *good* mood.

"Dr. Richardson, you never leave this early!" Cathy remarks. Her eyes are wide in surprise, and a huge smile curves her mouth. "Could it be because of that absolutely *adorable* woman I saw stomping out of your office on my way back from lunch?" She doesn't even try to hide being nosy.

I smile back at her. "Cathy," I tsk, giving her a wink as I open my phone to the apps. "It's because I have to make dinner, and I'm really looking forward to it."

Dinner for the adorable woman.

I listen to her laugh as I text, headed out the lobby doors of my practice. It's almost five, and I'd thankfully finished with my work early.

AR: Sarah Beara, do you like spicy chicken salad or regular? Blue cheese or ranch? You know what, I'll just get everything so you can have options...

Shamelessly using her nickname, I pocket my phone without a care. Because if dickhead David can do it, then so can I.

I tighten my lips and throw my briefcase in the passenger side of my vehicle, realizing this is my last night making dinner for her before she moves into her apartment the next day. My eyes narrow in displeasure. I don't like that. I know I haven't known her on a personal level long enough to be feeling like this, but I can't help it. She's crawled into me and settled herself in.

It's discombobulating, to say the least.

But I won't overstep boundaries, not all the time anyway. I know she will need her space. I can also acknowledge that I don't want to give her any.

Jesus Christ, what is wrong with me? We're practically strangers.

I pull out of my reserved spot and head to the store. *Except, we don't feel like strangers,* I muse, not turning the radio on, content to be lost in my own thoughts.

Thoughts of Sarah, the non-stranger.

I'm busy talking with Johnathan a couple hours later through google video, truly enjoying the vibe of my home tonight for the first time in a long time. The delicious smell of fried chicken permeates the air, and the sounds of "Land of 1000 Dances" gives the kitchen a playful ambiance that I hope lifts her spirits when she walks through the door. I wonder when she's going to show up because she should have been here at least forty-five minutes ago.

I debated calling her, but I don't want her to think I'm too clingy since that could possibly chase her away.

The satisfying sound of the sizzle of the grease frying pulls my attention away momentarily, and I work hard to get a grip.

"So, you're actually cooking for two, huh? You remember how to do that?" Johnathan teases.

I laugh, flipping the two cutlets in the skillet, hoping I didn't make them too salty.

"Come on, I'm not a Neanderthal," I joke, turning the screen to show him all the salad fixings chopped and ready to go on the counter, as well as the wine chilling in an electronic holder. Just then the hair on the back of my neck stands up, and I half turn my head, feeling her close. My skin tingles when I see in my peripheral that she's right behind me.

Sarah sings a line of the song, and it's beautiful, filling me with a shot of pleasure that's so warm it's almost dizzying.

She snuck up behind me, tapping me on the left shoulder before faking to my right. I turn to face her head on, and that shot of pleasure expands even more somehow at the sight of her long hair now out of its bun, swishing as she straightens back up. She greets me with a shy smile that makes my blood race in my veins.

I couldn't tell you the last time someone smiled at me the way she is, especially in my home, my sanctuary.

"Hey." I grin back at her, catching her gaze. Her spirit feels a bit brighter, and I hope that coming to my home with dinner cooking and some good music lifted her spirit the way I'd hoped. "I like this playful mood, Sarah," I murmur quietly.

For a split second our eyes clash. My chest tightens and fills with an almost unbearable heat. I lock myself down swiftly, resisting the urge to lean down and press my lips to hers. God, I bet she's a pleasure to kiss.

"*That's* Sarah? The girl who's been living with you? Ya 'iilahi, look at all that *hair*!" Johnathan's deep booming voice sounds out next to us, causing Sarah to suddenly scream in fright and throw herself at me.

She doesn't even wince as I catch her with an arm around her waist and press her close to me. Her hands fly up to my chest, and I see she's holding a thin black box with a black bow, but her face is more important than any gift.

However, even in the miss of sudden chaos I tuck the knowledge that gift-giving might be her love language deep inside for later.

I feel a rumble in my chest as her curves mold against mine. She's so short her breasts press high on my abdomen, and my hands instinctively move away from her back, one cupping the side of her hip and the other pressing her head into my chest. She fits me perfectly.

I have a brief moment where I feel tears sting the back of my eyes because I've missed true intimacy with another person, and to have her here like this is almost as painful as it is exhilarating.

Something about the simplicity of her head pressing right up to my heartbeat shatters me a little on the inside; although, she doesn't seem to be aware of how affected I am. I close my eyes briefly and turn my face away from the screen. I boldly press my lips to the hair at the top of her head, yet she doesn't notice. She's still gasping in fear, looking over with wide eyes to the monitor where Johnathan is laughing.

"Chill out scaredy cat-I don't bite. Can't say the same for *Alexander,* though," Johnathan gives her a wink before being shoved over by his wife, Vanessa, who's trying to force her way into the frame.

"Oh my gosh, you're *Sarah B*! I've been following you from the lounge! I love your voice so much.... *Ohhh*! We have to get together to sing! Please say yes! I'm Vanessa Reed. *Hi*!" the redhead half-screeches into the screen, her gray eyes widening with excitement at seeing Sarah.

I frown, furrow my brows and look down at her. I want to hear her sing; I want to see her at the lounge. Hell, I just want her.

Sarah blushes as she gingerly pulls away from me, and in the slowness and hesitancy of her movements, I see when she realizes just how compromising a position we were in. My thigh was pressed high and hard into the heat between her legs, and my hand that was curved around her hip falls away just as reluctantly, as she stares rather dumbfoundedly into the screen at Johnathan and Vanessa.

"*Wait*, you're with that band! Oh my God, I've seen you perform once!" Sarah's unease vanishes as her happy mood comes back.

She laughs, getting up close and personal with the google screen.

I'm left sort of reeling, wondering if I'm the only one as affected by this attraction between us. I hurriedly stop the trajectory of my thoughts; I can't be wondering how she feels about me. It'd be beyond selfish.

Sarah grabs up the video screen, and I don't like how close she is to the grease so I shoo her away from the stove, causing her eyes to meet me once more. Except now, there's a hint of something feisty in them. I give her a wicked grin.

"Please, Alexander, I'm *Black*; I think I know my way around some grease." She admonishes me, turning back to the screen and leaning her hips against the counter. The sizzle becomes louder as I add more cutlets into the pan, and I purposefully ignore her as she turns a questioning gaze to me. *"Who's going to eat all that?"* she asks softly, her brown eyes turning to meet mine as I finally allow myself to break out into a full smile.

I lean forward slightly, bringing our faces close together as if I'm sharing a secret.

"Well, you didn't answer my text, so I made two cutlets spicy and two not spicy." I throw her a wry glance as I back my way to our wine glasses, taking the bottle of wine out of its chilling station and pouring us each a healthy glass. "You eat as much as you want." I pause. "Well, just leave me one," I murmur.

Something like shame flits across her face, making me feel unsettled. "Ohhh...I'm sorry, Alexander. I didn't *not* respond on purpose." She turns back to my friends on the screen as she accepts the glass I hold out to her, tilting the video so we're both in it, and she's pressed against my side again. While the women are talking, I work to pick open the black box she'd shoved at me before her scare.

"Is this for me?" I murmur to her quietly, trying to get the damn thing open. I'm so excited that my fingers won't work right. When's the last time someone gave me something just because?

Sarah gives me a little look and nods her head, nudging me with her shoulder. *"It's yours,"* she whispers back before turning back to the screen where Vanessa's got a goofy smile on her face, watching us.

I inch to the side, feeling vulnerable as that fire creeps up my neck and makes me burn just a little bit hotter.

"Vanessa, I would *love* to sing with you. Give me your number, I'll save it and text you!" Sarah says, thrusting the video screen to me and turning to reach her phone, forcing me to put my present down.

Eyeing the food, I wait patiently while the girls exchange information before I confirm meeting with Johnathan at the boxing ring on Wednesday evening and hanging up. I look down at Sarah. The strands fall all around her in big bouncy waves as she sips her wine.

God, she's beautiful. How could that man fucking hit her? Worthless piece of shit.

"How's your back?" I ask, stepping into her and wrapping my arm around her shoulder. I pull her slowly into me, so she won't feel threatened, and press the side of my head into hers for a proper hug. I've missed her since she left my office. I feel sad at how stiff she goes against me, as if not used to the intimacy, and I'm sure instinctively wanting to protect her back.

"It's still bothering me, but I'm okay," she says softly.

She clears her throat, and I can tell this is something that she isn't wanting to discuss as she purposefully averts her gaze, quickly grabbing up the black box and handing it to me again. Like it's a buffer between us.

"It's not my birthday," I say with a teasing grin as I pluck at the box again, finally getting it open and seeing a nice leather wallet that has my initials on it. I break out into a wide smile. "Thank you, Sarah. I love it!" I fight the urge to hug her again; instead, I turn back to the stove and switch it off, taking the finished chicken off the pan and laying it on paper towels.

"I knew you would because you're a *Cancer*. I don't know how to feel about that." Her tone is light as she teases me.

I scoff as she grins back, and I realize this woman really is playful.

I muse this over as I take a bowl of homemade buffalo sauce and begin dipping the chicken in it, leaving two plain.

"What?" I admonish with a little laugh, turning to look at her and clacking the tongs together loudly. "What are you talking about, woman?"

Her eyes go wide, and her face flushes even deeper, causing my dick to tighten almost painfully hard. "You're a Cancer, the absolute emotional *crybaby* of all the astrology signs!" she says with a laugh of her own.

The way she calls me out on my emotions, even though I've attempted to be nothing but polite, stoic, and professional, melts me just enough that I snap, turning to face her. Sarah squeals and gasps as I slowly crowd her against the island. I place my hands on either side of her body on the countertop and lean into her. Her big doe eyes go even impossibly wider in her face, and her lips part slightly as she takes a breath.

Immediately the sweet yet bold marshmallow smell of her perfume assaults my senses, and I feel myself become a little bit more lost in her. The shudders in her breathing as my lips graze her ear verifies to me that I'm not imagining the attraction between us.

This illustrious pull intricately binds us together.

"Do you really want me to show you how big of a baby I can be about things, Sarah?" I rasp into her ear, leaning into her briefly to grab two of the salad bowls, and then pulling away to bring it over to where the chicken is resting. I'll let her think about that for a while. Hopefully, it tortures her the way I'm being tortured.

She bites her lip almost nervously as I begin to roughly chop up the buffalo chicken, spreading it evenly between the two bowls that I loaded with salad, and the various accoutrements. With a side of olives just like she likes.

"Nope, not necessary," she says, swallowing thickly. "I went ahead and ordered a swimsuit just as you requested, Dr. Richardson. You were *more than clear* in your office today." She makes a little shocking pleasant noise, making me wonder if she likes someone taking control. So, we're going to start with how I want her to address me.

"Good, and it's *Alex*," I quip.

I sprinkle feta cheese on top of our bowls and hand hers to her before grabbing the dressing and taking it over to the table. She follows a few steps behind. I set everything down and then pull out her chair with a little grin, giving her a wink.

She tucks a strand of hair behind her ear shyly. "Oh you don't have to—"

"Nonsense."

The tension immediately thickens between us.

She blinks at me, and we engage in another small standoff that I'm quickly discovering is our thing. She rolls her lips before murmuring her thanks and sitting down carefully.

"You're welcome." I'm so pleased she didn't put up a fight.

I round the table, sitting down across from her in the nook at the bay window. I notice the lights illuminating the property outside in the back where the sun has almost completely set, throwing the sky into dusky hues of lavender and pink. She's also staring out the window with a rather interesting expression, and I wonder if she likes the landscaping.

"Are you hungry?" I ask her.

Taking a sip of my wine, I watch as she blinks lazily and turns her head almost as if she's in a daze to meet my eye. I give her another smile, just wanting her to be with me, engage in conversation with me. I'm starving for something from her. Anything.

"Oh, yes," she giggles. "Your koi pond looks so beautiful, though, I can't help but stare when I sit here. I hope I don't look crazy—"

"You look beautiful." I interrupt quickly. My tone is low, deeper than what I'd like for it to have been, but I couldn't help it. She does something to me.

"Oh...well...thank you," she says quietly, setting my blood on fire. "And thank you so much for making this!" Her appreciative tone strikes right through to my heart, lighting me up, and begins to cleanse that part of me that's been so defeated, defiled, and colored black with bitterness from years of being rejected and neglected by my ex-spouse.

I take a second to unroll my linen napkin, placing it over my thigh. "You're welcome! It really was my pleasure. I enjoy cooking. It's one of my love languages," I share, watching her carefully.

She grabs the blue cheese dressing and pours a small amount on her salad. "Honestly..." she starts and then cocks her head to the side and stares back out the window, concentrating for a few moments. My brows rise as she frowns slightly. "You know, I don't think anyone's ever made me this before, and it's my absolute *favorite* salad!" she finishes with a smile, biting her lip and doing a little happy wiggle.

For a second she exudes pure joy, and I'm filled with joy myself at having done this for her. I wonder how she's going to like the pink roses that I put on her nightstand upstairs.

I feel the corner of my eyes crinkle as I smile at her before picking up my own fork and pouring dressing onto my salad, wishing it was her I was pouring dressing on so I could lick it off. I quickly dismiss the thought, promising myself I'll fantasize all I want when I get to the safety of my own bedroom, alone.

"It's the least I can do. I enjoy cooking, in case you couldn't tell," I joke, stirring my salad rather aggressively before putting a forkful into my mouth.

Sarah smiles so hard it throws me off balance. "Oh, I could tell alright. I can tell a lot of things about you," she teases me.

"Oh yeah?" I tease back. "Like *what?*"

My eyes drop to her mouth as she puts a forkful of salad in, preventing her from answering. A small bit of dressing stays behind on the corner of her lips, and I clear my throat softly before handing her a napkin, wishing I could lap it up with my tongue instead.

Would she freak out if she knew all the ways I've savored her already in my mind? I think, feeling my cock hardening again.

Sarah's phone dings; she checks it quickly, the screen light illuminating her face and momentarily turning her eyes a light brown.

"Oh, Vanessa has invited us to a pool party! It's the weekend we get back from Vancouver," she says absentmindedly. "It looks like she added us all into a group chat. How fun! She said we'd have an opportunity to sing together because her brother-in-law, Colin, has a studio in his guest house. That's *neat*!" she exclaims with a big grin across her face.

I wonder if she usually smiles this much or if I have something to do with it. If so, I pray I keep this up because Sarah truly has a beautiful smile.

Thank you, Vanessa. You just got me one step closer.

I nod. "Let's go. Johnathan's plenty of fun and so is his extended family. Albeit a bit crazy," I add with a laugh, crunching through a juicy cucumber.

Sarah turns sparkling eyes to me. “Well, who isn’t anymore, right?” she quips. "I'm sending her a VIP and asking if she needs me or you to bring anything." She taps for a bit and then places her phone screen-side down and concentrates on her meal and me again.

We eat and discuss what time she's going to be picking up her keys for the apartment tomorrow. She informs me she's going to go to the store after we eat, so she can pick up an air mattress and a few things for her apartment. She's surprisingly compliant when I offer to bring her a brand-new air mattress that I'd stored from when I fancied myself wanting to camp and never took the trip due to work obligations.

I'm lying, of course, as I'm not going to actually bring anything because I'd already purchased everything she needed; she just doesn’t know it yet. But I also want to be there when she walks in for the first time and sees she has furniture.

We finish up with the promise to dig into another documentary, having to break open another bottle of wine. This time Sarah stays awake, and I enjoy her nervous ticks and her little looks at me from across the couch. But I keep my hands to myself, not wanting to force anything on her.

Her eyes get heavy, and I turn the TV off, reaching my hand out to her. "Hey, come on. You need your rest; let’s go to bed." She puts her hand in mine, and I haul her up, carrying her up the stairs again. We pause outside the door, and to my surprise, she looks a little lost.

Does she need me the way I need her?

"What is it?" *You can tell me...*

"Can you...do you think—" Her voice is soft, and her eyes stay pinned to my chest. She's too nervous to ask for it, so I'll offer it.

"Yes. I'll be in in a moment. I'm going to take a shower real quick, and then I'll join you." My heart races with the knowledge she wants me next to her.

"Okay," her eyes raise up to meet mine. "I just...I don't want to be alone just yet."

I step into the room before setting her down, and bringing my hand up to brush my knuckles down her cheek. I'm blown away by how vulnerable her features are; her eyes are shiny as she looks up at me with that lost expression still on her face. I swallow thickly, fighting everything in me to lean down and kiss her. We're not there.

She may want the company of my body, the protection of it, even. But she's not ready for sexual intimacy.

Nowhere near ready.

"You're very brave to ask me for what you need." I keep my voice level, and purposefully calm and low; though, I feel anything but that. "You need to relax, so go take a shower, spray that perfume I know you love so much, and I'll be back in a little bit."

She gives me a little shy smile and averts her eyes again. "Okay. Yeah...that might help a lot. See you in a few minutes." I wait until she steps through the adjoining bathroom door, closing it with a little click behind her, before pivoting to make my way down the hallway and into my own bedroom.

But I don't get into the shower first.

No. I lay on my bed and pull out my cock, gliding my hand up and down my thick erection harshly, gasping as I imagine a certain little therapist bobbing up and down atop me. I groan, imagining her smell, and the sounds her heavy breasts will make as they slap against her ribcage. I wonder what she sounds like when she orgasms so many times she can't think straight, how those pretty features of hers contort with pleasure when she can't take anymore.

The helpless look on her face when she realizes just how thick I am, spreading her delectable pussy apart.

The visual tips me over the edge, and I orgasm with a guttural growl, feeling my seed spurting onto my stomach and hand. I rush through my shower, desperate to get back to her. As I pad down the hallway, I see the door is cracked, so I push through. I can smell the lingering humidity of her shower and the perfume she wears, and I rub my jaw hard, pausing before stepping deeper into the room.

I'm never going to sleep in my bedroom again. When she leaves, I'll be moving my things in here and sleeping on the pillow she lays on.

The room is dark, and the ceiling fan is on high, again. I make my way quietly to the side of the bed I'd been lying on and see the covers are already pulled back, but Sarah is still. There's just enough moonlight to show me she's not completely asleep, but she's somewhere in that holding spot.

"Sarah," I say curiously, quietly, seeing her eyes barely part; her breathing remains steady with the rise and fall of her breasts. "Are you meditating, sweetheart?"

"Hmm." She hums, her eyes closing back again.

Leaving her to her peace, I slide under the sheets next to her and relax on my back. I close my eyes and take a deep breath, feeling her saturate my lungs just right. My eyes open again when I feel her hand nudge my arm gently. I grab her hand, my touch gliding along her fingers before pausing at the air pod in her grasp.

"What's this?" I ask quietly.

"Put it in. Relax with me," she responds in a huskier voice, sounding like she's falling asleep.

I take it, placing it in my ear and hearing the gentle guided meditation she's listening to. I dare to wrap my hand back around hers, elated to be able to touch her like this.

We lay there in our own little world while listening to the meditation against a backdrop of a cello of all things. My hand tightens around hers, and my heart beats excitedly when I feel her pulse beat slow and steady in her fingers. I rub her thumb in response, right over the thrumming that lets me know she's slightly excited also.

It's the most intimate experience I've ever had with another person and makes me think about how this is the first time in my career that I hadn't gone to sleep while doing work for my practice. Hannah had spent years begging me not to work so much, and Sarah has seemingly gotten me to do the impossible.

And I haven't even kissed her yet.

CHAPTER TWENTY-SIX

DICKHEAD DAVID

THE NEXT MORNING I wake up early, needing to get to the office earlier than normal for an important evaluation. My eyes pop open, and my heart begins to thud heavily inside my chest because of how I'm wrapped around Sarah. My eyes lower down to where we're pressed together. *Fuck.* I'm gripping her breast over the sheet and holding her tummy in my other hand.

God, she's so beautiful and feels so soft.

Cradling her close, I feed that part of me that needs physical touch.

My eyes rise even further up her body to the tops of her bare shoulders, and I immediately see she'd shimmied out of her clothes sometime in the middle of the night. My eyes fly up to where her face is turned away from me. The delicate curve of her neck is tempting, begging me to run my lips along it. I bite back a groan, wanting to taste the flavor of her skin after she's been asleep all night.

My cock thickens as her scent hits me hard, and I want nothing more than to rip the sheet off her body.

The restraint I exercise is strangling me half to death, but I put my desire firmly to the side and work to extract myself from around her. She doesn't deserve to be lusted over the way I am right now. I pull away and move the cover up even more, slowly, so I don't wake her up and interrupt her rest.

And I'm ashamed to say that it takes every bit of my two decades of professionalism to keep my eyes off her as I leave the room.

Distracting myself, I dress in the main bedroom before heading downstairs to text Tyler to see how he's doing. Eerily content, I find I'm enjoying the hush of the early morning as I make lunch for Sarah. Turning, I stick it in the refrigerator, leaving her another note instructing her to grab breakfast out of the warmer and the tea I made for her, and then reminding her to get her lunch for the day.

Keeping my steps light, I sneak back into her room and place the note on my pillow, freezing when I see she shifted enough that the covers pulled away enough to expose her naked leg and hip. My face warms with renewed desire as my eyes roam greedily. Her skin is so creamy it looks like butter. It would be so wrong, but the fact that I can't run my hands along that flawless expanse of delicate skin is going to fuck my day up. I already know it.

Exercising an extreme force of will, I back out of the room, and the contentment I'd just felt melts away as I now dread the day ahead because I'm losing her. No—I'm being forced to let her slip through my grasp. And I don't want to, at all. *Nothing* in me wants to let her go. But I do it anyway because this isn't about me and what I want.

This is about Sarah and the time she needs to heal, to find herself, and grieve.

Locking the front door, the sound reverberates out like a bullet inside my skull because it feels so final, and it makes me hate my house even more than I already do. It's just one more thing to stand between us.

"We don't need to trauma bond" is my mantra, and I play it on repeat extra loud in my head on my drive to work. Forcing my brain to relent what it wants and kowtow to what's *best*.

Somehow I get through the first two hours of work, though I'm rather irritated with everyone and everything. With a heavy sigh, I close the door to my office after my client and her parents leave. My annoyance is at an all time high. I could see the looks the mother of my client was giving me, and I know I was coming across even icier than I normally do. I can't help it, though. I haven't heard a thing from Sarah, and it stokes the fire of my irritation.

Sitting back in my office chair, I take a rare second to myself, rubbing my hands roughly down my face, and forcing myself to get it together. "Dear God, help me," I plead, but there's no help to be had because I'm like a madman possessed.

Tightening my lips, I lean forward to pull up my work email, pausing as Sarah's name pops up on the screen. My chest loosens with relief. She's okay. She'd reached out about an hour ago, right when she got into the office it looks like. The relief is short lived, however, as my eyes skim her email. I clench my jaw in fresh agitation at her disrespectful greeting.

Mr.-Dr. Richardson,

It's Sarah Johnson asking for a rescheduling of our meeting for Client X. I can do Thursday 6p or Friday when you're free. However, I can't do after 4p on Friday because I'm performing at the lounge. Please let me know.

Hope your day is going well. I'm focusing on rescheduling the clients I thought I'd be seeing next Thursday, since you're making me stay an extra day in Vancouver. Smile.

A little anxious about my first night in the apartment. Maybe I should get a cat?

By the way, do you plan on being there? Frick and Frack want to know so we can properly plan for food.

Warmest of the warmest regards,

Sarah Bella Johnson, MA, LPC

I grin at the sight of her sign off with her full name; however, my grin falls fast when I realize Tyler is flying into town on Friday. He'd made plans to stay with me the night before going to his mother's for a couple of days before returning to Spain. My heart tightens with disappointment. It's a shame. I wanted to crash Sarah's performance and see her sing. Maybe enjoy a cigar. It's just what I need before speaking at the conference in Vancouver.

Dammit.

I narrow my eyes at my son's inconvenience. I love him, but Tyler is truly a pain in the ass at the worst possible times. And I just know that I'm going to have to give him some money at some point because at almost eighteen years old, the boy can't figure out how to keep a job for longer than two months. And his mother won't stop begging.

Sighing, I hit the reply button with a thunk of finality that feels just as serious as the click of my front door closing this morning.

Sarah Bella,

It's good to hear from you.

In an effort to be completely honest and transparent, I'm not having the best day. You know how you have one of those days when you wake up on the wrong side of the bed? Well, that's me. I wish I could just leave, but the clients' needs are greater than mine.

I would have loved to see you perform, but my son will be in town, and he will be staying with me that night. Would it be too much to ask if you could sing a little something tonight, perhaps?

I wouldn't miss you walking into your new apartment for the world. What are we having to eat? What are they thinking about ordering? Indian food is always a good choice.

Anyways, good luck at rescheduling your clients. I am going to have my secretary send you a few therapists who have become fully licensed and are looking for a home. I know you said you eventually want to fill up that extra room at your office.

And it's Alex. Just Alex.

I sigh deeply and hit send, leaning back in my chair, and squeezing the bridge of my nose between my fingers. A knock at my door has me turning my head in exasperation.

Shaking my head, I consider turning them away because I don't wish to be disturbed right now. I glance up to tell whoever it is to come back in twenty minutes; however, before I can utter one word, my office door cracks open without my permission, and it takes everything in me to not blow a gasket when *Dickhead David* walks in as friendly as ever. He's completely unaware that I'm on my last nerve of the day at just ten-thirty in the morning, and have adopted a sudden and irrational dislike towards him.

Staying stone sill in my seat, every muscle tightens as I fight to keep from cursing at him for invading my privacy. Ignorant to my feelings, David smiles brightly at me as he strolls into my office without a goddamn care in the world, running a hand through his hair.

"Hey, man. Glad to see you're in. Do you have a second?" David asks conversationally, gesturing to one of the two chairs across from my desk.

"Uh-huh," I say rather rudely, realizing this is becoming a new character trait for me. "I've got a few minutes before I have to see my last client of the day. What's up, Osterkamp?" I cringe, praying to all that is holy that he isn't about to ask me about anything to do with psychiatry. My brain feels too fried to be capable of helping with anything right now.

Actually what it is, is I'm unsettled.

I frown, realizing I'm only this upset because tonight Sarah won't be in my home. I slide cold eyes to David as he makes himself comfortable in one of the barrel seats.

"Nothing much, really. I just had a quick question," he says with a grin.

I manage a grimace, trying hard to turn it into a civilized grin. I cock my head and put an ankle over my knee, forcing myself to relax.

"I've got a second."

David clears his throat lightly before mimicking my posture. "Well, I was wondering if you were seeing Sarah?" he says, completely unaware of my dilemma...that I'm struggling within myself.

Not expecting the question, I fist my hand where it rests on the armrest.

I turn to the left slightly to hide the movement because I don't want him of all people to think I'm unhinged.

"No. We're not currently seeing each other. Why do you ask?" I ask, clenching my jaw.

"I was just wondering," he says cheekily. "She's never come in here before, and you *never* have therapists in your office. I was thinking about asking her out, if *you* weren't with her that is." I stay perfectly still as his gray eyes meet mine for longer than necessary, and damn it all to hell, but the man is *challenging* me.

Testing me.

If I'd thought I couldn't possibly be any more bothered than I was before David walked into my office, then I'd been sorely mistaken. In my mind I'm opening my office window and shoving him out, watching him bounce off the concrete sidewalk five floors below us. Maybe being mangled as he hits a parking meter.

I suck in a calming breath, giving him my most professional expression.

"Sarah and I are not dating, David. Now," I say lightly, leaning forward to tap a key on my keyboard, reawakening my monitor. "I'm not one to tell people's business, but I do not think right now would be a good time to enquire into a relationship with her. However, you'll have to bring that up with her," I say, sliding my psychiatrist mask smoothly on.

He taps his fingers on the armrest and nods his head, looking almost as if he didn't hear a goddamn word I just said.

"Good, because I've been waiting patiently for that piece of shit she was with to be out of the picture. I knew it was coming, and so did everyone else in our circle, and I can't wait to dig into that tender piece of flesh. If you know what I mean," David says with a self-satisfied smile.

My eyes slide to his, but I stay silent.

His words piss me clean off. The audacity of this fucker to have said what he just did is astounding. I've never been one for male locker talk or disrespecting women, but for him to have compared Sarah to a piece of meat makes me sick. However, I continue to stare at him impassively. I'm not into fraternizing with colleagues, either. And I don't plan to start or even insinuate that it's ever okay for any of them to come into my office and just start spewing off at the mouth about bullshit.

I lean forward and place my elbows on my desk, pinning him with my eyes; his eyes widen at my expression.

Good, you stupid piece of shit.

"I beg your pardon? What the fuck did you just call Ms. Johnson?" I quip, my fingers twitching as I steeple them together.

David's grin falls as he realizes his offense wasn't going to be left unacknowledged. "Okay, *my bad.* I probably shouldn't have said that...but come on, *you've seen her.* She's got the body of a—"

Heat creeps up my neck. Thankfully, though, his musing is interrupted by a loud ding from my computer, drawing my attention away. My eyes slowly slide to my monitor, seeing the woman in question replying to me. I flick my eyes back to David dismissively, ready for him to get the fuck out before I hurt him.

Coldy, I respond, *"If that'll be all?"*

I let the question hang in the air, the dismissal not going over David's head.

David gets up rather cheekily and slaps his hands on his thighs. "Yes, that's it. Good talk. Hey, do you happen to know her office address?" David asks, already halfway to my office door.

I scoff. *Fuck no.*

I can't.

Clenching my jaw so hard I feel a tooth protest painfully, I retort rather coldly, "You'll have to ask my secretary, *David.*" I arch a brow, uncaring when his face falls slightly as he walks out the door. *Dickhead.*

I turn back to my monitor.

Clicking on the email, I soften and smile as I read it. She's just so disrespectful. In the best way, though.

> Mr. Alexander,
>
> I will not be singing without a mic, band, and backup singers. Sorry!
>
> I am sorry you aren't having a good day. We all wake up on the wrong side of the bed sometimes. A little word of advice? Do this breathing exercise if you have a few minutes in between clients. Tap your chest rhythmically while you do it.
>
> I know you *have* to attend and speak to us worthless *peasants* at the conference, but maybe you can find some downtime, and the trip can just maybe feel like a partial vacation?
>
> I've let Frick and Frack know to get Indian food. I think they'll get a little of everything. But we always end up fighting over the butter chicken, so I guess it doesn't really matter to be honest. We may be fighting to the death tonight. Bring some boxing gloves.
>
> Sarah B.

The irony of her sports commentary makes my smile broaden upon seeing the boxing comment, along with the box-breathing exercise YouTube video she'd attached to the email. Figuring it can't hurt, I pull it up and begin to breathe along with it, closing my eyes, and tapping my chest the way she'd instructed.

After five minutes I note that I'm feeling much better and not like I'm going to jump out of my skin.

Before I know it, it's a little after four, and I say my goodbye to Cathy and make my way to my car. Jerome and Christopher had already texted me, letting me know I have about a thirty-minute head start on Sarah's arrival at the apartment complex, and they're waiting in the coffee shop for her.

Taking the extra time to stop at a nearby nail salon by her new place, I walk in, scrunching my nose up at the strong smell of acetone. The older, sweet-looking nail tech at a table looks up and greets me. "Hi, may I help you, sir? You here for a manicure?" she asks, glancing back down to the nails she'd been filing.

"Uh, no!" I huff sheepishly, rubbing the back of my neck, suddenly feeling embarrassed and *way* out of my element. The few times Hannah had begged me to get a pedicure with her, and I balked at the idea. I clear my throat, feeling myself beginning to perspire.

Jesus, why is this nerve wracking?

I clear my throat hard again to rid myself of the frog that's suddenly lodged itself in there. "I just wanted to know how much it costs to have a manicure?"

"Just a manicure? Or with gel or tips?" she asks, looking at me over her purple glasses.

I tighten my lips, pulling up a mental image of Sarah's nails. "*Gel,* I think?"

"Manicure is thirty-five dollars. Gel is fifty dollars, and acrylic is fifty-five dollars." She frowns, obviously irritated.

I grin at her, hoping to soothe her irritation at me. "Okay, then. How much is a pedicure?"

"Regular is thirty-five dollars. The extra deluxe is sixty-five dollars. It comes with seaweed scrub and oil massage."

I quickly do the mental math. "Could I pay for a years' worth of gel manicures and the deluxe pedicure as a gift to a friend?"

I bite back a grin as the woman who was getting her nails done snaps her neck to look at me with her mouth gaped open. "What kinda friend is that? Lucky friend, can I be your friend, too?"

The nail tech cackles. "*Close your mouth, Brittany, you look like a fish,*" she admonishes her client, letting go of the sputtering woman's hand and getting up to hobble over to the register, giving me a curious up and down assessment. "You realize people get two sets a *month* right? Otherwise they grow out." She eyes me once more over her thick-rimmed glasses.

Not really.

Not wanting to look stupid I smile, nodding and waiting as she rings everything up. When she's done, I pull out my card, not even balking at the total. I graciously accept the gift receipt and hurry back into my car to head to her apartment, pleased with myself. I don't want Sarah to have to compromise on her looks while she tries to figure out how to navigate this new way of life.

Speaking of new, I make the drive to her in silence, contemplating this new thing between us that has caught me so off guard. I wonder if she feels the way I do, slightly out of sorts at this thing we've just been thrown into haphazardly with no direction or guidance.

I know I can confidently say I'm so off-center I don't think I'll ever feel the same way again.

CHAPTER TWENTY-SEVEN

A NEW CHAPTER

WALKING INTO THE COMPLEX, I round the corner to the café, chuckling when I see the pile of balloons first before Sarah's friends come into my line of sight. They both smile as I make my way to their table where they stand and clasp hands with me, followed by a firm pat on the back.

"Hey, guys, how're you doing?" I smile broadly, clapping back just as hard.

I ignore the stares from nosy bystanders who are looking at us a little too closely.

Jerome gives me a curious up and down before giving me an approving nod. "My man! You look good! What did you end up getting her? I know you were stressin'," Jerome says with a chuckle as he sits back down.

He'd been the one that suggested a spa day gift card. We'd texted extensively with ideas for her, but considering she hasn't been too receptive to touch, I didn't think a massage day would be appropriate. *But* the woman loves her nails, so it was a pretty easy pick.

"I paid for her to get nails for a bit, just to give her some breathing room to get on her feet," I answer, glancing curiously at the array of cups in front of us.

"Yeah, that's cool. What's a *bit,* though?" Christopher chuckles, leaning forward to hand me a cup of coffee.

I grab it, briefly roaming his face. "A bit for me is a years' worth." Looking away, I take an appreciative sip of perfectly sweetened coffee.

Jerome chokes so hard it shocks me, and I whip my head over to him and set down my coffee in a rush.

"Damn." I frown. "Are you okay?" I ask, tilting my head as Jerome beats his fist to his chest.

"Yeah. You said a *year?"* Jerome's eyes water as he regards me just a little harder, his gaze turning shrewd. "Do you know how much a manicure costs, and how often you have to get them? Is your bank account okay?"

"Hmm-hmm. I just paid for it." I laugh. "The cost didn't matter to me," I say flippantly, "because I really wanted to take this off her plate. I hope she'll be happy with it." I glance at my watch. "She should be here any minute."

Suddenly, our phones ding at the same time with a text. A quick looks show's it's correspondence from Sarah, informing us she got her key.

"Well," Christopher says, standing up and grabbing the balloons, "our girl is punctual as always. Let's roll." Still chatting, we walk out of the coffee shop and round the bend to the lobby where Sarah's standing and looking like a breath of fresh air.

The vision of her makes me smile broadly.

She's balancing on the balls of her feet, waiting for us to get to her. When she see's us, she a hops excitely, making her pretty green dress sway enticingly around her beautifully sculpted legs, while grinning and waving at us. Christopher and Jerome get to her first. I hang back a few steps, wanting to see her interact with them before I greet her.

"Hi!" she says quietly, wrapping her arms around Jerome and Christopher both, closing her eyes as she snuggles in close. I feel a pang of envy because I'm remembering the night before when I went to hug her, and she stiffened. I wonder if I'll have better luck today. I want her to want to touch me like that. "Thank you so much for being here." She opens her eyes and locks gazes with me, causing my heart to skip a painful beat.

I wait for her cue, remaining standing slightly to the side, and decide she's going to have to make the first move.

Thankfully she does. Her face visibly softens even more somehow, and her cheeks stain a light pink as she closes the slight distance between us. "Hey, you," she says.

The abandon that she expresses with her friends disappears and is replaced with something more hesitant. Shyer.

"Hey," I reply as she carefully presses into my side, wrapping an arm around me and squeezing my bicep gently before giving me a little rub, which surprises me because it feels so intimate.

"Are you doing okay?" she whispers up to me, making my lips tip up in a crooked grin as I slowly roam the features of her face and drink her in.

"I'm doing good, much better now. Thank you," I reply back just as quietly, daring to pull her just a bit harder into my chest.

The hug we're sharing is longer than the one she gave them, and the extra contact does a lot for me emotionally. Turning my face away from the curious looks of the men, I sigh, feeling the stress of the day melting away as I stand there breathing in her warm, vanilla scent. I lament my long-sleeved work shirt, craving to feel her skin against mine.

"Thank you, *too*. You didn't have to come at all, especially since you didn't have a good day." She pulls away, looking up at me through her lashes. "I never would have expected you to."

Even though her touch is gone, something shifts inside of me, immediately causing me to feel better. The shitty day runs off me in swathes as I look into her eyes, and for a second Jerome and Christopher disappear. It's just me and her, connecting. I give her a smile, not able to help my eyes lowering to her berry-red, plump lips.

"It's nothing; I'm glad to be here. Let's get into your apartment so we can tackle this Indian food that I'm dying for," I joke, falling into step beside her as Christopher and Jerome lead the way to the elevators.

They hadn't seen the place yet, and I know Sarah wanted them to walk in first. She sneaks me a small smile, rolling her eyes as she listens to them argue about some football game they were watching yesterday.

"Do you know David emailed me?" she asks suddenly. "Did he say anything to you?"

The question makes my steps falter as we enter the elevator.

"No, he didn't. What did he want?" My fucking voice is back to being cold as I fight back a fresh, hot wave of jealousy at the mention of the man. *Jesus, he wasted no time, did he?*

Jerome hits the button for the floor, and I greedily fill my eyes with her. Her brows furrow, and I see she's genuinely curious as to my thoughts.

“I'm not sure yet; I didn't get a chance to open it. Was just wondering if you happened to know anything...*you know,* since he came into the office the other day."

"No."

"Well, it's just he doesn't normally email me first. *I* usually reach out to *him* about clients,” she says, ripping her gaze away to lower her head so she can dig in her purse for her keys. "Uhm, the way you two were acting kind of made me think there was some tension between you, and I didn't want to jump into the middle of anything."

I cock my head. She's very astute. "Oh, no. He's just an employee." I give her a wink as she looks back up to me and bites her lip. "All's good on my end. You should check it. See what he wants."

The elevator beeps, interrupting our conversation. We drop it, and Sarah teases the men about their bickering. As we walk down the fancy, expansive hallway, our footsteps are muffled by the lush rugs laid over the hardwood.

The excitement is palpable as she turns and hands Christopher the keys.

“Do me the honor, Chris!” she half-squeals, that spark glinting in her eyes as she softly claps her hands together and smooths down her dark green dress.

"I'd love to, babe!" Christopher smiles a cheeky grin back at her in response and unlocks the door, swinging it open wide and hurriedly walking inside with Jerome. "Ooohhwee! Holy shit, this is *niiceee!"*

Putting my hand on her elbow, I go to walk us in too, but Sarah freezes, slapping out a hand against my chest as her brows furrow and a confused look morphs her features. At the feel of her hand against my heart, my own hand comes up to wrap loosely around her wrist, pressing hers deeper into my chest momentarily. I look over.

She's frowning, not paying me any attention.

Not seeing me knocked askew at just the touch of her hand against my chest.

Does she have any clue how this makes me feel? What she's doing to me? My eyes sting at the feel of her warm hand there, right over my heart that suddenly aches painfully. Inhaling, I fight to not close my eyes. I've missed the intimacy of small gestures like this. Someone feeling your heartbeat.

I tilt my head and clench my jaw, wondering if I'd ever actually had it, or if I was wasting my time longing for something I'd never experience, but would always be doomed to crave. I'm so starved for touch that I'm weakened by the extent of the loss I'd been bearing for so long.

"Hey, *no!*" Sarah's confused voice rings out, swiftly bringing me back into the present. "No, no." The pulse thrumming away under her skin is strong, and I break, rubbing my thumb along her wrist.

Slightly though, so it's not obvious what I'm doing.

"Guys, *wait*, come back. Something's wrong. I think they must have given me the wrong apartment," she calls, tilting her head to double check the apartment number. As her frown deepens, my heart begins to race. The sensation making heat creep up my neck and robbing me of my breath. This is it; she's about to see that she's been given a gift.

I keep my hand around her wrist, holding her to me, and wondering if she feels my heart beginning to race with excitement.

"This one's furnished. There's been a mix-up, you guys; we need to go back downstairs. I'm sorry." Sarah pulls her hand away and glances at me apologetically through her lashes.

My lips part to reply, but before I can speak, our attention is drawn back into the apartment. I put my hand on her elbow, pulling her gently into the doorway where we see Christopher leaning against the peninsula in the kitchen, holding a white piece of paper, and Jerome next to him, picking through a huge gift basket of stuff.

"No, it says 5-D," Christopher calls. "They left you a note with your name on it, along with a bottle of some fancy wine *and* some snacks. Damn, woman, that's cool!" Christopher begins reading the note out loud.

Sarah,

Please enjoy this fully furnished apartment, courtesy of friends seen and unseen. Enjoy the wine as well! And welcome to Lanore Estates development.

-Shelly

"Hmm." Christopher hums, sneaking a peek at me, but I studiously ignore him. "Wonder what Shelly means by *unseen.*"

I clear my throat, arching an brow and giving him a tiny head shake. I don't want her to know it's me. I'm not important in this.

Sarah steps tentatively into the space and I watch her carefully, following a few steps behind. She glances around cautiously, eyeing Jerome who's now making himself comfortable in a chair in the living room. She advances to the peninsula where Christopher holds the paper out to her with a rather wicked grin on his face.

"You got the hook up, babygirl."

"Seems so...though, I don't know who'd do this for me. It couldn't be my parents, they don't know I'm here..." She takes the paper slowly from Christopher and reads it silently.

"Wondering who you aren't seeing?" Christopher eyes her before turning confidently, padding into the hallway and disappearing into the master bedroom. "Oh, my fucking God. *Look at this bathroooom!*" he shouts excitedly, making her jump in surprise.

"Don't take the Lord's name in vain," Sarah calls loudly, still eyeing the note. I chuckle, suddenly reminded of my mother.

"That's why she picked this one, baby," Jerome shouts back, pulling his phone out and turning on what sounds to be a football game.

But Sarah stays still, looking down at the note without moving. I walk farther, circling around her until I'm facing her front, needing to see her expression for myself. She's biting her lip, and her eyes are full of tears as she sniffs and looks up at me. I resist wiping a tear away when it falls onto her cheek.

"I guess it's a good thing because I *really* didn't want to give up my air mattress," I joke, a grin tilting my lips as I stare down into her dark eyes swimming with tears. I don't want her to cry, but she seems overwhelmed with gratefulness.

"Who would do this for me?" she whispers, laying the paper down and swiping carefully under both eyes with her fingers.

It breaks me, and I step into her and wrap her into a big hug, uncaring if it's improper or not.

Instead of stiffening, this time Sarah melts into my embrace. Her nose nuzzles into my neck gently, and she takes a breath so deep it makes my arms flex. My body reacts, warming up instantly with pleasure so acute that it momentarily sets me off course, and I work hard to prevent myself from taking the deep breath *I* need.

I don't want to be too obvious at how badly I needed a hug as well, how much I want to wrap her into my arms.

Sarah stiffens suddenly as a rhythmic squeaking sound comes from the bedroom, effectively yanking us back from our moment. She pulls back fast, her eyes flickering to and away from mine in embarrassment. The loss of the feel of her against me is paramount. I eye her warily when it suddenly hits me like a ton of bricks that I've never felt this way before about anyone.

I haven't known her any length of time, but she just feels so right...so *perfect* that it scares me.

"*Christopher, get off my bed!* The least I can do is take care of the furniture!" she half-shouts, turning away from me to walk down the hallway and peek into the bedroom where she disappears.

"Sorry, girl. I think this might be a problem for you." I hear Christopher tease and her say something back in reply, followed by a muffled smack that makes Christopher laugh good-naturedly.

He comes through the doorway and back to the kitchen and lounge area, rubbing his shoulder with a playful look on his face. I shake my head as he tosses a teasing grin my way before he digs back into the basket, grabbing one of the snacks and tearing it open then shoving a handful of chips into his mouth.

I settle on the barstool next to the peninsula and grin back at him.

Stop, I mouth, seeing him grin even harder. A slight rustling noise brings my attention back to the short hallway where Sarah's busy meandering around.

"It most certainly will *not* be a problem for me, thank you very much," Sarah admonishes before reappearing, looking into the spare bedroom curiously. Her foot pops up behind her as she balances herself against the doorframe. "Oh, it's an *office*! It's so cute!" she gushes, coming back into the kitchen with a big smile on her face.

Christopher scoffs. "Uhm, I actually think it's going to be a huge problem for you. Bed's going to break if it's rocked too hard. What do *you* think, Alexander?" he inquires with a husky laugh as he shoves more chips into his face.

This man's a fucking tease and a half if I've ever seen one.

I fold my arms and look to the side, watching amusedly as Jerome joins in on our chuckling from the living room. "I think bed-breaking is one of the better parts of being able to live life," I say simply, bringing my eyes back to hers and giving her a wink. "Being completely transparent, I might've broken a few in my day."

Her mouth drops open, and her eyes go wide, causing me to chuckle even harder.

"Ugh!" Sarah says, stomping her foot and throwing her hands in the air dramatically. "You guys are such *men*. I don't even know why I put up with you, honestly," she tisks, walking to the balcony door and sliding it open.

She steps out before almost toppling over, and I see her high heel caught between the planks.

I'm up and out there in a flash, squatting down beside her, grabbing her ankle, and firmly plucking it out before removing her cream-colored high-heeled shoe, and seeing her pretty toes appear. I tap her other ankle, looking up at her.

"You're so interesting. We say one word about breaking stuff, and the first thing you do is try and break your ankle?"

"Well." She bites her lip before swallowing hard. "I think you three are trouble. You're enough to make a girl want to jump off a balcony with all the testosterone floating around and choking a girl out."

I arch my brow at her use of words. "Can't have you throwing yourself from the balcony the first ten minutes now, can we? Then how're you supposed to find someone to help you break your bed in?"

She blushes a deep red, the sight filling me up with so much satisfaction, and her breath hitches as she looks away, back to being shy. "I don't think bed-breaking's my thing. But you all tease me all you want to."

"Hmm," I hum, tapping her foot again. We'd been so lost in each other, flirting, that she hadn't even lifted her foot for me.

I wrap my hand around her delicate ankle, feeling along the skin there. She's got blue-green veins that rope up her ankles and feet, and my mouth waters at wanting to trace their path with my tongue. "Come on," I say quietly, "Be a good girl and give me your foot." My breath burns in my lungs as she bends forward to steady herself on my shoulders while I get her other shoe off.

Standing up, I look into her eyes just as Jerome yells out the food has arrived.

A wary look passes over Sarah's features as she gently takes her shoes from me and turns to walk back into the apartment with me following close behind. I close the door shut, watching the gentle sway in her hips as she walks. That and the heady smell of spices makes my mouth water.

We spend the next two hours polishing off the Indian food and not one, but *three* bottles of wine between the four of us. I don't know how Sarah's disposition was when she was in her old home with her ex, but I can't imagine it was the same vibe she's exhibiting right now. Not under the same roof with an abuser.

The Sarah I see now is enjoying abandon, and I wonder when the last time was that she felt like this. This free. She's curled up on her knees in front of the wooden living room table, laughing at Jerome's college story of how he got locked out of some guy's apartment one time naked in the dead of winter, and therefore she needs to find a hiding spot for a spare key just in case.

I also notice with much pleasure that she's eaten almost her entire cartoon of food.

"Oh! Gifts! SJ! *We got you gifts!*" Christopher claps, dropping heavily onto the couch next to Jerome and putting his arm around him. He points to a spot next to the couch, showing her a big, plastic, clear see-through bag with dark blue bedding peeking through.

Sarah drags it to her and pulls it out. "Oohhh it has shams and everything." Her eyes flicker to his, and she smiles warmly. "And it's such a good thread count too, Chris. *Aww,"* she tilts her head, reaching out to touch his knee lightly. So she isn't scared of touching. "You didn't have to."

"And a spare set of sheets, for when all that squeaking gets too intense, you feel me?" Christopher teases, giving her a raunchy wink.

I can't help the chuckle that erupts from me as Sarah leans forward and slaps his arm playfully.

"*Christopher*!" she sputters, turning fire-engine red and pressing her hands to her cheeks. "I'm not even interested in *that. And* it wasn't good when I had it—*trust me."* She rolls her eyes.

I clench my jaw as her words process, and my heart skips a beat as I suddenly imagine myself laying my body on hers.

CHAPTER TWENTY-EIGHT

Letting Me In

It'd be good with me; it'd be amazing, in fact.

The hairs on the back of my neck and arms stand at attention, and my lungs constrict as the room suddenly feels like it's losing air. But Jerome interjects, saving me from feeling like I have to speak.

"I tried to tell you back in the day, remember? I said that fucker's *hips* weren't hipping. He just didn't have that swagger that's needed to be able to tell if a man is good in bed. He was seriously lacking," Jerome leans forward with a small piece of paper. "There you go, baby girl, a couple of massages for you. We need to get you healed up so you can start making the bedrock *rock,* baby girl." Sarah squeals and puts her hands over her face, giggling. "Hey, just promise me that the first time you break that bed in, you play Aliyah's Rock The Boat, okay? Promise me?" Jerome teases, chuckling harder as Christopher begins singing the chorus.

I let out a chuckle of my own, pressing my fist to my mouth to stem the sound and clear my throat. She's just too cute when she's embarrassed.

"No, I think I'll play that song by Queen B. I'm going to ride him with my surfboard instead of rocking the boat," she jests back at Jerome, pulling herself up on her knees and swaying her hips, tossing back her wine.

My blood boils.

Right on cue both men slide their eyes to me, but I'm studiously staring at Sarah. I work hard to keep my movements normal; though despite my best efforts, my toe taps on the floor in agitation as I fight like hell to keep my pants from tenting.

Jerome grabs the remote and starts pulling up various streaming services on the TV. Typing in an account and password.

"It's my turn," I say, cocking my head at Sarah as she puts another bite into her mouth with her wineglass held aloft in her hand. She looks like she's feeling very good. A bit uninhibited.

She nods and crawls to me, making Christopher throw me a hilarious look. I work to lock my body down seeing her inch closer and closer, and I wish to God her friends weren't here. Wish that we were in an actual relationship to where I could enjoy this to its fullest extent.

Wish I could tell her all the filthy things I want to do to her.

"I'm ready," she says breathlessly, sitting back on her heels and staring up at me with her big hazel eyes.

I grin at her, reaching into my inner jacket pocket and pulling out the card from the nail salon. Handing it to her with a half grin, my chin tilts down slightly to get a more direct look into her face.

“So you can keep your nails done for a bit and not have to worry about it,” I say quietly. "I got a few weeks taken care of for you, okay?"

My eyes flicker over her face, seeing her mouth drop open. "A few weeks?" Her eyes leave the card in my hand and rise to mine. "But...Alexander, that's *a lot."*

I keep my gaze steady on hers. "It's not enough," I say quietly.

Her brows furrow as her head tilts. "Alexander, I-*I can't accept this."* She sits back on the heels and goes to turn her face away, but I move fast, wrapping my hand around her chin and pulling her back to face me. I lean forward at the same time I tug her to me, and I place my lips to her ear.

"It's not enough. Not *near* enough," I whisper. "You deserve this, and so much more." My face is hidden in the curtain of her hair, shielding me from Jerome and Christopher, and it's just intimate enough for me to hear the sudden elevation in her breathing. She sounds almost as if she's panting. My lips brush against the delicate shell of her ear as I work to get a tiny bit deeper into her. "This entire time we've been circling around each other, I've been the one jumping through hoops to please you. And now, I think it's your turn to please me, and this would please me greatly."

Her head tilts slightly, and a soft smile graces her face. "Without a fuss, you mean."

"Yes, it would please me for you to accept your gift without *any* fuss. And it would make me even more pleased, if when you used it, you felt worthy of someone doing this for you." My thumb strokes back and forth. "Do you hear what I'm saying, sweetness?"

There's a half second pause where it's silent, and she nods ever so slightly against my grip, and I feel the card slowly pulled from my fingers. "Yes."

My fingers tighten. "Do you want to please me?" I dare, not letting her go. Wanting, *needing* to see something. And there it is: her breath quickens as she lets out a pant, before nodding a quick jerk against my fingers. I nod too, pressing my head to her temple so she can feel it.

"Tell me." I lower my voice even more. "I want to hear you say it."

Sarah's breath hitches making the blood race in my veins. My thumb strokes over her wrists, patiently waiting. "I want to please you, Alex," she says, so low that I almost don't hear her.

My heart skips a beat before thumping heavily in my chest, making the next couple beats vibrate through it painfully, and my dick twitches in response to her. The hairs on my arms stand up, and my own breathing gets slightly heavier. For just a minute, it's just me and her once again.

Sarah's plush breasts are nestled slightly against my thigh, and I notice with pleasure that she hasn't pulled her wrist away from my touch.

"Good girl." I press my lips to her ear, feeling her shudder. "I want to please you as well."

Firming my grip on her wrist, I keep us there like that until her breathing quiets, not wanting her to be embarrassed in front of her friends. When she pulls away, her eyes can't meet mine, and she's blushing a dusky red, biting her lip. "Thank you." She blinks and clears her throat, trying to stand up on shaky legs.

Seeing she's struggling, I stand and help her up.

“You’re welcome,” I say.

She tilts her head back and graces me with her eyes again but neither one of us grin. The seriousness of the moment is seared deep, burning to the core of something tentatively blossoming between us and beginning to mark our story with something more than trauma.

However, our privacy is short-lived. Out of the side of my eye, I see Jerome put a finger over his mouth, his eyes going wide as Christopher winks at me. "Squeak squeak motherfucker," he mouths to me.

"Ooohh, here's a good one. Let's watch it," Jerome says, turning the show on.

Sarah bends, beginning to grab up the trash from the table, but I grab it from her, taking everything to the kitchen. I lean against the counter, listening to the opening music of the show as she opens the dishwasher, and watch as she touches anything and everything she can to keep from facing me head on after what we just shared.

"Hey, there's one more container of butter chicken. Do you want to take it home?" she asks nonchalantly as she places the used cutlery and bowls into the dishwasher before closing it.

I shake my head slightly. "No. Thanks, though. Why don't you take it for lunch tomorrow? Do you think you're going to be ready to fly out super early on Sunday morning?"

She's got her arms around her torso, rubbing her hand down her arm rhythmically in a self-soothing motion. "Oh yeah, I'll be ready! *No one* can pack like me!" she says in a light-hearted voice, still not quite able to meet my eyes. "And besides, I'm just one person..." she trails off with a far away look, and I just know without her saying a thing that she's thinking about her baby.

I tilt my head, stepping a bit closer. *"Hey...* are you going to be okay tonight?"

Sadness floods her eyes, tightening her features as she now folds her arms and turns her back to the lounge, away from the men.

"I don't know..." she whispers, flitting her eyes to mine looking torn. "I've been trying to be brave today, keeping a smile on my face, you know...but it's *hard."* Her voice cracks, causing my heart to tug in sympathy.

She squeezes her eyes shut and works to wipe an errant tear away.

"Sarah." I walk into her, pushing us a bit deeper into the kitchen, out of the view of her friends. I put a hand up and caress her cheek with my knuckles, wiping her tears away and lower my voice, "I can stay tonight. If you need me."

She immediately shakes her head. "No, Alexander, you've done so much, *t-too much*—I could n-never ask—"

I silence her with a finger to her lips. "You're not asking; I'm *offering,"* I say gently, stroking my knuckles down her cheek. Doubt and fear replace the sadness, and I work to keep my motions gentle and non-threatening. Yet still her shoulders hunch up, and she grips her elbow with her hand, curling in on herself.

"You've had a bad day—" She tries, but I interrupt that, too.

"My day instantly got better when I saw you. Don't use it as an excuse, please, because I'm not."

Please see me, baby...see how badly I need this, too.

My chest tightens with anticipation. There in her little kitchen, squeezed up against her refrigerator and the cabinet, we engage in a very different stand off than we're used to. But she's too scared to break for me.

My spirit deflates just a little.

"How about this: you be brave, okay? And if it so happens you can't be brave anymore, give me a call, and I'll come right back." I stop stroking her cheek and instead hold her chin in my grasp, keeping her eyes on mine.

She licks her lips, shifting her weight to her other foot and gives me a head nod before rubbing her own hand on my bicep. The action makes my fingers fall away, and we leave her kitchen silently, back to the living room where she settles on a cushion on the floor.

"Do you want my seat?" I offer, standing next to the chair. Not wanting her on the floor.

"Oh, nooo, I'm fine down here," she says, looking up at me from her spot on the floor. "Sit and watch this with us! Have you seen it?"

Biting my lip contemplatively, I turn without answering and head to her bedroom, grabbing the comforter off her bed. Bringing it to the living room, I take off my jacket and slide to the floor next to her, spreading the blanket over both of us.

Hearing my phone ding, I take it out of my pocket to see texts from the guys.

Christopher: You got it bad, brother. We feel for yoouuu.

Jerome: Make sure she plays Rock the Boat by Aliyah the first time please? It'll just make my whole world complete! You know YOU got the hips that hip, right?

Christopher: Jesus, you don't have to answer that, Alex. Damn he's nosy.

I shake my head slightly in annoyance, discreetly putting up my middle finger for them to see. They laugh quietly, and one of them gently shoves my shoulder, jostling me.

Sarah takes the opportunity to check her phone too, pulling up her email. I tense at the unread email from Dickface David so blaringly obvious at the top. A raunchy moan fills the room, drawing our gazes to the TV where the main character is fucking his mistress against a tree in some raunchy scene. Sarah turns bright red. But I'm honestly very unimpressed and busy frowning, when the men on the couch behind us move.

"Well, hate to go, but we have to run!" Christopher says, standing up and pulling Jerome up with him.

Sarah looks up just as she clicks on the email from David, not reading it.

"Aww....but we just started it!" she complains. As she looks up at them, it gives me enough time to be nosy and see the contents of David's email to her. I stiffen and clench my jaw so hard I hear a grinding sound.

Christopher leans down to give her a kiss on the forehead, followed by a hug from Jerome. "Yeah, I know. I'm sorry, baby girl, but we'll be back soon to have a marathon. Jerome and I have something important to do," he says, pulling Jerome after him quickly before Sarah has a chance to get off the floor.

"Wait!" she sputters, furrowing her brows at them all but running to the door. I shake my head because I know their game. They wanted to leave us alone with a sex scene. As if we fucking need that right now with all the damn tension between us.

"Love you!" Jerome yells out right as the door clicks shut behind them.

"And then there were two," I say with a little chuckle, giving her a wink.

Sarah glances away from me shyly. Leaning forward, she puts her phone on the table without responding to David's request for dinner. The screen goes black.

"Well, let's take their spot. I'll finish it with you; then I'll leave, too, so you can have time to yourself before bed," I say, standing fluidly and holding my hand out to grasp hers to help her up.

Just like at my house, we sit on opposite ends of her new couch and finish the first episode of her show in comfortable silence. It's so pleasant. I have my feet propped up on the wooden living room table, and Sarah has her legs curled up underneath her, still sharing the comforter from her bed.

At almost nine-thirty I notice we're three episodes in and glance over at Sarah to mention it to her. Her head tilts as she nods off, then jerks back awake, blinking at the screen. When her eyes flutter shut again, I smile and reach over to grab one of her feet in a firm grip.

“Hey, go to bed. You look beat,” I say. My deep voice fills the space between us. Her eyes pop open, and she slowly looks over at me before nodding sleepily.

I get up and head for the door, but when I feel her close behind me, I turn, not ready to leave her yet.

We stare at each other for what feels like forever before I step into her and lean down, pressing a kiss to the top of her head. I tilt her head up to me, gazing down into her eyes and getting lost in them.

"You don't have to be brave all the time," I tell her softly. "It's okay to need someone."

"I have to try," she replies in a hurt voice, making my heart ache for her. "You can't always be here for me, Alex. I have to try to figure out how to do this without...” She looks down before trying to continue. “...Without..."

"I won't hurt you." I nuzzle her hair. "But I understand. Please know that I'll be here if you need me. It doesn't matter what time of the night." I breathe in her scent one last time before stepping through the door, making sure I hear the snick of the lock clicking into place before I saunter off to go sleep in my horridly cold and sterile house.

I'm sure disappointment fills me with equal measure to the sadness and pain that fill her. Feelings that are sharp, unrelenting, and that *do* deserve death.

I wonder if I'm ever going to deserve someone letting me in.

CHAPTER TWENTY-NINE

NEW LOVE

THAT FIRST NIGHT IN my new apartment was hard, and I barely got any sleep. It was my first true night alone since my miscarriage, and I was feeling almost irreparably empty. I cried most of the night away, with my phone in my hand and Alexander's number pulled up. But I needed to prove to myself that I could do this. That I didn't need to get on top of this by getting under someone else. And though it was hard, I made it through.

The next few days pass by uneventfully, and the sadness melts away bit by bit until I find myself floating on cloud nine under a new wave of peace.

I hadn't known how stifled and tense I'd grown under Brandon's ridiculously controlling and abusive energy. I had another night where I'd woken up crying, clutching my stomach. But I was able to breathe through it and calm myself, without having to worry about Brandon and constantly walking on eggshells.

Vanessa contacted me, wanting to see me perform at the lounge on Wednesday night, and in a surprise turn, she went up on stage and performed a couple of songs beside me, making me grateful for the change in pace. It excited and disrupted the rigmarole of the evening and did a lot to ease my anxiety of seeing Brandon in the crowd.

Vanessa texts me pretty regularly, and soon we strike up a tentative friendship. She reminds me a lot of my former client and her energy.

On Thursday, I'd finally mustered up the courage to read the email that David sent me the day I moved into the apartment, and I frown at the contents. He'd respectfully asked if I was single or dating anyone, and also requested my office address. Why he won't just google it is beyond me. Sighing, I tab the email to respond another time, wanting to word it just right and feeling like, due to our professional relationship, I didn't want to make anything weird between us.

I think about Alexander often, missing his light, easy and playful mood I'd gotten used to coming home to when I got off work. We traded emails occasionally. Mostly regarding work and my health.

He's very concerned with the state of my back and if I'd be able to travel comfortably, which is why he'd bought me a first-class ticket alongside his. His emails are pleasant and professional enough. Some are about the weather, some asked me about how I'm settling into the apartment, and others asking if I'd been feeding myself properly.

I ask myself multiple times throughout the days if I'm delaying responding to David because of Alexander. Honestly, the fact that I'm busy thinking about two men, when one had just literally landed me in the hospital, doesn't make me feel the greatest. So, not impressed with the direction of my thoughts, I contact a local trauma therapist, setting up an appointment as soon as possible.

On Friday, I spend my free day out shopping and splurge on a few new outfits for the Vancouver trip, utilizing the massage that my friends gifted to me, and got a manicure and pedicure with Alexander's gift. Already dealing with too many emotions, I blinked back tears when the owner revealed how much Alexander loaded onto the card. I sent him a text thanking him, and then sent him a bouquet of flowers to his office even though it's cheesy, and who sends men flowers?

He texted me a bit later with a simple picture of them at his desk, right next to his monitor.

One of the many stems of snow-white roses stuck out slightly more than the rest of them; its head leaned slightly in front of his screen, the petals almost touching my signature. He'd been reading an old email of mine from a few years ago, the one asking for an interview from him while I was in my internship. The image makes me smile because oh, how the tables have been turned. The picture lifts my spirits, thinking that I managed to break his icy exterior and cause him to be introspective, and I cruise through the rest of my day.

Later, I'm still thinking about him as I drive leisurely through my neighborhood with my windows down, and I slow when I spot an adoption shelter sign a few streets down a block I hadn't yet been able to explore. Before I can psych myself out, I pull into an empty spot and slip off my sunglasses as I walk into the cool building.

The animal smell suddenly hits me, causing me to smile. Memories of all the times spent on my great-aunt's farm come flooding back from when I was little, and my parents would take me to go horseback rid-ing. If my childhood hadn't been so fraught with unmet expectations and tension, I'd probably miss those days.

Thankful that I'm healing enough to carry my purse regularly, I sling my tote bag over my shoulder and make my way to the receptionist's desk with a bright smile.

"Hi! May I help you?" The receptionist, an older brown-haired woman with spectacles, looks up from her computer monitor.

Nibbling my lip, I can't help but second guess myself as I reply, "Uhm, yes. *Maybe.* I was considering adopting a cat. I wanted to see if you had any available here?"

Doubt and fear rises fast and hot inside of me. I've never had a pet before, and this is a huge responsibility. Though, not as big a responsibility as a baby. And honestly, I need something to curl up with at night to keep me from calling Alexander.

The receptionist regards me shrewdly before giving an approving smile and nod. "Yes, we have a few back there. I'll take you back, and you can look."

"Ok, thank you."

My phone dings, and I pull it out quickly, seeing a text from Alexander.

Alex: Hey you. Hope you're doing good...my son made it. Is it bad I want to say unfortunately? The demands are exhausting, I tell ya. Don't forget to start packing.

Sarah Bella: Ooohh Alex. I'll be sure to pack more than one pair of PJ's, ok? I'm a big girl. I know my way around a suitcase. And hey, I don't know much about kids, but hopefully he at least said hello to you before making any demands. The nerve. Hahaha.

My phone pings again.

Vanessa: I'm in the hospital! I can't believe this!

I frown before typing a fast reply. We're supposed to be singing together tonight.

Sarah: Girl, what? What's wrong?

The receptionist stays quiet while we make our way down the hall.

Vanssa: My fucking SISTER gave me food poisoning! I just wanted to let you know I wouldn't be able to make it tonight. I'm so sorry. We're all here. My husband, daughter, sister, and her husband too. Baby is with the nanny, fortunately. It's like one big freaking family reunion.

Sarah: Oh wow girl, that sounds like a nightmare. If there's anything I can do, please let me know. I can bring some chicken broth over if you need it?

Vanessa: No, the thought of putting anything on my stomach makes me weak. Thank you for offering though.

Sarah: Take care of yourself please.

Alex: A big girl huh? (smirk face). Funny. You don't feel so big when I'm carrying you in my arms.

Sarah Bella: Silliness.

"Here we are."

I put my phone away and walk through the door into the room with multiple cages, hearing various meows, and some barking through the wall coming from another room. My eyes scan the various cats as we walk past.

"Have you ever owned a pet before?" she asks, leading me to a back wall where there's a little Russian blue cat huddled in the corner of its cage.

"Nooo, never," I croon, sticking my face up to the cage. "But this one is *pretty*." I stick my finger through the little cage, hopefully.

The receptionist smiles at me. "She's quiet, and her name is Bunny. She's been here for a while, around six months or so. Always sits in the corner right there. She's a little reluctant and a lot scared." I feel her stare burning in the side of my face as I stay quiet. "We also have tabbies, and a tuxedo cat if you think you'd be interested in a more outgoing kitty?"

She quiets, watching me peer into the cage intently. I don't need to hear about the other cats. This one's mine; I can feel it in my soul.

"A cat named Bunny, huh? That's unique," I say softly.

She opens the cage and motions for me to reach in. "Her previous owner thought it was cute. Careful, she might bite. And just a warning, she doesn't seem to like men."

I reach my hand tentatively into the cage, my eyes melting as Bunny moves forward and sniffs my fingers. She reaches a beautiful blue-gray paw forward and inches even closer, butting her head against my fingers softly.

"I think she's fetching. I get you, little girl. I don't really like men much right now, either," I confess with a small smile.

I rub Bunny between her ears gently for a moment before picking her up and nestling her to my chest. The feline curls into my neck, purring prettily while nuzzling my chin. She gives me a tiny lick, making me giggle.

"How much is she?" I ask, looking at the receptionist.

Her face brightens. "There's a twenty-five-dollar application fee, and an adoption fee of one hundred and fifty dollars."

I wince thinking about the five-hundred-dollar pet fee at my new apartment. My heart sinks. *What am I doing here? I can't afford this.* I sigh. *Wishful thinking.* But the little voice in the back of my head, the one I've been ignoring for years, comes up strong to the surface.

Have a little faith.

I turn to the receptionist and give her an imploring look. "I really like her, but I have to travel out of town for a few days for a conference. Can I fill out the application, pay the deposit, and pick her up when I get back into town? Do you take a credit card?"

She brightens. *"Of course, you can!* And yes, we do! Let's go get the forms!" She helps me put Bunny back, considering she'd extracted her claws and tangled them into my hair to try to hold on.

"Don't worry, Bunny. I'll be back for you and get you out of your corner. *I promise.*"

I blow Bunny a kiss and follow the receptionist out the door.

CHAPTER THIRTY

BOX BREATH AND BRAIN CELLS

THE NEXT EVENING, I'M elbow deep in a heated argument with Tyler, who insisted on coming over for dinner even though it was his mother's night. No doubt we'll be paid a visit from her soon. The knowledge that she's going to pop up any moment distracts me from what he's saying; I stare unblinkingly as he talks, and force myself to listen to every word before squeezing my eyes shut in frustration.

Leaning against the counter in my kitchen, I listen to him ramble on about why he can't go back to Spain.

"What can I say to make you let me come back home, dad?" he queries sharply, his blue eyes, so much like mine, flashing with anger. "I don't want to go back!"

Frustrated beyond belief, my lips press together, and I fold my arms even tighter, working to keep my voice level as I address him. "Tyler, you have obligations. You made a *commitment.* We have sunk so much money into your education and all you've managed to do is fuck your way through your weight's worth in women," I admonish. "If *only* they could give out degrees based on being a man-whore, you'd be all set!"

Disappointment heavily laces my tone, causing Tyler to arch a brow.

"You're one to talk! You've had like *twenty* women since mom!" he throws back bitterly, not even knowing the facts to speak on my sex life. He leans his forearms against the island, uncaring about how disrespectful he sounds. In my house. "And you're screwing one now, too. Don't deny it because I found the longest fucking hair of my life in the bathroom drain a little bit ago."

I push off hard from the counter, walking the few steps to the opposite side of the island across from him. I can tell without even looking that my features are hard set. Tyler's eyes turn wary, but I couldn't care less. If you've got the balls to step to me in my house, then you better be prepared for me to step forward because I won't tolerate it.

Not anymore.

"I'm a grown man, Tyler! Who I'm dealing with has got absolutely nothing to do with you, nor is it any of your damn *business.* You better watch yourself and the way you speak to me, boy. *You* don't pay my bills; *I do.*" I point a finger. "The second you start is the second you can have an opinion," I snarl at him, angry but not surprised at Tyler's disrespect.

He's unfortunately just like his mom. Not knowing when to keep his mouth shut.

Tyler holds his hands up, backing off. "Look, okay, I'm *sorry*. All I'm saying is that I need a break."

I feel my face flush as all the blood rushes to my head. I clench my hands, truly irritated and taken aback at his words.

"A break, Tyler? You've barely even started!" My eyes narrow, and I gesture a hand. "You just began your studies in June! It's the end of *July*! What the hell are you talking about right now? Have you lost your ever-loving mind, Tyler? I have your tuition paid up until May of next year!"

Tyler narrows his eyes back and leans forward himself, betraying irritation, and dare I say it, jealousy? "Well, we can't all be super fucking famous psychiatrists who box with billionaires, *dad*. I'm not cut out for college."

"Then what *are* you cut out for, *boy*?" I don't even try to stem it anymore. My voice echos around the kitchen, rough and impatient as I tilt my head, wondering for the first time if this is the day I get into a physical altercation with my own son. My boy. "I had you in foreign language classes, instrumental lessons, sports, theater, martial arts. *Anything* that I could get you in to pique your interest, and you didn't want anything to do *with any of it*!" I take a few deep breaths, trying to calm myself. "Your mother coddled you. Every time you wanted to drop out of an activity, she let you. *I* wanted you to stick something out, to show you how consistency pays off. Teach you discipline. What I should have done was send your ungrateful tail to military school."

Pausing, because I feel my speech getting more rapid and cold, I take another deep breath and shake my head.

"All the opportunities in the world that you had at your disposal, and you squandered every one of them because you're lazy, Tyler." I gesture at him, trying to get him to see, to self-reflect.

"I'm *lazy*?" Tyler recoils his head back in obvious disgust as he narrows his eyes at me, his lips turning down into a frown.

The incredulously *clueless* look of denial makes me sick. As if we hadn't had this conversation dozens of times before.

"Yes!" I yell, slapping the side of my hand into my palm. My eyes flash angrily, beyond furious. "Lazy! You're *lazy*! If you had to *run* to fall into some pussy, I doubt at this point you'd even break a sweat to even accomplish that! You need to do better!" I finish, pointing my finger once more.

"*Hellloooo*," my ex's high, sickeningly happy voice sounds out from the foyer, making me wince.

Unaware of the argument we are currently embroiled in, Hannah walks through the threshold into the kitchen, just letting herself in like she still lives here.

My eyes go to Tylers. "You unlocked the door?" He at least has the grace to look ashamed.

What the fuck.

I close my eyes, throw my head back in defeat, run my hand down the back of my head and grip my neck hard.

Her tall heels click onto the floor as she sashays over to Tyler. I take a half-second to assess her: her blonde hair is styled into a long bob, and her wrap dress hugs her slender frame tightly. My teeth clench with irritation when her gray eyes meet mine cooly. I can tell she's had recent work done on her face, and the fact that I know she's stealing from Tyler's account to pay for it makes me want to punch my fist through a wall.

Backing up, I resume leaning against the counter, tapping my fingers rhythmically on the smooth surface while ignoring her. I'm seething mad at Tyler, and I just know that she's going to be nonchalant with him about this like she always is. She only feels this way because I pay for it.

Maybe if she'd ever cared to spare a dime for Tyler, she'd have been more invested in him.

My phone pings two times in a row, and I pull it out, turning my eyes away from the two of them.

Ever one for appearances, Hannah's busy obsessively picking her ridiculously pointed nails through his hair, trying to fix the strands. She murmurs quietly, asking how his trip was and if he'd forgotten he'd planned to see her tonight. As always, when they're around each other I'm forgotten, so I tune them out, their low voices fading to the background.

Leaving them to it, I read the two texts from Sarah. My shoulders relax out of their tense state as a rush of warmth fills me, replacing the almost unbearable irritation I feel towards the two of them. She sent a picture of her and a blue-grey Russian cat that she's smushed her face up against, making a kissy face.

Sarah Bella [5:25p]: Meet Bunny! I pick her up next week when we get back!

This woman named the cat *Bunny?*

I tap out a quick reply, ignoring Hannah fussing over Tyler's appearance.

Alex [5:26p]: That's the most adorable bunny I've ever seen in my life, almost as adorable as her new mom.

"Ew, why are you smiling like that?" Tyler's voice pulls me back from my momentary lapse of concentration.

I clear my throat, finding the sternness dissipating even more. Looking up from my phone, keeping my eyes on Tyler's as I slide it in my back pocket, not caring to grace Hannah with any sort of acknowledgment. The woman irks my goddamn nerves. The fact she's even standing in my kitchen is torture enough; I don't want to have to look at her, too.

"Tyler," I heave a slow breath, steeling myself, "you can finish out your studies for the year and figure out if foreign politics is something you really want to pursue, or you can drop out and then find a way to pay me back for the tuition I've wasted," I say decisively. "Up to you. This is your life; I can't live it for you, and I can't want these things more than you want them for yourself."

My mind starts to ease with this realization, the tight grip of years-long stress and worry loosening.

I swallow hard as emotions I didn't want to feel rise to the surface. I'd been harboring so many hopes and dreams for my kid that are obviously not welcomed, or wanted.

Despite how tense I am, Tyler pushes back, his eyes wide. "But, *Dad,* you won't even miss the money! You're *loaded—*"

My chin dips, and my eyes harden as anger takes the dominate role in my emotions. I will *not* let him go there. Not tonight, not anymore. I'm not a bank. I don't care how many zeros are in my account.

"Don't tell me what I won't miss," I snap. "Like I said, the choice is yours. *And my house is not a hotel.* If you drop out and have no ambitions, no goals, and no sense of direction, *then you can't live here.* Sorry. I'm giving you tough love, son." My eyes prick at the hurt look in his as I try my damnedest to let go.

It's hard, but doable.

"*Alexander Richardson*!" Hannah admonishes, turning to face me, her expression somehow managing to look shocked despite all the botox, fillers, and a mini face lift. "You'd abandon your own *son*?"

God knows I don't want to talk to this woman right now. Fuck.

My eyes slowly slide to hers, and unable to completely mask my inner feelings, my voice rises. "He's abandoning *himself,* Hannah! Why don't either of you two see that? I'm *done* fighting. Do what you want; it's your life. But *I'm* done letting people freeload off me like they're entitled to *my* money. I didn't drop out of school even when shit got hard. You think I didn't want to maybe a thousand times? *I* didn't whore my way through college instead of studying. You know this Hannah; *you were there!"*

Hannah blinks and recoils her head as a nasty look morphs her sharp features.

Scoffing, I give my head a slow shake. "You think I didn't want to fuck around with other kids my age and be irresponsible sometimes?" I continue. "Of course I did. But instead, I always kept *two jobs* to keep us afloat when we needed it. You forget about that? *Huh?* All those *years* I spent killing myself to make sure we had a roof over our heads so I could make *this* happen?" I motion with irritation around the house I can't stand, before pointing at Hannah who has the audacity to roll her eyes. "And I didn't even want this! *You wanted it!"*

"Now that's not fair—" Hannah hisses, her eyes narrowing.

But I narrow mine back, interrupting her. "And I did it all by myself while *you* sat back with your feet up and collected on the checks, with no desire to go to school or get a job yourself. I barely slept for *years*. I worked hard for *everything* I have, *everything* I was able to give you, and *you,* Tyler," I turn my gaze to him now, "while you were growing up. And the two of you put no effort into *anything*—"

"I was the fucking *trophy* wife! *That's what I was there for!*" Hannah yells, slapping her hand on the island. Her lips pull tight, and that grating voice washes over me, scratching over the overworked nerve endings and synapses like sandpaper.

Her eyes narrow impossibly further across the space at me, and I throw her a dirty look in response, truly sick of the woman.

"A trophy wife who didn't have *two brain cells* to knock together. If you were going to stay home, the least you could have done was raise our son correctly. That was literally your *only* job, Hannah! You enabled our son to fuck off all the time, and now look at him. *Look at him!"* I yell back, fighting for control over myself and breathing hard.
"I couldn't do it all by myself. I was just *one person*, trying to do the job of three people."

I shake my head, now bone tired and wishing I could just have had this time to talk with my kid without her interference. Which makes me even more upset, somehow, at the knowledge that there will never be a day I could be rid of this woman.

"I didn't want you to stand at my side and look pretty. I wanted a *partner*; I wanted you to show initiative, show joy in something other than spending money." My eyes narrow. "You had talent. Potential. I didn't want to be the only thing providing your happiness. What if I had died, and it all went away?"

"Your life insurance would have been fine enough for me to live off of," Hannah spits at me, her gray eyes turning colder than I'd thought possible.

The words ricochet like a gunshot throughout the kitchen before an eerie silence descends upon the room. It's broken quickly, however, when Tyler's head snaps to the side, and he gapes at her in horror. *"Mom, what the hell!"* he says in a hushed voice. "Why would you say that?"

I recoil slightly, feeling like she stabbed me in the heart.

That was by far the worst thing she's ever said to me, and she's said a lot of nasty things to me throughout the years.

A muscle ticks in my jaw as I just stare at her for a second, disbelieving I'd ever, and I mean *ever,* dropped my seed inside this hellacious bitch.

"Do you know how difficult it was for me to hold everything together for this family without any appreciation, or even a smidgen of effort from either one of you?" I meet her eyes with a tired sadness, not even feeling strong enough at this point. "That's why I couldn't give you what you wanted, Hannah. All you wanted to do was take. And all I did was give. And I don't believe I even got so much as a thank you, *from either one of you.* That's all I needed to hear."

My eyes flicker to Tyler, who's busy looking down at the island. I stare for a moment, but he won't even lift his head to meet my gaze.

"We did so much wrong, Hannah. I take responsibility for the part I played in the failure of our marriage. You know from our counseling sessions how incredibly burnt out I was from working two jobs and trying to get through school. I was so depleted physically and emotionally that I had nothing left to give you. Our balance was off... but you know as well as I do that I truly did the best I could with the hand I was dealt." I glance down, knowing my next words will be harsh, but I need to get them off my chest. Finally say what's been on my heart, and what I never allowed myself to say before tonight. Looking back up, I firm my voice. "I want you to know that even though I am so thankful for Tyler," my eyes go back to hers, "you are my only regret in life. I wish to God that when I first saw you, I would have kept moving and never looked back." Her face flushes, and her eyes widen, stunned. "Now get your disrespectful ass out of my house, and *knock* the next time you come over."

I turn and walk out of the kitchen to my study, not understanding why she's so stunned. Other than me regretting her existence, we've talked about all of this in marriage counseling before I decided to divorce her. I figure she's just putting on an act for Tyler. Like she always does.

Closing my office door, I pull up the picture of Sarah again, wishing I could just leave and see her perform tonight. But even though I'm frustrated with Tyler, my son *is* here, and I'd promised to have dinner with him.

We might not see eye to eye on everything, and we for sure have a great deal to figure out, but I'm not going to just fuck off on the one night I get to spend with him in weeks, no matter how much I desire to see Sarah. There would be other times, hopefully. But tonight, Tyler needs me. And no matter what Hannah says, I won't abandon my son for a woman, for anyone.

The start of that behavior could lead to the beginning of something unhealthy.

I give myself a few minutes alone in my study, following the box-breathing video Sarah had sent me, and wait until I'm sure Hannah is gone. Striding through the threshold of the kitchen, my heart lurches at the sight of Tyler sitting at the island, looking more dejected than I've ever seen him.

Slowly and quietly, I walk to him and put a hand on his shoulder, waiting patiently. After a second, Tyler glances up at me, his eyes red.

"I can't believe she said that to you, Dad—about the life insurance. I'm so sorry," he says thickly. "You didn't deserve that. I *know* I've been fucking up, and I am sorry. I just don't know what to do. I feel so lost. I love you. And I'm sorry if my choices and the way I've acted makes you feel like I don't."

Fuck.

"Come here, son." I hold my arm out. I'm cautiously relieved when he leans forward and places his head on my shoulder. I swallow past the lump in my throat. "Well, we're going to start by getting into family therapy, son. Me and you. And I love you too, boy, even if you piss me off." I place a hand on his head and press him into my shoulder harder, wrapping my other arm around Tyler's shoulders. I sniff as my eyes well up, making the room blurry. "You're my son. I'd do anything for you...*give* anything for you, Ty."

My chest tightens painfully at the small sob that issues forth. His tears are the final blow for me, and I let my emotion out. All the years of pent-up frustration and shit that I've been fighting so hard for bubbles up, and I shudder. A tear slides down my face, and I roughly wipe it away.

"I'm sorry, dad," Tyler croaks.

I nod, firmly patting his back. "We're going to be okay, Ty. Because we have each other. I'll always be here for you. I hope you know I only want the best for you, son. I love you more than anything in the world."

Tyler and I stand leaning together at the island and cry for long minutes.

We'll be okay. I think. As I listen to him cry, my mind whirls with so much regret. My heart breaks for him because I didn't choose the right mother for him. I wish things were different...wish I had a chance at a do over. Because I'd do it so differently. Starting with the woman I would pick to have my children.

At that thought, images of Sarah pop in my head, and I think of her pain.

Of how sorrowful she was the night she lost her baby. And I wonder about the unfairness of it all. That someone like Hannah had such a blessed, privileged life and a child, and she couldn't do right by him. Squandered her blessings with her selfishness.

And Sarah, who I instinctively know would have been eternally grateful for having the kind of life Hannah had, and the opportunities therein, got handed the life she was dealt. It's senseless.

We break apart and scrub a hand down our faces, each of us giving each other a sheepish look.

"You alright?" I ask, and he nods, before getting off the stool to walk to the fridge. Noting that he's embarrassed, I put some music on to help ease the tension as we start dinner. We talk about his latest love interest and his friendships in Spain while he stands next to me and chops the ingredients to make a broccoli alfredo and salad. It's Tyler's favorite; I only eat it when he's home.

As we work I can't help but smile, secretly thinking how well Sarah would fit in, if she ever wanted to. Maybe if she was here, we'd be having bolognese.

I pick up my phone to text Sarah back.

Alex [6:02p]: I can't wait to hold Bunny! Do you think she'll like me?

Sarah Bella [6:04p]: =D Crying laughing.

Alex [6:04p]: What's so funny?

Sarah Bella [6:05p]: Nothing at all. Let's just cross our fingers and hope for the best. Are you having a good day?

I contemplate telling her what's going on, not wanting to worry her by sharing the fucked-up issues between me and Hannah. She has her own ex to think about.

Alex [6:06p]: It's gotten so much better now that I heard from you. Can I save that picture as your photo on my phone?

Sarah Bella [6:07p]: Lol, sure, send me one of you to save as well. Have a great night with your son. Gotta go.

CHAPTER THIRTY-ONE

Flighty Conversations

Utterly exhausted, I spend Saturday morning sleeping in after my performance the night before. I know I've been pushing myself too hard since my miscarriage, but I just don't have the time or the finances to take the break I know I need. So the band offered to have last night be a love ballad night, and thankfully I was able to sit and sing easy love songs for the audience. But it still wore me out.

The audience loved it, nevertheless, and gave us an extra-long standing ovation, which helped to bolster my self-confidence in my hobby.

I go back to the animal adoption center and spend time playing with Bunny. Alexander texts me again, seemingly just as anxious about this trip as I am.

Alex [2:30p]: Are you sure you have everything you need? Here's the room. I booked us a double bed.

He sends me a picture of the suite, and honestly, it somehow makes me even more anxious seeing two beds instead of one. Because all I'm going to be thinking about is how we've shared a bed before, how badly he wanted to stay with me my first night in my apartment, and how I didn't call him because I wanted to prove to myself I could be strong.

Smiling, because he's such a gentleman, I reply back.

Sarah Bella [2:31p]: Yup! I have everything I need, and maybe a bit extra too. haha. You didn't have to show me the booking, silly. I trust you.

Alex [2:32p]: Do you?

My heart pounds at those two words, and I flush at the sudden memory of how he wanted to hear me tell him that I wanted to please him. What do I say, what do I say, what do I say?

The truth?

What if the truth....*starts something?*

Sarah Bella [2:34p]: Yes. I think I can trust you.

I head to my car and sit for a minute before pulling out, letting myself feel these foreign feelings of arousal that I haven't been able to feel for so long. And though I wanted to prove to myself that I can be brave, I apparently am not brave enough yet to flirt back so boldly. So, I chicken out and send him a couple of pep talk videos of how to not be nervous and how to be animated with the crowd for his upcoming speech.

However, it's probably stupid because he'd been in his line of work for years. But I do it to be helpful anyway, just in case. Honestly, I need a pep talk myself because I'm so nervous about sharing a room with him. Not because I'm nervous to be with him, but I'm nervous at being around him. Because somehow, *someway,* I'm developing feelings for him, and it scares me.

Thinking to soothe his anxiety once I'm home, I send him a picture of my purple luggage and carry-on that's stuffed to the brim with hair products and anything else I could need. I also made sure I packed my brand-new credit card that has a twenty-grand limit, just in case anything should go sideways while I'm out of the country.

I don't want to ever be stuck in a situation where I feel helpless like I did with Brandon.

Jerome and Christopher come over as promised later in the evening for dinner, and we binge on our favorite show and rice crispy treats, chocolate chip cookies, M&Ms, and wine. Enjoying each other's company. And let me tell you, I've missed them like hell, and it's *much* needed. They annoy me to no end asking about Alexander, and I can't help but catch the disappointed look on their faces when I explain to them that he's just a colleague.

No matter these feelings inside of me, it's true. He is just a colleague that happened to be in the wrong place, at the wrong time.

The reminder sobers me.

What do I look like trying to rush right into dating or anything else after what I went through? But...I'm lonely. And I miss how easy it was with Alexander when I was at his house for those few days. Yet, things continue to feel much easier when Brandon isn't present, and I chalk up the feeling to me finally being free from the clutches of an abuser.

I reaffirm myself to stay committed to my healing journey. Yet I long for the day where I won't be lonely anymore.

Early the next morning, I yawn and stretch, waiting in the lobby for Alexander to show up in the ride he'd ordered for us.

I glance at my luggage, feeling another blast of relief because I didn't want to embarrass myself in front of him with a ratty suitcase. It's a nice set. A gift from my parents a couple years ago when I'd started making enough money to travel frequently back and forth.

Anxious, I smooth a hand down my sleek ponytail, pulling the long strands over my shoulder to the front. I'd had to get up at one-thirty in the morning in order to make sure I was ready enough to leave at three, when Alex said he would be pulling up. A little self-conscious about my appearance, I turn my head to glance in the mirror of the lobby. My cheeks are still flushed because I'd used my vibrator right before I came down, trying to get a last minute orgasm in before the trip.

I straighten my simple white tank top and gray low-slung sweat-pants, and look down at my toenails. They're a fun dark blue, and would normally cause me a lot of joy; however, right now I feel guilty for letting Alexander pay for them. Even though he insisted it would be a housewarming gift, that guilt still eats at me because I'm not used to a man doing things like this. I haven't been able to stop thinking about it since then...I just wasn't prepared to find he'd given me a *year's* supply. I was in total shock standing at the register in the nail salon yesterday.

The manicurist patted my back while I broke down in tears.

Lost in my thoughts, I startle when my phone pings loudly.

Alex [2:53a]: Are you downstairs? We're pulling up, around the corner at the light.

Sarah Bella [2:53a]: Yes, been down in the lobby waiting for five minutes.

Alex [2:54a]: Did you double check you had your passport, your ID, and backup credit card? Not that you'll need any money... but I know you'll feel better with it.

I smirk, sending him a picture of my travel wallet that houses all my necessary documents with my thumb in the way, showing slightly longer nude-colored nails.

Alex [2:55a]: Good girl, so prepared. I like it.

Alex [2:55a]: Your nails are nice. What shape is that?

Alex [2:56a]: We're here, come outside.

Putting my fingers to my lips, I feel my face turn red and shake my head. I'm giddy at seeing him call me a "good girl," never imagining myself having a praise kink.

When the car pulls to the front, I stand and roll my luggage out into the humid night air and am hit with such a wave of shyness that I don't quite know what to do with myself. The car hasn't even pulled to a complete stop yet before Alexander opens the door and jumps out. He strides to me with a wicked grin, and I can't help the soft smile on my face when he leans in to take my bags. The trunk pops open with a click, and I watch while he quickly places them next to his.

He turns his head to look over at me, that grin of his deepening. Despite the smile, his effortlessly smoldering stare is so intense I take an involuntary step back. He acts unfazed though.

"Hey you," he murmurs. His voice, a bit deeper and huskier than normal, has me floundering, as does the smile he treats me to. To my shock, it makes me weak and my panties wet. I'd brought several extra pairs, just in case.

"Hey." Dammit, why do I have to sound so *breathless?*

As he turns his back to me, reshuffling our luggage, my eyes lower slowly, taking a second to admire his outfit. He'd also chosen gray sweatpants and a dark gray t-shirt, ironically. A rush of pleasure flows through me at how good he looks and how good it's going to feel to match with him. Though it wasn't planned, something akin to confidence blossoms inside me at the prospect of doing something so mundane with Alex that I'd never really done with Brandon.

“Squoval, by the way,” I say with a grin.

I cover a yawn and lift a hand, trying to rub my eye in a way that won't mess up my mascara. Alexander closes the trunk with a bang and turns back around, looking me up and down. "Good morning," he says in a playful tone, bending down to give me a hug.

A full body shiver wracks my body when he runs a hand down my ponytail in a gentle caress.

As his arms pull me in, I melt slightly as his clean masculine scent also envelopes me, and I can't help but let out a small moan at the smell of him. My nipples tighten, and my pussy clenches at just the feel of him so close. The warmth of his body seeps into mine through the thin fabric of his gray t-shirt, making it all worse.

Unbeknownst to my suffering, he pulls away and chucks me under the chin, giving me a little squeeze. "So, what's squoval?" He turns, opening the rear car door for me.

"My nail shape," I reply with a small smile, getting in the car. I lean forward, greeting the woman who's driving us. "Hello, thanks for getting us so early!" I return her cheeky grin through the rearview mirror.

"No problem, miss," she replies before putting her eyes back to the front.

Clicking my seatbelt, I try to keep my eyes averted as Alexander slides into the seat next to me smoothly. I wonder if I affect him as much as he does me. He shuts the door, then reaches over to smooth a heavy hand down my thigh in a move so quick and absentminded that I don't even know if he realizes he did it before his hand disappears, and he shuts the door with a firm bang.

"Ma'am, to the airport please," he rumbles in his deep voice, quickly snapping his seatbelt. I stay still in my seat, blinking and contemplating how on earth he manages to take over all the space in the backseat, especially when he moves to stretch a leg, and then leans to the side to grab his phone from his back pocket. Our driver pulls off, and I watch, amused, as he turns on the flashlight.

"Wh—What are you doing?" I ask, furrowing my brow with a curious grin.

To my surprise, he reaches over and picks my right hand up in a gentle hold before shining the light on my fingers. "Squoval is quite the sexy shape," he mutters, taking me completely aback. So much so my vocal chords freeze. The traitors.

As if he can tell, he flicks me a rather wicked grin and smooths his thumb over my fingers, making my skin tingle.

"Thanks," I say, blinking rapidly and feeling heat creep up my neck.

"Oh, I got you something." Alexander lets my fingers go and reaches to the seat between us. "Here you go, sweetness," he says, handing me a travel coffee.

I'm still not sure how to feel about this nickname I've acquired. But I can admit, it sets me on fire in places that are truly making me suffer because I can't ask him to quench them.

"Oh." The heat creeps from my neck to my cheeks as I take it from him and wrap my hands around the warmth. *"Thank you so much...*I should have brought you something..." I shake my head, feeling stupid. "I wasn't thinking. It's early, and I'm *not* an early bird I'm afraid." I huff a sigh and throw him an apologetic look. "You're getting the room and everything—"

"You like to sleep in, hm?" he interrupts quickly and gives me a chuckle, dropping his gaze to my lips before he turns his face back to the front. "Leyla, when are we supposed to arrive at the airport?"

"We're set to be there in twenty minutes, Dr. Richardson," she replies, turning onto the highway.

We fall quiet, but I can feel his gaze on me. I try to ignore it, a little intimidated by him still. However, Alexander continues to stare at me until I relent and turn to face him.

"Did you get your toes the same color?"

"No, my toes are blue," I giggle. "Party on the bottom, professional on the top." Leaning back into the leather seat, I cross my legs, happy that it doesn't pull as bad on my back anymore.

He gives me another slow, assessing look. "Why are your cheeks so red... are you okay?" he enquires with an arched brow.

I quickly avert my face from his piercing gaze, embarrassed at having been caught in the after effects of pleasuring myself. "No reason. I guess I'm just excited is all," I answer softly, hiding a smile. His eyes bore into the side of my face for a long second, and I fight breaking out into a full on sweat because I feel like he knows what I did.

"Hmm," he hums, finally looking away and setting me free of all his intensity.

He swipes his phone unlocked, pulls up his itinerary, and begins to scroll through it. I pull out my own phone when it dings with an incoming message from Vanessa, who I nicknamed Nessie.

> Nessie [3:06a]: Hey lady, I emailed you a demo to listen to. I know it's early, but I figured that you guys are heading to the airport right about now, right? Unless you slept in and missed your flight. In that case, that SUCKS.

"So have you been working on any songs on your cello?" I ask him kindly, not wanting to be rude while I'm tapping back a reply. Alexander side eyes me curiously, but I keep my attention on my phone. "Like, do you know a lot of songs?"

"Yes. I can play a lot of pieces, actually. Any you want to hear or you'd recommend?" he replies.

Sarah [3:09a]: No, we didn't sleep in. We're in the uber headed to the airport now. I'll give it a listen while we're waiting to take off. This the one for B, right? I'm so excited for you! You're so lucky!

Sarah [3:10a] Why are you up so early any-ways?

"*Well,* that really depends solely on if you can do Braveheart justice?" I tease, throwing him a wry grin and giving a little laugh before looking back at my phone that dings with Vanessa's reply.

Nessie [3:11a]: Soooo what do you mean "we" didn't sleep in? You and Alex spent the night together? Also, got a baby remember? He takes his feeding this time of night normally. Yes, it's for B. I hope you like it. Also, are you and Alex for sure coming to the pool party next weekend? We need to expand our friendship group.

Alexander grunts softly. "You don't have to insult me," he says quietly, giving me a scowl before looking back at his phone.

"Shouldn't be an insult. Your fingers look *insanely* talented when you play." I look over to see him now flipping through pictures of the resort. His eyes suddenly snap to mine. My heart skips a beat, and I swear all the air leaves the car as we stare each other down.

"*Very* talented. In more ways than one," he replies lowly.

My eyes widen in shock, and what air that *is* left in the car thickens between us, causing my lips to part as I attempt with everything in me to breathe normally. By some act of divine intervention, I manage to turn my face away and fight back an embarrassed smile when I see our driver eyeing me with a little grin of her own in the rearview mirror.

Flushing, I peek over shyly at Alexander. He wets his lips, his eyes darting down to mine before turning his attention smoothly to his phone.

He clears his throat, sounding a bit hoarse as he says, “So, I looked up that hostel you were telling me that you had originally booked, and I’m so happy I made you leave that place. Did you see the reviews?" He taps rather hard on his screen. "It’s barely two stars and looks like a place someone takes you to *kill* you,” Alexander mutters, pausing on a picture of the resort's pool next to the Pacific Ocean.

“Look, beggars can’t be choosers, and we can’t all have deep pockets, you know? It would have been fine. You just didn’t want to see me in a run-down hotel with your *snobby self*,” I tease, shamelessly flirting while typing out a quick reply to Vanessa.

“You’re damn right about that." Alexander glances over at me for a second before looking back down. "And it wasn’t even a *motel*; it was a hostel. You were about to share a room with a *stranger*. A potential ax murderer.” He pulls up another picture of a dining room and narrows his eyes, giving it an interestingly close inspection.

He's quiet for a second when a picture of chocolate cake pops up on the screen, and I *swear* that I see his fingers shake ever so slightly.

Grinning, I tilt my head, thinking this guy's really got a thing for food. It's kind of cute because you'd never tell it by looking at him. “Aren’t *you* kind of a stranger, though?” I say, purposefully digging at him.

Grinning down at my phone, I ignore him. The sound of my nails tapping lightly on the screen fills the silence while I go back and forth with Vanessa. In my peripheral I see him look at me sharply. He recoils his head slightly in obvious offense.

“See?" I whisper quietly, still concentrating on my phone. "*Cancer baby.*”

The energy that emits from him shifts slightly, making me burn up even more somehow with a mixture of nervousness and arousal. I'm ashamed to say that it pleases me that I'm able to get under his skin just a little.

"No, no *Cancer nothing*. I am not a stranger, Sarah." The way he says my name makes a shiver roll through my body, but I keep my eyes studiously on my phone in an attempt to appear at ease. "We've known each other since you were in grad school, technically," he continues. His deep voice sounds out harshly across the small space between us, and I can tell I've touched a pretty sensitive nerve.

I turn my face and give him my best smile. That burn deepens when his eyes lower to my mouth before sliding back up to my eyes. I try to keep my gaze from wavering at the intensity because, man, I wonder if he truly knows just how deep his pierces when it's trained on you.

"Nooo, I've known your colleague *David* since I was in grad school," I correct, twisting my lips at the way his brow lowers. "You know, the psychiatrist who actually *bothered* to give me the time of day? *You* I just met. For real." Not able to help myself, I smile softly, wondering just how deep I can dig.

I don't know how it's possible, but his eyes turn even more stormy.

He narrows them at me before clearing his throat and looking back down at his phone. "Hm. Alright, well, we'll be seeing about that. Won't we?" he mutters, still shifting through pictures on his phone.

Sarah [3:19p]: No, Vanessa, we didn't sleep together. He picked me up from my place in an uber. I'll text you back when I listen to the demo. Can Alex listen to it?

Nessie [3:20a]: Yes. So, are you two sharing a room at the resort?

Nessie [3:20a]: Is it a king bed?

Sarah [3:21a]: Why do I have a feeling you're trying to get me laid so bad? LOL!

Nessie [3:21a]: Becaauussssee. It seems like you two have mad chemistry, and I want to know when it finally happens!

Sarah [3:22a]: Vanessa, I'm trying not to. Like so hard. Please don't tempt me!

I shove my phone back into my purse on a deep exhale and lean my head back on the headrest. I stare out the window, watching the lights whiz by as I lose myself in my thoughts. I know Alexander and I have chemistry; I just don't know if I have the energy to trust again. I don't know if I *want* to trust again. It just seems like too much of a risk.

My last relationship cost me *everything*.

When we exit the ramp, and the runway lights of the airport shine brightly in the distance, I yawn widely. Alexander chuckles as if amused.

I turn to face him. "Hey, you want to listen to Vanessa's new demo? It's the one for B. She just sent it," I say, plugging in my earphones. I don't want the driver to hear it in case of some sort of confidentiality rules.

"Oh, man. Why's she up so early?" Alexander queries, accepting the ear bud and leaning in closer so it'll reach. His warm, clean scent hits me even harder along with the minty scent of his toothpaste, and

I feel myself slicken between my legs. It surprises me because it's been so long since I've felt desire like this.

"Baby feeding," I whisper back, hitting play right as we pull into the terminal. We have to wait a bit in line before being dropped off, but not that long because we're pulling up to the curb right when the song ends.

"Damn, I can't wait to hear that in concert," Alexander says with a short smile.

He hands back the earphone when our driver comes to a stop to let us out. He unloads our bags, and we stay quiet while we check our bags in and make our way to the gate. In a companionship so comfortable that I'm afraid I've made a monumental mistake agreeing to come on this trip with him, because I feel myself falling.

And the last time I fell like this, the glass shattering wasn't near as loud as my heart splintering to pieces.

CHAPTER THIRTY-TWO

PUSHING THROUGH

"THE FLIGHT IS A little over five hours. Are you going to sleep, or are you going to push through?" I ask conversationally, placing my carry-on bag next to hers in the seat between us.

"Well, considering we're gaining three hours of time, I might nap on the plane and then explore the resort. Those pictures you sent me looked nice! And right off the Pacific Ocean, too? This place has a very pretty view, and it looks like they set you guys up so well..." She smiles, ducking her head down in an adorably shy move. "I'm a little jealous, to be honest," she says in a low tone.

"Well, now you get to see it in all its glory for yourself." I smile, pulling out my phone to let Tyler know that I'll be temporarily out of service until we get to Vancouver.

To my surprise, he texts back immediately with a thumbs-up emoji and good luck message, which is a great sign because it means he didn't sleep the morning away and is hopefully in class.

Admittedly, I'm *really* looking forward to being out of the country with Sarah. And the fact that we're going to be staying in such a beautiful, lush plot of land at the five-star resort in Vancouver really stokes my anticipation to be alone with her. Selfishly, I hope she loves it. It's right off the ocean and boasts great views and opportunities to see wildlife, but I'm especially anticipating watching a sunrise with her more than anything.

We have a room with private patio, and I'm already concocting scenarios to get her out there.

"Would you like to get a drink while we wait? Plane doesn't take off for an hour," I say, seeing she's craning her head and looking at the various restaurants and stores within the airport. It's so early there's only a handful of places open, though, so we'll have to settle.

"A drink this early in the morning?" she asks playfully, turning her head to look at me with a mischievous grin that I meet with one of my own.

"Why not? Airport rules defy the laws of society. Didn't you know that? It's the only place we can be in pajamas at four in the morning and drink alcohol, and no one bats an eye," I say, rising out of the seat and holding my hand out to her. "Come on, I won't tell anyone if you don't!"

She bites her lip before shrugging her shoulders and letting me pull her up. My skin tingles at the first touch. I attempt to be smooth about it while I work to entwine my fingers with hers and hold on, praying she doesn't pull away.

She doesn't.

Ten minutes later, we've found a quaint breakfast place and are sitting down with mimosas, a breakfast sandwich for me, and a breakfast wrap for her. Her phone pings a couple of times with a notification, jogging my memory about my colleague and his intentions towards what I want.

"So..." I flick my eyes up to Sarah's, who's busy sipping on her mimosa. "Did you ever figure out what David wanted?"

She gives me an adorable crooked grin and leans forward a bit, eyes sparkling like she has a juicy secret. "Well, turns out he wanted me to join him for *dinner*," she says.

I tense, watching as she picks up her wrap and takes a big bite, blissfully unaware of how bothered I am.

I already know that. I just wanted a way to broach a subject that had been bothering me and figured this was the most organic, non-confrontational way. But I don't care for the way she said "dinner" as if she knows that's a hot spot for me.

"*Hmm-hm,*" I hum slowly. "And what did you say back?" Curiosity gets the better of me, but I'm somehow strong enough to feign nonchalance, picking up my drink for a healthy swallow.

Her eyes fall to my throat, and the look that enters her eyes for a fleeting moment is positively mesmerizing.

"Oh...*uhm...*" Her gaze falls down to her wrap, and she spends a second ripping off a piece of the tortilla. She places it carefully on the wrapping paper and pauses for a heartbeat. A tense moment passes before eyes rise once more to mine with a sadness I haven't seen since she was recovering at my home. I shift in my seat, uncomfortable with that knowledge. "It's rude, but I didn't reply to him," she says, pursing her lips contemplatively.

"Why not?"

Her brow furrows. "The truth is I just don't know how to say it in a way that's not going to ruin our professional relationship."

I hum, tapping my fingers on the table.

"Another truth is I don't know if I can trust myself to be in a relationship right now." She takes a deep breath, and it takes everything in me to prevent myself from reaching forward and taking her hand back into mine. She waves a hand absentmindedly, her eyes becoming vacant with a faraway look. "I compromised and ignored *so* many red flags with Brandon. I need to build myself up stronger, you know?" she finishes, crossing her legs and swinging a foot nervously.

"Yeah, I understand completely. Thank you for sharing."

We fall into a weighty silence, but on the inside, it's anything but.

My heart squeezes rather painfully, and I take a minute to chew my sandwich while I probe all the emotions surging throughout me. There's a healthy dose of relief because Dickhead David isn't going to be a problem, at least not right now, anyways. And pride because I know she's been through a lot and is taking the steps to build herself back up. Yet there's disappointment also because I really, *really* want this woman, but I'll wait for her.

Dickhead David can just fuck right off as far as I'm concerned, I muse, tilting my head when she turns her eyes back to mine. Finally gracing me again with her gaze.

"That's very smart of you, Sarah," I continue, in a desperate bid to break the silence, since she isn't. "Many people tend to jump back in too fast after a bad break up. So, it's good to see you taking time for yourself."

At her slightly coy expression, I allow myself to reach forward and graze my fingers across the back of her hand, wholeheartedly believing my words. Also I want a reason to touch her soft, silky skin again. A little freckle at the knuckle at the base of her thumb catches my attention. For some reason that's allusive, every little thing about her enthralls me. As if in a trance, I stare at her fingers, that beautiful thumb of hers giving away that she's double-jointed.

Her bones feel so fragile beneath my touch, and the urge to protect her wraps even tighter around my heart.

Sarah huffs a breath, averting her eyes in obvious shyness as the heat of our hands seep into one another, becoming the perfect temperature. It's something so simple, yet causes me such pleasure. We pull our hands back at the same time, and she raises her eyes in amusement, momentarily losing her shyness.

"Thanks, I try. Don't always succeed...but, boy, am I the world's hardest *trier*," she teases. I smile when the corner of her mouth tips up adoringly before she parts her lips to eat another bite of her wrap.

Does she know what she's doing to me? What her little whispers, soft moans, and sounds she makes do to me? It's as if she's divulging riveting, juicy secrets for me to savor.

And savor I will.

Bringing up a hand, I rub my jaw thoughtfully. "Well, at least you have the wherewithal to do that. A lot of people don't try; they're just content on skating through life," I respond, my words coming out a bit more rapid and harder than I'd intended them to.

Like my ex.

My son.

I grimace at the thought. I could give a shit about Hannah, but *Tyler*...that hits personally.

At the unwanted thought, I drape my arm over the back of the chair next to me and shift in my seat. I don't even want to be having these thoughts. But when I'm around Sarah, I don't feel like my mind is my own, and I can't help but compare the two women and how different they are.

Not just physically, but *mentally.*

Sarah nods. "I get that," she says. That vacant look enters her eyes when she's thinking about her ex and her trauma. "I paid our mortgage and all of our bills, started my practice, and took on its financial upkeep without his help. I drive a piece of shit Hyundai, and he paid for next to nothing and spent all his money on a Lexus. I mean.... the shit I *put up* with because he was my first love. I should be committed because I was so stupid. Putting up with so much nonsense was just dumb. Blind as a freaking bat," she states quietly.

She looks down at the table, swaying slightly in her seat.

Understanding that she needs a moment, I sit with her in silence, instinctually knowing that there's nothing I could say to her in this moment that'll matter. She didn't share this with me for advice, or attention, or reassurance. No, I'm noticing she shares bits and pieces of herself with me with no expectation other than for me to listen, though I want to give her more.

As I assess her, the sounds of the airport become louder as more people filter in for their flights. Her eyes finally lift from the table, and shift to the side. Quietly, she watches people walk by with their rolling suitcases, a few of them dragging along crying kids. Everyone's in a hurry. Everyone's anxious and stressed. I feel it. So does she.

Her eyes tighten when a woman walks by us with a baby stroller while arguing with a man, and she suddenly turns her head in the opposite direction, looking back into the café we're at. Her eyes well with tears, and just as I'm about to reach forward and take her hand again, she suddenly speaks up, rubbing lightly across her brow and keeping her face averted from me. "I think I'd like a cookie. Want one, Alex?"

She stands abruptly and walks away without waiting for my reply.

Watching her disappear down a snack aisle and out of my view, I look back and people watch, knowing she needs a minute to herself and not wanting to push too hard. Especially when she's trusting me to bring her on this trip, and I don't want to betray this bud of possibility or her trust in me before it's even started.

She hasn't yet talked about her feelings about the baby she'd lost...Bumpy. And I wonder if she ever will. Or if she's the type to never bring up something like that again, burying it deep inside to never deal with again.

The only glimpse I'd had at any sort of emotions on the matter was when she was crying in my arms on the floor of my office while she was losing Bumpy, and when she'd cried in her sleep that first night at my house.

I collect our trash while she stands at the register to pay for our cookies and throw it away in a nearby receptacle. When I get back to the table, I see her phone light up with an email from *David*. A hot, sickening wave of jealousy washes over me at seeing his name before the notification disappears. I can't even take a slight comfort in the fact that she'd listed him as "psychiatry referral buddy" in her phone.

I clench my jaw with irritation.

Speak of the devil and he shall come, apparently.

Glancing quickly at my watch, I see it's almost four in the morning and scoff, curling my lip with displeasure. It doesn't matter that I've emailed her many times, sometimes around the same time. That's me.

What makes me so special compared to him though? the rational part of my brain muses, right as Sarah comes into view and plops down rather hard onto her seat, scattering five cookies on the table.

"Okay," Sarah says breathlessly, looking rather pink in the face. "We've got marshmallow, which looks delicious, chocolate chip—*my favorite—* oatmeal raisin, *ewww*, and sugar cookie." She nibbles her bottom lip, shifting on her seat and lifting a shoulder. "I don't know what you like, so take your pick."

My eyes roam her face greedily, curious at her change in attitude so soon after being as visibly upset as she was. She shifts in her seat again nervously, her right eyebrow arches, and she brings up a lithe hand and strokes slowly down her ponytail where it lays spilled across her breasts to her navel. I lower my eyes. Breasts are a trigger for me, and if I'm not careful, she'll catch me staring.

She'd only grabbed two of the chocolate chip cookies, so I snag up the marshmallow and oatmeal raisin, leaving her the sugar cookie and chocolate chip ones.

Sarah scoffs, pushing the sugar cookie at me, leaving me with three and her with two. "You know how I feel about sugar," she mutters.

"Yes." I glance down at her lips. "You've made yourself very clear about it, in fact. I think it's very sweet, no pun intended."

Bringing my gaze back to hers, I chuckle, watching as that blush paints her cheeks pink again. It's such a beautiful sight that my laughter trails off into a hum. I tilt my head as that blush in her face and chest deepens, and she ducks her head down once more to break our eye contact, informing me I make her nervous. Emboldened by the knowledge, I can't help the truly inappropriate grin that tilts the corner of my mouth. Making her blush is quickly becoming one of my favorite things to do.

I pitch my voice a little lower and whisper, "One of my goals this trip is to change the way you feel about things that give you pleasure."

Sarah inhales sharply, causing my own body to respond in kind.

Her lips part, her eyes go hooded for a millisecond, and her tongue flicks out to caress her top lip. My dick swells thickly in response, becoming painfully hard where it rests against my thigh. Reminding me how long it's been since I've felt a woman around me in this way. I feel my facial expression settle into the one that I wear at the office as I work to beat my erection down, and it takes every ounce of effort on my part to control myself. I manage it, though.

She looks away nervously, her slender fingers picking at the package of her chocolate chip cookie. The plastic crinkles for a moment before she tightens her grip, tearing it open. "Uhm. I started by buying Bunny," she says hesitantly.

I watch greedily as she picks off a minuscule piece of cookie and puts it between her lips.

Her juicy, plump lips that would look fucking delectable swallowing my cock—I cut my thoughts off, harshly and thoroughly, and I clear my throat. "Yes. She's adorable, by the way," I reply, standing up and swiping up the cookies and my bag. "Let's head back to the gate; they'll be announcing departures soon."

I don't trust myself to take her hand again, so instead I walk a step behind her. Allowing myself to watch her hips sway as she walks. I take in the swishing of her ponytail against the round globes of her ass, flexing my fingers because I'd like to run my hand down it again.

Boarding the plane, we accept our drinks, and both nap on the plane ride to Vancouver. Resting our heads against each other as we sleep.

CHAPTER THIRTY-THREE

Girl's Be Slangin'

A FEW HOURS AND one short connecting flight later, we walk into the plush resort rejuvenated from our nap, and I can't help but glance over at Sarah, seeing her mouth gaped open.

"Careful. A mosquito will fly in there, and you'll have a bite on your throat," I laugh, chucking her under her chin gently and successfully shaking her out of her daze.

She laughs at my joke, and I delight at the sparkle in her eye, wondering if she knows it's there.

"Are *all* the presenters staying here?" she wonders curiously as I walk her to the receptionist area and proceed to check us in.

"How are you doing, ma'am?" I greet the receptionist and then tilt my head to eye Sarah. "Just about, yes."

Sarah watches with an arched eyebrow as the brown-haired woman flirts with me, audaciously sliding me a card with her personal number on it when she hands me our room key. I arch my eyebrow back, not even bothering myself with the woman. She looks away with an amused grin as I slide the card back to the receptionist. "I'm with someone," I clip, giving her a polite smile before turning away and jerking my chin at Sarah to walk with me.

We board the swanky all-mirrored elevator, and I use the reflection to gaze down her body in a quick assessment that she misses because she's busy staring at the numbers going up as we ascend to our floor.

"I made reservations for dinner at four," I say lightly. She's quiet since the interaction, and I work to get us back to where we were. "I figured we might be hungry due to the time difference. We feel like it's seven when it's actually four here." The doors slide open, and I hold out my arm, letting her exit the elevator first.

Walking through, she makes a sharp left, following the signs to our room. "I could eat. What do they have?"

"Not sure," I lie. A white lie. I of course know everything on the menu and have already spent a few nights torturing myself with fantasizing about watching her eat half of it. "And anyways, don't worry about it because I'm paying for your food while you're here."

She stops at a door hidden at the end of the hall and turns to look at me with an arched brow. "Alexander—"

"*Alex*," I shoot back, arching my own eyebrow at her in amusement.

"Alex," she replies slowly with an adorable smile, making my chest tighten. "That is *completely* unnecessary. I can pay for my own food while I'm here. You already got the room." She sucks her bottom lip through her teeth, and I feel my skin catch on fire. Because I want to kiss her so bad I can taste it.

I step forward and look down into her face, getting nice and comfortable staring in her eyes which dilate wider with every microsecond that ticks pass.

"Sarah, don't be rude," I say just as softly.

There it is; her pupils dilated. I rejoice in my head and watch, amused, as her lips part, and she sucks in an indignant breath.

"I wasn't being *rude.* I'm sorry, but I just—*you don't have to—*" Sarah stutters before going silent.

Her face heats up. She glances down at my feet, and I just know that she feels this thing between us. I'm not alone in how badly I want what is growing between us. It's planted deep, and it's so strong I can feel it in the silence.

"Sarah, look at me, please." I tilt my head at her, putting a finger under her chin and pull her back up to meet my eyes, giving her what I pray is a gentle smile and not predatory. "I was only teasing you. You don't have anything to worry about. You're my guest, sweetness. Now, can I not treat my guest how I want?"

Sarah narrows her eyes at me and scrunches up her nose. "Within reason. Yes. Fine, you can pay for my food," she grumbles, adopting a rather adorable pouty face that I've never seen from her before.

"Thanks a lot," I laugh, sliding the room key in the door and pushing it open, gesturing for her to proceed ahead of me.

"Oh, this is so *darling,* Mr. Richardson!" Sarah coos, flicking on the light and going straight to the air conditioner.

My dick swells so hard at her words that a flash of pain radiates through my lower abdomen. *"It's Doct—"* I start to say before pausing, feeling a perplexed then annoyed look cross my face.

"Are you a seventy-two or sixty-eight degree person, *Alex*?" she asks while pausing in front of the thermostat to look over her shoulder, clearly teasing me.

Jesus fucking Christ. I shake my head before attempting to respond.

"Definitely a sixty-eight degree person. Especially at night," I quip, striding through the small sitting area into the bedroom where I pause upon seeing only one bed.

It's a king. Adorned with a plush comforter and lit with dimmed lights above. And it's perfect for fucking. I just know it. I lick my lips and feel my blood boiling, imagining Sarah and me in bed together again. I tense when she walks up behind me.

"I turned it to sixty-eight—" she starts, before her words cut off when she gets a look at the lone bed in the room. *"Oh..."*

There's that silence that says so much.

I clear my throat, flicking my eyes to hers quickly. "Sarah, I swear to God I requested a double bed. I didn't know." My speech is rapid as I try to explain quickly. "I'm going back down to see if we can get another room." I turn to walk back out, but Sarah stops me with a hand on my arm, scrunching her nose at me teasingly.

"Oh, stop. And besides, you know as well as I do that this resort is booked full, and there are no rooms available. It's okay. We've shared a bed before, haven't we?"

I tilt my head, giving her a noncommittal grunt in response before folding my arms. I mean, sharing a bed with this woman is simultaneously the easiest and hardest thing. I hesitate, unsure.

"And it was fine, right? So, if I'm okay, can't *you* be okay?" she nudges me out of my musing, arching a brow at me just as a mischievous smile tugs her lips.

But I keep my gaze on hers, my tongue slicking over my lip. "Yes...I can be okay with that," I reply softly, unfolding my arms to turn back to the living room to get my bag.

She follows me out to grab hers as well and takes her toiletries into the bathroom, placing them neatly, and comes back into the bedroom, looking at me quizzically. "What are you doing?" she laughs, seeing I'd pulled out all the drawers on the left side of the dresser.

"I'm putting my clothes away." My eyes flash to hers humorously, seeing hers wide in her face as she stares at me rather stunned looking. I go back to my task, stacking my clothes neatly.

"Woooww... I thought only women did that."

I snap my head back up to look at her, amused. "Hey now, don't be sexist!" I admonish, taking a stack of shirts and placing them into a drawer.

She holds her hands palm up. "Oops. Not my intention. It's just been a keen observation over the years," she throws back, unzipping her own luggage.

She begins to hang up dress after dress in the closet space, humming some tune while we work in comfortable silence. The both of us are obviously a little mellow from the travel and time change.

I try not to be obvious as I watch her, wanting to see what clothes she'd packed. "You like the TV on or off while you go to sleep?"

"Off. I can't have that type of noise when I try to go to sleep. But I *do* need a fan for a little white noise and to keep me from sweating through my hair. Is that going to be a problem?" she asks, plunking a small pink portable fan onto the shared nightstand and pointing it towards the pillow. She clicks the button, and it hums to life, making me smile.

That's adorable, I think with amusement before pausing, wondering if I can make her sweat bad enough to curl the strands of her hair. My eyes slide to hers, constantly tortured with ways of how to get her to open up to me in this way.

"No," I laugh, quieting as she suddenly gets a grimace on her face. "What's wrong?" I ask, noticing her distress.

"Uhm...so I know we shared a bed for a couple of nights when...*you know*," she emphasizes, sitting on the side of the bed and drawing her legs up in a crisscross style.

Seeing her playful mood has bled into something more serious, I close the last drawer before walking over to her side and sitting in the blue chair.

"I do know," I say, biting the inside of my cheek to keep from elaborating.

" *Well*....well..." She licks her lips, and her eyes flicker from mine to my chest and then back again.

"Just spit it out," I clip, arching my brow but not able to bite back the grin spreading across my face.

"Okay, uh, it's just that sometimes, but not *all* the time, I take my clothes off at night. Like by accident. I'll wake up and won't have anything on." She bites her lip, turning an incredible shade of red.

My heart races, and I'm extraordinarily proud of myself that I'm able to even control my breathing, because her words engorged my already massive erection. Leaning back, I put an ankle over my knee and drape an arm across the armrest, trying to look casual.

"Hm-hmm... I see. *Very unfortunate*," I drawl slowly, keeping my eyes on hers. Not giving into the urge to rake my eyes down her body like I want to. We're supposed to be two platonic professionals sharing a living space for five days. "I already know you do that."

Her eyes fly to mine and widen with surprise. "What? *How?*"

"You did it at my house. But I didn't see anything, I promise," I confess, keeping my eyes steady on hers as the silence of the room drapes over us and magnifies our tension to an almost unbearable level.

I purposefully stay quiet for long moments, letting the silence become heavier and heavier. Letting her know plainly that I want her, and I'm not above making us sit through extended moments of quietness to drive home that fact.

"Oh." She blinks, putting a shaking hand up to her cheek and then over to her nose ring where she starts fiddling with it.

"I'll tell you what though, Sarah," I lean forward to clasp my hands together between my legs, planting my feet on the floor and leveling her with a stare. "If in fact, I should get up before you do, and I see more nude skin in my peripheral vision than is normal, then I will blindly cover you up without looking. Just like I did at my house. Scout's honor." I hold up two fingers.

What color are your nipples? What do they taste like? I think, keeping my expression neutral. *Fuck, the shit I want to do with this woman should qualify me to go straight to the insane asylum.*

"Were you even a scout?" Sarah asks doubtfully, narrowing her eyes at me.

"Not for a single day." I smile my best smile at her, not even crossing my mind to lie to her. My eyes roam, seeing the long length of her hair peeking out from the curve of her hip.

How do we keep from getting it snagged if we're fucking—

"Okay, well, you *could* have lied about that, so good enough for me. Just don't act like you're going blind if you wake up and you see my breasts slangin' here, there, and everywhere, okay?" Sarah says, rolling her lips.

Her cheeks are bright red as she puts a hand to her mouth, her eyes going wide as she stares at me.

I have a half second of awareness before seeing her jump as I suddenly roar with laughter.

I put my my fingers up to the bridge of my nose and squeeze as I lose all control of myself, and just laugh at her fucking *hilarious* joke. Not able to help it, I carry on for a minute before I'm able to calm down and take a deep breath. I have tears in my eyes as I look at her.

She's got her fingers to her lips and is giggling with me, her brows are pinched, and she's looking at me like she thinks I might be going crazy.

"I swear to God, when I get up on stage, and I get a weird case of stage fright or get bored, I'm going to think about what you just said. It might just give me the push I need to finish my speech. Like, instead of imagining the audience naked, I'll just think about their breasts slangin' and stuff." I heave a deep breath, wiping a tear out of my eye. "Oh, shit." I clear my throat softly. "Thank you. Because that was fucking *funny*."

I get up and go into the bathroom, wet a towel, and wash my face carefully. Thinking how no woman has ever made me laugh the way she just did.

I smile at my reflection, and something rises in my chest. An emotion that feels a bit like...fulfillment.

See, you're not the cold-hearted psychiatrist everyone's making you out to be, I think, replacing the towel and checking my teeth in the mirror. Giving my teeth another good brush, I look over and see Sarah's travel makeup case, a small pointy tube of oil, and a white travel tube of what looks to be lipstick.

Turning my head quickly to try to listen for her, I reach over, pick up the heavily embossed plain white tube, and open it. I'm curious as to what color lipstick she likes because I never see her wear any.

My brows rise as the top uncovers *perfume*, not lipstick.

I spit, rinsing my mouth and the sink quickly before taking the small vial between my fingers at the top, and carefully pull, plucking the spray out of the holder, before turning it to read the words engraved on the side. I look around before landing on the tissue on the side of the vanity. I grab a couple, fold them over, and wrap it around the spray before pumping one spray into the tissue. Carefully replacing the perfume where I found it, I double the tissue again.

Holding it to my nose, I groan.

It's her. That's why she smells so fucking amazing. Oh, Jesus. I lament, letting myself have a couple more seconds to savor her scent before shoving the tissue into my pocket.

Walking out of the bathroom I pause, seeing her standing at a full-length mirror and struggling to zip up the side of her dress. She rises on her toes and does a cute little bounce before making a frustrated sound, scowling at herself in the mirror. I hold back a wicked grin, knowing her issue is the full size of her breasts.

My eyes lower slowly down her body, taking in her lush figure.

I fight back the sharp, dizzying wave of arousal that hits me at the sight of her delectable body, and I can't believe I'm so lucky as to be graced with her presence for dinner.

She's wearing a soft, leather-pleated dress that hugs every curve from the waist up before the pleats taper down in a flowy pattern, cutting off at her knee. She continues to struggle with the zipper, the tip of her tongue touching the corner of her mouth. My eyes pause on the long, creamy expanse of bare skin exposed by the zipper halfway up her torso. My groin tightens painfully at the knowledge she's didn't put a bra on for this dress

I inhale deeply, praying for calm.

"Here, let me. Before the girls start slangin' or whatever you said," I joke, seeing her pretty smile as she twists to the side to let me have access to the zipper. She holds her arm up in the air and puts her other hand to her ribcage and pushes.

"It's gotta freaking go *up*," she mumbles, looking down at my hands on the zipper. "Oh God, please don't accidently zip me up in it; I'll scream!" she says, sounding half like she's going to cry. I meet her eyes, giving her a teasing smile as my fingers brush her skin softly. I tug, hearing the teeth of the zipper lock together.

It's going up alright, not because it can't, but because I'm going perfectly slow, enjoying my fingers caressing her naked flesh and the goose bumps that are pebbling on her skin that she probably isn't even aware of. When I get to the top, I fasten the tiny hook and then step back, giving her a thorough perusal.

"Spin," I say, twisting my finger, pleased as she does so easily. I watch the pleats in the dress spread. "I didn't know leather could do that. You look wonderful." My eyes land on her five-inch heels, the tiny straps fastened delicately against her ankles. A little fissure of displeasure enters me because I don't know that she should be wearing heels this high with her back possibly still bothering her.

"Aww, thank you, Alex," Sarah coos, obviously in a good mood and effectively quieting my desire to bring up my unhappiness at her possible discomfort.

She flicks her hair behind her suddenly and bends forward, trying to adjust the top slightly. There's only so much willpower a person gets a day, so I squeeze past her, knowing if I watch her touch her breasts, then I'm a goner.

I pull out my phone and grab a nice pair of slacks and a white button up shirt before heading back into the bathroom. I line up my permanent five o'clock shadow and splash on some aftershave before changing my clothes. Glancing over at her makeup bag again I grin.

Because I definitely have a type, and it's high maintenance women. And it's putting me through hell that Sarah's checking all my boxes but is currently unattainable.

"Alex, it's three-forty! We have to go!" Sarah's soft voice calls through the bathroom door, interrupting my thoughts.

I quickly step out with my travel clothes, put them all into a laundry service bag and grab my wallet off the small side table.

"Well, let's get going then, Ms. Promptu," I tease, flashing her a smile as she walks past me and out the door I hold open for her.

Dinner is a success, and I'm pleased that she doesn't pout anymore after our initial conversation regarding who was paying for dinner. Truthfully, I'd expected more pushback and just knew it was coming when she saw the prices at the resort restaurant. Her face fell slightly as she desperately tried to find something cheap to order, but everything was expensive, so she took a deep breath and ordered a salad and an entrée.

Accompanied by exactly two alcoholic drinks. A red merlot.

We ate together over a small candle on the white linen cloth-covered table, going over things to do in Vancouver, and found she really wanted to take a day just to sight-see. So, we looked up a few things to do on her phone and reserved what we wanted. At the end of the meal, we shared a chocolate cake dessert. The napkin I'd sprayed with her perfume suddenly began burning a hole in my pocket.

I ate the dessert slowly, instinctively knowing how well it would go mixed with the taste of her skin.

If I ever get to, that is. The two licks I got when I'd lost my mind and lapped up the droplet of syrup off her collarbone doesn't count in my opinion.

When we get back to the room, Sarah falls immediately into bed, high heels and all. I chuckle, crouching down to pick up one foot, taking the shoe off before repeating with the other one. "Sarah," I grasp her hand, shaking her gently. "*Sarah*, you need to get into your pajamas."

It's like she doubles down on being limp, so I haul her up by both of her arms and sit her up against my chest. She scrunches her face at me and opens one eye.

"But I'm so *tiirreed*," she moans, trying to fling herself back, but I catch her before she can hit the mattress.

"I know, sweetie," I say back quietly. "But you're not going to blame *me* for the reason you have a pimple on your face tomorrow. Let's get up; I'll help you get your makeup off and unzip your dress."

I pick her up, carry her into the bathroom, set her on the vanity, and pull open her makeup case, finding the makeup remover wipes. She wakes enough while I take her makeup off that I can give her privacy for her to change into pajamas. Then we both fall into bed. Exhausted.

CHAPTER THIRTY-FOUR

BIRTHDAY WISHES

I WAKE UP IN the middle of the night sweltering hot. I try to turn my head but realize I'm weighed down. Disoriented, my heart races in my chest before I realize it's Alexander wrapped around me *again*.

His arm is wedged under my neck and bent at the elbow. One hand is cupping my breast, and his other hand is wedged tightly in the leg of my shorts that had ridden up and is currently trapped between my legs, cupping my pussy. Like, *all* of it.

My breath hitches as heat suddenly floods me all the way from my cheeks to the flesh between my legs that he's encompassing in his wide hand. Biting my lip hard, I realize that's why I'd woken up; I'm aroused. I bite back a whimper, feeling one of his fingers pressed deeply against me, resting against my clit and in between the lips of my sex

Holyyyy shit. Oh my God, how do I get his hand out without waking him up?

I force myself to be still, realizing my shorts and panties are snagged tightly around us both, and every wiggle of my hips ensures I'm a hair's breadth away from waking him up. I try to move gently, cutting off a surprised cry with a hand to my mouth as he suddenly tightens around me, pulling me flush against him as he buries his head into the crook of my neck on a deep groan before settling back into sleep.

How does he sleep so deeply? I wonder, feeling my entire body catch on fire.

"Alex! Alex, I have to pee," I whisper, lying.

Taking his arm and moving it firmly, I grasp his wrist and pull it out from between my legs and roll off the bed in one smooth motion.

"Uh-huh," Alexander breathes, rolling to his back and flinging his arm across his chest. I watch carefully as he settles back deeper into sleep, unaware of what just happened.

I frown, giving him an incredulous look as I stay crouched there next to the bed for a moment just watching him.

I get up, walking to the little bar area and quietly get myself a glass of water. Looking at the open door of our bedroom, I sip my water, putting a hand self-consciously to my hair. Hating that I didn't feel comfortable enough to be able to sleep in a scarf or bonnet around him, and now my hair routine is going to suffer because of it.

Putting my glass down, I crawl back into bed quietly.

Laying there, I silently watch the clock, determined to suss him out. It's not even three minutes before I feel him getting closer. It happens gradually, and I bite back a giggle as he wedges his arm under me to cup my breast and feel him adjust himself minutely until I'm back in the nook of his body.

His hand moves incrementally until it's in a comfortable position against me, and then it's only another minute before I feel his hand sliding along my hip slowly before cupping me over my shorts.

It's exactly fifteen seconds before he make a displeased noise in his throat and restlessly moves his hand, searching until he finds the leg of my shorts and shoves his hand through and presses against my warmth with a deep sigh. As if it settles him to be as close to me as possible.

Wow, this is freaking crazy, I think to myself.

After a couple minutes, I realize I'm completely relaxed and find myself blinking lazily. Also finding that I quite enjoy the heavy feeling of his hand on my pussy, and it's comforting. I close my eyes, feeling Alexander's breath wash warmly over my neck and cheek and lulling me rhythmically back to sleep.

I let go and drift off in the silence, feeling completely safe in his arms.

The next morning I wake up very early, carefully extracting myself from Alexander's hold. I place the comforter back over him and smile at how peaceful he looks. My fingers shake a little as I reach forward, letting myself stroke the hair back off his forehead. Turning, I grab my phone and make my way into the bathroom to start a bath, sitting on the toilet while I wait and flicking through my messages.

Reading them all, I smile, feeling very fortunate for my friends.

David: Happy Birthday Sarah Beara!

Nessie: Hey baby girl, you're 29, can you believe it?! Almost to the dirty thirties! Wish you were here, we could have gotten mad drunk!

Jerome: Sarah Beara, Happy Birthday boo! Tell me, I haven't heard from you, you bitch. Do that man's hips do what I dream they can do? Whew!

Mom: Happy Birthday my darling, sweet, exceptional girl! I love you, sending you big hugs all the way from California! Let me know when you're about to fly back and I'll ship your gift to you!

Christopher: Oh SJ! What was your birthday wish this year?

My eyes widen at the reminder, and I pull my robe back on quickly, hastily making my way out of the bathroom, back through the bedroom, and to the balcony outside, not even casting Alexander a glance. With my heart pounding, I blow out a relieved breath when I realize there are still some stars in the sky. Finding the brightest one, I tilt my head back, close my eyes, and make my wish.

Feeling something cool touch my neck suddenly, I startle. My hands fly up, slapping at it.

Awareness that Alexander's behind me hits me hard, and I calm quickly, feeling a chain begin to settle alongside my neck. I reach up and brush my hands over his, feeling his strong fingers manipulating a necklace slowly underneath my hair.

He was so quiet I hadn't even heard him come out behind me. As he fastens the clasp at my nape, tears flood my eyes, and I'm grateful that I'm facing away from him because right now I'm so vulnerable I don't know that I can look in his eyes. I hadn't been expecting anything from him. Or anyone, really.

He got me a gift? I think, as my fingers trace the necklace delicately, trying to feel what it is. My fingers clasp on a circular stone.

"Alex," I whisper, *"what's this?"*

Touched, I close my eyes, feeling a lone tear slip down my cheek as he places his lips tenderly against the back of my head.

"Happy Birthday, Sarah." Do I imagine his usually cool demeaner softened with warmth as he speaks to me?

Alexander's muscular arms loop around me from behind as he cradles me carefully to his front and begins to quietly sing the "Happy Birthday" song in his deep, strong, and clear voice. He rests his chin on the top of my head and rocks me through it while we stare at the fading stars together, watching the sun rise over the Pacific Ocean.

My heart swells too big to maintain my emotions, and I bite back a sob and turn, throwing my arms around him. "Thank you so much. You know you didn't have to," I whisper in his ear, giving him an extra tight squeeze.

He's bare chested, and my fingers slide over his naked skin that's almost too familiar, as if I've touched him like this a million times. His muscles jump under my fingertips, responding to me. My breath hitches as I feel his strong arms band around my body, splaying against my back, and pull me into him slowly. Molding my curves into his hardness.

He knows just how to touch me. Like *he's* done this a million times.

My nose grazes his neck, and I tense, getting a welcome whiff of his scent. His lips graze my temple and, not able to help myself, I let out a little moan, praying he doesn't hear. But from the sudden and unexpected hardness I feel pressing into my belly, I know he did, and everything in me wants to tell him to take me inside and take me to bed, but this isn't what he brought me here for.

And I instinctively know that some, if not most of this, needs to be on his terms emotionally, just as much as it needs to be on mine.

Throwing abandon to the wind, not caring about propriety and unable to help myself, and just daring to let myself lean into the one thing that I've always wanted but never have been able to attain, I melt into his embrace. Letting myself go at the feel of his hands softly stroking down my hair and my back, while he rocks me gently side to side as the sun rises over the ocean behind us.

But right now, all we have eyes for is each other...

His touch ends at just the curve of my lower back, and I'm reminded of Jerome's text as a shiver of desire makes its way up my spine. It's been so long since I've felt like I've desired another person.

Pulling back reluctantly, I pray my nipples aren't poking through my robe, revealing my desire to him. But his eyes are unwavering on my face, grasping my chin between his thumb and forefinger and then tilting my head up to him.

"Look at me," he says, tilting his own head down to meet my gaze.

As our eyes clash, the pure blue sucks me in. It reminds me of the unmistakably vibrant hue off the coasts of California during some of my happiest times when I would surf without a care in the world, traveling through a wave, headed toward the azure of nothingness to come out on the other end exhilarated that I managed to ride a wave all the way to the end.

Even though its waves often pulled me under, I never felt unsafe. Only happy. A pure, innocent joy. And in this moment, unbeknownst to Alexander, he's taking me on a unique ride that feels like home.

I wet my lips, wanting to say something, to put a voice to how I feel. His eyes go slightly hooded, his knuckles brush over my cheek as he gives me this smile that makes my tummy flip, and I swallow hard. I bite my bottom lip as he tilts his head, flickering his eyes between mine. Silently communicating, no words needed.

In our profession, where we build our trust with others by talking, it's so intimate that this is all we need.

He strokes my cheek, tucking a strand of hair behind my ear before encompassing the side of my face in his broad hand. We're just staring into each other, letting our souls weave a masterpiece that words don't need to interrupt.

The wind blows just right, ruffling my robe around my thighs and making me realize just how much of the robe was gaped open, exposing rather a lot of my bare cleavage to his gaze. I can't help but notice his stare turn hot as he looks at me unashamedly. His eyes flicker down slowly, and I see his chest tighten minutely as the seconds tick past without a word.

This desire seems to be mutual.

Alexander's eyes flick back up to mine, and he gives me a sexy, knowing grin. He grasps my chin in his hand once again, stroking me slowly.

"Good morning, sweetness," he says softly. I think it's so endearing that even though we've been out here for probably a good ten minutes or more, he's just now saying good morning. Ever the gentleman. "I turned your bath off so it wouldn't overflow."

I can't help the little grin I feel break across my face. *I think I'm the one overflowing.*

I scoff, peering up through my lashes at him. "You play entirely too much with this nickname because you *know* I don't like *sugar,*" I tease.

His grin becomes even more devilish. "Now, what have we talked about in regards to *balance,* Sarah?" Alexander's eyes crinkle as he smiles down at me.

Shyly meeting his gaze, I will myself to hold it despite how intense it is. Burying my fingers in my hair, I take a second to think about my attraction to him. Feeling desire that I didn't think I'd feel again for another person, I tilt my head and lick my lips.

"Thank you. *Sorry."* I lift a shoulder, looking away shyly. "I was trying to get out here to make my birthday wish before the stars went away," I admit.

I bite my lip as he takes another step into me and puts his own fingers into my hair, right above mine, and slides the strands through his fingers. Gliding over my hand lightly.

I shudder when his fingertips brush feather soft across my nipple as our hands lower through the strands to the ends, where he gives me a cheeky little tug and makes me jerk on a slight squeal.

"We're forgetting a birthday tradition," he says suddenly.

I feel my heart skip a beat at the absolutely hungry look that crosses his face. I swallow hard. "Oh yeah? And what would that be?"

"Turn around, and let me show you." He grins. "Everyone gets birthday swats on their birthday."

CHAPTER THIRTY-FIVE

FUCK ME HEELS

I STUMBLE BACK A step at what he suggests. My eyes widen even further as my heart decides to stop thumping all over the place and instead draws to a stop, stealing my breath. *"E-Excuse me?"*

"You heard me." Alexander says, smiling wickedly as he reaches forward and grabs my arm.

"Alex-" I can't help a crooked smile that breaks across my face when we struggle playfully against each other, laughing as he tries to get me to turn around, and I arch against him, giggling. *"Nooo!"*

His eyes flash at me as he wraps his hands around my wrists, holding them up between us. "Actually, stay just like this. I'd rather you face me while I do it; I want to see your reaction."

Of course he does.

My mouth opens in shock as he pulls me firmly to him. Forcing me to lean back as he presses me to his body once more, and I look down quickly as the wind swirls a bit more intimately against me, feeling the hem of my robe lifting as he grasps it, pulling it up and out the way.

The simple action causes me to become wet between my legs, and I realize then that I'm not scared at the prospect of him hitting me in this way. I'm turned on. Alexander firms his hands on me.

"*Alexander Richardson,* you naughty boy-*AAHH!!*" I shout, hearing my tone laced with shock as his broad hand meets the skin of my bare hip with a light popping sound. My hands rest against his chest, and suddenly his thighs are brushing against me as he walks me backwards, pressing me back against the balcony.

I feel my vagina become heavy, throbbing at how lustful he's making me.

"Come on, cooperate so I can get in there the way I need to; otherwise, it won't count," Alexander says quietly, tugging the robe out the way and baring my leg all the way to the skin of my ribcage where the robes belt cinch me tightly under my breasts.

He doesn't chuckle, and the words come out harsh, letting me know he's about close to breaking. I've successfully dug under his hardened exterior and am currently running my finger across all the nerves that I'm sure he works doubly hard to make sure aren't touched.

I keep quiet, not wanting to break this spell between us.

He tilts his head, leaning down to caress me with his gaze. I stiffen, feeling his hand stroke me all the way from my hip to my knee, then back again in a bold move. "You've got the most flawless, *prettiest* legs

I think I've ever seen." His eyes flicker back to mine and hold my stare, making my heart skip a beat.

I feel my face turn bright red. Gasping, I bury myself in his chest shyly.

He gives me exactly two seconds to hide before I feel my hair being tugged gently, and my neck arches, making me stare up into his face. I swallow hard at his expression. His color is slightly flushed, and a vein is engorged in his temple. I shiver as he suddenly grabs me behind my knee and hitches my leg around his hip on a soft grunt that slams need inside me so deep I don't think I'll ever be rid of it.

"You need to look at me while I do this sweetheart." His voice is low, rough.

"O-Okay," I let out a gasping moan, slapping a hand over my mouth, and stare at him, trembling from deep inside.

I lower my hand because I don't want him to see me trembling so visibly, but he's catching *every* movement. His gaze turns darker as his eyes eat up every movement I make. I suck my bottom lip between my teeth instead and hold his stare, determined to be just as bold as he is.

Alexander's eyebrow arches rather haughtily, reminding me of his stoic and usually unphased disposition. "Keep it there. Twenty-eight more to go," he says darkly, and I can tell he's enjoying this as much, if not more, than I am.

Staring wide-eyed at him, my breath hitches again as he gives me another light pop to the fleshy skin of my ass, making my thigh jiggle with the movements. Pausing, he rubs the spot with a broad circular motion before slapping me lightly two more times, then slowly rubbing the sting away.

I bite back a whimper as he continues on, slowly, forcing me to feel every inch of his hand rubbing on me. He doesn't let me retreat from him, hauling my leg up even higher. The lush burn spreads throughout my ass and hip, congregating in my swollen pussy and setting the burn there even more miserably than it was.

I lick my lips, feeling my juices slick down my thigh. His mouth sets in a tight line, and his chest and his neck flush a bit darker as his eyes narrow, crinkling at the corners as he stares down at me. His eye contact is so intense I bet it's enough to burn an Amazon forest down.

He takes another step further, pressing even harder into me, and the next pop stings. Making my lip quiver.

"You like that?" he asks quietly as his eyes fall to my mouth.

I can't even begin to speak, so I just nod once.

I'm thankful for the sound of the ocean behind me, praying it's hiding the majority of my ragged breathing from him. My heart beats wildly in my chest, and his does, too, as it's beating hard under my hand. I press deeper into his chest, seeing his eyes dilate and his nostrils flare as he takes a deep breath suddenly, and by the look on his face, I know he can smell me.

He stills with his palm against my ass once he gets all my spankings out of the way. I think we went over the twenty-nine, honestly.

"Go," he orders, jerking his head to the sliding doors of the room. "Take your bath and enjoy yourself. We've got a couple hours before the meetings start. I'll sit with you for them, but at three I'll have to leave for the last two hours."

I wet my lip, lamenting the feel of his hand leaving my skin as I lower my leg, just now realizing it's still wrapped indecently around his hip. I clear my throat, hoping I sound normal.

"Oh really? Why... more presentation preparation stuff?" I turn to walk back into our room, looking up at him.

"Yes, lots of preparation," he replies, following ne into the room.

We stay silent, and the closing of the sliding door sounds loudly between us as I avert my gaze from him, feeling my cheeks pinken.

When I take my robe off to get into the bath, I see my reflection in the vanity.

The skin on my ass and thigh is flushed a hot pink, and when I lower into the water, my flesh burns slightly, almost feeling like his hand is still there.

Hours later, nothing has cooled this burn inside of me, making it a horrible first conference day. Because though I'm *supposed* to be paying attention to the speakers, all I can think about is my and Alexander's encounter on the balcony. I sneak a peek at him through my lashes, remembering the way his hand felt on my bare flesh.

Feeling my core heat I look away, flushing and nodding my head when he asks if I'm okay. At three, just like he stated, he gets up to go.

"I'll see you in our room at five, okay? Don't be late."

He places his hand on the side of my head and rubs his thumb against my temple firmly, the only time he's touched me since this morning. I bite my lip and nod again, grateful that he's out in the aisle and walking away before he can see how badly I blushed at the contact.

No longer distracted, I'm able to pay attention to the last two speakers, and even write notes about different tips and tricks that I plan on utilizing in my work. When the last speaker's finished, I make my way slowly to our room, feeling down that I still hadn't heard from my dad with birthday wishes.

I pause outside the door and fish my phone out of my bag to check again, feeling a tear slip down my cheek when I see he still hasn't messaged.

What more could you have expected, stupid? He doesn't even like you!

Wiping my eyes roughly, I jam the key into the door, determined to take a shower and see if I can convince Alexander to let me hog the television in the bedroom for the rest of the night. Maybe order a chocolate cake through room service and veg out in bed, eating my sorrows away.

Knowing Alexander, I don't think he would mind it at all if he got to have some, too.

Pushing through the door, I draw to a stop, seeing dozens of red, pink and white balloons, and red and white roses in glass vases littering the inside of the small living area. I look behind me, expecting to see Alexander there, but he's not.

I shut the door softly, grabbing my phone back out but not seeing a message from him, nor hearing him inside the hotel room. *"Alexander?"* I call out, listening, but I don't hear anything.

Walking into the bedroom, I see on our bed there's a white box tied with a red bow with a note on top. My eyes widen, and a thrill races through me, seeing another singular rose on my pillow. I reach for the envelope with shaky hands, opening it.

> Sarah,
>
> I hope you don't think this is too forward, but I would like for you to wear your present out for dinner with me. I got two, just in case I didn't pick the right size; although, I did my best. We wouldn't want your girls slangin' unnecessarily, now would we?
>
> Meet me in the lobby at six.
>
> Alex

Wiping another tear away, I immediately pull out my phone.

Sarah Bella: You ridiculous, impossible, beautiful man! The first-class tickets were enough!

Opening the box I let out an excited screech at the beautiful satin and lace red dress that's carefully folded inside. I pull it out and nestle it against me. Going to the mirror I give myself a little twirl with it against my front, running my hands down the material and knowing he spent a fortune on it.

Looking back in the box I see another one in there, in a different size just in case, like he said. And nestled amongst the tissue paper is a beautiful, obviously expensive red lingerie set, a garter for my thigh, and another note.

Thank you for trusting me to deliver your birthday spanks this morning. However, gorgeous thighs like yours should never be naked. Here's a present to doll yourself up.

Alex

I don't think I've ever been so excited in my life to tear off my clothes. Standing there naked, I pause, taking out my phone again and snapping a picture of everything before sending it to Jerome and Vanessa.

Sarah: OMG look what Alex got me for my birthday! It's RED!!!!!!

I grab the lingerie set, walking into the bathroom to get ready and see two small boxes, both wrapped with red ribbon.

How the hell does he know I love red? I think, remembering the fights I'd used to have with my mother over wearing red ribbons in my hair when I was a girl.

I open the flat box first and gasp, seeing a tennis bracelet inside. My fingers tremble, going up to caress the diamond necklace he'd gifted me with just that morning. Mentally, I try to tally up everything he's done for me so far, and my lips roll as I come up with an amount that has me flushing.

He wants to fuck you. No man does this for a woman he's not trying to screw, Sarah!

I look myself over in the mirror, standing here naked while wondering what the night has in store for me. My fingers brush over the swell in my tummy before my eyes land back on mine in the mirror.

But you want to fuck him, too. My consciousness whispers like the devil in my ear.

Curiously, I pick up the last box, put the ribbon to the side and open it. My eyes widen upon seeing a full-sized bottle of my favorite perfume that I'd never let myself buy because it's too expensive. I melt at the sight. *He knows my perfume?* Overwhelmed, I bow my head, sobbing with my hand against my mouth.

With shaky hands, I gather the ribbon, carefully tie it in the tissue paper from the box and place it in my purse for safekeeping. Hopping into the shower, I wash and am ready in record time, only having to refresh my makeup lightly. But I decide to surprise him by putting a deep, rustic-red lipstick on.

I'm surprised with how much of a difference lipstick makes; I instantly look sexier, worldlier.

More womanly.

I turn to see myself in the dress before putting my foot on the chair, sliding the garter up my leg and nestling it high on my calf. The daring hip-high split in the dress shows the curve of my leg off perfectly. I smooth my hands over the lace that molds my breasts before slicking over the satin that's draped from underneath and flows all the way down to my ankles.

He'd bought me Louboutin fuck-me red heels to match the dress, and I suddenly have an almost irrational fear I'm going to leave a damp spot on the seat of my dress because I'm so turned on. I snatch the white fur shawl he'd bought to go with it and drape it loosely over my elbows, and then give myself one good lookover.

I'd fuck me. I think with pleasure, seeing how skin tight the dress was on me. I don't even mind that my waist isn't completely flat. Alexander seems to have a knack for picking out the right type of dress, and not only does it look amazing on me, but I feel drop-dead sexy.

I shove my items into a clutch, and pausing by one of the vases with the red roses, I grab one, then exit the room to make my way to the lobby. Six pm on the dot.

CHAPTER THIRTY-SIX

TORTURE

I WAIT NERVOUSLY AT the bar, drinking the scotch I'd been nursing for the last half hour while I attempt to convince myself for the hundredth time to not go upstairs and interrupt Sarah getting ready. I didn't even respond to her text, afraid it was going to make it too tempting.

So, I sit here and drink, torturing myself with how she'll look when she gets down to the lobby. My chest tightens, wondering what her reaction to all her gifts were, and I desperately hope that she feels how I see her: priceless.

I turn in the direction of the lobby, wanting to have a clear view when she comes down, and am pleased to see I don't have to wait long. I can tell she's in the area before I can even see her as multiple individuals turned their heads to openly gawk in the direction of our elevator bank. And sure enough, thirty seconds later, she appears in the lobby.

Getting my first look at her, I groan as my dick jerks painfully. It swells so fast I have to grit my teeth and will it down, breathing hard through my nose.

Holy fuck, she's exquisite. I moan to myself, jerking the lapel of my suit jacket, willing myself to get a grip.

I walk slowly to the bars entrance, wanting to observe her while she looks around for me. My heart begins to race as my eyes flicker over her body. She's turned with her back towards me. I enjoy the swish of her long hair against her swaying backside on top of the fur shawl I'd picked out for her. But it's when she turns again, and I'm treated to the side profile of her with the lace that perfectly cups her breasts, and the high slit in her dress that reveals the garter I'd tortured myself picking out for her, that I know I've made a huge mistake.

Monumental.

How am I going to be able to sleep next to her tonight and not touch her?

I stop breathing when her eyes lock onto mine, and I relish her doe-eyed stare before she gives me a bright smile. At the sight of her red lips, my heart begins to race, making me involuntarily suck in a deep breath in order to get it to calm down.

"Alexander!" she trills, almost singing my name as I approach her in the lobby. I ignore the multiple stares everyone's giving me.

I throw her my best smile and watch the blush start in her cheeks before spreading to her nose, and even her ears turn bright red.

"It's *Alex*. How do you feel, sweetness?" I ask confidently.

My hand glides up her arm as I approach her, then lean down and press my lips to her cheek in a chaste kiss. Trying to let her know without words that I didn't do any of this because I expect sex from her. I did this because I want to see her smile, I want her to feel pleasure, and I desire for her to feel cherished.

Feeling my skin warm as a tingle races down my spine that causes me to straighten slightly and lock my body down, I breathe deeply, catching something slightly different with her scent tonight.

Her blush deepens. "Hey, isn't that *my* line?" she jokes.

I feel my heart skip a beat when she places her hand softly on my chest. My eyes flicker from hers to the gentle swell in her arm, seeing the smooth expanse of skin there decorated with delicate gold bracelets. I move my hand, seeing her flush again when I encircle her wrist to inspect her new bracelet.

"Do you like it?" I ask inquisitively, tilting my head as I pierce her with a stare that I know is full of lust. She can tell, too.

Sarah shivers, her arm breaks out into goosebumps which makes me give her a wry smile, but I don't draw her attention to it. No, my attention is on her eyes and on fighting down my erection. My desire is heightened at the knowledge that she feels this deepening connection and simmering desire between us. She bites her lip, glancing away shyly before flickering her gaze back to mine.

When I make love to this woman for the first time, I'll be damned if I let her take her eyes off me.

Sarah wets her lips. "I do! Thank you, Alex! Everything was so...It's all soo..." she trails off, stumbling over her words. She steps back a step and flashes me another shy smile. *"Do you like it?"* she says, doing a small turn and showing off her dress.

Caught off guard by her question, I slap a smile on my face, hoping it hides what I feel is a near *feral* desire that I'm sure has been plain as day on my face.

"You're a vision, sweetness," I answer, hearing my voice come out too hoarse, too sexual. My eyes flit down her body as I contemplate this thing growing between us that's equal parts sexual attraction and something even a bit deeper.

The way I'd ravish you in this dress is sickening. You deserve to be thrown onto your back and serviced until you don't know your name anymore. Until your only purpose in life is to feel pleasure. It doesn't even make sense the shit I want to do with you, to you, for you, I think. Exhaling a hot breath, I clear my throat gently, grab her elbow, and begin to lead her out of the hotel double doors.

The wind flickers her dress and my jacket lightly, and I put my arm around her waist, feeling the fur of her shawl caress my arm as I draw her so close to me her hip brushes my leg.

"Thank you. I actually think I feel like one." Sarah pauses when we get to our ride waiting outside. Turning to face me, she keeps her eyes on my chest while she twirls the flower she'd brought down with her, sliding it in the pocket of my jacket. "Because you deserve flowers, too," she says breathily, her eyes rising to meet mine once more as she smooths her hand over my jacket.

My heart skips a literal beat. It takes everything in me to not snatch her up and haul her back up to the room, toss the flowers all over the bed and then fuck her on top of them.

"Thank you," I grit, fighting against the tightness in my throat.

"You're welcome." She smiles. "Do you like flowers?"

I've never been given any. No one's ever thought to gift me with anything, much less something as sweet as a simple flower.

She stares up at me patiently, her eyes flickering between mine while I mentally pull myself together. Her brows scrunch, obviously waiting for me to say something. I manage a nod and grin at her once more as I open the door, taking her by the hand to help her into the car.

"So, where are we going?" Sarah asks, not even wincing as I settle in next to her and reach for her hand.

My blood rushes in my veins as I thread our fingers together and begin to stroke her knuckles with my thumb, gliding over the tips of her fingernails while we ride.

Dismissing the thoughts of not feeling worthy, I look over at her playfully. "You'll see. The anticipation is in the surprise." I relish her giggle as she turns to stare out the window, and I tighten my hand harder on hers, loving the feel of her skin against mine.

CHAPTER THIRTY-SEVEN

Do I Intimidate You?

I CAN BARELY CONTAIN my excitement, and I vibrate in happiness next to Alexander as he walks me in on his arm into the fancy restaurant. My mouth falls open at the intimate room complete with a live singer, band, and tables covered with white linen and intimate candlelight.

It's elegant and miles more sophisticated than the lounge I sing at at home.

"*Alex...*" I'm breathless, tugging on his arm and drawing him to a stop. His eyes flash as he looks at me.

"No, Sarah. No complaining tonight. Let me spoil you, *please.*" Alexander looks down at me, and I hear his breath catch, letting me know that I affect him. Good, because I feel so much for this man it would be devastating to think that I'm in this alone.

I tighten my lips, feeling myself go hot at the look on his face. He's so handsome it almost hurts to look at him.

"I enjoy putting that color on your face, sweetness." As he leans into me, his lips scrape the shell of my ear, causing my pussy to become heavy and warm with need. My nipples tighten, and I pray to all that's holy that he can't see. "I hope you won't deny me getting to watch you eat in your pretty red dress, and then taking you for a spin on the dance floor afterwards?"

His words are like a literal wave of fire that he just tosses atop me without a care. His warm, spicy cologne fills my lungs, and when his hand settles against my waist, my body breaks out in goosebumps. I nod my head yes, wanting to know what it feels like to dance with him.

"I'd love that very much," I whisper back, unable to bring my voice to a normal level.

We follow the hostess to the table set back in an intimate alcove which hosts dimmed glowing candles on the wall, as well as real ivy twining in the wall and ceiling above them. I'm looking around, trying to avoid his stare, but it's too intense to ignore. I bring my eyes to meet his right as the server walks up to fill our water glasses and take our drink order.

"We'd like a bottle of your most expensive merlot," Alexander orders, not even sparing the server a glance as he keeps his eyes trained on mine.

The waiter raises an eyebrow as she looks from me to Alexander. "Sir, would you like to know the cost-"

"No, ma'am, I wouldn't," Alexander states simply, keeping his eyes on me.

Tearing my eyes away, I give the woman a small smile. "Thank you so much," I say, picking up my glass of water and taking a small sip.

Alexander's eyes tighten as I place the glass back down, nailing themselves on the lipstick print left behind. I stay silent as his eyes fall to my lace clad breast, and he visibly tightens even further. Shy, I glance down, seeing the hint of my puffy nipples erect and straining against the lace.

"You're welcome. *You look...*" Alexander pauses, gaze licking from my cleavage to my face. "*Ravishing...*" he trails off, reaching for his water.

His throat bobs as he swallows, drawing my gaze to the smooth expanse of skin over the collar of his button up dress shirt. His lips twitch, looking like he's holding back a smile. I feel my ears burn, I turn red, and my gaze flickers from his as he tilts his head with a curious, yet *knowing* look on his face.

I flush even deeper.

"You're very shy," Alexander states. It's not worded as a question.

I put my gaze to the stage where the band and the singer are crooning softly, providing much to the already romantic atmosphere. But when he talks, it makes my blood rush in my veins.

"Eyes on me, Bella." His use of my middle name makes my heart skip a beat. It's intimate, familiar in a way you wouldn't expect. Despite his coaxing, I can't look at him. I can't. "You can do it." He quietly encourages me to look at him. "I know how I look; a lot of people find it hard to meet my eyes, but I don't want *you* to feel that way."

I settle my gaze back on him, arching my eyebrow in shock. I lick my lips, leaning forward as Alexander leans closer as well, indulging him with a generous view of my breasts. "You don't intimidate me," I whisper, holding my hair back with one slender arm as I somehow inch even closer, feeling my breasts smoosh even harder into the table. Alexander swallows hard, noticing. I nibble my lip, feeling rather vulnerable. "Not in that way, anyways."

"No?" Alexander tilts his head. I stiffen as his eyes flicker to the pulse in my neck before returning to my eyes, pausing so long the silence becomes almost intolerable. A muscle ticks in his jaw, and his eyes become even icier somehow, yet I'm on fire for him. "So, in what way *do I* intimidate you?" His brow arches as he waits for me, expectantly.

His words cause my pussy to twitch, forcing me to press my legs together as my clit begins an uncomfortable pulsating. I lick my lips as I struggle to take in the next breath of air. I'm stuck, can't speak.

He grins slowly. "Professionally?" His voice is calm, steady.

I shake my head no, blinking in reply.

"Sexually?" His voice comes out a bit deeper than normal, and his eyes firmly land on my lips as my chest shudders with the next breath.

Images of him on top of me, straining as he pounds into me, fill my head, and it's all I can do to keep my eyes on his. I fail, lowering my eyes to my plate. Despite my bravado, this man is *so* intimidating.

I sit back when the server suddenly comes back with our wine. Again, he holds my gaze as the server takes her time pouring us both a glass. Unfazed by our interruption, he refuses to look away from me, waiting for my answer. With wide eyes, I give him a minuscule nod, seeing his jaw tick again.

"Are you two ready to order?" The server who'd been standing patiently asks quietly. But Alexander is refusing to look away from me, and I feel myself literally melting into the seat under me.

"Yes," I say slowly, keeping my gaze on Alexander's for two seconds too long before turning to the server. *"Mr. Richardson* here-" Alexander chuckles, shaking his head lightly. His eyes flash teasingly at me, but he doesn't say anything, letting me have my fun. I keep talking despite his laughing. "—will have the spaghetti, extra meat sauce, accompanied with a side salad and the house dressing. And please bring him a glass of scotch." I throw him a cheeky smile that has him shifting uncomfortably in his seat. However, he continues to stare at me as I keep going, giving the server my order now. "*I'll* have your half plate of salmon alfredo—"

Alexander interrupts me, letting me know fun-time is over. *"Full.* She'll have the full plate."

I turn my head to face him and narrow my eyes.

"Well, if we're going to do this, then we're going to do it the right way. Wouldn't you say, beautiful?" His term of endearment barely has time to sink in before he reaches forward and grabs my wineglass, turning the lipstick mark to face him. He sips deeply from my glass before putting it back down in front of me, ignoring my shocked look. Seems we're full of surprises tonight. "She'll have a full plate of the salmon alfredo, blacken the salmon, and give her a side of pimento stuffed olives please. As well as your house special cocktail with an extra shot of alcohol. And if you could bring us an extra plate to share, we'd be most appreciative." And as if to drive the point home, I feel his calf suddenly press into mine.

My eyes widen as the feel of him sinks in.

"Will that be all?" the server inquires.

"No, it's this beautiful woman's birthday today. May we please have a piece of chocolate cake to share? As well as one packed up to go, please?"

I cock my head and arch an eyebrow, slowly raising my foot up his leg teasingly. I jerk slightly in surprise when I feel him grasp my ankle, digging his fingers in just as the server confirms our order and leaves.

"You love playing with me, don't you?" he asks boldly. His fingers begin to rub firm circles into the delicate bone of my ankle, causing me to shudder at the contact.

"Maybe a little," I say to him with a teasing smile. "It's just so fun to watch you squirm."

"Hm..." he replies simply.

The sound hangs in the air between us, and my fingers rise to nervously caress the necklace he gifted me. We stare each other down for a moment while he rubs my calf and ankle, and I rub my diamond. The sexual tension between us is so thick it could be cut with a knife. He looks at me with a hungry expression.

"Sarah, will you dance with me tonight for your birthday?" He tightens his fingers on me, ignoring my squirming.

"Uhm, Alexander...I have a secret to tell you," I reply. My eyes leave his shyly to glance to the side, seeing two servers coming out with our food and drinks. Attempting to pull my foot back, I still when he just tightens his fingers on my calf, keeping me still for him.

"Thank you," we both say to the server as she pulls the domes off the plates keeping our food warm and walks away.

I give him a pointed look. "Now, *whooo's* going to eat all of this?" I wave at my full plate of noodles.

"You are, either now or when we're in bed later. I'll feed it to you after I feed you your chocolate cake," he says, finally releasing my leg and picking up his scotch. He drinks deeply, putting the drink down with a contented sigh as if he didn't just light me on fire with his words. *"Man,* that's a good scotch." His voice tumbles from his throat rough and unrestrained.

Making me wonder yet again what it'd be like to make love with him.

Sarah and Alexander Dancing by Alice Anderson

CHAPTER THIRTY-NINE

Intimate Birthday Dances

I MUSE OVER HIS words, wondering how we tumbled so thoroughly into dangerous waters. Not having much experience in seduction, I approach warily. However, I'm brave enough to dip my toe in, and I decide I like it.

Alexander picks up his fork and gestures to me. "Unless you need me to feed you now?"

Taking the hint, I pick up my knife and fork to cut the delicate fish for him, placing it on the little dish in front of us meant for sharing.

"No, ma'am." Alexander's eyes snap to mine and hold my stare. "Give it to me from *your* fork," he demands, keeping still while his challenge processes.

I pause in the act of taking my first bite at the simmering desire within his gaze. Bold, I swallow slowly and lick my bottom lip before tearing my eyes from his to twirl a small amount of noodles onto the fork. "Salmon?" I ask quietly, glancing back up through my lashes to see him nod. Biting back a small smile, I take my time stabbing a bite of salmon, then hold it across the table.

Alexander gives me a wicked grin and leans forward, attempting to take the bite, but I playfully pull back, making him miss.

He arches a brow. "Is this the game we're going to play?" he asks.

His grin broadens in his face at seeing just how delighted I am at besting him.

"Maybe." I hold the fork out again. He wraps his hand firmly over mine and keeps me still for him as he takes his bite, releasing me and sitting back while chewing. He twirls some of his spaghetti on his fork and holds it out for me to take a bite. Surprisingly, I'm still able to hold his stare, which turns hot when he slides the tines between my lips. I can't help my little moan as the spicy flavor hits my tongue. *"It's so good,"* I whisper, closing my eyes. *"But* it's not yours," I tease sadly.

Alexander's quiet chuckle has me tightening all over. "It's kind of tough to beat perfection," he quips, taking a slow sip of his scotch. "I've been practicing that recipe for damn near twenty years."

"Hm. That's a long time."

It has me musing on his age. His experience. Not just in life, but in the bedroom. As he speaks, my eyes lower from his face to peruse his neck, caressing the broad expanse of his chest and shoulders. My eyes go even lower; however, sadly, I can't see through the table.

We eat a while, talking about work and what we would normally do for our birthdays when I break and reach into my clutch. Thinking of my dad, I pull out my phone, disappointed as I see he still hasn't tried to contact me.

"What is it?" Alexander asks curiously.

I nibble on my lip. "It's nothing...it's just it's getting late, and my dad *still* hasn't wished me a happy birthday," I reply softly. Putting my phone back in my clutch, I turn back to him and give him my best smile, carefully hiding the hurt I hadn't intended to show.

The very minor tilt of his head and the flash of his eyes has me suddenly on edge. *"Hmm..."* he hums, "there seems to be some tension there."

"There is," I say quietly.

"I'm sorry he hasn't contacted you," Alexander says simply, sitting back in his seat and swirling his wine glass between his fingers.

Thankful he's not pressing the issue, I put my fork down and sit back against the cushion, gazing at him silently. The music swells in the background, causing my eyes to slide to the dance floor.

"So, what was your secret? You forgot to finish telling me earlier." Alexander's sudden question has me coming back quickly.

"Oh!" My eyes widen with humor. "Just that I can't dance." I let out a little laugh as Alexander chuckles at me.

"What? I have a hard time believing that!" When he takes another drink, I mirror him.

"Well, it's the truth. So believe it. I've never been dancing before. The closest I get to it is when I am on stage, but that's it."

I put my glass down hastily when he stands smoothly out of his seat and holds his hand out to me.

"Well, join me. Because I'd love to share a dance with you." I feel my muscles tightening in excitement at the thought of him pressing me against him. He leans closer, obviously sensing my nervousness. The rich scent of his cologne fills my nose, robbing me of my common sense and making me almost woozy with desire. My heart begins to beat faster, but it's his next words that knock me completely askew, "Let me lead you." His eyes bore into mine unwavering and every inch the man who knows what he wants.

The deep cadence of his voice has a shiver rolling through my body. I swear time stops. The sounds of the restaurant and the band fall away as we continue to stare, the both of us searching for something. Longing for it.

"Trust me," he says softly. Running his hand down my forearm, he grasps my hand firmly.

When he gives me a tug, I nervously wet my lips, feeling butterflies erupt in my stomach. My tummy trembles, forcing me to press a hand there. He affords me enough room to rise from my seat, and I let him pull me to the dance floor where a romantic instrumental song begins to play.

Alexander turns me to face him before crooking a finger under my chin to tilt my head up, and I obey every silent command without a word. So enraptured I am with every movement this man makes. I hold my breath when his hand rises to brush my hair to my back, exposing the upper swells of my breasts to him.

He stares for just a moment longer than proper before his eyes flit back to mine.

Burning me up from the inside out, the stark intimacy threatens to eviscerate me.

"Touch me," he commands. And I do; I place both palms flat to his chest and fight like hell to not meet his searching gaze. The taut muscles flex under my hands. To my horror, I begin to shake with nerves when he slowly runs his fingertips down my spine and presses his left hand into my lower back, pulling me flush against every hard line of his body. He bends to my ear, barely brushing my skin, "Shhh."

I swallow hard, but in an unexpected movement that ramps up my nervousness, he lowers his hand to the curve of my ass and firmly presses me even *further* against him. A teasing grin tips his mouth, and something hot and sensual flashes in his eyes, making him harder. On *fire.*

My lashes flutter at the feel of my hips settling into his, and that incessant throbbing that's been tormenting me deepens.

Peeking up at him through my lashes, I settle my right hand onto his bicep at the same time that he takes my right arm and grasps my hand, holding it out and to the side. I try to ignore my warm cheeks and focus on the feel of his body against mine.

I glance to the side nervously, slightly embarrassed that everyone else has already begun dancing, and we're just standing still. "They're already dancing," I say quietly.

Clearly nonplussed, he cocks his head to the side, and the crinkles next to his eyes deepen slightly as he smiles. "Let them worry about themselves," he replies, his hand firming onto my back and forcing me even further into him somehow, "and I will worry about you."

His words settle deep into my core, affecting me in ways I cannot express. Rolling my lips slightly, my eyes raise to his, and I give a tiny nod.

When his thigh presses against mine, I take a step back, and we begin to move gracefully, following the beat of the song.

"Wow." I giggle.

"Wow is right," he murmurs.

My eyes widen at the realization that Alexander knows what he's doing hits me. As we sway together, I can't help but imagine our bodies entangling in bed.

Alexander presses me even harder against him, now molding my upper torso to his front. He suddenly pushes me out and gives me a turn, making my hair whip out wildly, and then yanks me back to him. He lowers his face to my neck as we sway, running his nose down the sensitive spot there and nuzzling me rather blatantly.

What the hell is this between us? I relish his thigh thick between my legs, rubbing me there as we sway intimately. As I gaze up at him while we move in sync, feeling vulnerable, I can't help but wonder...*is this love?*

Tilting my head back I half-close my eyes, letting him lead me just like he asked. I quiver, feeling myself falling.

Alexander tilts his head down and rests his jaw against the side of my face. "See, in the game of dance, the man is the frame, and the woman is the picture in the frame. And the frame's entire purpose is to show off his picture. And you, Sarah...you make such a *desirable* picture."

Ducking my head shyly, I flood my panties at his words. Turns out, Alexander is quite the seductor.

I give a breathless giggle.

"And on the contrary, what is the picture without her frame surrounding her so beautifully? I think they need each other to balance it out," I retort.

Our eyes meet as he continues to lead me through the dance, and in a bold move his hand lowers just a bit more, once again cupping the top curve of my ass and pressing me even harder into him just as the music switches into something sexier, more sultry.

My heart rate begins to ramp up, and I glance at him nervously. "Alex, I-*I don't know*...I don't think I can dance to this! The other one was easier."

Alexander smiles devilishly. "*Breathe.* I won't let you fall, sweetness. Look at me." I glance up nervously, but I'm unable to say anything. "You're okay; I've got you. Don't think. Just move with me. Here we go."

Tightening his hold on me, Alexander moves us with purpose, lowering his lips to my ear once more as he steps into me four, five, six times, before suddenly turning me, holding me to him by my waist and my hip as we sway.

"Alex!" I gasp, thrilled.

Alexander whips me around again and yanks me to him, molding every inch of us together. He puts a hand to my chin, tilting my head up to look him in the eyes. I can tell, just know, something is changing, shifting, between the two of us. My fingers on his chest flex, feeling Alexander's heart pounding wildly in his chest.

"Are you with me?" he asks quietly.

"*Yes,*" I smile at him, feeling a bit dazed and dreamy.

"Then be alive with me, baby." Alexander lowers his hand and snatches me up by my leg through the split in my dress and hitches it around his hip, making me squeal into his neck. His thumb caresses the sensitive skin under the garter as he whirls us several times in a circle before stopping and bending me into a daringly low dip just as the music ends.

Our lips are so close we're almost kissing.

Just when I think he will, his face morphs from one of desire to serene joy as he raises me back up, and he breaks out into a chuckle when I throw my arms around his neck in excitement. My feet leave the ground once more, and he gives me a couple more twirls. When he sets me down, I can't help how excited I feel as he keeps my hand in his and leads me off the dance floor

"Oh my gosh, that was *wild!"* I giggle, stumbling a little as I attempt to keep up with his pace as he guides me back to our table.

We sit back in our booth, finishing our drinks as the server brings out our decadent chocolate cake, complete with a candle in the middle. The server lights it, and I clap as the band and singer lead the restaurant through the "Happy Birthday" song. Alexander takes out his phone and records me laughing and swaying in my seat. At the end of the song, I blow the band a kiss before turning and blowing out the candle, giving Alex a wink.

Alexander stops the recording and puts his phone away. "Hey," he stops me right as I'm about to stab my fork in the cake, "do you mind if we take this back to the room?"

I smile, putting my fork down. "No. But I'm starting to think you really have a thing for food, mister," I breathe, watching the server come back over after Alexander calls for her. I wait patiently as he pays and packages up my cake, and then brings the other one to go.

My mind races at the possibilities for the rest of the night.

Oh God, are we going to have sex? The thought is incessant, swirling around in my brain during the ride back to the hotel. I'm giddy, thinking about Alexander between my legs. It's been so long since I've felt the weight of a man's body on top of mine, and the anticipation is eating me alive.

When he looks at me, those butterflies in my tummy get worse.

"Alex," I say nervously. Dragging a nail up his arm, I lower my voice so the driver can't hear, "What can I do to repay you for such an amazing birthday?" My anxiety ramps up, becoming almost unbearable in the small space between us when he tilts his head and regards me with an unreadable expression on his face.

"What would you like?" Alex asks hesitantly, rubbing his hand across his jaw.

"I think...I'd like to dance some more i-if *you* would?" I look at him shyly.

Alexander smiles, brushing his knuckles down my cheek. "Then let's dance, baby."

He leads me into our room and out to the balcony where we kick off our shoes, and he loosens his tie.

We dance another hour under the moonlight until my eyes grow heavy. Picking me up, Alexander brings me back in the room and places me on the bed. The silence swells between us as he takes off my dress, leaving my lingerie on. To my surprise, he takes my garter off. I tense because I feel it's still wet from my arousal that slicked down my thighs, but he doesn't leave me any doubt that he knows. I know he feels it because his eyes go half-lidded when he closes his fingers over the delicate fabric, and the thick bulge between his legs twitches. But he doesn't act on it.

Yawning, I lay back, working to get comfortable. He shoves it in his pocket and pulls the covers over me.

"Goodnight, sweetness," he rasps, sounding far away, but I feel him kiss my forehead.

The next thing I know, I gently wake up a few hours later to him deeply asleep and wrapped completely around me, with his hand between my legs per usual. Rubbing my hand down his arm, I wedge mine over his and snuggle even more into him on a contented sigh.

This has been the *best* birthday of my life.

CHAPTER FORTY

DON'T BE FRESH

I TWITCH IN MY sleep, deep in my dream.

"Alex." Sarah looks over at me, wetting her lips. "What can I do to repay you for such an amazing birthday?"

"Well, that depends on what you're prepared to give me." I turn my head to face her, piercing her with a direct gaze.

Sarah inhales, eyeing me warily as I lean forward into her space and snatch her hand into mine, placing the back of it to my lips at the same time my other hand settles on her bare thigh. Right over her garter.

"I think I would very much like to be allowed to take this off of you," I say. The feeling of her melting into me makes me feel a thousand feet tall.

Keeping my lips to her hand, I turn it over to kiss the inside of her delicate wrist at the same time I hook a finger around her garter and caress her flesh. Same as I did while we were on the dance floor. Looking down, her breasts heave with barely controlled emotion, and her eyes widen, watching me observe her.

I groan miserably at the sight of her nipples sticking through the lace of her top, so delectable looking that my mouth waters.

Feeling bold, I continue to hold her hand to my mouth until we pull up to the hotel. I help her slide out, holding our cake in one hand and her hand in the other. We remain silent as we journey to our room. She shivers against me, and I caress her fingers in slow, soothing intervals.

Walking into our room that's currently only illuminated by dimmed recessed lighting at the bar, Sarah shyly stands to the side as I put our cake on a small table by the couch. I grin to myself, seeing her fidget, wringing her fingers together and shifting her weight from foot-to-foot.

Relishing her nervousness, I remain quiet as I work to shrug off my jacket and unbutton the first two buttons of my shirt.

I turn, sinking down into the cushioned couch, spreading my thighs as I settle in with a deep sigh, and give her a blatantly slow drag of my gaze from the top of her head to her toes, then back again. Slowing at the juncture between her legs.

My heart skips a beat as my straining cock jerks in my pants. God, I bet you're so warm and juicy. *I wet my lips. "Come here," I command.*

Sarah tugs her bottom lip between her teeth, her eyes going wide as she takes a hesitant step, then another, and another. Bringing herself to stand between my spread legs. I take several long seconds to caress my gaze all over her body again.

"Do you like what you see?" Sarah whispers.

Contemplating her question, I tilt my head, seeing her flush so hard her ears turn red. "Do I like what I see?" I repeat, parroting her question back to her in a serious tone. "Hm." I place a hand to my erection and squeeze hard, giving her a guttural grunt as I do so.

Sarah's eyes flutter as she watches me.

She parts her lips to speak before I suddenly reach forward and pluck her clutch out from where she had it cinched under her arm, rendering her silent. Tossing it to the side I reach forward, grasping the hem of her fur shawl, and pull it slowly from her shoulders and down her right side. A growl starts in my chest at the sound of her whimper, knowing she's feeling the material scrape her already sensitive nipples.

My eyes lower, seeing them distended tight and hard against the lace of her dress. My mouth waters.

"Alex," she whimpers again, swaying slightly on her feet as I toss the shawl to the side as well.

"Shhh." I shush her, putting a finger to her lips and tilt my head. "Just a second, baby."

Sarah's lips quiver against my finger, clearly overwhelmed with my blatant icy stare.

I'm not cold for you, baby; I burn so hot for you, can't you tell?

"What color are they?" I ask, squeezing my erection even harder.

Her brow furrows. "What color are w-what?"

"Your nipples."

Her eyes lower, and she rolls her lips again in embarrassment. "Oh. Uhm..."

Releasing my cock, I drape my arm lazily on the arm of the couch and tilt my head. "I imagine them a light brownish-red..." I edge.

She nods, the flush in her face deepening.

"Same color as your pussy?" I grit through the tightness in my throat.

Sarah's inhales sharply, thrown off by my boldness. Her eyes—wide and innocent—fly up to meet mine. Damn near drowning in desire, I manage to give her an unbothered smile as her lips part. "Alex..." she breathes shakily.

"You have to know I've thought about it," I murmur, reaching forward to now slide my hand up her thigh to grip a firm hip and squeeze. "Desperately." My gaze lowers to her cleavage. "I love sucking both." Leaning back against the cushions, I tap my right thigh, letting her know silently what I want. "All I can think about is your clit between my teeth and how you taste."

Sarah's eyes meet mine for a couple seconds before she reaches her hand out to me. I take it, helping her maintain her balance as she lifts her leg up to place her foot on my thigh. I raise my other hand to the clasp at her ankle and undo it one-handed, pulling her shoe off and letting it fall to the floor with a careless thunk. She tilts her head back and moans softly, no doubt feeling relief from getting out of her heels after dancing and being in them for so long.

I let her have her moment before tapping my other leg, and we switch hands as she puts her other foot up, and I make quick work of taking it off, then tossing it to land next to the other one. Sarah goes to pull her foot away, but I grab it before she can.

There's a split second where we're connected by our extremities: one set of hands clasping with my other hand on her ankle, holding it in the air to keep her from retreating. We stare at each other for a long, tense second. My gaze lowers to the juncture between her legs, sucking in a deep breath of my own and smelling her delicious scent. My heart thumps hard in my chest at the sight of the perfectly plump mound of her pussy, barely covered by the dress.

I take another deep breath in a bid for self-control. Sarah whimpers when I firm my hold on her hand and ankle and slowly press her leg outward, opening her up even more for my gaze. A low, rough sound of longing rips from my chest when the red, lacy panties I'd picked out for her peek out under the slit in her dress. I swallow hard, denying myself throwing her to the couch and fucking her the way I want to.

Denying myself smearing cake all over her body and licking it off, my true desire and kink is to eat food off of her and mix its flavor with hers, giving myself a one-way ticket to nirvana.

I pull on her ankle, making her inch closer to me carefully. Lowering her leg, I place her foot back on my thigh and slowly drag my fingertips up her calf to her knee.

"Oh God," she whines breathlessly.

I lean forward and place my lips to her knee, giving her a wet kiss there. Letting go of her hand, she places it on my shoulder as I run both of my hands up underneath her dress to the back of her leg until my hands encompass her ass and squeeze, making a moan fly out of her mouth.

We stay there like this in the quiet, while I knead her ass and keep my lips pressed to her knee. "I love the way you respond to me. And I haven't even kissed you yet," I murmur against her flesh. "Fuck, you're so soft. So pretty."

"Alex, I want you to touch me."

Amused, I look up to see her eyes widen, and her hand flies up to her mouth as if embarrassed by her sudden outburst. But it doesn't phase me.

I stay quiet, trailing my lips further up the sensitive, vulnerable flesh of her inner thigh. Her scent gets stronger, intoxicating me. "I didn't bring you to Vancouver to fuck you, baby." I keep my voice quiet while lashing my tongue against her skin and groan at her taste.

"I know!" she gasps. "I know you didn't, Alex, b-but-"

"Sssshhhh. You talk so much, Miss Counselor," I chastise gently with a dark chuckle, nipping at her skin.

I smile when the muscles in her thigh begin to shake uncontrollably.

Thinking of all the ways I can fuck her, the images torture me even as I also torture myself with her scent. The same scent I smelled on my hand this morning. "Tell me, do you enjoy it when I have my hand on your pussy at night?" I ask. My hands tighten on her ass when she jerks in surprise.

"Wh-What—"

"You heard me, beautiful. I said, do you enjoy it?" I wrap my teeth around her garter and give her a little snap, making her jump. I lick my tongue underneath, soothing the sting away before scraping my teeth against her skin in a warning. At her silence, I pull back slightly. "Answer me, sweetness."

Her response is a rapid, "Yes."

The features in my face tighten at her admission. "Were you going to tell me, sweetness," I ask gently, "or was that supposed to be your naughty secret?" I smile, delighting in the slightly overwhelmed look on her face. "As you should see by now, not much gets past me."

"I—" Her eyes lower, and the flush in her face deepens.

"Do you think about me placing my fingers inside you?"

"Yes," she breathes.

"Do you think about me fucking you?"

"Y-yes."

I take pity on her, slowly pulling down her garter until it falls to her ankle. Our eyes stay locked. The tension between us sweltering, I slide it off before sitting back and handing it to her. "Put it in your panties."

Sarah bites her bottom lip, unsure.

"Do it."

My chest tightens so hard I don't know if it's actually healthy to let oneself become this aroused, then stay there on the precipice with no relief for as long as I'd been.

Sarah sucks in a sharp breath through her nose, and my eyes flit down to her covered mound, watching her slowly shove the garter under the lace. When her fingers hesitate, I lift my gaze to her and arch a haughty brow, not able to help my stern tone. "Don't be fresh. All the way so it's snug right against your cunt."

Sarah's eyes are burning pools of desire, and her lips quiver as she pushes it lower. My cock jerks again with the knowledge she's feeling her fingertips and the rough lace of the garter scrape her sensitive clit. As if to reinforce this knowledge, she lets out a desperate whine that turns into a small cry as I roughly yank her to me. She tumbles into my lap and falls onto my chest hard. Her breath washes over my mouth, our lips so close they're almost touching.

Everything in me wants to close the distance between us and take her mouth. But instead, I slowly lower her down my chest, our clothes softly rustling as she makes her descent, until I settle her to where she's straddling my hips. Right on the thick bulge of my cock.

Our breathing's the only sound in the quiet space as I keep her tight against me and then begin to rock her, dragging her sweet pussy over me.

"I'm going to make you feel very good, love," I say hoarsely. "You want me to make you feel good?"

I grip her hips tightly and circle her hard against me, raising my hips up into her.

Sarah's eyes go half-lidded. She makes a ragged sound then shivers, biting her lip and throwing her head back to expose the vulnerable expanse of her throat. I bend to her, making her flinch as my lips land on her neck, right over her ticklish spot, to suck and agitate her flesh. My hands tighten on her hips, reluctantly pulling away from her with something else on my mind.

Sarah opens her eyes, curiously watching me reach for the container of chocolate cake.

Biting back a smile at her still absentmindedly grinding her pussy into me, I open the wrapped cutlery and scoop up a small portion and hold it up. "Open," I order.

My desire ramps to dangerous heights when she parts her pink lips and lets me put the cake in her mouth. Before she can swallow, I place the cake on the couch cushion beside her calf and put my hands back on her ass, and begin to rock her against my thick bulge. Watching her chew, I lean forward to lick the corner of her mouth.

"Is it good?" I bring a hand up to cup her breast and she stills, stiffening at the feel of me squeezing her.

We stare into each other's eyes. "Yes," she whispers. When her eyes move to close, I firmly drag my thumb over her taut nipple.

"You're so hot, baby, I can feel the warmth of you against my cock," I rasp, tightening my fingers around her, taking pleasure at the glazed look in her eyes as I start to pluck her nipple with tight pulls. Alternating pinching and tugging on it.

As she rocks on me, I remove my hand to feed her another bite of cake. The sight of her pink tongue caressing the fork has me jerking against her. Seeing her mouth work around the desert, I know my eyes are just as lost as hers are.

"I'm not fucking you tonight," I say quietly. "I don't want to hurt you. And as turned on as I am right now, I won't be gentle."

Sarah squeezes her eyes shut, and lets out a small, disappointed sound before I resume playing with her nipple. I grip her ass hard with my other hand and give a rough roll of my hips into hers.

Over and over we repeat this until she's gasping and turning her face away from the next bite I feed her. She's shaking, her eyes are glassy, and she's now moaning softly through her panting, letting me know her orgasm is looming.

Sarah startles as I bring her head back around by a fist in her hair and make her face me once more. Her fingernails dig into my shoulder, but I disregard the slight pain.

"Open," I command again, my eyes stern on hers.

Sarah whimpers, and I match her with a groan when she heavily drags her pussy over my hardness again. "Please, I need to come—" she gulps, "Want to come—" She squeals with excitement as I firmly place the spoon into her mouth and scrape the cake off of it against her teeth, making her take it.

Tossing the spoon to the side, I grasp her ass again and drag her pussy fast and hard over my straining cock.

"I'll let you come," I say. "But when you do, don't hide from me. I want to see it."

Bracing my feet on the floor, I circle my hips into hers, grunting my own pleasure.

The sound of our heavy breathing fills the air as I work our flesh together roughly. Our clothes rustle, and the couch bangs slightly against the wall with our efforts. A light sheen of perspiration makes her face glow, and her eyes are wet as she stares helplessly at me, as is her mouth. Eager to see her succumb to her orgasm, I raise a hand once more to pinch and roll her nipple, my eyes narrowing as she suddenly flinches and makes a high-pitched noise in her throat. She throws her head back on a tortured sound as she orgasms. Her entire face flushes red, her brows scrunch together, her lips part, and her buttocks flex under my fingers as her hips twitch weakly against mine.

"Ohhhh," she moans softly, her heaving chest flushed and shiny with sweat. Despite the pain of my erection, I firm my hold on her, keeping her moving against me and rubbing as much pleasure out of her as I can. Her knees slide along the couch cushions as she tries to clamp her legs shut against my hips.

And it's the most humbling, beautiful sight I've ever had the privilege to observe.

"So fucking beautiful when you orgasm," I praise her quietly. My eyes stay tight on hers, not looking away even when I feel her fingernails scraping against me as she clutches at my shirt.

Sarah collapses weakly against me, panting and laying her head on my chest as she blinks sleepily. Content. We say nothing. We don't need to.

I smile against her hair, feeling her go lax against me in sleep a couple minutes later. I reach over to pick up the rest of the cake and eat it with her laying against me.

"You know, I must admit, this is the best fucking day *I've ever experienced in my life," I whisper to her, licking the spoon. "What do* you *think?" Chuckling at her silence, I place my lips to her temple. "Ah, well. Maybe one day you'll tell me."*

I jerk awake, sitting straight up with my chest heaving and my heart racing. I look down at my cock tenting the covers and take a deep breath, trying to calm myself. Keeping my eyes straight ahead, I don't chance even looking at Sarah, knowing if I do, I'll wake her up and start something we have no business beginning right now.

Breathing, counting to five-hundred, all the usual distraction methods don't work, so I slide out of bed silently so I don't wake her up, and jump in the shower, taking care of it.

Thirty minutes later I'm lowering my head back on the pillow. I bite back a groan, lamenting that I didn't even fuck her in my dreams. This time, I'm calm enough to glance over at her, but all I can see is the beautiful pink slash of her mouth through her mountain of hair.

Rolling over, I turn myself away from the object of my desire and attempt to get a grip on myself.

CHAPTER FORTY-ONE

DENYING ONESELF

I WAKE UP EARLY the next morning to find Sarah's side of the bed empty. Yet again disappointed that I hadn't seen anything I wasn't supposed to, I pull out my phone and check the time. We'd both gotten up before the alarm. A wonderful side effect due to the time change.

Hearing some rustling, I turn my head just in time to see Sarah walk out of the bathroom. Her hair is pristine as usual, and she has a very light amount of makeup on. Though my body fills with warmth at the sight of her, I frown slightly, desiring more than anything to know what she looks like when she wakes up not perfect. This is our second morning here, and selfishly I'd expected to not see her so put together by now. But like with her unnecessarily restricting her diet, she's unrelenting in her search for perfection.

It burns me up, honestly. If I'd just let myself fuck her the way I wanted to the night before, then she'd be sleeping in, and I'd have had my chance.

"Good morning, sleepyhead!" she chimes in her soft, sing-song voice, throwing me a bright smile without quite meeting my gaze and hopping onto her side of the bed. I turn my head lazily when the action bounces us both gently.

I furrow my brows; she's in a robe and back to being shy.

I bite against the wicked grin struggling to break across my face. "Good morning," I rasp. "Sleepyhead might be correct for *you.* I had to endure your snoring." I soften my words with a teasing look.

Obviously offended, she scrunches her nose. "*I don't snore!*" she exclaims, her voice going an octave higher.

Sitting up on my elbows, I level her with a pointed look. "If you want some medical advice, you might want to do a sleep study. Thank God for your fan because it helped lull me to sleep. I think I needed it more than *you* did!" I retort, falling back to my pillow and laughing as she throws her pillow at me.

She grumbles as I scrub a hand down my face. But I'm suddenly too distracted to appease her because my arousal comes back full force at the unmistakable scent of pussy on my skin. My brows furrow.

Before I can help myself I'm breathing deeply, letting out a rough groan right as a rush of desire so painful flashes down the length of my dick, causing it to stand erect under the covers. I throw her a look. Sarah turns her face away before rising and hurriedly walking to the closet. Keeping her face averted, she throws both doors open and then steps back. Biting her lip, she studiously examines the contents, trying a little *too* hard to ignore me. I bet she knows something about this and isn't letting on.

I force my hand down, keeping silent.

"What are you wearing today?" she asks. Her arms fold, and her fingers tap anxiously against her upper arms, continuing to peruse her clothes.

I sit up and swing my legs over the side of the bed, clearing my throat. "I think I'm going with a light blue suit."

"Well, our styles have to coordinate. Otherwise it'll look weird if we *clash* as we're walking down the hallway or seen together, you know," she iterates. Reaching into the closet, she picks out a cream pantsuit before holding it out for me to see. "Will this match?" she brings it closer.

I nod. Her style is a spot-on compliment to mine, and it is such a turn on. "It'll be fine," I assure her hoarsely as I rise out of the bed. "Let's go to breakfast. I have to be at the conference at nine, but I don't go on stage until ten."

Sarah tilts her head up and finally looks at me full-on. *"Good morning,"* she whispers playfully. Every muscle in my body tenses when she steps into me, wrapping me up in a surprisingly tight hug. "You got this; you're going to *rock it*. You know your stuff!" She pulls away and smiles at me brightly, making my heart skip a beat.

Goddamn, she's beautiful. My brain momentarily glitches at the sight of her happiness. Despite my self-assured response, I have genuine fear that I might not have it as in-the-bag this year as I normally do. Her presence affects me in ways that don't make sense.

"I hope I have it; all these years I've been servicing our community," I tease, wrapping my arm around her waist and squeezing briefly.

"Oh yeah, Mr. Old Psychiatrist man. *Poor you.* Wonder when the gray hair is going to start?" She screams softly when I pick up the same pillow that she'd thrown at me, and slap her lightly across the face.

"What gray hair?" I growl, getting up close and personal in her face.

Her hazel eyes widen, and she shakes her head, laughing. "Oh God, I'm *sorrryyy*. Okay, none yet!" she breathes, stepping away and flinging herself back to her side of the bed, snuggling under the covers with a self-satisfied smile.

"Don't go back to sleep," I admonish, my eyebrows knitting together at how comfortable she's making herself. "We're about to leave."

Sarah's eyes snap to mine wryly. "Excuse you, *mister*. I'm going to relax while *you* take your sweet time getting ready. I did the hard part already; I just need to pull my clothes on." She stifles a yawn and pulls the covers up to her chin.

I shake my head, making my way to the bathroom with my clothes tucked under my arm. "Wear the black shoes with the thin straps; they'll show off your toes perfectly," I call as I walk into the bathroom and close the door.

My eyes roam. The light steam from her shower embraces me in it's lingering humidity. I reach into the shower and turn it on hot. Putting my hand to my nose I groan as my erection jerks painfully, and I hiss, grabbing it as I step under the spray. I jerk off roughly in the shower, imagining her naked in here with me.

God, her body is luscious and succulent. Worthy of being worshiped. And I'd worship her *properly*, sucking and nipping at every sensitive spot that makes her squirm and cry out for mercy as I make her come over and over again, until that beautiful voice is hoarse. With that thought, I reach out of the shower to open my grooming kit where I'd stashed her garter, and finish jacking off with it held against my nose. Pleased to find it's still a little wet from how I'd folded it.

Oh fuck, she smells amazing.

I orgasm with a pained groan, and not able to exercise an iota of self-control now that I'm by myself, I suck on the lace of the garter. I muffle my growls of ecstasy with it. Pumping my cock hard and inhaling her scent until thick, white ropes of my ejaculate spurt from the tip of my cock to paint the shower floor.

When I walk out of the bathroom forty-minutes later, I'm freshly lined, and my hair is styled perfectly.

Sarah's leaning against the desk with her back to me dressed in her pantsuit with the blazer slung over her arm and typing out a text on her phone. I clear my throat gently and hold my arms out, wanting to show myself off to her. She turns and gives me a rather appreciative once over, her eyes widening slightly.

Sarah arches a brow. *"My.* You clean up very well don't you, mister?" she says with a cute grin as she flicks her eyes to my hair. "Has anyone ever told you your jaw line makes you look like that one actor?" she muses gently, tapping her finger against her cheek. "Why can't I think of his name..."

I smile, sitting down at the end of our bed and putting on my dress shoes, noticing she'd put on the black strappy heels I'd suggested. "A time or two," I reply, finishing my job then standing up. "And you look sensational as always. Breakfast?"

I place my own suit jacket over my arm and wave a hand to escort her out of the room. She slides past me with a small smile, and I eagerly watch her hair swishing against the round globes of her ass the entire way to the buffet room.

"So, you don't get nervous at these things?" Sarah asks around a bite of cantaloupe.

We're sitting at the same restaurant we'd gone to last night, except today it's transformed into a lavish buffet.

I narrow my eyes at her plate in judgment seeing she'd chosen all fruits, a yogurt, and a tiny scoop of scrambled eggs. She gives a little wiggle when she pops the rest of the cantaloupe in her mouth and moans appreciatively.

You can't be too upset; all the fruit is why she smells so good, I chastise myself.

"Every now and then something will throw me off," I admit, putting down my fork. I'd been working through a loaded omelet. But craving something more light, I reach forward to grab a piece of fruit off her plate.

She sticks her tongue out playfully. *"Get your own,"* she teases, her husky laugh making me smile as I pop the fruit in my mouth.

"Letting you know right now..." I wipe my mouth with a napkin. "We're eating at this local restaurant our last night here, and I'm making you order all unhealthy food," I warn.

She throws me an incredulous look. *"Come on, Alexander!"*

"No." I raise my brow, sitting back in my seat and crossing my arms. "You're not restricting yourself here the way you do at home. It's all about balance. *Balance, Sarah,*" I stress, giving her a stern look.

"If you keep shoving food down my throat, I'm going to be in the hospital being intubated because I can't breathe," Sarah jokes, shoving one of the three bites of eggs into her mouth and chewing slowly.

Does she realize her eyes are sparkling at me?

I don't want to just shove food down your throat, baby. There's other things that need to go down there as well. I could intubate you with my cock.

I sneak another piece of fruit off her plate, wondering how far she could take me down her throat before she gags.

I laugh when she slaps the back of my hand lightly. "You got a long way to go before that happens," I shoot back, winking at her and then pushing my own plate away, now full. "Listen, I know that I can come across...*intense*...but I really just want you to take care of yourself. Find a balance that works for you and makes you happy without having to deny yourself." I give her a cheeky wink when she nods at me.

Because trust me, denying yourself is not fun.

Though she doesn't verbally respond, I can tell by her active listening skills that she really tries to take my words to heart when I bring up touchy subjects. My chest tightens at the thought that she feels like she needs to not eat sometimes because her ex made her feel insecure.

We finish up and then make our way to the auditorium, passing by tables laden down with mental health paraphernalia littered amidst goodies like small hand sanitizer bottles, stickers, pens, and pop sockets with company logos.

Drawing to a stop at the double-door entrance, I pull my badge out of my pocket and show the security guard, who lets us through. Walking into the space, I pull her to the side gently by her wrist, ignoring the stragglers who make their way in behind us.

"I have to go meet with the other presenters. I'm on at ten," I say hurriedly, nodding at the staff member by the side door who waves at me. "Grab a seat up front and save me a seat next to you so when I'm done, I can come and sit through the rest of the presentations with you." I lean forward and squeeze her arm briefly.

"Okay," she says quietly. "Knock 'em dead."

I smile, sweeping my thumb down her arm when I walk past her. "That's something you'll never have to worry about."

CHAPTER FORTY-TWO

Icy Reminders

I BLINK MY EYES at his touch. Nodding as he turns and makes his way through a side door, quickly shaking hands with another infamous mental health pioneer. Turning on my heel, I make my way to a seat about five rows from the front and at the inner aisle, wanting to get the best view possible.

I sit through the introductions, and the admittedly boring MC droning on about the speakers for the day. The first presenter comes out and sits across from the interviewer. The spotlights shine brightly on them, and I'm quickly swept up in the excitement of it all, impressed at how at ease they look up there. Though I feel at ease when

I'm singing on stage, I don't think I could ever be in their position with thousands of eyes all at once watching me talk.

Worried about how he's doing, I pull out my phone and send Alexander a quick text.

Sarah Bella: Don't be nervous. Remember, envision everyone's tits slangin.'

I send the text with a smile, seeing him respond back with a laughing GIF.

Alex: Naughty girl. You're going to make me mess up my presentation.

Sarah Bella: You can punish me later.

I grin at how comfortable I am at blatantly flirting with him. The speaker suddenly announces his name to come onto the stage, drawing my gaze from my phone. The audience begins to clap, but he's not walking out. I glance back down at my phone curiously. There's a pause as the three dots come up on the screen, and my eyes flicker again to the stage. No Alex.

The speaker calls his name once more, and I bite my lip, nervously furrowing my brow.

Just then, his text comes through. It's a GIF of a man crowding a woman against a wall in a dark space, and the woman looks up at the man helplessly as his hand comes up to spread itself against her jaw, before sliding to the back of her hair and pulling her up gently for a kiss. The fact that he'd just made thousands of people wait so he could respond to me first makes my pussy slick with desire, forcing me to press my legs together hard to control it.

Alex: No punishments, not for you.

Suddenly he appears on stage. A thunderous applause reverberates throughout the auditorium, but when I look up, the noise falls away when we lock eyes, somehow able to even amongst thousands of people. We share a glance for a heartbeat, and he gives me a sexy, mischievous smile before cooling his face into a neutral, pleasant expression. He rewards the auditorium with a quick glance, holding up his hand in greeting.

"*Jesus, that man is so handsome*. Do you know he's single?" I stiffen at the grating female voice behind me.

"For a *reason*, Susan!" A higher-lilted voice responds. "The man is cold as *ice*."

"Really? How do you know that? Do you know him?"

"Me?" She laughs. "No. I have a girlfriend who dated him for a month a while back, and he *never* brought her to his house, never drove her around when they went places, and always had her meet him wherever they went. And he dropped her quickly after maybe five or so weeks?"

The woman gasps. "Really? That's fucking rude as hell."

Her friend hums. "Hm-hm. Said she wasn't what he was looking for and that's it. And apparently, he *never* wanted to sleep with her. Weird."

"Well, *I'd* heard he only keeps them around no longer than a month. And he doesn't date often, but when he *does,* it's usually open and shut. I thought I might give him my number while I'm here. Maybe he'll melt for me?" The other woman giggles.

A sickly hot wave of jealousy hits me, causing my back to stiffen further. Pursing my lips, I fight the urge to turn around and look back at them. Instead, I'm intent on focusing on Alexander, but they just won't shut up.

She makes a thoughtful sound. "I don't think he's all bad, though. And honestly, my friend is a bit of a slut so she probably did something to turn him off." Her friend laughs, but she continues, "You know, he sure has a reputation for having a soft spot for the women clients at his job. My colleague told me he takes more care and consideration with women who lose their kids to the foster care system and spends a ton of his time advocating for them in court. Maybe that's what you need to do, lose a kid to get his attention?"

"I'll be sure to tell him I have two kids."

At her words, the jealousy quickly gives way to nausea, and I snatch up my purse. Just done.

I turn in my seat and throw them both a filthy look before getting up and moving to another part of the audience. My face flames, and anger has my movements more jerky than normal. Alexander pauses in his speech as I gracelessly make my way out into the aisle and a few rows further back, luckily finding two empty seats next to each other. Thankfully, he begins talking again when I settle, but his words are more stilted than they were prior to me relocating.

My playful mood of the morning evaporates, and I sulk, trying to keep my attention on Alex, who's now regained his stride and is answering all the interviewer's questions confidently. Assessing his reaction to the questions, I take a few seconds to observe his demeanor on stage and note that he *is* rather cold: his blue eyes are icy, and his responses are clipped, short, and to the point.

Alexander finishes up his set and then exits the stage to another round of thunderous applause. I clap along with them, then curiously turn my head to see the woman from the seat I'd left eyeing him hungrily. Another wave of jealousy hits me, and I curl my lip, ignoring the pain in my back as I cross my legs.

I pull out my phone and text Vanessa about the interaction, having just hit send when Alexander appears and slides smoothly in the seat next to me. I glance over at the two women. They're still caught up deep in conversation and haven't noticed him enter the back of the auditorium and sit next to me.

He leans into my ear. "Hey there. Why did you change seats?" he asks. He spreads out, draping his arm along the back of my chair.

I turn my phone slightly when I see Vanessa respond with a very long text. The scent of his cologne has me clench my legs together tightly. A dull, achy pressure moves through my thighs. They've been getting quite the workout the last couple days.

"There were a couple of women behind me who wouldn't stop talking, so I moved," I say, lying by omission. Not wanting to embarrass him that others were talking about him in that way. I become very still as his fingers suddenly touch my shoulder in a gentle, soothing caress, making my heart skip a beat as a hesitant pleasure fills me at the contact. "You did great up th-there by the way." I stammer. "The people in the audience loved you."

When he turns his head, his eyes pierce mine, and he gives me that same sexy grin from earlier. "Thank you. I imagined someone naked."

Oh my God.

My eyes widen. "Y-You mean *everyone*...not *someone,*" I stress. Because surely...

His grin gets a little wider as his eyes flicker to my lips, and his voice goes deeper. Lower. "No...I said it right. I meant *someone.* Singular."

My heart begins to race out of control, and my breath hitches as we lock eyes again. This weird tingling sensation fills me, and before I know it, our faces are slowly tilting towards each other. He's so close his breath washes over my lips. His hand tightens on my shoulder, pulling me slightly into him, and my pussy becomes heavy and hot with need. My clit pinches with arousal, as do my nipples, which draw tight under my blouse.

His are slightly hooded and single-mindedly focused on mine. The sounds of the audience dull to a slight murmur in the background as everyone and everything falls away, leaving just the two of us and this moment. His hand slides up from my shoulder to cup my nape warmly under my hair, causing me to break out in goosebumps.

"Come here..." he whispers, bringing me in even closer.

Just before our lips touch, the room explodes in another round of applause, forcing me to jerk away and breathing hard.

I don't miss the frustrated groan or the searing hot look of desire he gives me before he scrubs a hand across his jaw and places his arm back around me. His fingers begin a calm rapping, and as I glance over, I see his foot is bobbing along to the same beat of his fingers. I'm aware that whereas *I* meditate to calm myself, *he* uses music. And he's no doubt probably going over a piece in his head.

We watch the next two speakers, and I fidget, wanting to open my phone and look at Vanessa's response. Even tell her about our almost kiss. But I hold off, not wanting to risk him seeing it. I breathe a sigh of relief when the host announces a brief intermission, and I get up quickly, wanting to read the text message. I look down at him shyly, not quite able to make eye contact.

"I'm going to stretch my legs and use the restroom, and maybe look at the mental health flyers they have over there," I say, carefully sliding by him as his long legs preclude me from easily brushing past him.

Alexander stands up anyways right as I make it past him. "I'll join you," he says, lazily smoothing his hand down his suit jacket before following me out to the aisle.

I draw to a stop just outside the aisle, tensing up as a tall, older gentleman accompanied by another younger man suddenly comes out of nowhere, stepping forward and thrusting his hand at Alexander with a big, familiar smile on his face.

"Dr. Richardson!" The man drawls in a deep southern voice, making me smile. "So nice to see you!"

I stand awkwardly silent as the other man glances at me curiously and flicks his eyes down my body in a bold look. My mouth twists as Alexander suddenly places his hand on my lower back and inches me forward slightly.

"Dr. Phillips, this is Sarah Johnson. She's a wonderful therapist who's stationed near me in Connecticut." I fight from tensing up at how uncomfortable the other man makes me feel.

Though my fingers tremble with nerves, I hold my hand out to the older gray-haired man who takes it but then bends forward and surprises me by kissing my cheek in greeting. I bite my lip, blushing furiously as the man steps back, patting the back of my hand.

"Ma'am, please don't think me too forward, but you smell absolutely delightful," Dr. Phillip says kindly. "Do tell me your scent so I can buy it for my wife."

"She wears Kilian's Love, Don't Be Shy," Alexander interjects smoothly, but my throat is so constricted I can't say anything. "It's pricey, so just go on ahead and kiss the wallet goodbye now!" He laughs; his blue eyes warm, looking down at me teasingly.

Our eyes lock again, and I stare, beginning to tremble and almost scared to smile back at him.

Breaking our eye contact, I look away nervously and take a step back. "Excuse me," I say softly, turning and leaving them to their conversation.

I make my way out of the auditorium and use the restroom before coming back out to the lobby and seeing Alexander surrounded by people. I take my time going over the pamphlets, looking up when the announcer speaks over the intercom announcing the resuming of the program in ten minutes.

Looking back over, I tense when I see the woman from earlier, who'd bragged about wanting to give Alexander her number, standing rather close to him. She's pretty, long, dirty blonde hair, and bright blue eyes like his. They're speaking. I'm sure it's innocent, but I can't help but heat with jealousy once more, so thick I want to scream with it. I nibble my bottom lip, aware I've got it pretty bad for Alex. Somewhere along the way I've caught feelings, and I don't quite know how to deal with them. My eyes slide to him.

He bends over slightly to her short frame and nods at her once, holding out his hand for the card she's giving him.

I bite my lip as she places her hand on his arm rather suggestively. But what happens next makes me frown; Alexander stiffens the moment she touches him, the icy mask falls back into place, and he pulls away sternly but still keeps his demeanor rather professional. I catch the hurt look on the woman's face, but Alexander continues to talk with her as if he didn't just reject her.

"Hey, there you are. So, I couldn't help noticing, or rather *overhearing,* that you're a therapist?" a husky voice sounds out next to me, startling me.

I turn, shoving my papers into my bag and meet a pair of chocolate eyes, seeing it's the man who'd been standing next to Dr. Phillips. I take a hasty step back and clutch my bag tighter to me. I hadn't liked his energy earlier, and I don't like it now. Though I try to relax my posture, my shoulders hunch of their own volition.

I stay quiet even as small trembles wrack my body. I'm painfully aware I don't know this man and don't wish to judge him, but something about him feels familiar.

Too familiar.

It clicks. *He reminds me of Brandon.*

I feel my skin suddenly break out into a sweat at the realization. The man holds his hand out to me, and I just stare at it, my fingers like a vice grip around the handle of my purse. I make myself take a deep breath and unclench my fingers, grasping just the very tip of his in greeting and a *very* tiny smile. That's all I can manage.

"My name is Charles. I have a practice in New York, and I believe I'm only a bit away from you. Maybe we could hang out one day, get to know each other more?" He looks at me expectantly, and though his smile is warm, there's an edge to it I don't trust.

Determined to not look like a freak, I open my mouth, trying to find the words, but they won't come. In my mind I hear Brandon screaming at me. My heart races, the small amount of lingering pain in my back heightens, making my stomach knot. Charles has me stuck; I can't look away from him.

"Uhm. *Uhhh...* "I stammer, swallowing thickly and wetting my lips. I flinch hard when I feel a hand on my back and bite back a scream of terror. Looking over, I see it's Alexander. My heart draws to a sudden stop before racing at a breakneck speed.

"*Baby*, are you alright?" He looks down at me with a stern expression. However, there's nothing but veiled concern in his eyes, which slide rather sharply to Charles.

My knees buckle as I sag in relief, but Alexander pulls me to him smoothly, hiding me from embarrassment. He leans down, pressing his lips against my temple as he rubs soothing circles on my lower back. I tremble, and my heart rate starts to slow as his scent washes over me, making me relax and feel safe.

Charles' eyes go wide.

"Oh, I'm *sorry.* I didn't realize you were together," Charles says. His eyebrows knit together as Alexander suddenly slides his hand from its spot on my lower back to grip my hip.

Pressing me rather indecently against his side, Alexander's lips are still in my hair as he replies in a curt tone, "I was standing right next to her. You should have known better." Alexander's tone is so icy with the man that I feel myself shiver as I break out into a full-body flush. *"Excuse us,"* he says rudely, turning us both and putting his hand around my waist, keeping us pressed close as we walk back to our seats.

I'm thankful for his intervention. I can't believe I've had such an embarrassingly horrible public reaction. Not able to help it, I chance a look over my shoulder as we walk away, seeing a put out look on Charle's face that erases almost the moment our eyes lock. I turn my head forward...

Safe.

CHAPTER FORTY-THREE

WARM BLUE SKIES

I KEEP HER CLOSE to me, seeing an immense shift in her body language. She's tight and uncomfortable. Morose. Guarded.

"Thank you," Sarah says thickly.

As she looks up at me, I observe her eyes swimming with tears.

I glance at her briefly as I work to steer us back to where we were sitting. "No thanks needed, sweetness. Are you okay to sit through the rest of the seminars, or do you want to go back to the room to lay down?" I ask quietly as we approach our row.

I wait as she settles herself into her seat, fussing with her hair and getting comfortable before I sit.

She looks at me as I adjust my suit jacket before leaning back and settling my arm across the back of her seat. "I'd like to sit through some more; I mean, that's the reason why I came. Not to hide the whole time because I had an unfortunate flashback..." She trails off, putting her purse in her lap.

She nonchalantly pulls the program out of a side pocket and opens it. Her eyes flicker back and forth, following her finger sliding down the page. Though I can't blame her, I can tell she's putting on a façade to hide what just happened, and I'll be damned if this woman hides anything from me. I want it all. Every emotion, dirty or clean.

I lean a little more into her space, making sure to keep my voice low. "*Sarah*, what did he say?"

A hesitant look flits across her features, and she fusses with the leather handle of her purse as if she's trying to find something to comfort her. The interviewer and new speaker begin to talk as she places her mouth to my ear. My hand, braced on my thigh, trembles slightly when the soft tresses of her hair suddenly tumble into my lap. She's not aware of it, though.

Nor is she aware that I've tangled my fingers in the strands, rubbing gently.

"It wasn't what he said; it was the way he made me *feel,*" she whispers quietly, and a hot shiver rolls its way up my back at the way her lips lightly brush the shell of my ear. "Something about him reminded me of Brandon; it was his energy. Thank you so much for stepping in when you did." When she pulls away to settle back into her chair, her long hair trails through my fingertips whisper-soft.

I'm reluctant to let her go, so I put my hand in hers and thread our fingers together. She makes no movement, but I can feel her eyes on where we're clasped. My heart beats a bit harder at how right it feels, and I wonder if she thinks so too, but her phone pings suddenly, distracting her.

"Oops, sorry." She glances apologetically out the side of her eye before moving to pull out her phone with her free hand. Something like anger swirls deep in my chest when the screen lights up, and I continue to stare. I don't mean to be nosy, but I want to know if that idiot fucker of an employee of mine has texted her. The fingers of her left hand twitch in mine as she inhales a sharp breath, and my own narrow upon seeing Brandon's name. *Not* Dickhead David.

My fingers tighten on hers as I read the text.

> Brandon: I was thinking about what we would have named our baby... and I think we could have picked a simple name like Katherine. I miss you, Sarah. I think about you all the time, and I just want you to know how sorry I am. For everything.

That motherfucker.

Immeasurable anger slices through my being before being replaced by concern. My eyes slide to her face, assessing her quietly.

Sarah visibly stiffens before making a choked sound. The phone dims, and she goes deathly still, still staring at the screen. I don't react, aware that she needs a minute to let his words sink in to her consciousness. She blinks, and my chest tightens with sympathetic hurt when tears leak out of her eyes onto her cheeks.

I'm five seconds from snatching her phone and breaking it when she jerks in the seat, dispelling that thought quickly. My hand tightens on her shoulder, but she stands up in a rush, stumbling as she tries to get out of the row.

"I'm sorry, Alex. *I c-can't do this,*" she chokes out, swiping her tears away as she makes it past me and out into the aisle.

Rising, I'm quickly behind her, mindfully keeping a step behind as she briskly walks through the auditorium doors. Letting herself out before I can even hold the door open for her.

Her short gait is nothing for me to catch up to, and soon I'm step-in-step beside her fighting to not break the silence. Painfully aware she needs a moment to process.

Sarah's face is flushed with emotion. My eyes prick at the tiny whimpers bravely trapped in her throat as we journey silently through the marble lobby. I can tell she's fighting as hard as she can to walk to the elevator calmly. To her credit, she manages it quite gracefully. Though, to my utter dismay, she seems like she can't even tell it's me behind her she's so desperate to flee. That man turned her inside out. Made her wary and scared. Even of me.

My fears are validated when she flinches when I join her in the empty elevator. Her wide eyes meet mine, full of shock and shiny with tears. I feel my jaw tick as I reach my hand out to grab her; however, she promptly turns her back to me. In the mirrored elevator, she clasps her hands together hard, obviously trying to stem the shaking. Her eyes are squeezed shut even harder.

My heart, already pounding, breaks in half at how lost she is.

"We're almost to the room, baby," I reassure her quietly, keeping my distance. Not wanting to startle her or make her feel even more overwhelmed than she already is. "It's going to be okay."

A small tingle of shame flows through me.

I discard all pretense that the attraction I already knew was between us hasn't blossomed into something deeper. Tangible. It snuck up on us like a secret in the night, and all it needed was an opportunity to deepen its roots. I have no time to muse over it because the sensitive situation at hand requires every ounce of attention and care I can give it, and I can't have my focus being muddied by whether or not I should've used a term of endearment.

The elevator pings before the doors open. I settle my hand on her lower back in a move as familiar as her scent has grown to be and press, steering her forward. Worry fills me when she lets out a pained sound in her throat as we exit and head left for our room. Pulling out the key, she tries to put it in the door, but her hand is shaking so badly she can't get it to fit into the slot.

I hear her teeth grind as my hand closes over hers and make her steady, helping her to get the keycard in.

My concern ramps up. A sweltering trickle of trepidation creeps down my spine as she begins to pant now, and her skin breaks out in a fine mist of sweat. The door clicks, and she grabs the handle with everything in her and pushes. She wipes a hand across her top lip on a muffled sob.

"Sarah, *breathe,*" I remind her calmly as she bursts through the door, dropping her phone and her purse into the foyer floor as she flies through the living space towards the bedroom.

I don't even stop to pick up her things.

Closing the door, I step over them and head through to the bedroom as well, keeping my eyes tight on her. At the bedroom, I linger in the doorway, one hand on the knob as she turns furiously to face me, her hair whipping. Though she's in such a state of distress, my mind can't help but whirl. I've never seen my ex-wife out of sorts like this. The only other experience I've had with women and panic attacks are through my clients, and I become uncomfortably warm myself, shrugging out of my suit jacket and slinging it across the end of her bed.

"Oh, god," she says in a strained voice, turning to now pace back and forth.

My brows knit with dismay as she yanks off her blazer, lifting her hair off her neck and fanning herself with her hand. Though it's not hot in here, I head to the thermostat.

"Sarah," I say quietly, reaching over to turn the air a bit cooler. "Slow down, honey. You're working yourself into—"

Sarah suddenly claws at her necklace, tearing the necklace off with a shrill cry and then begins yanking off her blouse. It tumbles to the floor at her feet, leaving her in a lacy black bra, but it doesn't seem to offer any relief. Her eyes go slightly unfocused as she keeps tearing at her body.

"*Off*. Get it off," she grits through her teeth, yanking her fingers down her arm and ripping off her bracelet.

Seeing she's completely losing her senses to a panic attack, I walk to her and lower, unclasping the strap of her high heel and tugging it off. She jerks against my hold to help, but in her haste she stumbles and trips. I move quickly, catching her before she hits the floor. I sink down to my knees beside her and lower her to the carpet, hearing her pained moans as she now struggles to get her pants off. Her nails hinder her from unclasping the button.

"Don't push me through the table," she yells, undulating in my arms.

My eyes widen. *Oh God.*

No.

My heart races as she violently arches. The shadows of her ribcage straining against the thin skin of her torso as she still desperately tries to get her pants off, but she's fumbling too hard.

"Fuck," I curse. Throwing caution to the wind, I unclasp her button and yank, thankful when the material gives and lowers over her hips. She falls to her back on the carpet, and I pull harder, trying to help get them off around her thrashing. I get one leg free before she makes another high-pitched noise.

"I can't breeaatheee," Sarah whimpers hoarsely, flipping to her stomach before the other pant leg can come off. *"Oh my God, I can't breathe!"* Her lace clad chest heaves as she coughs. Leaving red marks on her delicate skin, she claws at her breasts, fighting for air that's wheezing out of her throat.

"Sarah, I'm here. I'm here, sweetheart."

"No!" she gasps, her hand sweeps fast along the carpet, trying to feel for something.

But there's nothing. Nothing except me.

I reach over, grasping her hand and squeezing her fingers. "Sarah, I'm right here. You can breathe. You're having a panic attack, sweetie. Please listen to my voice and let me lead you."

Tension tightens her face, and she lets out another sob. Helpless, my heart begins to pound out of control, and the hair stands up on the back of my arms and neck as another uncomfortable shiver rolls through my body. Sarah reaches around to her back, but then her arm jerks and she lets out a pained cry at the soreness she no doubt still feels there. Working fast, I finally get her pants off, now revealing a lacy pair of black panties, and I shuffle back a bit to give her room as she flops around on the floor and reaches around once more, trying to find the clasp on her bra but still can't reach it.

And I can't find it in myself to compromise her dignity while she's at her most vulnerable.

My chest tightens even more when she begins sobbing. *"He doesn't want to be my friend; he's only doing this because I'm pathetic, just like Brandon said."*

My eyes widen, and I stiffen as I hear the words, strangled and full of pain, rip from her throat. I ignore my heart pounding and reach forward to smooth my hands down her hair, her shoulders, trying to comfort her. I don't care that she's half dressed and flip-flopping all over the floor or if this is improper at all. I just want to help. However, at this point in her panic attack, I don't even know if she can recognize my efforts or not.

I fight through the tightness in my own throat. "No, sweetie, that's not true at all. You're not pathetic, and I *am* your friend. Listen to my voice. Let yourself reach for my voice. *I'm right here.*"

"Get it oooffff!" she screams.

She bends her arm and scratches for her bra clasp again. The choked gasping torn from her throat is my undoing. I give up trying to preserve her dignity at this point, reaching around and unclasping her bra. The result is so fast its as if I'd performed a miracle. Every straining muscle relaxes as she immediately lowers herself into a downward dog position. Placing her cheek against the rough wool of the carpet, crying big heaving sobs that finish cracking what's left of my heart.

When our eyes lock, she brings her hands up to her face, covering herself.

"Oh, sweetness," I murmur. "You don't ever need to hide herself with me."

Ever.

Standing, I walk a couple feet to the foot of the bed and grab a pillow, before sinking back to the floor with her. "You're safe," I repeat.

I cradle one hand under her head and shoulder, and then lift her to settle across me. While I work, I try my hardest to make sure her breasts stay out of view, protecting her modesty. Shifting my legs so I can make her as comfortable as possible, I can't help but notice how her breasts feel squashed in my lap as I settle her across my thighs on the floor.

She cries for long, torturous minutes. Every sob and wet drop that soaks into my thigh fucks with my head.

Tears flow in unrestrained streams down her cheeks as she lays there, trembling. She stares at my bare forearm, making me aware that at some point I'd pushed up the sleeves of my dress shirt and loosened my tie. She blinks and sniffs. The tears begin to recede when my hand comes up to rest on her head, just over her left ear. I press gently, hoping—wishing—to ground her. My other hand raises to the top of her back and makes gentle sweeping motions all the way to her nape and then back down to her hip.

I can't believe she's letting me touch her like this.

"Sarah... tell me five things you can see."

Though I try my hardest to keep my tone soft, I still jolt her.

She trembles, her eyes flickering. "Uhm...I see your watch, the blue of your suit...the platform of the bed, the w-window...the desk chair there."

"Give me four things you can touch," I say, matching her tone, stroking her hair now. My wrist brushes her cheek as I move, and she takes a deep breath.

"The carpet, your legs, this pillow, my hair," she breathes on an exhale before dragging another deep breath into her lungs.

"Good girl," I say, keeping my touch light. "Tell me three things you can hear."

"Your voice, my voice...the—the air conditioner." Her eyes flutter, and she sags on another slower breath, relaxing even further into me.

"That's it," I croon. "Relax. You're safe here with me, sweetness. Now, take another deep breath and tell me two things you can smell."

Sarah takes a deep breath before furrowing her nose and frowning slightly. "My perfume. Coming from your hip very strongly for some reason," she whispers, glancing up at me, and I feel my face turn hot and my chest tighten at being caught. "And *you*. I smell you. You smell very good...like a man."

I chuckle humorlessly. "Thank God I'm a man. Now, one thing you can taste." I lean my head back into the mattress, looking up at the ceiling, feeling pained.

But I have to finish talking her through this before I can focus on myself.

I wait a few moments before I suddenly feel the warm wet lash of her tongue on my wrist. To my dismay, my cock hardens immediately at the contact, and I'm grateful she's not that far on top of me to feel. I tilt my head, looking down at her and raise a brow.

"You just...*licked me,"* I say rather stupidly, wincing as disbelief colors my tone.

"Well, it was only fair since you licked me first, remember?" she says, closing her eyes and going silent once more. I lean my head back to rest against the bed again and continue to stroke her back.

"Your bruises are almost gone," I say conversationally. "Your skin is so beautiful." My fingers slow as I let myself enjoy the feel of her skin against mine. I refuse to look back down at her. Seeing her body like this is going to give me a one-way ticket to hell, and I have a sickening thought that if I look back down at her, there would be no going back. She's too vulnerable and doesn't need another man coming onto her. "Sarah," I harden my voice, "I didn't see anything. Your hair covered your breasts, baby. I just wanted you to know that in case you were worried." I swallow thickly. "I didn't look."

Fucking hell, I can't believe I didn't look.

My chest expands on a deep breath as I try to get ahold of my emotions and traitorous desire.

"Thank you," Sarah says in a soft tone, turning her head slightly to face away from me and heaving a deep sigh as if she's content. As if she's settled.

As if she's safe.

I can't remember the last time I felt like someone felt settled in my presence.

"My pleasure. Are you okay to get up? I'd like to get you a washcloth for your face; then, you should probably lay down and rest. You just had a pretty bad panic attack." I wait a couple of seconds, but she doesn't respond or move. "I'm going to call room service and have them bring something up since we missed lunch and dessert, which you're going to eat first. You need something sweet to help," I say roughly.

"Some chocolate might be nice," she replies in a tired tone before raising to one lithe arm with her back to me. My hand settles at the delicate curve of her back into the swell of her hip. It takes everything in me to not tighten my grip there.

I keep my face averted as she clutches the pillow to her front. I stand and help her up, watching as she walks slowly to my side of the bed and crawls in silently, not bothering with trying to pull any clothes on.

I walk to the bathroom and wet a washcloth before walking back out to her. I kneel next to the bed and wipe her face gently, careful not to smear her makeup. I stay quiet, understanding that she needs time to recover, and reach over for the phone and order us some lunch and another piece of chocolate cake, stroking her cheek the entire time.

I may have a one-way ticket to hell for having my hands all over her right now, but I'll be damned if I deny myself these small moments of intimacy. We both need it.

Hanging up, I stay kneeling on the floor, enraptured by her wide, dark-pink mouth and thick lashes that lay just right on her cheeks. She'd closed her eyes, and her chest rises and falls softly, looking like she's slowly falling asleep. I'm so lost staring, watching her features settle into being calm, that I inhale in surprise when her hazel eyes suddenly open and lock with mine.

I meet her gaze patiently, wanting with everything in me to close the distance between us and kiss her soft, full lips. She's beautiful. Absolutely breathtaking.

I can't believe I'm this close to you, baby.

My chest tightens hard at the pain in her eyes.

"I'm *s-sorry*," she whispers, her voice cracking as tears suddenly fall down her face and then onto the pillow beneath her. "I didn't mean to. This was supposed to be *your* week." Her face contorts with pain and embarrassment, and she brings a hand up to cover her face. "Oh my god. I didn't mean to make it all about me, and I couldn't even make it through the second *day* w-without—"

"No, don't." Tugging her hand from her face, I put my hand gently across her mouth, hushing her words. "Please, stop," I plead hoarsely, leaning forward to place my forehead against hers. "You have nothing to apologize for, sweetness. *Do you hear me? Nothing!*"

We stay like this for long minutes, pressed intimately together. Her warm breath glides over my hand. I reluctantly let her wrap her fingers around my wrist and gently pull my hand away from her lips. Her eyes meet mine warily, as if she's worried. I tense when she tugs our clasped hands to her mouth.

"She said you were cold," Sarah says quietly, pressing her lips to my knuckles and closing her eyes briefly.

Though I relish her affection, her words give me pause. I frown and tilt my head, my brow furrowing in confusion. "Hm, sweetheart? Who said?" I ask gently, feeling my heart starting to race again. Perplexed. Her wet eyes flicker between mine, somehow warm and sad at the same time.

Cherishing how intimate this is, I allow myself to brush my thumb across her bottom lip, marveling at its plump, smooth texture.

"The women behind me when you were speaking. They were talking badly about you. *That's* why I moved seats. They said a few things...but what they said wasn't true," Sarah says harshly, releasing my hand and reaching for my face. "You're not cold. Not to me."

Her hand molds against the side of my face, warm and soft.

I lean into her hand. So touch starved I feel like a man deprived of oxygen, and she's offering me my first breath in so long I forgot what it felt like to breathe. My eyes flicker between hers, and I hold my breath at the first caress of her fingers against my cheek.

A single tear slips from her eyes that I wipe away gently. "People might look into your eyes and see ice, but when *I* look into them, I see a bright, clear blue sky with no clouds to bring thunderstorms or darkness. Just beautiful, soft warm blue as far as the eye can see. It reminds me that I'm alive, and I'm grateful for that. I don't see what they see, Alex. And I *really* hope you don't either."

Her words ring soundly in my head, my eyes widen as they stare into hers, and my body flushes from head to toe. Tingles erupt everywhere, and I realize...

I'm in love with her.

My heart stops beating as I kneel here, staring at her for several quiet seconds. So much passes between us. Sacred, intense, indescribable.

Inevitable...

When my body stops betraying me, I let out a ragged exhale.

Tearing my eyes from hers, I snatch her hand up and put my lips to her inner wrist before pushing off the floor, making my way to the bathroom, and closing the door. Turning the handle to the shower, I go back to the vanity and strip out of my clothes, tossing them to the side. Her words swell inside my head; the torturous echo on repeat, reminding me I'm so close to what I want but can't have. Placing my hands flat on the vanity, I lean forward as the steam begins to tumble out of the shower and invade the room around me. The humidity mists my skin, cocooning me in a warm embrace. But I don't want the steam.

Memories of my ex swirl inside my head. Of the times I'd let my guard down, thinking I could be vulnerable with her. But I never could. It was always a trap. Fake, much like her.

But with Sarah, I want something real. I don't want the steam's embrace...

I wish it was *her.*

I glance up, looking at myself in the reflection of the mirror, reaching out a hand to caress down the image of my eyes. The same ones I'd spent my whole life hearing how cold and lifeless they are. How closed off I could be.

The shower roars, pounding against the tile and highlighting how alone I am right now. Glancing at the bathroom door, I temporarily lose my mind and take a step forward to grab her and bring her in here with me before coming to an abrupt halt. *"Alex,"* I chastise myself. I look to the side sharply and will myself to get a grip.

Balling my hand into a fist, I fight against walking back in the bedroom and asking her to join me. Instead, I turn away from my image to step into the shower, alone.

Placing my hands flat on the tiled wall, I hang my head. The hot water pounds down on my head, soaking the strands. Tears prick the back of my eyes, and I bite my lip on a harsh sob. Because I'm *not* icy like everyone's made me believe I was all these years. I'm warm. A soft, clear blue sky.

Like *Sarah* said.

Keeping my head hanging down, I shudder—weak—on a bit-off sob, letting myself cry. Cry for myself, and cry for the woman in the next room whom I'm in love with...and she's not ready.

CHAPTER FORTY-FOUR

LIFE'S NOTHING BUT A DREAM

TOO WIRED TO SLEEP, I lay next to Sarah after our lunch, my eyes greedily roaming the exposed brown skin of her back calling to me as she naps. I turn my head back towards the ceiling, wishing I could scoot closer and curl around her, instinctively knowing her body heat and her touch would help lull me to sleep. I'm restless. My mind races with all the feelings I feel for her that are so different and unlike anything else I've experienced before.

Seeing a bright light suddenly glow against the ceiling above us, I turn my face to my phone and pick it up. Hannah's name on the screen has me tensing with anxiety and irritation because the fact she is reaching out to me personally instead of going through Tyler means these phone calls are going to become more frequent. Which means my blood pressure is about to be through the roof all the time.

"Fuck." I groan quietly.

Swinging my legs off the bed, I get up quietly and answer the call as I walk through the bedroom door into the sitting room. I keep the door cracked and my voice low so I don't wake Sarah up.

"Hello, Hannah." I greet her in my usual, impassive tone, already bracing myself for the vitriol that usually comes during an interaction with her. I consider forwarding the call, but I answer on the off chance something's happened with Tyler.

"Hey, Alexander."

I pause at her sad tone. "Hannah, is everything okay with Tyler?" My chest tightens, always worried about my boy.

"Yeah, everything's fine." She scoffs softly. "Calm down, I'm not calling about him."

"Oh," I state simply, feeling the knot in my chest ease up. Walking to the chair, I sink down. "What do you need now, then? More money?"

Hannah pauses on the other line. "No. I didn't call for that, either. Gosh, you make me sound like a beggar."

Because you are. I make a small sound, refusing to acknowledge that one way or another.

She continues, never realizing how uncomfortable she makes me. Or when to stop. "No, um...I was actually kind of hoping maybe we could have dinner when you get back in town." She huffs a quiet, awkward laugh.

My eyebrows raise. "For what reason, Hannah?" I ask sternly.

"I was hoping we could... well,...*reconnect."*

"No." I don't hesitate in the slightest. "There's no reason to, Hannah. Tyler is eighteen. We've been divorced for nine years. We don't need to go down that road. As long as we can stay cordial, then we're good."

As if I'd ever give up a possible life with Sarah to go back to this headache. This *nightmare* of a woman.

"Are you seeing someone?" Her voice is breathless, desperate.

I take a deep breath. "Respectfully, I fail to see where that's any of your business."

"Alexander," she snaps. *"I'm the mother of your son—"*

"A fact that I do not need to be verbally reminded of, *I assure you,*" I clip back.

"God, what the fuck is *wrong* with you?" she cries in a shrill voice, immediately causing my hackles to rise. "Must you *always* be so fucking cold?"

"No. Apparently to someone else I'm a warm, blue sky." And with that I hang up, feeling validated.

I leave my phone on the round table next to the chair and then make my way back to the bedroom. Sarah's scent envelopes my senses and calms me instantly. Heading to the sliding door of the patio, I close the curtains tighter to shut out the evening light, then get back into bed, placing a soft kiss against a fading bruise on her shoulder blade. Carefully, I mold my body to her back and bury my face into her neck. Giving myself permission to wrap myself around her. Though I can't see them, I boldly palm her breasts, memorizing the feel of her.

My fingers glide over her softened nipples, memorizing the way her breasts smash against each other as she lays on her side.

I smile, loving the weight of her in my palm, and slide my other hand in between her legs and over her panties. I relax instantly, settling in, and fall asleep quickly, lured in by her body heat as Hannah's words dissipate like they were never said.

It doesn't matter if I'm cold...she's warm enough for the both of us.

I stare into Sarah's eyes as I lay myself on her body and rejoice at the feel of her naked skin on mine. I chuckle against her lips as she moans so sexily as I cup her breast in my hand and squeeze, leaning down to place my lips against hers. I deepen the kiss, desperately eager to finally taste her.

She tastes like life.

Our tongues dance as my hand roams lower, trailing down her belly and to her smooth mound.

"Ahhh, sweetness. Are you ready?" I ask, searching lower until I find her clit. Grasping and rolling it, I lower my mouth to hers, swallowing her high moan.

Sarah rips her lips away with a gasp. "Alex," she whispers, her fingers clutch my shoulders tightly as I slowly place two fingers inside of her. A shudder ripples down my spine as her tight flesh ripples around me. So soft and velvety that I know right then and there nothing else will ever do for me except her.

"God, baby, you're so warm," I praise quietly. I tangle the fingers of my other hand into her curls, making her keep eye contact though she's blushing so hard she's trying to avert her face. I smile at her, loving we're like this. Our hearts are free, connected. "So luscious. So worth waiting for, my love. You're worth everything...you know that?"

Her eyes flicker between mine as I press deeper, parting her flesh relentlessly. "Ohhh!" she cries out again, arching her head back as her mouth parts in pleasure.

I thrust hard, hearing the wet muted sound of my fingers working against her. I rejoice, feeling her wiggle before she bends her knees back and spreads her pretty legs even wider for me. My heart swells inside of my chest as my eyes roam her face, finally feeling connected.

The one I'd waited for and cherished was finally here for me to love.

Love.

To rest secure in the knowledge that someone who deserved everything in life was underneath me. I just want to treat her well. Make her feel good, deserve her in return.

"Alex." She moans, wetting her lips. "Ohhhh...." she cries out with her orgasm.

Her hips buck against my hand, and her fingers dig deeper. Perspiration makes her face glow dewy and soft, and her eyes are warm liquid pools of love and desire. I close my eyes for a moment as a rush of every sensation possible fills me bone deep.

God... am I worthy? I just want to be worthy of her...

I groan as her giggles mix with whimpers as she wiggles under me, trying to get away from the pleasure. Smiling with happiness, I lower my head to take her nipple into my mouth—

"Alex, wake up!"

At the sound of Sarah calling my name anxiously I startle awake, sitting straight up with my chest heaving and my aching cock tenting the blankets. I pull up a knee to hide it and scrub a hand down my face on a deep inhale that does nothing to calm me. I turn my face to her and see Sarah sitting up in bed next to me, clutching the covers to her naked chest. My eyes roam the bare expanse of her arm and her shapely shoulder that flows into her delicate collarbone, and lower to where her cleavage is barely covered. Her thick dark-brown hair is slightly mussed, and her eyes are wide on mine, letting me look as much as I want.

"Are you okay? You sounded like you were having a bad dream." She turns her face to look at the clock on the nightstand, giving me a peek of the flawless side of her breast. Fuck. "We overslept," she says simply.

I nod, feeling my heart rate start to slow, but my erection won't let up. She's too warm. Too fragrant next to me.

"I'm pretty sure we missed dinner, so we'll have to go out. The resort's restaurant has to be closed by now." Not able to help myself, my eyes lower once more down to the sheet clutched to her breasts, relishing the blush that spreads across her cheeks.

"Well, I feel refreshed. Late afternoon naps are the best!" she says with a small smile that doesn't quite reach her eyes, clearly still feeling vulnerable after her panic attack.

I clear my throat gently. "I'm glad. I think I needed the sleep too," I say, rubbing a hand down my face.

It's interesting when awareness hits her that she's only in her panties. It hits her slowly; her lips twitch, her eyes dart away from mine, and her hand hauls the sheet higher under her chin.

"I'm sorry....this must be uncomfortable for you. I just—*the clothes thing*... I'm sorry," she repeats, closing her eyes in embarrassment.

I give her a smile, hoping it doesn't look as predatory as I feel. Under different circumstances, I'd have her on her back.

"Don't apologize. I think it's an incredibly sexy quirk." I ignore the surprised look on her face that draws her eyes even wider. "You seem to have a lot of those," I tease before hauling myself off the bed. "Let's get ready to go. Go take a quick shower; I'm sure you'll feel much better.

I'm going to head to the front and ask the receptionist what's a good place to eat nearby, and call us a driver. Give you a little privacy."

"O-Okay..."

Kneeling, I slide my shoes on and pull on a jacket before making my way out of the room.

CHAPTER FORTY-FIVE

Lead Me

I NOD, ROLLING MY lips together and feeling my face flush from his words. I stay silent as he leaves the room, hearing the door shut with a click. Now alone, I jump in the shower and take my time scrubbing, thinking about the attraction between us.

How safe I feel around him.

Getting out of the shower I put on some makeup and carefully slide into a form-fitting strapless dress that hugs my curves and accentuates my breasts. I pull my hair over one shoulder and apply hair oil, making the long tresses shiny. I take a second to put my bracelets back on, seeing he'd put those by my travel bags in the bathroom, and clasp my necklace back on. I pause for a second, feeling so bad that I'd ripped off his present.

Though I'm horrified that he saw me this way, I'm glad it was him that I had a panic attack with. I just hate that he seems to be privy to all my worst moments, for some reason. So, I take a little extra care with my appearance, desiring to give him something good to look at for once instead of the crazy, discombobulated person I seem to have morphed into.

Finished, I turn and eye myself in the mirror, pleased at what I see. Giving my lips a little smack, I exit the bathroom and glance around.

"Alex? *Are you back?"* I call out, looking at my phone as I turn the corner into the room.

Picking up my phone, I tap out a quick text to Vanessa, asking to meet up when I get back into town. Suddenly a chill races through my body, and the hair on the back of my neck stands. I sense his gaze on me before I see him. My heart begins to pitter-patter, and my face warms as I look up. Alexander is standing across the room, eyeing me with the same hungry look that he had when we woke up in bed together. I swallow thickly when heady, red-hot desire slams into me once again.

But it's brighter this time. Deeper.

My breathing turns fast and shallow at the way his eyes drag down my body, stopping at the short hemline of my dress.

"Hm-hm. I'm right here," Alexander says softly, in the middle of switching out his watch for another one. His eyes flick back to mine, and he gives me a sly smile. One that lets me know he's in control despite the almost suffocating tension between us. "That dress is... *sensual."* He stares for another achingly slow heartbeat before turning his attention back to his watch.

Wanting to be brave, I approach him and take his wrist into my hands.

"Let me help." My fingers snap the clasp gently before smoothing over the band of the watch. Though he's tilted his head to try to meet my eyes, I keep my gaze averted and step away, turning back to the bedroom door. Desperately in search of liquid courage because I think I need to tell this man how I feel. What I want. *"Hey,"* I say teasingly, "how bad would the tab be if we broke into the mini bar? I think I'd like a shot before we go out."

Alexander chuckles, causing me to grin. His face breaks out into a wide, handsome smile before winking at me. "Sweetness, you can break into *whatever* you want. Don't worry about it."

I giggle, clapping my hands excitedly before exiting the bedroom and going into the mini-kitchen. I open the little refrigerator, perusing the many options. "Aleeexaannddeerrr," I call, still bending down into the fridge, "do you want whiskey, vodka, or gin?" I think for a second before reaching forward to grab two shots of vodka for myself.

He approaches from behind, and I stay bent over, waiting patiently. "Whiskey, please. Two as well," he answers.

"Whiskey it is!" Grabbing his drinks, I stand, awkwardly tugging on my dress. It's ridden up so high it's a wonder he didn't get a load of my panties.

Alexander leans a hip against the counter, giving me a rather sexy once over as he takes his sweet time settling in. He grins as I toss him a shot, forcing him to catch it midair. I twist the top off mine and walk slowly to him before setting my shots down on the counter. Turning my back to the counter, I haul myself rather ungracefully up to sit on the marble surface, wincing when my heel bangs against the lower cabinet. So much for trying to be sexy.

I cross my legs and glance through my lashes at him.

His blue eyes are twin pools of searing intensity, burning my skin everywhere he looks. I flush when his eyes lower even more, silently watching my breasts bounce as I wiggle around on the counter trying to adjust myself into a more comfortable position. Thrilled with his attention, I probably exagerate my motions further in order to keep him enthralled. My dress slips down rather dangerously low on my cleavage, but I ignore it, wanting to see his reaction. His eyes slide slowly up to mine. He wets his lips, and I can't help but wonder what he's thinking.

I know *I'm* thinking about him sucking on my breasts.

He twirls the shot, looking at me rather darkly, and I feign nonchalantness, crossing my legs and making the dress ride up all the way to my hips. My heel bangs rather hard against the cabinet, and he grins another wicked smile at me as his eyes lower to the skin of my legs. Heat fills me as his eyes snap to meet mine.

Holding eye contact, he steps forward and reaches for my chest, grabbing the neckline.

His fingertips caress the tender skin of my breasts, causing my lips to part and a ragged breath to rush out. *"Oh."*

Even though he's staring at me, I keep my eyes averted as he jerks my dress up firmly over my cleavage. I laugh, feeling my breasts jiggle slightly with his efforts.

"It seems like you need a lot of help with your clothes, ma'am," he teases. Removing his hands, he untwists the lid to his shot and tosses it carelessly to the counter next to my hip.

"It's just 'cause I'm curvy." Sticking my tongue out playfully, I snatch up my second shot and hold it out between us. Alexander rests a hand on the countertop next to my hip and raises his shot to press against mine. "To our exes. May they stay in their place, and may we be thankful for the harsh, yet lifelong lessons they've taught us," I say, tossing my hair to the front of my body and smoothing it down.

I go to take my shot, but his hand flies up and stops me before I can put it to my lips.

"Nu-uh. Not yet," he says, his lips tilted in a half-smile. "May we also not let the damage they've given us go into the next relationship."

At his words my heart beats rather uncomfortably, and we stare each other down for a couple of tense seconds before he lets go of my wrist when I nod my head in agreement. My eyes are wide, and I avert them bashfully. Intimidated by the intense, handsome blue. We slam our shots and open the other ones, holding them up again.

I raise my brow haughtily, and give him a sly grin. "You first," I say softly, licking my lips.

Alexander tilts his head, regarding me for a moment. "May we never let our professional rivalry get in the way of our new friendship." His eyes lower to my bottom lip, which is caught between my teeth. "May you never stop challenging me and being a smartass—" He fake ducks and belts out a laugh when I gasp in offense and push his shoulder. He inches closer, his eyes smoldering as he stares me down, his voice darkening. "I'm serious. *Promise me*, Sarah."

He pins me with a hard stare, placing his shot once again between us.

I tilt my head with a teasing look. "Oh, Alex... we don't even need to toast to this," I laugh huskily. He clears his throat; his gaze roaming my face quietly. "I won't ever stop challenging you. That's a threat and a promise all rolled into one, handsome." I wink at him and suck my second shot down.

He drinks his shot much more slowly as we regard each other, feeling something shift between us. Something that started during my panic attack that I don't think either one of us can explain even if we tried. I know I can't explain it.

His phone dings, signaling the driver has arrived.

"You ready to go?" Alex asks, holding his hand out to me and helping me off the counter. He throws our empty bottles away as he pulls me out the door behind him. Tingles erupt on my arm and make my pussy clench with desire when he doesn't let our grip go.

"Am I ever! I can't wait to try this Jamaican place you found for us!" I gush, squeezing his hand.

Alex pulls me in close, tucking me in under his arm and placing a kiss on the top of my head. I stiffen with shock and keep my eyes straight ahead, too scared to look up at him. "We're going to eat with our fingers, and it's going to be *sloppy."* He laughs, making my heart warm because this man is so much more than the icy persona he's developed over the years. So much more.

We joke and laugh the entire way to the restaurant, and I mimic my best Jamaican accent the whole ride there, making him laugh hilariously.

"Yah, man," he teases back.

I'm glad to feel comfortable enough to be free with him. Happy to see that he can be free with me as well.

We order way too much food at the restaurant and eat sitting in a booth across from each other. Fun multi-colored neon lights, masks, and plants hang on the walls and from the ceiling, lending a fun vibe and perfect ambience. Especially for us two professionals. Alex is looser than normal, too, eating across from me with his sleeves rolled up. I can't stop staring at his forearms. Man, he has to know he's built like a god. The muscles flexing keep my attention and cause me to be more careless with my eating.

When he sucks the tip of his finger into his mouth, I'm surprised I don't feel drool sliding down my chin. My pussy thuds dully, and my entire body is thrumming to life just at being with him. I still feel a bit vulnerable after my panic attack, and my emotions are heightened, leaving me reeling. Wanting.

A splash of sauce hits the exposed swell of my breast, and I squeal quietly. Alex sits back in his seat, an amused expression on his face when I swipe it up with a finger and stick it in my mouth to suck it off. I'm so relieved to see that my affect on him is the same as what he does to me; the skin around his eyes tighten, as does a muscle in his jaw. And his face flushes slightly. Feeling desired, I give him a shy smile but stay quiet.

Everything in me wants to lean in and kiss him. To just get it *over* with. Taste him. Feel his tongue and lips and taste if his hunger is as fierce as mine is.

"Damn, woman. How much food are you going to spill on yourself?" he chuckles, wiping his hands roughly with the napkin. His eyes flit to my lips. "Do you need some help getting it off?" The unspoken question hangs there, but my shyness gets the better of me.

"Sorry! It's the freaking curse of having big boobs," I lament with an apologetic look. Picking up my drink, I take a deep sip and close my eyes. I feel so good right now, swaying in my seat to the music and sipping on my third vodka cranberry. It's been months since I was able to let my hair down like this.

God, he makes me feel so free; when's the last time I had this much fun? Opening my eyes, I blush when I see he's still watching me, but he no longer looks amused. He's back to being cold. Almost stone cold, based on the tightness in his jaw. Even so, *fuck...*

He looks so handsome.

I feel my pussy swell with need as I stare back at Alexander, greedily. I feel my pussy become even wetter with need when I realize he's staring rather blatantly at my breasts.

As if he can't sit still, Alexander adjusts himself rather sexily in his seat. "*Hm-hm*. I see that," he says with a half-laugh, placing the last forkful of food in his mouth. The waiter comes and discreetly places the black check at the edge of the table with a smile before moving on to the next table.

I go to take another drink, but gasp when I accidentally slosh some down my front. *"Oh no."* He turns his head away and hurriedly places his card in the sleeve. I giggle, looking up at him through my lashes as I try again. "Alex, help me," I say, barely able to get the words out through my laughter.

"I'll do no such thing, beautiful," he says in a slightly rougher voice than I'm used to. His eyes go hooded again. "I'm enjoying this *very much* over here."

I tip the drink again, spilling some onto my chin now.

He gets up, smoothing his hand in a lazy movement down the front of his shirt to sit in the booth next to me. I slide over to give him some room. That attraction between us simmers even hotter as he puts an arm around my shoulders and leans in. Without a word, he takes his free hand and steadies my glass, helping it to my lips.

I take a tiny sip before pulling away and relaxing into his side. "Thank you."

"I can tell you don't let loose like this often," Alexander notes quietly. His fingers curl around my shoulder and tuck me into his side. I take full advantage of how open he's being with me; I turn my face into his chest, nuzzling and breathing his scent in. "You feel good, baby? *Safe?"* he whispers the last word, now placing the glass down onto the table. He puts a finger under my chin and tilts my face up, staring into my eyes. My soul. "Do you feel safe with me, Sarah? *Hmm? Tell me, Princess."*

My eyes widen. *Princess?*

"Yes," I say breathlessly. "I know I'm safe with you. Thank you, Alex," I whisper, my eyes lowering to his mouth.

I lick my lips, tensing at the pure electric current of pleasure racing through my body. I raise my eyes back to his, and at what I find in their depths, I fall completely. I can't help it.

Sliding my hand up, I press against the hard planes of his pecs and then rub. "I can feel your heart beating," I whisper.

His head tilts, a muscle jerks under my hand, and a flush rises in his cheeks. Leaning forward, I place my lips against his on a low whimper.

I whimper again when his heart skips a beat under my palm.

His chest rumbles under my fingers before he groans low into my mouth. His flavor hits me harder than I'd expected. My senses whirl, and I press deeper. Boldly pushing my breasts tightly into his chest, my hand slides to the hair at the nape of his neck and grips it. Alexander inhales sharply, and his lips part mine. I arch my back when our tongues touch. Our tongues dance, tangling slowly, and my own heart races out of control.

His muscles flex against me, and his arms wrap around me on a deep groan.

I let out a quiet squeal when one hand sinks into the hair at the back of my head, and the other goes to my hip, hauling me slightly off the booth and into him in a rough movement.

As Alexander sucks in another deep breath, his chest tightens under my fingers. Our lips make a small smacking sound as he pulls back only slightly, breaking our kiss. Emotionally shattered, we breathe hard, and he keeps his hands fisted in my hair, holding me still for him to look into my eyes.

"What is this between us?" he whispers in a hoarse voice.

I swallow hard, unable to speak yet.

I bite my lip, my eyes flickering between his and searching for the answer that he just asked of me. My heart flutters painfully and then begins to beat slower at the sudden, mind-numbing fear that I've pegged this wrong. I mean...I don't think I have...

Seeing my hesitancy he leans forward and runs his nose along my jaw in a wildly intimate move, making goosebumps dot my arms. His breath washes along my skin as he inhales. My face feels hot, and I squirm, trying to get closer, nuzzling him just as blatantly as he's nuzzling me.

His lips trail along my cheek. *"Tell me,"* he grits, those two words so strained and sensually charged that I find myself becoming even wetter.

To my utter horror, I begin to pant lightly, causing him to pull away. As his blue eyes meet mine and pierce deep into my soul, searching for his own truth, that wall I've erected over my heart crumbles completely. And I know, I just *know I'm not wrong.*

But I have to hear him say it.

"I want you...and I *think* you want me, too..." I close my eyes and nuzzle against his hand, reveling in his skin on mine. I feel my heart grow weak at the feel of him so close, making me feel so connected with him. "Am I wrong?" I whisper, opening my eyes to gaze up at him.

God, please don't let me be wrong.

It takes everything in me to say what I admitted to him earlier when he held me after my panic attack. I'd never been this vulnerable with anyone in my life. Ever...

Alexander furrows his brow before taking a deep breath. "I don't just want your body, baby. Do you understand?" His voice is rough with unrestrained emotion.

I nod, unable to speak. I clear my throat softly, trying anyways. "I do."

He looks at my empty glass before pinning me with a pointed look. "You've been drinking, *a lot,*" he states quietly, his gaze boring even deeper into mine.

"I have...yes. I know." I blink.

He looks away. "We need to go," he says, followed by a rough noise in his throat that nestles inside my aching pussy. Letting go of my hair, he grabs my wrist and pulls me out of the booth behind him. "We can talk about this back at the hotel."

I let him lead me...and God, it feels so amazing.

So right.

CHAPTER FORTY-SIX

MAKE LOVE TO ME

I HOLD HER CLOSE as we make the short ride back to the resort in silence, the sexual tension between the two of us palpable. Our fingers are entwined, and every now and then I bring her hand up to kiss her soft skin, letting my lips linger against the pulse of her wrist. It flutters fast. I relate. Desire hums just below the surface of my skin, thrumming through my blood, and making me hyper aware of every little fidget and move she makes.

I help her out of the car, settling my palm against the curve of her lower back, and the quietness continues as we make the short journey to our room. We're scared to talk.

To break this new, fragile bit of possibility between us.

When we exit the elevator and into the hallway, she stares up at me with such a look of longing that it takes what's left of my breath away. "*God, baby. Me too,*" I murmur quietly.

Forced painfully face-to-face with my values, I'm at war with myself.

Tamping down the desires of my body is proving harder and harder, but I find myself weakening. Everything about Sarah chips away at my stoic resolve, leaving me emotionally and mentally floundering. My heart pounds as I pull her to the room with a hand around her wrist. Jamming the keycard in the door, I begin to pray, hearing her pant softly next to me.

I stiffen when she presses herself into my arm, and her breasts nestle softly against me.

God, just please give me the fucking strength. She's not ready. Not emotionally, not physically, not mentally... She's drunk, and she's still hurt.

I grind my teeth, ashamed to admit that I'm slightly upset as I push the door open. Keeping her facing me, I back her into the room, my eyes lock hard on hers, and I know without having to look at a mirror just how icy my gaze must look. The source of my torment is actively throwing herself at me, and I'll be denying us both out of a sense of honor.

Is it maybe misplaced?

The moment I close the door, she flings herself into my chest. I grab her to me hard. Just as desperate as she is. Her leg lifts to wrap around my hip, and I grunt in surprise as she wraps herself around me in a tight hold.

I break the silence between us first. "Slow down, love," I say quietly, wanting to ease her urgency.

"No," she says breathlessly, pressing even harder. *"No, I don't want to go slow."* Her voice quivers. "I'm burning up for you."

My eyes narrow. "Whatever you're thinking, baby, just know our first time *won't* be fast."

She gasps, her eyes widening.

Taking a couple steps deeper into the room, I break, putting an arm under the fleshy curve of her ass, and haul her higher until her legs wrap around my waist; I feel her heels digging into my lower back. My cock jerks with arousal so acute it might as well be pain. Fuck, her core is so warm nestled against my abdomen, almost like she's not wearing panties. Closing my eyes, I bite the inside of my cheek hard when I get a hint of her desire, and my mouth waters.

"Kiss me. *Now,"* I plead, not even ashamed for her to know how badly I want her mouth on me. So desperate for a taste of her that I'm currently cemented to the floor in the middle of the little foyer, unable to move.

Sarah makes this small sound in her throat before slanting her lips onto mine and wrapping her arms around my neck, one hand sinking into my hair. At the feel of her lips rubbing over mine, I groan, needing to go deeper. To truly taste her. Feeling her nails scratching my scalp gently, I tilt my own head, licking into her mouth and searching deeper.

Goddammit, her flavor is amazing.

"You're heaven," I whisper, my tongue slicking along hers. Though there's so much passion, I can sense her hesitancy and naivety in the way she kisses. My cock throbs so painfully that I slide my hands under her dress and into her panties, palming her ass. I give her a grind, trying to find a little relief. At her sharp moan, I pull back enough to speak. *"Give me your tongue when I kiss you."*

Her eyes dilate at the rough command, but her lashes lower, and her cheeks blush a deep crimson.

Leaning forward, I lick the plump flesh of her bottom lip. My body heats with an uncomfortable layer of perspiration when I feel her entire body shiver. I seal my mouth over hers and part her lips firmly, touching the tip of my tongue to hers, then waiting patiently.

But she doesn't make me wait for long; her tongue touches mine back, and I begin to rock us as I suck her into my mouth.

Tilting my head, I groan miserably as Sarah overtakes my senses. Feeling her soft lips moving against mine gently, my mind races as something substantial shifts inside me, something crucial that I know has never been touched or moved before. The closest I think I've ever felt to this was when Tyler was born.

"Make love to me," Sarah mumbles against my lips. Instead of shying away at this point like I normally do when a woman asks me to fuck, my need becomes even deeper. More enhanced. Making my entire body flush hot with an unbearably intense arousal. Before I can answer, she moves fast, putting a hand to her side and struggling to unzip her dress. *"Alex, help me."*

She tugs even more erratically, but the zipper isn't going down.

Honestly, I don't even care right at this moment because she tastes too good to stop.

Lost in the bliss of her mouth, I feel the hair on the back of my neck and arms stand up as I give myself permission to lose myself in the intimacy of this moment. I pull my hand from her ass to cradle the side of her jaw as I kiss her back roughly. It's messy. Hot. Sensual and forbidden all at once. Our lips smack together, and precome drips off the tip of my dick at the next roll of her hips into me, and God, there's nothing inside me that wants her to stop. But we need to before we cross a line we can't come back from.

She's not ready, but our bodies don't understand. Electricity sizzles between us so strong it's a wonder we're not catching on fire.

I pull away reluctantly and note that she's still trying to jerk the zipper of her dress down. A little line between her brows appears with her frustration, and her cheeks tint red the more she struggles. Wanting to calm her, my hand presses against hers, stilling her movements as I work to look into her eyes. She meets them with a wide-eyed, slightly confused look.

"Sarah," I say in a soft tone. "If you show me your breasts, I won't be able to stop, sweetness."

I bite the inside of my cheek hard, suddenly wishing I had something to sink my hand into because I can't believe I'm actually saying this. Apparently, neither can she.

Sarah recoils her head slightly, clearly offended. "*Wait, what...*what do you mean?" she says in a small voice.

My eyes drink her in greedily. Her hair is slightly mussed, and the tip of her nose and cheeks are red; her eyes are wide and shiny with the pupils blown wide, dilated with desire. And eagerness. My gaze roams lower, seeing her breasts slightly heaving as she works to catch her breath. My eyes flit back to hers, seeing hurt begin to override her arousal, and it makes my chest tighten in pain because the last thing I want to do is hurt her.

I have to explain.

Needing her to understand, I wet my lips, speaking hastily, "I can't, Sarah. You're not ready, baby. You're drunk. You still have some bruising on your back... it wouldn't be right. I can't make love to you right now, *not like this*."

My heart cracks in half as Sarah's bottom lip trembles. "You don't want me..." she whispers with a finality that lets me know she really thinks I don't. Her eyes lower to my chest before welling with tears, and I see a sadness inside her that makes my heart pound uncomfortably.

I make a rough sound. "Look at me, *now,"* I give her a little shake and wait until her eyes return to mine. "How can you fucking say that to me? You know *damn well* how badly I want you. I've *been* wanting you, Sarah."

She sniffs, and her eyes widen as she furrows her brows. "Then why won't you make me feel good? *I just want you to—"*

I squeeze my eyes shut for a second, wishing I was a different person. Wishing just *for once* I could let myself sink into her lush body without a care in the world about the repercussions. My eyes snap open.

"Because once I get in I am *not* leaving. That's why," I pin her with a hard stare, seeing her eyes widen even further. "And you are not ready for everything that comes along with an intimate sexual connection. I'm not doing that to your psyche; you're too fragile right now." My voice is about as hard as my eyes, yet I don't attempt to soften my approach. She needs to understand. "You mean way too much to me for me to fuck you right now."

"Please, please, *Alex, please,"* she pleads. A tear travels down her cheek and drips onto the naked upper swell of her breast. To make matters worse for me, she lets out a tiny sob, followed by another. I stand still for a moment, regarding her. My heart tugs painfully, and tears well in my own eyes at the sight of her vulnerability *and* the feeling of mine, because I want her just as badly, if not more.

I stay silent as I look unwavering into her eyes; they're shiny, full of desire and fear. I know without looking that she sees something similar in my gaze. Slowly, I bend, burying my nose in the crook of her neck where I just breathe her in.

The woman I'm in love with.

"Make love to me," Sarah says again. "I know...I know you want to. *I* want to....The bed's right there!"

She's unrelenting.

I relax out of our hug, and I pull away on a deep inhale. I'm not ready to do that yet. I'm not. Because my fucking spirit needs something deeper than the flesh craves. And because I *know* this woman, what I need on the inside has got to match what she needs on the inside. I refuse to believe any different.

Placing a hand on her cheek I hold her stare as I begin to walk through the suite, carrying her through the threshold of the bedroom.

"You want me to make love to you?" I ask, my voice hoarse and deep.

"Uh-huh. I do," she whispers, nodding.

"Then take your dress off for me, sweetness." I brush my thumb over her cheek, setting her down onto the carpet and stepping back, giving her a look. Not even trying to hide my hunger. I crave this woman, and everything that comes with her, and she should see exactly how deep this runs for me.

She blinks at me for a second before wetting her lips. A wave of nervousness radiates from her, hitting me with a blast that makes me almost ejaculate in my briefs. Distracting myself, I turn and take my watch off and place it on the nightstand, waiting patiently until she unzips her dress and slides it off.

My eyes drag down her body in a slow, thorough perusal. Fuck. She's nothing but soft, bountiful curves and smooth skin. Her areolas are twin dark shadows beneath the lace of her bra, teasing me. I can tell she's smooth under her panties. That swell in her lower tummy is enough to drive me insane.

She's got a slight smattering of dimples across her hips that I just know I'm going to lose my mind when I sink into her. But not tonight.

I cut the lights off, throwing us into complete darkness. Heart pounding, I round the bed, taking care to go slow as I approach her, pressing myself against her softness, and sinking both hands into her hair. Cradling her head gently with both hands, I look down. We're just close enough to make out each other's eyes in the darkness, but that's it.

"Are you going to—" Sarah's breath hitches with her shyness, and I shush her even further by pressing a chaste kiss to her lips before deepening it firmly, until she's whimpering against me and squirming in my hands. I pull away, giving her bottom lip a little lick as I do so.

"No, baby," I croon. Picking her up, I place her down gently on the edge of the bed before stepping back to pull my pants and shirt off, leaving my briefs on, and then crawl under the silky sheets behind her. My voice deepens as I address her. "I'm not going to make love to you tonight because you don't *need* me to make love with you. What you need and want is intimacy."

My heart pounds, excited at the prospect of us bonding this way.

"I do?" she asks breathlessly. Her eyes go almost half-lidded as she settles deeper into the pillows. Rubbing a hand down her hair, I smooth it off her shoulder to lie on the satin.

I raise a brow and lower my voice. "You don't trust me?"

She holds her breath for a few seconds. *"I do."* It comes out confident. Sarah watches me warily. She's got a slight flush on her face, and her chest rises and falls slowly with her breathing. "But I *really* want to have sex with you," she whispers so quietly that I almost don't hear her.

"Hm-hm," I hum, now running my hand down the length of her arm. "And I want to have sex with you too, but you don't *need* sex, though. You just want to feel close, and I can provide that."

She nods, exhaling deeply. "I think you can, too."

A smile tips my lips. *"Do you, now?"* I tease.

"Well..." a cute grin tips the corner of her mouth, "you've been close this entire time."

She's not incorrect. The silence settles around us as we just lay there for a minute. I'm busy stroking my fingers down her cheek when I feel her head turn towards me in the darkness.

"Alex?" she says hesitantly.

I love the way she says my name. It's so intimate falling from her lips that it affects me almost like I've never heard it before. Like she personally chose it for me, cradled it within the palm of her hand, and offered it to me. Like she offered me back to myself.

"Yes, sweetness?"

"Can you...*c-can...*"

Hearing her hesitancy, I lift up on an elbow and prop my head on my hand. "What is it?" I ask softly. At her silence, my fingers move to her lips, and my thumb smoothes across her bottom lip. "You can ask me anything."

"Can you take my bra off and....and rub my back please?" Her voice is so small as she trails off.

My heart damn near pounds out of my chest, enthralled at the gift she's just given me. "Come here." Moving closer, I slide my arms around her and unsnap her bra.

Though the covers aren't pulled over us, it doesn't matter. It's dark in here; there's not enough light to see her nipples, but I *can* see the round outline of her breasts, and I feel my cock jerk before thickening the most it's ever done that I can recall.

Placing my temple against hers, I give us a minute to relax into each other like this before I work to pull her closer to me.

I tense at the feel of her erect nipples pressing into my chest before her softness settles against me, and let me tell you, it's the best thing I've ever felt in my entire life.

As my fingers press into her back, I gentle my touch, knowing I'm touching the fading bruises that still grace her flesh. She wanted me to make love to her... but this? This is miles more intimate than me putting my cock into her, and I am so grateful that she's gifted me with her trust.

So I decide to give her a gift of my own. I keep my voice low, within the confines of our little bubble.

"I oftentimes wonder if the nights he was doing this to you were the same nights that I cried myself to sleep." I pause for a minute as my fingers stroke her repeatedly, going slow. In the darkness her head tilts slightly, letting me know she's trying to find my eyes. Her fingers tighten on my shoulders, grounding me. "My life had been hell the last few months, and I couldn't figure out why. For some reason, I kept spiraling and *spiraling*. Becoming more agitated and closed off. Now I know. My soul was responding to you, baby. It was you all along."

Pressing my hand into the middle of her shoulder blades, I give her a long stroke down the entirety of her back, keeping my touch light, aware that I'm touching a part of her that'd so far been closed off. The spot on her body where that fucker took his anger out on her. The fact that she's allowing me to touch her here says so much more to me than her ever letting me have access to her breasts or her pussy.

This is it...what I've been searching so long for. Finally.

This is love.

I press my lips to hers, kissing her softly, slowly. Our bellies rub together, and our thighs touch as she works to maneuver closer. Her foot meets mine, then presses, dragging its way up my calf, and then my thigh, before settling around my hip.

"Make love to me."

She gasps as I seal my mouth around hers, stealing her words. "I am."

My hand firms on her back on the next downward stroke, but instead of stopping at her lower back, I go lower. I slip my hand into her panties to settle my hand on the curve of her ass and her hip and squeeze. I groan in pleasure at the feel of her. She's silky soft there. Warm. My thumb settles into one of the twin dips at the seam of her ass and presses. Sarah shudders against me, flexing her foot against my thigh, straining.

But we can't get any closer.

"I'm so in love with you," I say, pulling back and meeting her eyes, showing her how much I mean it before pressing my lips to hers again in a kiss I never want to end.

"I love you, too." Her breath hitches. "Alex."

I work my other arm under her, settling my head down on the same pillow as hers and deepen our kiss. I splay my hand on her upper back, holding her steady. Letting her know I've got her. I want her to feel like I'm wrapped all around her.

I'm here, baby, so you don't have to look over your shoulder and watch your back anymore.

My tongue touches hers, whisper-soft, and I revel in the moan she gives me. It's my turn to shudder now as I taste salt.

She's crying.

"Make love to me." Her voice cracks as she pleads.

And I don't know why, but something about her saying it just the way she said it cracks something deep inside me I wasn't aware existed. I can't remember the last time anyone has said these words to me. I squeeze my eyes shut as my breath shudders out of my lungs, and I make a tortured groan that I fail to cut off. But it's too late, she's heard.

"I am." My voice breaks in the silence of the room as our breathing, somehow desperate and soft at the same time, fills the empty space between us. "I am, my love."

Her hips roll into mine, her hand goes to my hair, and the other on my back holds me just as firmly as I'm holding her as she cries and breaks under my hands. She pulls away and then tilts her head down to my chest, pressing a kiss directly over my heart. My hand cradles the back of her head as I shudder at the first contact of her lips against where I swear I'm most sensitive.

My heart.

It races as she pauses there, giving me another soft kiss and making my fingers tighten against her head as the tears fall. Laying myself bare for this woman is painful. What we're experiencing is painful, like we're trying to carefully dance on the edge of a sword.

"Why are you crying?" Her head tilts back, and her hands come up to cradle my nape tenderly. "Please tell me."

"Because it's been *so long* since I've had this with another person," I admit, my voice thick with emotion. "Having another person touch me, *want to touch me..."* In response I tighten my arms around her, pulling her even closer.

"Make love to me," she whispers again, making my cock jerk painfully hard.

Oh, God. I am weak for her...

I swallow hard. *"Sweetheart, I—"*

"No, *shhh...Listen to me."* Sarah puts a finger against my lips, silencing my words. She moves her hand away and grabs my forearm, making me rub my hand up and down her back again. *"Make love to me,"* she stresses.

My heart beats wildly out of control because I know then that she *gets it.* She's giving me permission to love her in this way that I need right now. Because even though sinking into her body would be heaven on earth, I didn't bring her to Vancouver to fuck her; I meant that.

I brought her to Vancouver to acquaint myself with her. And as we rock against each other, kissing, whispering, and touching deep into the middle of the night when everyone else is asleep, I know without a shadow of a doubt that this woman has melted me completely.

As long as I have her, I don't ever have to worry about being cold again.

CHAPTER FORTY-SEVEN

More By...

INTERCONNECTED WORLDS

Psychological Thriller

In You

With Me (2026)

The Romancing Me Series

Sarah and Alexander's Story:

Will You Reach For Me (book 1)

Coming 2026...Will You Love Me (book 2)

Coming 2026...Will Your Heart Beat For Me (book 3)

The King Dynasty Series:

The Heir

The Spare

Coming Soon: The Reign

The Billionaire's Assurance Series

Colin and Olivia's story:

The Pain We Nurture (book 1)

The Pain We Allow (book 2)

Unmasking Me Series:

Lola and Hudson's Story:

Lola Unmasked part. 1

Lola Unmasked part. 2

Lola Unmasked part 3

CHAPTER FORTY-EIGHT

CONTACT ME

Follow My Socials

www.presleyauthor.com

TikTok, Patreon, IG:

S.K. Presley Author

Please join my Facebook ARC group: **S.K. Presley ARC/Street Team**

Please do not forget to review/rate!

CHAPTER FORTY-NINE

ACKNOWLEDGEMENTS

THIS STORY HAS BEEN almost three years in the making, and one that was so special to me that I sat on it until it was the perfect time to release! I want to offer my sincere thank you to all who have helped bring this story and these characters to life.

To my PA Paige, you are a God send, and one of the most amazing people I know. Thank you for your continued friendship, support, the hard work you've put into my brand. I appreciate you more than you know, hun.

To Sarah, my bestie, girl, I'll call you before I start crying, but honestly, what would my life be without you? I don't know. I love you, babe.

Mari, Emily, Haley, Merr, Lauren, Jehn, Paige, Jenny, Brittany, BWills, Tris, ya'll are my sisterhood. I hope you know that. You're held close to my heart and I couldn't be more grateful.

To my editor, Traci, this one was wild, wasn't it? Getting this from it's original form of 3rd person to 1st was an insane task, thank you for helping this release go smoothly. Again, I'm so sorry. I feel like you have to perform miracles for me, and I am so grateful for your grace and understanding.

To my street and ARC team, are you kidding? Do you know how wonderful each and every one of you are? Without you I'd be nothing. Thank you for your continue support and encouragement. Without your backing, I'd be in the weeds. Authors are nothing without a great team behind them, and I've got some amazing people behind me.

To my family, I know I tell you all everyday, but you are the reason I can do this. Your shenanigans fuel my imagination and helps me to make our lives just that much more bright. You are my universe.

To my readers, well, you get the piece of me that lives on, and that's supremely sacred and special to me. I hope you all know how much I adore and love you. Thank you, thank you, thank you.

Until the next,

S.K. Presley